MIND
GAMES

OTHER BOOKS AND AUDIOBOOKS
BY STEPHANIE BLACK

The Witnesses

The Believer

Twisted Fate

Methods of Madness

Shadowed

Rearview Mirror

Cold as Ice

Fool Me Twice

Played for a Fool

Not a Word

MIND
GAMES

a novel

STEPHANIE BLACK

Covenant Communications, Inc.

Cover image *Gazebo* © Lee Yiu Tung

Cover design copyright © 2017 by Covenant Communications, Inc.

Published by Covenant Communications, Inc.
American Fork, Utah

Printed in the United States of America
First Printing: September 2017

22 22 21 20 19 18 17   10 9 8 7 6 5 4 3 2 1

ISBN-13: 978-1-52440-437-6

To Sue McConkie, the Wonder Woman of test readers.
Thank you for wielding your speedy and insightful superpowers
for the benefit of my books.

ACKNOWLEDGMENTS

I OWE MY DAUGHTER, AMY Black, a colossal thank you. If I ask her *one more question*—which I will—she'll probably rue the day she set out to earn a doctorate in counseling psychology, but it's too late now. She knows things, and I want to know the things, and I know where to find her. I'm also indebted to Monique Luetkemeyer, my accountability partner, source of medical knowledge, and partner in crime.

Much appreciation also goes to Sue and Marshall McConkie, Jean Newman, Suzanne Lucas, Shauna and Justin Rasband, Hydi Hoeger, Zohar Mamet, Nichole and Gary Giles, Robert O'Callaghan, Buffie Iu, and Michael Young.

Working with my wise and delightful editor, Samantha Millburn, is one of my favorite parts of being a writer. Thank you, Sam! Thank you also to Christina Marcano for designing a marvelously spooky cover. I'm grateful to all the people at Covenant Communications for the skill and hard work they put into bringing my stories to readers.

Love and endless gratitude go to my husband, Brian. I deeply appreciate his support.

CHAPTER 1

NATALIE MARSH PEERED AT THE miniature purple blossoms floating in a glass the server had handed her. Either the server had brushed against a flowering bush on one of the paved garden paths or this wasn't a drink she'd tried before.

"Lavender lemonade, madam." The server's diction matched his formal livery. He turned toward Gideon Radcliffe, who was standing next to Natalie. "Sir?"

"Yes, please." Gideon accepted a glass. "I'm all for drinking a shrub."

The server moved toward the next group of guests.

"The catering staff makes me feel underdressed." Gideon tapped his bowtie with one finger.

With her free hand, Natalie straightened the tie for him.

"Is the dashed thing crooked again?" An English accent appeared in Gideon's voice. "Do forgive my disheveled appearance. My valet is new at his job."

Natalie laughed. She'd seen Gideon in formal dress only a couple of times—dark-haired Gideon with his attentive gray-blue eyes and warmhearted smile was attractive enough in button-down shirts and khakis or jeans and a T-shirt. Deck him out in a tuxedo and Natalie wanted to ignore the rest of the people filling the gardens of the Stoker Office Building and sit and stare at just Gideon.

Or maybe not. Contemplating him for too long would stir her questions about the trajectory of their relationship, and she couldn't ponder that tonight. She needed to focus on doing her part to make this opening gala a success. Besides, overt admiration would kill Gideon with embarrassment. She scaled down her appreciation to "You look anything but disheveled."

"Aww, thanks. And you look great, as always. Nice hair jewels."

"Thank you." Natalie touched the rhinestone comb holding one side of her chocolate-brown hair back from her face. "It's from 1880-something. I found it on eBay. I'm trying to get into the spirit of Victoriana."

"All hail the nineteenth century." Gideon surveyed the newly restored brick office building. Most of the arched windows in the four-story building were dark, but the central lobby on the lower level glowed. The doors to the lobby were fixed open, and classical piano music—Elgar was Natalie's guess—glided from the lobby into the June evening.

"Actually, all hail a twenty-first century renovation of the nineteenth century," Gideon amended. "I hear the Victorians had lousy Wi-Fi."

A baritone voice spoke from Natalie's left. "At least they had the sense not to parade their nutcases through art galleries and financial offices."

Natalie pivoted to confront the man—a handsome thirty-something with a hawkish face, a balding head with the remnants of his hair shaved close, and a smile that challenged her to fight with him.

Hiding the anger she knew he hoped to see, she responded with calm words. "If you're nostalgic for nineteenth-century treatment of the mentally ill, may I recommend *Ten Days in a Madhouse* by Nellie Bly. It might widen your perspective."

"I'm not advocating a return to barbarism, Dr. Marsh. I'm advocating for common sense."

"If that's the case, I suggest you choose less crass ways of presenting your concerns," Natalie said. Gideon stepped closer, probably preparing himself to speak up for her or to grab her if he feared she might slosh her lemonade down the man's formalwear. "Baxter, may I introduce Gideon Radcliffe? Gideon, Baxter Quincy."

Baxter extended a lean hand. "A pleasure to meet you."

Gideon shook his hand. "Mr. Quincy." He didn't echo Baxter's polite greeting. Natalie suspected Baxter had already pitched his tent on Gideon's bad side.

"You work here too?" Baxter asked. "Where at?"

"I don't work here. I work for the city—civil engineer. I volunteer here when I can. At Nefesh Bria."

"Should have known," Baxter said. "Nefesh Bria—what kind of name is that for a mental health clinic? Sounds like a synagogue."

"The Hebrew words mean 'healthy soul,'" Natalie said. "Bob Chapman chose it in honor of his Jewish grandmother."

"When you fund it with your millions, I guess you get to name it," Baxter said. "So what's your volunteer gig there, Radcliffe?"

"Whatever they need. Fix a leaky sink, vacuum the carpet, sort the mail, answer questions. The less money they need to spend on overhead, the more there is to spend on serving the community."

"You ought to work security," Baxter said. "We're going to need more of that. Nefesh Bria is a noble cause, but it's in the wrong location."

"Why do you say that?" Gideon asked.

"This is a high-end office building. The clinic will attract a different clientele. It's good business sense to put it in a part of town where those clients live."

"The clientele will come from all over Ohneka," Gideon said. "That's the point of sliding-scale fees—to invite people of all financial situations to seek help."

"Good job on memorizing Dr. Marsh's press releases. You know a free or cheap clinic will mainly attract people who can't afford better. Dr. Marsh is making us a magnet for every destitute and dysfunctional person in central New York. Financially solvent clients will go to private practices."

Gideon swept one hand toward the landscaped gardens and the other toward the tiled patio area where shimmering veils of water flowed over a tiered marble fountain. "You have a point," he said. "Nobody would come to this dump unless they had no other options."

Hard dents appeared in the muscles crossing Baxter's temples. Natalie could have quoted the predictions he'd trapped behind a clenched jaw: the Stoker Building was elegant now, but no one would care about the architecture or the gardens once there were "homeless lunatics" and "mass shooters in training" loitering near the doors, snoring on benches, and scaring away the clients of other businesses. She'd tried to disabuse Baxter of his assumptions and stereotypes. It hadn't worked.

"You're aware that Chapman Development has offered to cancel the contracts of any tenants who've changed their minds about leasing space here," Natalie said. "If you think the clinic will be catastrophic to your business, move your travel agency elsewhere."

"It makes far more sense for the catastrophe to relocate than for dozens of businesses to have their plans disrupted."

"If Chapman Development thought we were a catastrophe, we wouldn't be here," Natalie said.

"Robert Chapman is a nut himself." Baxter glanced across the garden to where short, white-haired Chapman was using someone's cane to demonstrate fencing moves.

"He's a savvy businessman," Natalie said. "He knows better than to create a catastrophe."

"He knows better. He doesn't care. He can do his community-relations stunt and make himself look like a holy philanthropist. If he loses his investment in the Stoker, so what? What's a few million lost? Meanwhile, the rest of us go bankrupt."

A young couple strolled past Natalie's group: a red-haired woman in apricot satin and a tanned man with muscular shoulders. Natalie watched them—Ainsley MacKerron, and the man must be her husband, Stuart.

"Excuse us," Natalie said, deciding to use the MacKerrons as an excuse to escape Baxter. "I wanted to introduce Gideon to a new member of our office staff. Enjoy your evening." She grasped Gideon's arm and followed the couple as they headed toward the group watching Chapman slice the air with a cane.

"Nice guy," Gideon muttered as soon as they were out of Baxter's earshot. "He's worse than you described him. If he's that spooked by the clinic, why doesn't he leave?"

"He doesn't want to give up his prime spot. The Stoker is worlds classier than his old location next to that heavy-equipment rental warehouse on Watkins Road."

"Once he figures out you're not the local Serial Killer Expo, I hope he settles down."

"So do I." Natalie stopped next to the MacKerrons, who stood at the perimeter of the crowd around Chapman.

Ainsley smiled at her. "Hi. I saw you got cornered by Baxter Quincy. Is he any happier?"

"No."

"How big is his ego to think he can go up against Robert Chapman?" Ainsley tapped her husband's arm, drawing his attention away from Chapman's hijinks. "Stuart, this is Dr. Natalie Marsh, the psychologist who founded the clinic."

"Good to meet you." Stuart shook Natalie's hand in a grip that made her glad she didn't bruise easily. He offered his hand to Gideon. "Stuart MacKerron."

"Gideon Radcliffe, Natalie's bodyguard—which I didn't know she needed until five minutes ago when Baxter Quincy educated me on how dangerous Nefesh Bria is."

"I'm Ainsley." Ainsley shook his hand, her brow furrowing. "You look familiar. Have we met?"

"You look familiar too," Gideon said. "Maybe we've already crossed paths at the clinic?"

"I don't think so. I've only been there a couple weeks, and I don't remember . . . Wait. Where do you live?"

"Innes Hill Apartments. Ah, you're there too, right?"

"Yes," Ainsley said. "Number eighteen."

"I'm in twenty-six. Glad to officially meet you, neighbors."

"Glad to meet you too," Stuart said. "As long as you're not the joker who parks his white Escalade over the line and keeps dinging my car."

"Not guilty."

Stuart's gaze swung back to Chapman, who was lunging toward an invisible opponent. "That guy's a trip."

"I hope I'm that energetic at his age," Natalie said.

"I hope I'm that rich at his age," Ainsley said. "He's paying Stuart's cousin an insane amount of money to serve as his"—she made air quotes—"*Trekmeister*."

"His what?" Gideon asked.

"Private trail guide," Stuart said. "A few years back, he got into hiking. Now he's ramping it up and wants to hit long-distance trails. They're heading to California in August. Three weeks on the John Muir Trail."

"Three weeks!" Natalie said. "Are you sure Mr. Chapman is paying him for this? It sounds like your cousin is kidnapping him. Who would voluntarily hike for three weeks?"

"Best vacations are backpacking trips," Stuart said. "I've done the JMT a few times."

"I'd be willing to backpack across the parking lot to the Marriott," Natalie said.

Gideon laughed.

"Stuart would be a fantastic guide, better than his cousin." Ainsley fiddled with the pendant she wore, a small, silver-trimmed crystal globe containing a sprig of white flowers. "If you've heard of a hiking trail, Stuart's done it."

"My dad and I used to hike, but never for more than a few days," Gideon said. "I'd like to get back into it. What East Coast trails do you recommend?"

As the conversation progressed into a detailed discussion of backpacking, Natalie's gaze wandered around the gardens—the sculpted granite benches, the strings of white lights glimmering in huge, old trees, the new beds of rose bushes, the people celebrating the completed renovation of a long-abandoned building. The gardens were beautiful; the building was stately and classically appealing. And the mental health clinic that occupied the east wing of the ground floor was funded, staffed—mostly staffed—and opened.

She'd labored for the clinic, battled for it, dreamed of it, ached for it. Now she had to make Nefesh Bria a sustainable long-term benefit to the community. She ought to circulate as much as she could tonight to meet Stoker tenants and attempt to assuage concerns. Thank heavens that most people were more reasonable than Baxter . . . Natalie's gaze stalled on a woman moving through the courtyard, lingering so close to the perimeter that her flowing skirt grazed a wrought-iron lamppost. Was that . . . no . . . maybe . . . Security was supposed to be watching for her . . .

Natalie craned her neck, trying for a better view of the woman's face. She'd moved into a patch of shadow, and Natalie wasn't confident she could recognize her anyway. She turned back toward Gideon and the MacKerrons.

". . . can fit in a bear canister, you're not going to be packing lobster and rib eye no matter how much money you have," Stuart was saying.

"Dehydrated lobster pellets and Kobe beef jerky for all," Gideon said.

Natalie spoke quickly. "Excuse me for interrupting. Ainsley—that woman in the long black dress." Keeping her hand at her side, Natalie made a subtle gesture in the woman's direction. "Is she the one Bob warned us about?"

Ainsley looked where Natalie had indicated. "The one who was arguing with him the other day? The ghost woman?"

"Yes."

"Ghost woman?" Stuart asked.

Ainsley squinted. "Could be. But with her hair down . . . and I can't see her face that well. Better call security though."

"I don't want to set security on an innocent guest just because I'm jumpy," Natalie said. "Excuse me for a moment. I want a better look at her. I'll be right back."

Moving as rapidly as she could without drawing attention or falling off heels higher than she usually wore, Natalie strode after the woman, who was now approaching the open lobby doors. Gideon kept pace with her.

"I didn't mean to pull you away from your conversation," Natalie said.

"You're pursuing a ghost. You think I'll let you waltz into danger while I hang back and talk about freeze-dried lasagna?"

"She's not a ghost or dangerous. I told you about her. Heather Osbourne."

"Yeah, the woman who thinks her grandmother is haunting the Stoker."

"Great-great-great-grandmother."

"The woman who desperately needs to visit your clinic."

"If she ever did seek help, we're the last people she'd go to. We're the invaders of her ancestor's mausoleum."

The woman meandered toward the grand piano in the lobby, layers of black chiffon rippling around her legs and long black hair brushing her waist. She paused, her back to Natalie, and stood with other guests who were watching the pianist. A server with a tray of pastries stopped near the woman. She took one.

"Looks like she's just enjoying the party," Gideon said.

Natalie nodded, slowing her pace. "I'm paranoid," she said. "Too worried about everything going smoothly tonight."

"No harm done. Let's wander to the other side of the piano so you can get a clear look at her face and ease your mind. Then we can go back to eating filet-of-history on sliced cucumbers."

"And chocolate-dipped nostalgia." Natalie took a sip from her glass of lavender lemonade and strolled toward the side of the lobby opposite where the woman stood. Before she'd reached a suitable vantage point, the woman turned and drifted away from the piano, heading toward the first-floor corridor that led to the interior staff entrance to Nefesh Bria. The clinic was closed. Where was she going?

"I'm starting to think someone should call security on *me*," Natalie whispered as she trailed the woman. "Creeping around, spying on other guests."

"What is Chapman worried she might do tonight?"

"Something disruptive. Embarrassing. At the end of the argument I overheard, she was telling him how her grandmother wouldn't put up with his trespassing and her ghost would get revenge." Natalie reached the corridor that dead-ended at her clinic. It was empty. A plate holding an untouched raspberry tart sat on the marble-topped table across from the elevators. The woman hadn't taken the elevator. Natalie hadn't heard the musical *ping* that would have sounded if the doors had opened.

"She disappeared," Gideon said. "I thought you said she wasn't a ghost."

Natalie set her glass of lemonade next to the raspberry tart. Gideon abandoned his drink as well and accompanied Natalie toward the stairs.

She opened the stairwell door. The tap of footsteps echoed above her. Footsteps, much louder, rapped behind her. She turned and saw Stuart and Ainsley approaching.

"Yes, we're following you," Ainsley said. "She went upstairs? It *is* her."

"We still don't know," Natalie said. "But it's not your worry. Please go back to the party."

Ainsley shook her head. "If we let her make a scene that ends up on the news, Mr. Chapman will kick us all out."

"We don't all need to get arrested for stalking her," Natalie said. Footsteps still echoed from the stairs, distant now. She hurried into the stairwell with Gideon and the MacKerrons tailing her. She'd rather not approach the woman like an advancing army, but once the word *danger* had come out of Gideon's mouth, he wouldn't leave her side, even if she insisted the danger didn't exist. And she didn't want to argue with the MacKerrons, making this a bigger deal than it needed to be. Forget being sneaky; she'd catch up to the woman, call out to her, and get a clear look at her. If it *was* Heather, Natalie would try to keep things calm while Ainsley called security. If it wasn't, she'd apologize with an "I thought you were someone I knew" and scuttle back to the party.

Each running step hammered the balls of her feet, and her toes felt squashed into about a quarter-inch of shoe space by the time she reached the third-floor landing. *Stupid heels.* Above her, she heard the fourth-floor door close. She rushed up the last flight and pulled the door open.

The woman was standing in front of an office door, an access card in her hand. For an instant, Natalie felt like an idiot—plainly she worked here—but as Natalie exited the stairwell, the woman whirled toward her. Her face was ghastly white, her eyes dark, ethereal splotches.

"Heather." Natalie halted and flung her arms straight out from her sides, mutely ordering Gideon and the MacKerrons to stay back. "Can I help you with something?"

Heather stared at her. "You're the shrink."

"Yes." Winded from galloping up the stairs, Natalie tried not to pant. "My name is Natalie."

"I've read about you. About your clinic. You're like Chapman. Using the building like it's up for grabs, trampling sacred ground." Heather slid the card through the slot. Her hand shook, and she didn't position the card well. The door remained locked.

Natalie took a few careful steps closer and saw the lettering on the brass panel next to the door. Quincy Travel. *Marvelous.*

"How did you get an access card?" Natalie didn't check behind her, but she was certain Ainsley had slipped into the stairwell to call security.

Heather switched the card to her other hand, wiped her free hand on her skirt, and switched the card back. "Tabitha."

Ghost-Grandma Tabitha, dead for over a hundred years. "How did she help you?" Natalie asked calmly.

Heather swiped the card again. The lock clicked.

"Did Tabitha tell you what to do tonight?" Natalie asked.

Heather opened the door and glared at Natalie. Her face was steel-gray. "I'm here to show everyone the . . . horror . . . the death beneath these pretty new bricks. He thinks he can handle one ghost? Let him fight with two."

She whisked through the door and slammed it.

Natalie lunged for the door. Locked. Stuart and Gideon surged forward.

"Heather." Natalie leaned close to the paneled wood. "Heather, please open the door. Let's talk. You don't have to—Gideon!" Natalie tried to shake off his grip, but he hauled her down the corridor. She staggered; her ankle turned, and one shoe fell off. She kicked the other shoe off as well. "Let me talk to her!"

"She could have an arsenal hidden under that skirt." Gideon stopped but didn't release her. "That office faces the courtyard. We could have a massacre on our hands."

Horror and death. Natalie pictured the travertine-tiled courtyard filled with guests. Quincy Travel had large windows, old-style, that swung open instead of being sealed shut. *Two ghosts.*

"She's not going to massacre the guests. She's going to jump," Natalie said as Ainsley rushed from the stairwell, phone in hand. "Two ghosts. She said two ghosts. Tabitha Ferguson died here when she fell from a window. That's why Heather's obsessed with the building, why she's been wandering the corridors for years—"

Stuart slammed his foot against the office door with an ear-piercing concussion that boomed through the corridor. Ainsley screamed. Gideon dragged Natalie back a few more yards.

Stuart rammed his foot against the door again, and what was left of the doorframe splintered. The door swung open. He dropped to the floor and army-crawled into the room.

"Stuart!" Ainsley shrieked, heading toward the open door. From inside the room came a screech and a thump.

"Stay back! She might be armed!" Gideon yelled.

Ainsley stopped, both hands over her mouth.

"It's okay!" Stuart shouted. "No guns. Everything's under control."

Ainsley sprinted into Quincy Travel. Gideon released Natalie, and they looked at each other.

"Sorry," he said. "I need practice on the bodyguard thing. Are you okay?"

"I'm fine, and thank you." Natalie started toward the shattered doorway. "You were right. We had no idea if she had a gun. Or guns."

Gideon picked up Natalie's shoes and handed them to her. "Let me guess." He eyed the wreck of the door. "That guy's Special Ops."

"He's a high school athletic trainer." Natalie put her shoes on, and she and Gideon entered the office.

Near the window, Heather lay prone on the floor. Stuart had pinned her arms behind her, bending them at such a severe angle that it had to be excruciating for her. Her hair hid her face. She drew loud, ragged breaths, and her body trembled.

Natalie opened her mouth to tell Stuart to loosen his hold, but Gideon spoke first. "Hey, easy on her. She's not going anywhere. You don't need to pop her shoulders out of joint."

Stuart adjusted his grip, allowing Heather's arms to straighten. Heather shook her head to clear hair away from her face, but it didn't help much. Natalie could see only a sliver of midnight-colored eye studying Gideon from among black strands of hair.

The window was ajar, with the key in the lock. Natalie hurried to close it and claim the key.

"That was in her hand." Stuart tilted his head toward a cream-colored envelope that lay on the floor near Heather.

Natalie picked it up. Robert Chapman's name was written on the envelope.

The ping of the elevator and footsteps sounded in the hallway.

"Well played, Stuart MacKerron," Heather whispered. "You win. He'll reward you. What's your dream? You want a new car. A new truck. You'll get it. What else? You want to be at his side on his crazy wanderings. You can have that too."

Two security guards rushed into the office. Stuart rose to his feet and stepped back, allowing them to take custody of Heather. While Stuart answered their questions, Natalie, Gideon, and Ainsley retreated to stand next to a wall decorated with posters of beaches, mountains, and medieval castles.

Knowing she probably shouldn't, Natalie ripped Heather's envelope open and read the message.

"Suicide note?" Gideon asked under his breath.

Natalie nodded.

"I already called the police," Ainsley said. "I assume this is more than security can deal with."

"Yes." Natalie folded the note.

The security guards drew a handcuffed Heather to her feet. Natalie approached and handed one of them the note and the window key. "Mr. MacKerron found this letter next to her."

"Thank you, ma'am. We'll pass it on to the police. You people need to remain here until they arrive."

"We'll do that," Natalie said.

As the guards led Heather toward the door, she fixed a piercing gaze on Stuart. Stuart averted his eyes and tugged his tie loose.

Once Heather and the security team were gone, Stuart tossed his tie and tuxedo jacket onto a desk. "That girl had the window open when I tackled her. Would have dived right in the middle of the party." He frowned at Natalie. "How did she know who I am?"

"I have no idea," Natalie said, her emotions a blend of deep relief that Heather was safe and horror at how close she'd come to dying. "Well done, Stuart. Thank you."

"Let us know when that new truck shows up," Gideon added.

Stuart snorted. "Yeah, I'll keep you posted. That creepy chick needs to reboot her crystal ball."

CHAPTER 2

At a tap on her open office door, Natalie looked up from her computer. Building manager Regina Santiago stood in the doorway observing Natalie with eyes like blue-tinted diamonds—exquisite, sparkling, and able to drill through anything. "Good morning, Natalie. Do you have a few minutes?"

"I do." Natalie closed her computer. "Have a seat."

Regina sat on the couch and ran her hand along her neck, freeing spikes of highlighted hair that had slipped beneath a ruffled scarf. "Thank you for your help in averting Saturday night's near disaster. Two security guards are hunting for new jobs."

Natalie winced. Guests hadn't been required to show their invitations at the doors, and there had been multiple entrances to the building and gardens through which they could enter. It seemed harsh to condemn the guards because they hadn't spotted one woman in the crowd.

"An agent at Quincy Travel is out on her ear too," Regina said. "The access card Heather Osbourne used belonged to her. The agent claimed she kept it safely in her purse and has no idea how Heather got it, but when we investigated, she admitted she keeps her purse on an open shelf under her desk. A woman who fits Heather's description was at Quincy Travel on Friday with one of those flyers Baxter sent out offering a free messenger bag to anyone who brought the flyer in and inquired about booking a trip. It was a credible excuse for Heather to be in there—I suppose that's why she picked Quincy Travel, though I don't know if she tried to steal an access card anywhere else first. She pretended to be interested in a trip to Morocco. She had a coughing fit—a fake coughing fit, no doubt—and this woman left Heather alone for a moment while she went to get her a glass of water. *And* she didn't realize her access card was missing until the police took it from Heather. Mr. Quincy fired her as soon as he heard."

Baxter's punitive response didn't surprise Natalie. "Firing people seems draconian. At Bob's request, those of us who knew about Heather Osbourne's obsession with the building were keeping that information quiet. The travel agent couldn't have known to be wary of her, and security at the party wasn't set up to—"

"Their incompetence almost led to an incident that would have tarnished the Stoker's reputation and hurt every business here. You know the way people think. Our lovely gardens would have become the place where Heather Osbourne's body smashed to the pavement. We'd have had ghoulish tourists searching for bloodstains, everyone else avoiding us, and newspaper reports painting Chapman Development as the greedy, heartless entity that drove her to suicide."

While Natalie understood and agreed with Regina's assessment of what Heather's suicide would have done to the building's reputation—at least in the short term—she had to stop herself from asking Regina to show some sign that she valued Heather's life more than the reputation of the Stoker. "I'm grateful Heather didn't succeed."

"So am I. Poor lady. I hope I don't sound callous. I feel terrible that she's suffering. I'm in a bad mood after getting harangued by Vanessa Parisi. She gave me an earful before I could even get inside my office this morning. She's certain Heather was nearly the ruin of her art gallery and wants guarantees that we'll keep everything out of the papers. Thank you *so* much, Vanessa; it never *occurred* to us that publicity would be a bad idea—" Regina's phone rang. She pulled it out of her blazer pocket. "Pardon me. It's Bob." She lifted the phone to her ear. "Hello, this is Regina."

While Regina talked, Natalie flipped her computer open and reached for the cup holding the remainder of the strawberry smoothie she'd bought on the way to work.

". . . at Nefesh Bria, actually, talking to Dr. Marsh." Regina paused. "Let me check." She lowered the phone and looked at Natalie. "Bob's pulling into the parking lot, and he'd like to see you, if you have time."

"Of course." Natalie had planned to respond to e-mails and sign off on her intern's therapy notes before the clinic opened this morning, but if the man who was funding the clinic wanted to talk to her, she'd be wise to make time for him.

"She's available," Regina said into the phone. "I'll come out and meet you. On my way." She hung up.

Assuming they'd meet at the building management office, Natalie started to stand, but Regina said, "Stay put. He's coming here." She exited.

Natalie drank the rest of her smoothie, threw the cup away, and wiped her lips with a tissue. She stood, smoothed the overlapping fabric of her green wraparound blouse, adjusted her skirt, and straightened the emerald-cut tourmaline ring on her right hand. Wearing the ring Camille's mother had given her after the funeral always made her feel a little bolder—a little more like her longtime best friend had been.

Bob Chapman cantered into the room, longish white hair tousled as always, a glittery magenta necktie a startling combination with his striped Oxford shirt and plain black trousers. Natalie stepped forward.

"Ah, *mein Schatz*. My dear." Chapman clasped her hand and kissed it. "*Wie geht es dir?*"

"*Mir geht es gut,*" Natalie said. Behind Chapman, Regina arched her brows at Natalie, plainly wondering what had provoked an exchange of German when neither Natalie nor Chapman hailed from *Deutschland*.

"A while back, I learned Bob was fluent in German, and I mentioned I'd always wanted to learn it," Natalie said. "He's been tossing German at me ever since. I had to start studying it to figure out what on earth he was saying."

"You may thank me, then, for the blossoming of your linguistic talents," Chapman said.

"I don't know about blossoming," Natalie said. "But if I'm ever lost in Munich, at least I'll be able to say '*Hilf mir. Ich spreche kein Deutsch.*'"

"Meaning?" Regina asked.

"Meaning 'Help, I don't speak German.' Please, have a seat." Natalie gestured. Chapman sat in an armchair, and Regina took a seat on the couch.

Natalie returned to her own chair. "What can I do for you?"

"You may accept my thanks, *meine scharfsichtige Dame*—my sharp-eyed lady. I've been informed that your lovely brown eyes—or are they green?—are the instruments that spotted our much-disturbed friend, Heather Osbourne. Had it not been for your alertness, she would have succeeded in her sad quest."

"I'm grateful I was in the right place to notice her," Natalie said. "But she still would have succeeded if Stuart MacKerron hadn't kicked that door down."

"Yes, the noble Mr. MacKerron saved the day with panache worthy of the silver screen. I am indebted to him. But I'm here to talk about you, Dr.

Marsh. I enjoy showering my gratitude on the worthy, and I believe I have enough insight into your soul to know what you desire. You may begin the process of bringing a full-time nurse practitioner on board."

"*Thank you*," Natalie said. "A psychiatric nurse practitioner would be a huge help."

"Good thing you have so much office space," Regina said. "Didn't you just hire a few new people?"

"Yes, a receptionist to replace our original hire, who moved to Long Island to take care of family issues. And a licensed clinical social worker, and I have an intern from NYU. We still have plenty of room. Our three part-time psychologists share office space, and our marriage and family therapists are—"

Regina held up a hand. "I believe you. Don't recite the whole seating chart."

Chapman laughed. "Ah, Regina, if you invite Dr. Marsh to speak about her clinic, you should prepare yourself for an enthusiastic and detailed report. Dr. Marsh, the funds for the nurse will be made available to you. My excellent assistant, William the Prepared, will send you the details."

"Thank you."

"I'm also here to ask a favor." Chapman tapped the toe of one high-top sneaker against the carpet. "I know you are as concerned as I that Ms. Osbourne receive the necessary treatment and not return to haunt us— either in the flesh or as a ghost. The police took her to the emergency room on Saturday night, and she has now plunged into the catacombs of confidentiality. The hospital will tell us nothing, including whether or not she is still a patient."

"That's how it works," Natalie said. "I'm sorry. It can be frustrating."

"We've discovered she has a brother who is blessed with a few more marbles than she. Considering Ms. Osbourne's obsession with this resurrected edifice, William asked the brother if he would be willing to stay in touch with us regarding his sister's situation and state of mind."

"Was he willing?" Natalie asked.

"After some persuasion," Chapman said. "I'd like you to serve as our liaison. You wouldn't be involved in whatever treatment Ms. Osbourne is receiving. You would simply meet with her brother as soon as possible to get updated information and then stay in touch with him. Please persuade him to contact us immediately if anything occurs that might affect us."

"I'd be happy to keep in touch with him."

"Excellent." Chapman plucked a folded paper out of his shirt pocket and extended it to Natalie. "His contact information. His name is Kenton Lowery. He said he knows you."

Natalie blocked a surge of dismay before it damaged her businesslike smile. Kenton Lowery was Heather's brother? That gave her a measure of insight about Heather's struggles—insight she couldn't share with Chapman or Regina. "Bob, I apologize. I'm always willing to help, but I recommend that someone else function as Mr. Lowery's contact. My serving in this position might create a conflict of interest."

Chapman gave her a knowing smile and lowered the paper. "Ah, *mein Schatz*, I wondered about this when I heard Mr. Lowery was acquainted with you. I'm told he's dazzling to the female eye. Is he perhaps a former suitor?"

"No," Natalie said. "But the situation would be a better fit for someone else. If it involves getting and relaying reports, you don't need a mental health professional in the role. Maybe Regina . . . ?"

Regina shook her head. "William said that until your name came up, Lowery wasn't willing to speak to anyone about Heather. He's willing to talk to you but no one else."

Chapman still looked amused. "Are you concerned about the good Mr. Radcliffe's reaction if you begin intimate communication with the very pinnacle of male beauty?"

Heat began to singe Natalie's composure. "Not at all."

"Ah." Chapman leaned forward, curiosity displacing the teasing in his eyes. "A professional complication, then? Not surprising, given his sister's difficulties. Mr. Lowery is your client?"

"I didn't say that."

"Does he struggle with the same type of issues as his sister?" Regina asked sharply. "Could he end up focusing his delusions on us?"

Natalie ignored Regina's questions. "I'd prefer that someone else meet with him."

"I see." Chapman leaned back in his chair and scrutinized her. "How will it affect Mr. Lowery's willingness to help us if we tell him the one person with whom he's comfortable refuses to speak with him?"

"William can phrase it more gently. Tell him I'm unable to serve in that capacity, not that I'm unwilling."

"*Are* you unable?" Chapman asked.

Natalie hesitated. She wasn't, strictly speaking, unable. Ethically, interaction with a former client was a gray area, one she didn't want to muddle through.

Nor did she want to tell the financial backer of her dream that she refused to help. Kenton was extremely private; he *would* refuse to talk to anyone else. It had taken her considerable work to gain his trust. She didn't want to shatter that by giving him the impression she was now rejecting him.

"If you are able, my dear, I would greatly appreciate it," Chapman said. "It's for your benefit more than for any of the other businesses here. Though Heather Osbourne has never received services from Nefesh Bria, any news reports discussing her will inevitably link her difficulties with those of your clientele, luridly creating the impression that you are flooded by delusional people ready to submit themselves to a bloody end at the whim of a ghost."

"I will . . . attempt it," Natalie said.

"I have faith in you, *mein Schatz*." Chapman bounced to his feet, tossed the folded paper with Kenton's contact information onto Natalie's desk, and headed for the door. "*Auf Wiedersehen*."

When Chapman's exuberant footsteps had faded, Natalie picked up the paper and said, "This isn't a good idea."

"Thank you for being willing to try," Regina said. "I'm sorry you're in an uncomfortable position, but the fact that Bob would come to ask you personally shows how important this is to him."

"I understand."

"It's never a good idea to get in Bob's way when something is important to him." Regina stood. "The Stoker Building is his new pet. He doesn't want problems here."

"I understand." Natalie slid the paper into her center desk drawer. "I don't want problems either."

CHAPTER 3

GIDEON SET HIS LAPTOP ON the kitchen table and draped his tie around his neck. A guy could tie only so many full Windsors before the lure of YouTube tutorials drew him to experiment. A dinner hosted by a surprisingly friendly Baxter Quincy—who claimed he wanted to express his gratitude to everyone involved in preventing Heather's dive from the window of his travel agency—definitely called for a new knot. Gideon hit play on "Twenty Necktie Knots to Try."

Fifteen minutes later, after a lopsided Prince Albert, a reasonably dignified Cape, a valiant attempt at the Trinity, and three increasingly improving Eldredges, the ringing of the doorbell reminded Gideon that he had no socks or shoes on, the cuffs of his shirt weren't buttoned, and he ought to glance in the mirror to make sure his hair hadn't gone feral since he'd combed it at 6:00 a.m.

He checked his watch. He'd planned to meet the MacKerrons at their apartment ten minutes from now, but maybe they were antsy to leave. Natalie was coming straight from Nefesh Bria and would meet them at the restaurant.

Gideon shut his laptop and patted the current Eldredge knot—good enough. He buttoned his cuffs as he trotted toward the door.

It wasn't Ainsley or Stuart at the door. The sight of a police uniform hit like a blast of grit in his eyes and throat. He blinked, swallowed, and yanked his thoughts out of paths they detoured into all too quickly. *Take it easy. It doesn't mean someone is hurt. Or dead.*

"Good evening, sir." The woman spoke briskly. "I'm Officer Kalili. I'm sorry to disturb you, but we've had another burglary reported in the complex."

"I'm sorry to hear that." Gideon attempted not to sound too relieved. He doubted his neighbors would appreciate an attitude of "Hey, I was sure glad to hear you were burglarized."

"The break-in occurred around 1:00 p.m. today," Kalili said. "Were you home at that time?"

"I wasn't, unfortunately." *Another burglary.* He'd forgotten about the flyer tacked on his door a week or two back warning tenants of recent break-ins.

"The burglary took place in your building this time," Kalili said. "Have you seen anything lately that might help us apprehend the thief? Suspicious behavior? Cars that don't belong? Unfamiliar people in the complex?"

Gideon pondered the questions. "Sorry. I haven't noticed anything."

"What's your name, sir?"

"Gideon Radcliffe. Would you like ID?" Gideon reached into his back pocket, pulled out his wallet, and passed Kalili his driver's license.

She jotted his information on her notepad and passed the license back, along with a business card. "Please contact us immediately if you learn anything that might help. Keep your doors and windows locked, even when you're home. This time the thief broke in while the tenant was there."

"Yikes," Gideon said. "Is everyone okay?"

"Everyone's fine. If you do see anything suspicious, please don't confront the person. Call 911 immediately. If you have valuable jewelry or pricey knickknacks, you might want to put them in a safe-deposit box for a while."

"Nothing exciting for a jewelry or knickknack thief here," Gideon said. Unless the thief wanted to swipe his silver Gucci cufflinks. He had no clue what they were worth, but ex-fiancée Tamara had presented them to him like they belonged in a vault at Fort Knox. He ought to donate them to Goodwill. He never wore them.

"Thank you, sir. Have a good evening."

"Thanks." Gideon closed the door and went to put on his socks and shoes.

Five minutes later, he headed outside and down the stairs to the MacKerrons' ground-level apartment. Ainsley answered the door. "Come in. We're almost ready."

Gideon stepped inside. Ainsley disappeared into the back of the apartment, and he stood in the living room, admiring how clean the place was and thinking he ought to dust off his own vacuum and use it. A deep cleaning was definitely overdue. He contemplated the crystal vase of silk tulips in the middle of the MacKerrons' kitchen table. It looked about a thousand times more elegant than the scattered work papers and piles of Lego pieces decorating his own table. One of these days, he ought to get some class.

Ainsley returned to the living room, Stuart following her.

"Thanks for offering to play chauffeur," Gideon said.

"Our pleasure." Ainsley picked up her purse. "I figured you'd go with Natalie until she told me she was going directly from work. It's a waste of gas for neighbors to take separate cars, and we'd like a chance to get to know you better."

"Likewise," Gideon said.

Stuart opened the front door and held it as Ainsley and Gideon walked out of the apartment.

"Did the police stop at your place just now?" Gideon watched Stuart dead bolt the door behind them. "Asking about another burglary?"

"Yeah," Stuart said. "We'd already heard about it. It was a lady two doors down who got robbed." He gestured behind them on the walkway. "Number sixteen."

Gideon grimaced. "The officer said someone was home when the thief broke in?"

"Yes, she was there," Ainsley said. "She was taking a nap and heard noise and came out to see this guy in a ski mask."

"She's okay?"

"Yeah," Stuart said. "The thief grabbed something and bolted. One of those fancy eggs."

"A Fabergé egg," Ainsley said.

"Huh." Gideon fiddled with his tie knot. "The officer said the thief was a fan of pricey knickknacks. Are jeweled eggs a hot item on the black market?"

Stuart shrugged. "Who knows? I'm changing our locks. I don't care if management doesn't like it."

As they reached the bottom of the stairs, Ainsley said, "Oh, Stuart, we got a note saying there's a FedEx package for us."

"What is it?"

"I don't know. Did you order something?"

"I'll grab it." Stuart detoured toward the office. Ainsley and Gideon remained on the sidewalk next to a concrete planter box where petunias rustled in a cool wind.

"Feels like summer got canceled," Gideon remarked.

"It's supposed to rain late tonight." Ainsley smiled at him. "How long have you known Natalie?"

Oh boy. Relationship questions. "Uh . . . just under a year."

"How did you meet?"

"Uh . . . actually my stepmother has known Natalie since she was a kid. We met when I moved to Ohneka after my father's death. How about you and Stuart?"

"I was a secretary at Larraway High, where Stuart works. He's an athletic trainer. Works with the teams, deals with injuries, helps keep the kids safe."

"Sounds like a satisfying job."

"It doesn't pay much though. So you and Natalie are dating?"

Gideon's face heated up. "I should go see if Stuart needs . . ." *Needs help carrying the package? In case someone shipped him a piano?*

"Sorry," Ainsley said. "I was just curious. It's not my business."

Gideon figured he shouldn't respond with, *Natalie is curious too. And so am I. And I'm an idiot.*

"I hope Baxter has the decency not to pick a fight with Natalie tonight." Ainsley changed the subject. "If it weren't for her and Stuart, his travel agency would be haunted for real."

"At least he appreciates their help enough to invite us all to dinner."

"Yes." Ainsley's red hair fluttered in the wind. Repeatedly, she smoothed it down as though wanting to make sure she looked perfect. "You'd think he could do better though."

"Maybe he's planning to hand out travel vouchers to the Bahamas."

"I doubt it. Stuart's cousin Drew recently started working for Quincy Travel. He says Baxter is pretty tightfisted in how he runs his business."

"Guess I won't bother hinting at how much I'd like to visit Machu Picchu," Gideon said.

Stuart walked out of the office carrying a FedEx envelope. Ainsley resumed walking along the sidewalk, and Gideon started to follow, but after a few steps, he realized Stuart was still in front of the office ripping the envelope open.

Ainsley paused and glanced back at Stuart. "What is it?"

Stuart unfolded a stack of papers. "Lamb, come look at this. *Now.*"

Ainsley hurried to his side. Stuart passed her the papers, reached into the FedEx envelope, and removed a small, bulky envelope.

Ainsley read the top sheet, then grabbed Stuart's arm. "Is this real?"

"It can't be." Stuart ripped open the small envelope. "It's a joke."

"It's not a joke." Ainsley raced in the direction of the parking lot, her heels pattering like hailstones against the concrete. Stuart followed her.

Feeling like an intruder—Gideon barely knew the MacKerrons, and judging by their agitation, something significant had happened—he called out, "I'll meet you at Il Giardino."

Without looking back, Stuart beckoned curtly for Gideon to follow. Not wanting to be rude, Gideon trailed after them, deliberately not catching up.

"*There,*" Stuart called to Ainsley, pointing into the parking lot.

Gideon looked where he was pointing but wasn't sure which vehicle had caught his attention. Stuart and Ainsley rushed between parked cars and approached a pickup truck, a glossy-black Dodge Ram.

Ainsley threw her arms around Stuart's neck and kissed him, a kiss so long and passionate that Gideon made a firm decision to retreat. "I'll see you at dinner," he said loudly and started walking away. Behind him, he heard Stuart laugh.

"Come check out my new wheels," Stuart yelled.

Gideon turned. Stuart tapped the hood of the Dodge and grinned. "A thank-you gift," he said. "From Robert Chapman."

"Seriously?" Gideon walked toward the truck. "Nice!"

"Guess that crazy girl really is a fortune-teller," Stuart said.

Ainsley flapped the paperwork in her hand. "Do you know how much this cost?"

"Nope," Gideon said. He hadn't researched the prices of pickup trucks lately. "More than I paid for my seven-year-old Honda, I'm guessing."

Stuart pressed the button on the key fob he'd taken from the envelope. The truck beeped, and the locks clicked open. "In Drew's *face.*" Stuart climbed up to settle in the driver's seat.

"Sur*priiiise.*"

At the sing-song word, Gideon wheeled around to see Heather Osbourne approaching.

Ainsley gasped. Stuart thumped to the ground and faced Heather. "You're supposed to be locked up," he said.

Heather stroked the tailgate with her index finger. "I'm not insane."

Stuart started toward her, but Ainsley caught his arm. "*Don't.* She might be armed."

Stuart shifted so his body blocked Ainsley. "How'd you escape?"

"Give Robert Chapman my regards." Heather swung around and walked away, her long black hair whipping in the wind.

"I don't think she has a gun," Stuart said. "I'll grab her. Radcliffe, call the police. How'd she sneak out of the loony bin?"

Heather fired a glare over her shoulder. "Touch me and you'll be the one locked up, Stuart MacKerron."

"Let her go," Gideon said. "I doubt she escaped. They've released her."

"But she tried to throw herself out a window," Ainsley said as Heather glided around the corner of a building and disappeared.

"They must have decided she isn't in acute danger at the moment," Gideon said.

"Maybe *she* isn't, but what about us?" Ainsley gripped Stuart's arm. "She's stalking us! How else would she know where we live?"

"Google?" Stuart turned back to the gleaming new truck. "Don't worry. I can handle her. Let's go for a ride."

* * *

Stuart drove carefully—more carefully than Ainsley had ever seen him drive—but her pulse was speeding as they walked through the doors of Il Giardino. She'd wanted to spill all her excited thoughts to Stuart, but with Gideon Radcliffe sitting in the back seat of the extended cab, she'd limited herself to commenting on Chapman's generosity and Heather Osbourne's creepiness.

She'd hoped for a reward from Robert Chapman but hadn't thought Heather's predictions were worth anything. Maybe they were. Maybe Heather wasn't insane—maybe she had the second sight. Maybe she could see things other people couldn't, like ghosts and the future. Heather had predicted exactly how Chapman would show his gratitude, and the truck hadn't been her only prediction. *"You want to be at his side on his crazy wanderings. You can have that too."*

That prediction had startled and confused Ainsley. Heather could have heard about Chapman's hiring a trail guide—Drew was always bragging about the Trekmeister job, and Heather could have heard gossip while wandering around the Stoker or even heard Drew boasting about it when she'd gone to Quincy Travel to steal that access card. But how could she have known Stuart coveted the position? Stuart had insisted he'd never said anything about it to anyone and it must be Ainsley who'd blabbed, but Ainsley had never told anyone either. The closest she'd come was mentioning to Natalie and Gideon that Stuart would be a great trail guide.

Maybe Heather *did* have a gift—a curse?—of seeing things. Knowing things.

At the direction of the hostess at the front of the restaurant, Ainsley, Stuart, and Gideon headed through the wood-and-marble-paneled restaurant toward the stairs that led to private banquet rooms on the upper floor.

Stuart hadn't put his new keys in his suit pocket. He kept jiggling them, fingering them, grinning at them. "This is crazy," he said. "Crazy. Let's bail early and go for a drive."

"Welcome!" Baxter was standing at the doorway to the banquet room. "Ainsley, you look fantastic."

"Thank you."

Stuart shook Baxter's hand. "How's business?"

"Hot, thanks to you. You're the man, MacKerron. I've heard a lot about you from Drew Drummond. Glad to have Drew on board." Baxter offered his hand to Gideon. "Welcome. Gavin, right?"

"Gideon." Gideon shook his hand.

Baxter touched the arm of the woman next to him. She reminded Ainsley of a 1950s movie star—tall, elegant, small waist, her hair unnaturally perfect and styled in a retro way that made the strong bones of her face look queenly. Her mint-green cocktail dress was a fashion Ainsley doubted anyone had worn in the last sixty years, but it flattered her. In fact, she looked so stunning that Ainsley felt instantly tacky, expecting her sister-in-law's voice to come out of the woman's mouth: *"This isn't really a Walmart occasion, Ainsley. Don't you have anything nicer?"*

"This is Lauren Bell," Baxter introduced her. "She works at the Stoker too, at the Parisi Gallery."

The art gallery, Ainsley thought. *Of course.*

"Good to meet you, Lauren." Gideon shook her hand. Stuart offered his hand too. Ainsley would rather have made a catty comment about how the 1950s called and wanted their dress back, but she smiled and shook Lauren's manicured hand.

"Baxter told me how you all saved the day," Lauren said, her voice as polished as her appearance.

"It was Stuart." Ainsley glanced at her husband to see if he was ogling Lauren. He wasn't.

Stuart rested his hand on Ainsley's shoulder. "Ainsley's the one who told me to follow Heather."

Lauren smiled with lips so flawless they belonged in a Photoshopped makeup ad. "Obviously, you make a wonderful team. Baxter has told me many times how grateful he is."

"I brought the gang. They all want to thank you." Baxter waved toward a group of people clustered near a table of appetizers. The only person in the group Ainsley recognized was Drew.

"Is Mr. Chapman coming tonight?" Ainsley asked.

"He can't make it for dinner, but he'll try to stop by for dessert," Baxter said. "Natalie, welcome." As Baxter's attention shifted to Natalie, who had just entered, Ainsley clutched Stuart's elbow and steered him farther into the room. Stuart, still fiddling with the keys now in his pocket, didn't seem to care where they were going and let her guide him until they were standing alone in front of a window.

"Stuart," she whispered, "if Mr. Chapman does come, this is your chance." She tipped her head toward Drew, who had picked up one of the stained-glass candleholders from the table and was showing the candle to a woman—probably mansplaining how fire worked. Stocky, curly-haired Drew was a girl magnet, which made Ainsley wonder if there was a limit to how dumb women could be. "You have to impress Chapman. Convince him you're a better choice to be his hiking guru."

"Give it *up*. He's not going to ditch Drew. Drew's a solid choice."

"Chapman picked Drew because he crossed paths with him when Drew was working for his company. Drew was lucky. *You're* a better choice. He gave you a *truck* as a thank-you gift. If you can—"

Stuart nudged her. Drew had set the candle on the table and was walking toward them, grinning.

"Hey, hero." Drew gave Stuart a bro hug. "Too bad they kept things so quiet. Your ugly face should have been on the front page."

"Nobody wants publicity about what happened," Stuart said. "Especially not Quincy."

"Yeah, whew, boss man wasn't happy." Drew kissed Ainsley's cheek. "How does it feel to be married to a guy who finally did something great? I got the whole scoop from Bob. That woman's a total nut. Good thing she's off the streets."

"She's already free." Ainsley hated Drew's constant digging at Stuart, but if she called him on it, he'd say, like he always did, that he was joking. And Stuart would say, like he always did, that he didn't mind, though Ainsley knew he did. "We saw her tonight."

"She's *free*? It's only been, what, like a week? Two weeks? I thought they'd clap her in a padded cell and eat the key. Does Bob know she's out?"

"How would we know?" Ainsley asked. "You're the one who has the whole scoop."

"I haven't talked to him for a few days. But you did well, Stu. He's one grateful dude."

Stuart held up his truck keys. "He sent me a thank-you note. With four-wheel drive."

"Cousin!" Drew hammered Stuart on the back. "You're welcome!"

Ainsley tried not to sound irritated. "What did you have to do with this?"

Drew laughed. "Who do you think told Bob what Stuart would want as a reward?"

Stuart grinned at his cousin. "Thanks."

Ainsley forced herself to smile as well, though she'd sooner have smacked that smug expression off Drew's face. "Did you tell Heather Osbourne too?"

"Who?"

"The woman Stuart stopped from throwing herself out the window."

"Sorry, I forgot her name. What do you mean, did I tell her? I never saw her that night. I missed all the fun."

"She predicted Chapman would reward me with a truck," Stuart explained, flicking a warning glance at Ainsley—he was afraid she'd say something about Heather's other prediction. "After I tackled her."

"She did?" Drew snickered. "So she's psychic, eh?"

"I guess so," Stuart said.

Drew plucked the keys out of Stuart's hand and examined them. "You happy with the Dodge?"

"Yeah, for sure."

"Told you Bob's generous. Every time I blink, there's a bonus. Being *der Trekmeister* is like living in a gold mine." He tossed the keys to Stuart. "Kiss up to him and things might get cushy enough that your wife can quit working as a desk flunky at that clinic."

A flash flood of heat swirled into Ainsley's cheeks. She was finished with Drew's putdowns and bragging. Stuart, not Drew, deserved that appointment with Chapman. Heather had been right once. Ainsley would make sure she was right twice.

How?

"She doesn't want to quit," Stuart said. "She likes it."

"It's a step on the ladder," Ainsley said sweetly. Drew was too oblivious to notice how she'd reddened. "Drew, you need to come over and see Stuart's new truck. You guys ought to christen it on a camping trip."

Stuart slipped a baffled glance at Ainsley, obviously confused at her encouraging him to spend time with his cousin when usually she griped about it. She beamed at him. "Stuart needs to squeeze in some fun before sports practices start ramping up again."

"Name the date," Drew said. "I set my own schedule with Quincy. As long as it doesn't conflict with one of the prep hikes I'm setting up for Bob, we're good."

"I'm clear next Friday," Stuart said. "The twentieth."

"Drew could come to dinner that Thursday night," Ainsley suggested. "You guys could catch up, get sloshed, sleep late. Then leave Friday afternoon. Maybe head for the Adirondacks."

"I'm on board with that." Drew fist-bumped Stuart. "Ainsley, make that pulled pork, will you?"

"Sure," Ainsley said. "It'll be the best home-cooked meal you've had in years."

"Can't wait," Drew said. "You're a prize, Ainsley."

Ainsley made her smile as bewitching as she could. "Thank you."

* * *

Glad to see Gideon, glad for a chance to eat and relax, and grateful for the unexpected—the *very* unexpected—chance to improve her interaction with Baxter Quincy, Natalie intertwined her fingers with Gideon's. He squeezed her hand but released it so quickly that it reminded her of the time he'd absentmindedly grabbed the handle of her heated cast-iron frying pan.

Natalie subdued an urge to ask if he'd prefer she not touch him. He hadn't been this reticent when they'd started dating last fall, but she'd noticed it more and more over the past two or three months—at least she'd noticed it when she'd had time to see him between the countless jobs involved in getting the clinic running. A warm good-night kiss had become a good-night peck, then a kiss on the cheek, then a hug. One of these days, she'd be lucky to get a handshake.

Did he want to end the relationship—whatever the relationship was? He still seemed to want to be with her, contacting her and seeking her company, and he'd been a godsend with his volunteer work at Nefesh Bria.

But did he want a friend, not a girlfriend?

Give him a break, she told herself. Just over a year ago, he'd been engaged to someone else. Was it any wonder he was sending mixed signals? He was probably steeling himself for the possibility that Natalie would dump him as Tamara had. If he kept at least a little distance between them, maybe he wouldn't have to be devastated again.

Whatever his reasons, they needed to talk about it. She'd procrastinated that conversation for too long, and the silence wasn't healthy for them.

They meandered toward the table of appetizers. "Thanks for meeting me here," Natalie said casually. Baxter's dinner party wasn't the place to corner him about what he wanted from their relationship. "You can keep me awake on the ride home."

"Hitching a ride with the MacKerrons was no problem," Gideon said. "I got to be part of a historic occasion. The inaugural ride of Stuart's new truck."

"New truck?"

"Brand-new Dodge Ram. A gift from Bob Chapman."

"Are you serious? Ainsley didn't mention that at work today."

"Just happened tonight."

"That's fantastic. I figured Bob would do something grandiose for . . . Wait. Isn't a truck what Heather Osbourne predicted . . ."

"Yes." Gideon's grin went grim. "Heather showed up while we were gawking at the truck. Startled us."

More clouds gathered over Natalie's hope for a relaxing evening. "What did she do?"

"Not much. Said to say hi to Chapman and walked away."

"Did she act threatening?"

"No. She seemed calm. Sane but creepy, if that makes sense. Her showing up right when Stuart found the truck was eerie enough on its own. How did she know?"

"Natalie." Baxter caught up with them, Lauren at his side. "I just heard the ghost lady is rattling around free. What's up with that? They let her go, and we get to wait until she sneaks into the Stoker and knifes someone on Grandma's orders?"

"They wouldn't have released her unless they were confident she wasn't a threat," Natalie said. This wasn't an auspicious time to mention that there *had* been occasions when she'd hospitalized clients and seen them released sooner than she thought wise.

"Yeah, that's not money in the bank," Baxter said. "I'd like her doctor's name so I know who to sue after Grandma attacks me."

"Grandma is 125 years old and dead," Gideon said. "If you can't take her on, forget the lawsuit. Hit the gym."

Baxter scowled. Lauren raised an eyebrow. Natalie tried not to laugh. Obviously, she was the only one in the conversation who appreciated Gideon's snippet of dark humor.

"I doubt there's reason to worry," Natalie said. "As far as I know, Heather has never threatened any of the Stoker tenants or shown aggression toward them. She didn't attempt to hurt anyone besides herself the other night, and her doctor must be confident that she's not imminently suicidal."

"Maybe her attempt at the party was more an effort to stir bad publicity for the Stoker than a genuine desire to die," Gideon suggested.

"'As far as I know.'" Baxter mimicked Natalie. "'Must be.' 'Maybe.' Neither of you knows anything for sure."

"No, we don't know," Natalie said. So much for hoping she could mend fences with Baxter. The news of Heather's release seemed to have wiped out whatever goodwill he'd felt when he'd invited Natalie. "How often can any of us predict anything for sure?"

"We know for sure Heather Osbourne is insane," Baxter said. "That's a fact. It should be enough to keep her off the streets."

"There are laws that control the circumstances under which a person can be involuntarily committed and for how long," Natalie said. "If she no longer meets those criteria, they can't hold her."

"It astounds me that you'd take her side after what you saw."

"Baxter, I'm not taking anyone's side. I'm stating what we're dealing with legally. It's a complicated issue, and hospitals have limited bed space."

"Complicated because her rights get put before our safety."

Lowering her eyes, Lauren rubbed a fingertip against her ivory-leather clutch purse as though cleaning away a spot. Natalie was glad she looked embarrassed. She didn't seem to share Baxter's attitude.

"The idea that mental illness makes a person likely to commit acts of violence is a myth." Natalie tried not to sound exasperated. "You know that. We've discussed this before. There's no reason to think Heather is going to harm anyone."

"Baxter doesn't mean to sound harsh," Lauren said graciously. "He's concerned for Heather's well-being. When Mr. Chapman asked if he would agree to let the matter go if they could persuade the district attorney not to file charges, Baxter was in favor of that. He didn't want poor Heather in prison."

Baxter's face softened and settled into a more temperate expression. "The woman needs a hospital, not prison, but I expected they'd *keep* her in the hospital. Natalie, I assume you've talked to her brother. Bob said you were going to meet with him. What did he say?"

"I haven't spoken to him yet. We have an appointment."

"What are you waiting for?" Baxter's tone hardened again; apparently Lauren's gentle tact couldn't mellow him for long. "Shouldn't it be your top priority?"

"This was the soonest our schedules matched up," Natalie said. "Even when I do talk with him, I can't force him to share anything he doesn't want to share. Nor do I have any control over Heather or over the decisions of her health providers or law enforcement."

Baxter opened his mouth, and Natalie braced herself for an angry response, but Lauren touched his shoulder and said, "I'm sure Natalie's doing everything she can."

"I understand that," Baxter said in what Natalie assumed was a kinder voice than he would have used without Lauren's intervention. "After what almost happened at my office, I get wound up about this, especially because it's what I've been warning Bob about all along. Her clinic doesn't belong at the Stoker. Clients and customers should feel comfortable there, not worried about running into a lunatic who thinks we're disturbing her grandmother's ghost."

"You realize Heather has no connection to Nefesh Bria, right?" Gideon said.

"Fine, yes, but she could be your poster child. There's more where she came from, and you're putting out the welcome mat."

Natalie sighed. "With respect, Baxter, when you invited us to dinner, I was under the impression that you wanted to express appreciation, not harangue me with old arguments."

"You're right," Baxter said. "I apologize. I *am* grateful for your part in stopping Heather. I want you to know that."

"I'm glad I could help," Natalie said. "Like you, I sincerely hope Heather will get the help she needs and that nothing like this will happen again."

"Exactly. But before we drop the subject, you should know there *have* been problems already with your clinic. Someone who works in the Stoker told me that a man coming from Nefesh Bria followed her while she was walking home and kept trying to talk to her. She was ready to call the cops when he finally gave up and left her alone. Now she's nervous whenever she leaves work, and she's driving instead of walking, even though she likes the walk. It shouldn't be that way."

Dismay prickled through Natalie. "When did this happen?"

"Last week."

"Did she report the man to security?"

"No. She thought she was overreacting and didn't want to make trouble. But the guy gave her the willies. He didn't approach her until she was off the Stoker grounds—I'll bet he was avoiding security cameras."

"Did she give you a description?"

"She said she didn't get a good look at him."

"I'd like to talk to her."

"She wouldn't want to get interrogated by you. She doesn't want the guy arrested or anything."

"She doesn't want anyone to do anything about it? She wants to continue being creeped out?"

"No matter what you do, it'd be swatting one fly while a thousand more swarm in. You're in the wrong place, Natalie. Quincy Travel is willing to kick in some of the funds to help you relocate to a more appropriate location."

Now he was trying to pay her to clear out? Was it impossible for Baxter to talk to her for more than thirty seconds without condemning the clinic's presence at the Stoker? "Thank you for the offer. We're not moving."

Lauren's elegant fingertips touched Baxter's arm. "Let's talk business another time. I'm sure Natalie and Gideon would like to eat and relax."

"Great idea," Gideon said. "The melon with prosciutto is calling my name." Clasping Natalie's elbow, he propelled her toward the appetizers.

"Calling a time-out?" Natalie said drily.

"Yeah. I was afraid one of us would say something that would get us kicked out before I get my fried ravioli."

"It wouldn't have been me," Natalie said through gritted teeth. "My self-control is forged of steel."

"So were those daggers your eyes were hurling at Baxter." Gideon handed her a plate. "Bruschetta?"

CHAPTER 4

NATALIE PARKED IN FRONT OF a small, white clapboard building. A hanging wooden sign displayed a river otter floating on its back and clutching a baguette in its paws. Cheerfully crooked font read *Playful Otter Bakery*. Though Kenton Lowery had helped found the bakery, Natalie doubted he'd had much to do with either the name or the logo. Both were too whimsical to be his style. The location *was* his style on this narrow, quiet street in East Rochester. The bakery must have a strong reputation to draw customers here. Not much random traffic would pass this way.

The clock on her dashboard read 5:58. The Playful Otter closed at five. Kenton had told her to arrive at six and he'd talk to her in the empty bakery. She would have preferred a more public location but knew that would cause him stress. Sitting with him at a table near the storefront windows would have to be public enough.

Black clouds and a grumble of thunder played prelude to rain as Natalie stepped into the damp July evening. She walked toward the bakery door, contemplating how best to gain Kenton's confidence so he'd update her on Heather—and how to gently convince him to meet with Regina for future updates.

Raindrops splattered her hair, and she rushed the last few steps to get under the brick-red awning. She rapped on the locked door.

Through the glass, she saw Kenton approaching. He unlocked the door, and Natalie stepped to the side so he could push it open.

"Good evening," she said.

"Hi, Dr. Marsh." He spoke quietly. She'd never heard Kenton raise his voice, no matter how upset he was. "Thanks for driving all the way here."

"I'd be more comfortable if you'd call me Natalie. I'm not here in a professional capacity."

Kenton offered an edgy smile. He wore a white T-shirt, white pants, and a flour-covered apron with the Playful Otter logo on it. A white cap covered his thick black hair, and flour powdered his face like marble dust from the chisel of a sculptor who'd created a god. Kenton Lowery was, without question, the most physically beautiful man Natalie had ever seen in her life.

"Come in," he said.

Natalie stepped into the bakery. Four rectangular wood-topped tables were set near the windows. On the back wall, a glass case and two wall shelves were empty; earlier they must have displayed baked goods. A menu board listed items for sale—mostly breads, Kenton's specialty.

Kenton watched her, waiting for her to take the initiative. She was a guest in his domain, but he automatically elevated her into a position of control over the situation: she the therapist, he the client. Changing that dynamic would be difficult.

"Should we sit down?" she asked.

Kenton gestured uncertainly toward one of the tables. "Is here okay?"

"Yes, thank you." Natalie pulled out a wooden chair and sat. Rain blew under the awning, speckling the windows. "Your bakery is charming."

"Thanks." Kenton removed his white cap and ran his fingers through his hat-and-sweat-flattened hair. "It's doing pretty well."

"Congratulations. You're enjoying your work?"

"It's great. Jenny and Josie—my business partners—you remember Jenny and Josie?"

"I do." Jenny and Josie were part of the reason Kenton's ex had objected—repeatedly and violently—to his dream of opening a bakery, a dream that had started moving forward when he'd combined forces with two women he'd met while working as a hotel chef. Never mind that they were both happily married and twenty or thirty years older than Kenton. Natalie had never met Jenny or Josie, but she was grateful to them. They had been the ones to notice the injuries Kenton persistently tried to hide and to finally persuade him to seek help.

"They take care of the customers and everything else," Kenton said. "They're bossy as all get out with me, treat me like one of their kids. Protective of me, right? But I don't mind. I like being able to focus exclusively on baking, and it's good to know they have my back."

A loving mother figure, bossy or otherwise, was something Kenton hadn't grown up with. It sounded like he now had two of them. "I'm glad it's working out so well."

"Want to . . . sample this month's special? It's a grape-rosemary focaccia."

"Grape and rosemary?"

"Concord grapes, fresh rosemary, sea salt, coarse sugar. We always sell out by noon, but I held some back for you today. Hope that's okay."

"That's very kind. I'd love to try it."

"Help yourself to a drink." He pointed at a refrigerated cabinet holding bottled water and soft drinks. "I'll be right back."

Kenton headed through the swinging door behind the counter. Natalie fetched herself a bottle of water.

Kenton returned carrying a piece of parchment paper bearing a flat loaf of bread cut into squares. He set the bread on the table and placed a square on a napkin for Natalie.

"Thank you." She picked up the golden bread glistening with crystals of salt—or was that the sugar?—and dotted with deep purple.

Kenton stood watching her as she tasted it. As she'd expected, it was delicious. "I see why you sell out," she said. "My compliments to the baker."

He rubbed a smear of flour off his arm. "Thanks."

Natalie took two more bites of bread, waiting for Kenton to sit, but he remained standing.

"Will you sit with me?" she asked.

Kenton pulled out a chair and sat, still monitoring her progress with the focaccia. Was he afraid her compliment had been phony? Natalie finished the square of bread, took another piece, and set it on her napkin before launching the conversation. "I hope you know how grateful Mr. Chapman and the management of the Stoker Building are about your willingness to keep us updated on your sister's situation."

He took a square of bread and picked a bit of rosemary off the top. "You want to know why I didn't tell you more about Heather."

"No. I'm not here to ask about what you didn't share in therapy or why you didn't share it. That's none of my business now. I'm not your therapist, the circumstances are different, and please understand that whatever we discuss here is not confidential."

"I know that. You're reporting to your people at the Stoker Building." Kenton's crystalline violet eyes were uncomfortably familiar. Right now, the expression in them was guarded, similar to how he'd appeared when he'd first come to Natalie. Through session after session, she'd worked to penetrate his defenses, and she'd succeeded. She'd witnessed those eyes filled with agony, with rage, with tears. With determination. Finally, with serenity.

Being face-to-face with Kenton made her uneasy about her plan to first discuss Heather, then try to convince him Regina would be a better contact. On the one hand, if she opened with her concerns about serving as liaison, she might learn nothing from him, and neither Chapman, Regina, nor complainers like Baxter would be pleased. But the prospect of accepting and using his trust and then whipping around and shoving him toward Regina . . . no. She needed to be forthright.

"I'd like to discuss our situation for a moment," Natalie said. "I don't want to offend you, but meeting with you like this is uncomfortable for me. I normally don't associate with former clients—not because I don't want their company but because I don't want to do anything that might impede their continued progress. Trying to alter roles and create a healthy relationship independent of—" She stopped. Under the flour, Kenton's face was crimson.

Realizing what he was thinking, Natalie said quickly, "I apologize. I'm not explaining myself well." Eye-candy Kenton was accustomed to being drooled over by nearly every woman who saw him, and he was reading her meaning through that lens. "I'm not speaking of romantic relationships. I know that's not your intention. I'm saying it's difficult to shape any kind of new relationship—friendship, business, and so forth—without patterns of interaction carrying over from therapy and for one or both of us to view things from that perspective."

"I . . . make you uncomfortable?"

"Not you personally. I'd feel the same if it were any former client. I was told you refused to talk to anyone but me, but would you be willing to reconsider that?"

Kenton picked off another fragment of rosemary and lined it up on his napkin with the first bit. "I don't want to talk to *anyone* about this," he mumbled. "I already got my arm twisted by that guy who tracked me down. Robert Chapman's assistant."

"In what way did he twist your arm?"

"Grilling me about Heather." Kenton's voice got quieter. "Wanting me to agree to give updates. Warning about legal action against our family if things go south again."

Internally, Natalie winced. "I understand how you would have felt uncomfortable with his approach. I'm not suggesting you meet with Mr. Chapman's assistant. I can recommend someone who—"

"I'm not obligated to share anything about Heather." Kenton ripped the square of bread in half, staining his fingers purple. "I don't want to get hounded by some business person who thinks Heather is a psycho. They don't care about her. They care about their property values, that's all."

"I know you have no obligation to do this," Natalie said. "We're all worried and, honestly, aren't sure what we're dealing with. The police can't tell us much. We want to do what's best for Heather and for everyone involved."

Kenton didn't respond.

Natalie started on her second piece of focaccia, debating how to proceed. Kenton was avoiding eye contact now and sitting on the edge of his chair as though preparing to escape. If she kept urging him to confide in someone else, he'd withdraw his fragile cooperation entirely and she'd be heading home with less than nothing. "All right," she said. "I know this is difficult for you. I won't press you to handle it differently. If you're willing to talk to me, I'm grateful for that."

"I understand this isn't therapy," he said, some of the stiffness in his spine relaxing. "I'm not thinking of it that way. But at least I know you care. You don't think people with mental problems are freaks. And you already know the family history."

"Anything you told me in therapy is still confidential," Natalie said. "I haven't—and won't—give out any information about you or your family other than what you expressly tell me under these new circumstances. And, of course, I didn't tell anyone you're a former client."

Kenton slid back in his seat, even more visibly at ease. "Have you seen Heather? Talked to her? Before you helped stop her from killing herself, I mean?"

"I saw her arguing with Robert Chapman a few days before that. They were in the hallway outside Nefesh Bria."

"Nefesh Bria?"

"My mental health services clinic at the Stoker."

"What did Heather say to him?"

"In the part of the argument I heard, she called him an invader and said your ancestor Tabitha would get revenge. He told me later he'd invited her there that day so he could tell her he planned to create a memorial alcove and bench in the Stoker gardens to honor Tabitha Ferguson. Mr. Chapman likes to take the diplomatic route and change enemies to allies when he can. Heather wasn't placated, obviously. Would you be willing to tell me more about why Heather is so fixated on your great-great-great-grandmother's death and the place where she died? More information would help us understand how better to de-escalate this situation."

"Yeah, okay, I can do that." Kenton folded his arms across his apron. "It . . . When Heather was a kid, she found these ancient letters. There was this old shed on our property, full of junk. Heather would hide there when Mom would . . . when things got bad. In the shed, she found a bunch of letters from this lady, Tabitha Ferguson, written to her daughter. Heather loved the letters. Read them a million times."

"How did she learn about the way Tabitha died?"

"Library. A librarian helped her figure out Tabitha was our great-great-great-grandmother. Or two greats or four—can't remember. This lady found Tabitha's obituary for Heather and some newspaper articles about how she fell out a window at work. Can't remember how it happened."

"I looked up the articles," Natalie said. "She was standing on a chair, dusting curtains, and lost her balance. The window was open."

"Oh yeah. I thought it had something to do with cleaning. Heather got obsessed with the story. She'd break into the Stoker Building, or whatever it was called back when it was abandoned, and wander around. She had this antique candleholder, and she'd light a candle and carry it around. She told me Tabitha would talk to her there. I told her she was loony. Got a black eye over that."

"From Heather?"

"Yeah. She took Tabitha seriously. Swore Tabitha loved her."

It didn't surprise Natalie that child Heather had fantasized a substitute mother, given the abusive mother and absent father she'd had in real life. "How old was Heather at this time?"

"Uhhhh . . . when she found the letters, I think she was maybe ten? Twelve? She was obsessed with them for years, until she got involved with this Osbourne guy. I guess he distracted her. They got married like a month after she finished high school."

"Is he still around?"

"Nah, he ran off awhile back. That's when she got interested in Tabitha again. Chapman Development had started renovating the building, and she'd call and beg me to help her drive them out. I told her forget it. I wasn't up for anything that might cause trouble. Last thing I need is my name in the news. I never know if . . . *she* might notice it, might . . . get interested in me again."

Natalie knew *she* didn't refer to Heather. Kenton was tracing his thumb along the scar that ran down his left forearm onto the back of his hand—his wife's work with a shard of a crystal goblet Kenton had dropped.

Natalie fought her instincts to ask about his ex. She'd feared throughout the entire divorce process that he'd cave and return to her, submitting to her abuse, but he'd made it. Was she leaving Kenton alone now? If she did contact him, was he refusing to let her manipulate him?

Striving to stay focused on Heather and not delve into things that were no longer her business, Natalie asked, "Have you spoken to Heather recently?"

"Yeah, she called me from the hospital."

"What did—?" Natalie hesitated, discomfort stirring again. It was too easy to ask questions, too easy to expect Kenton to answer them as they settled back into former patterns. "Before we go on, I want to make something clear. You don't have to answer any questions you don't want to answer. Feel free to tell me if you'd rather not share something."

He nodded. "You want to know what Heather was like on the phone, right?"

"Yes."

"She was crying." He watched the rain streaming down the windows. "Said she thought dying at the party would help Tabitha, but now she was afraid she'd been wrong."

"Has she ever been suicidal before?"

"Not that I know of. She begged me to talk to the doctors and tell them she wasn't crazy. I said trying to jump out a window so you can help a ghost haunt a building sounds crackers to me. She hung up. A few days later, she showed up here to say, 'I told you so; they let me go.' I said, 'Great.'"

"How did she seem?"

"Okay, pretty much. She has her act together most of the time. She did say some weird stuff about your clinic."

"Weird stuff not connected to Tabitha?"

"She said something evil is happening there."

"Did she get more specific?"

"No. Just said there were wicked people there. Wicked hearts. That it was a dangerous place."

She'd get along wonderfully with Baxter Quincy. "Do you know if she's receiving counseling now?"

"She said she'd promised to see a therapist and had an appointment set up, but she didn't go. The doc at the hospital started her on medication, but once she got out, she stopped taking it." Kenton picked up a new square of focaccia and prodded the interior of the bread with his little finger as though assessing the structure of the bubbles. "She mentioned you," he said. "She doesn't know you were my therapist. She doesn't know I know you at all."

"What did she say?"

"That you pretend to be nice but you're Chapman's minion. You have to kiss his boots to keep your funding."

Natalie wanted to respond that her lips had never touched Chapman's footwear, but the fact that, under pressure from him, she was here talking to Kenton—an assignment she hadn't wanted and had tried to reject—made her reluctant to open that argument.

Kenton drew several hasty, shallow breaths. He made eye contact, didn't breathe at all for a long moment, then averted his eyes and repeated the shallow breaths. Natalie had seen that pattern from him countless times: he ached to say something but was struggling to find the nerve. She waited.

After the third time through the cycle, Kenton spoke. "She said you've . . . you've experienced a lot of evil in your personal life."

Startled, Natalie said neutrally, "Did she?"

Kenton scratched a fleck of bread dough off the back of his hand. "She said your mother hated you."

"I wouldn't use the word *hate*. It was more complicated than that."

"Heather said she went years without speaking to you. Is that true?"

Feeling emotionally naked in front of Kenton Lowery was not something Natalie had expected to deal with. "Yes, it's true."

"That your sister tried to steal your inheritance and the whole mess led to a friend of yours getting killed. And you . . . nearly got killed yourself."

Natalie pressed her thumb against Camille's tourmaline ring. Kenton had ended therapy over a year before these shattering events, he wasn't a fan of reading depressing news reports, and he didn't live in Ohneka, so she hadn't expected him to be familiar with her history. "Yes, those things are true, but my personal life is irrelevant. Let's focus on Heather."

Kenton lowered his gaze and muttered, "Heather doesn't think anyone's personal life is irrelevant."

Natalie wanted to force the change of subject, but Kenton's neck had turned hot pink. He'd taken a risk, revealing he knew things about Natalie beyond their professional interaction, and she'd shut him down. After she'd made the point that this was no longer a therapist-client relationship, she, not Kenton, was the one having trouble adjusting.

"I take it Heather researched me," Natalie said, careful not to sound disapproving.

"She learns everything she can about anyone who interests her."

Being interesting to Heather Osbourne sounded like an uncomfortable honor, but if Heather was curious about people in general, Natalie couldn't blame her for being intrigued by such a sordid history. "Does my past make her think *I'm* the evil at the clinic? Beyond my conspiring with Robert Chapman to invade Tabitha's territory?"

"I don't know." Kenton stared at the wood planks of the floor. "Your . . . mother didn't speak to you?"

Natalie tried not to let her demeanor show how acutely she didn't want to talk about this. "We had a difficult relationship. She struggled with bipolar disorder but refused to acknowledge she was ill. I tried to urge her toward treatment. She didn't like that and accused me of trying to control her."

Kenton kept staring at the floor, a bewildered look on his face. Natalie suspected he was processing the fact that she was human and, like Kenton and Heather, had a problematic family history. "Can I ask if she was abusive?"

"You can ask anything. I may or may not answer. She wasn't physically abusive, but at times, she was verbally and emotionally abusive. She died of cancer a few years ago." This was the first time anyone had asked her about these events while zeroing in on her relationship with her mother. People were usually more interested in the fact that her own sister had conspired against her and someone she'd trusted had tried to murder her.

"I'm sorry," Kenton said, though his expression didn't match the words. He appeared relieved—almost awed.

Gently, Natalie steered the conversation back on course. "Do you know where Heather is living now?"

"Sure. She works at an apartment complex in Ohneka. At the clubhouse. The job comes with an apartment. I thought they'd fire her after what happened at the Stoker, but I guess they don't know about it. Heather said it wasn't in the paper."

"It wasn't."

"While she was in the hospital, she had me text her boss and tell her Heather was out with the flu. The boss was cool with that. Just wanted her to get better."

"How long has she been at her job?"

"I don't know. A year or two? She likes it."

This was positive news. Heather sounded more functional than Natalie had assumed. "Do you think she'd be willing to talk with me? Not for counseling. Just in an informal meeting?"

"I don't know. Are you going to try to talk her into leaving your building alone?"

"First, I want to help her understand that we care about her and we aren't the enemy."

"If she's interested enough in you, she might agree to a meeting. Go on and try it." He reached into the pocket of his apron and took out his phone. "I'll text you her contact info."

"Thank you."

After sending the message, Kenton returned the phone to his pocket. "Will you let me know how she reacts?"

"Yes, I'll do that. Will you contact me if her situation changes or if you think she's planning anything related to the Stoker—or planning anything at all that worries you? I *am* concerned about her, not just about property values."

"I know. Yeah, I'll keep you posted." Kenton rose to his feet, so Natalie stood too. She was about to thank him and exit, but he started drawing shallow breaths again and twiddling the sides of his apron.

"Would you like to add anything?" Natalie asked. "I'd appreciate any information you can give, and I'll treat it with respect."

"Yeah, I just . . . I know Heather's quirky. But the stuff she said about evil at your clinic . . . Heather's smart, and she's usually right." His anxious amethyst eyes focused on Natalie. "Be careful, okay?"

CHAPTER 5

IT WASN'T RAINING ANYMORE, BUT thanks to the clammy wind and gray sky, there weren't many people on Lake Ohneka. This was an ideal place to talk, and Ainsley was ready. She paddled vigorously to catch up with Stuart. When they kayaked around the shoreline, he always tried to stay with her but inevitably pulled ahead by accident.

She reached him, smiled at him, and began. "We need to talk about Drew."

Stuart set his paddle across his knees. "Wishing you hadn't invited him to dinner next week? I figured you'd change your mind, but I'm not uninviting him. If you don't want to cook, we'll order pizza."

"I'm fine cooking, and I don't want to uninvite him. But, Stuart, you have an opportunity here. I don't want you to miss it."

"To be Chapman's *Trekmeister*?" Stuart slipped one blade of the paddle into the water and raised it again, moving in slow motion. "Lamb, we talked about this."

"You've impressed him. At Baxter's dinner, did you notice he talked more to you during dessert than to anyone else?"

"Yeah, he's fun to talk to. Total loon."

"If Drew weren't in the way, he'd take you in a heartbeat. You're a better planner. You're a better guide. You have medical training. You're bigger, stronger, have more stamina."

"This isn't about that crazy girl's prediction, is it?" Stuart whisked his paddle across the surface of the water, splashing Ainsley. "An endorsement from Kooksville won't impress Chapman."

Ainsley didn't return the mischievous splash. "She was right about the truck."

"Drew's the one who told Chapman I wanted a truck."

"Heather said that *before* Drew had the chance to talk to him about it. How did she know?"

He shrugged. "She floats around picking up gossip. Making guesses. Who cares?"

"She might have the gift of seeing the future," Ainsley said. "Some people do."

"You're welcome to your superstitions, but you know I don't buy into that stuff."

"You're going to be Chapman's choice. We'll make this come true."

Stuart pushed his paddle into the water and maneuvered so his kayak touched Ainsley's. He reached over to her kayak and grabbed the edge of the cockpit, keeping them side-by-side. "What do you mean, 'make' it come true? No way can we talk him into dumping Drew. I hear if you have his respect, he's loyal."

"We need to get Drew to back out."

Stuart laughed. "He's been bragging about this for a year. Big salary, bonuses, perks. There's no *way* he'd back out. The trip is next month!"

Ainsley dipped her fingers into the water on the opposite side of her kayak, then lowered her hand to the wrist. With the overcast sky, the water appeared black and opaque as a whole, but her white fingers were starkly visible a few inches beneath the surface. She spread her fingers, then clenched them into a fist.

"Ainsley! What's going on with you?"

"We need to *force* Drew to back out," she said.

"Force him how?" Stuart's tone went caustic. "Get him locked up for being a blowhard who thinks he's the backpacking king?"

Ainsley lifted her wet hand and wiped it on her shorts. Stuart liked his cousin, but it didn't take much work to stir his antipathy. He'd spent his life watching Drew win and gloat. "We need to take him out of commission for a few weeks. Chapman won't cancel the trip now. He'll replace Drew, and you will be his choice."

Stuart's tanned face looked bleached out. "What do you mean, 'take him out of commission'?"

"I mean force a few weeks of rest." Ainsley pushed his hand off her kayak and started paddling. "Like . . . a minor injury."

With a couple of strokes, Stuart caught up. "Like *cause* an injury?"

"Nothing serious." Ainsley paddled faster. She couldn't hold still while saying these words. "One fracture. You've both experienced a lot worse, and it was no big deal. One minor broken bone. In a few weeks, he'll heal, but he won't be up to hiking yet. *You'll* be Chapman's man. On the hike, you'll impress him so much that he'll keep you. Drew's had enough good luck. It's your turn."

"You're saying we do what? Push him down the stairs?"

"No. We need more control. It can't be . . . too much. Or not enough. When he's staying overnight at our place, we stage a break-in."

"Are you *crazy*?"

"You know how they keep warning us about those burglaries? And how the most recent break-in happened while the lady was home? We can use that. The stage is already set." Ainsley's arms were beginning to hurt from her paddling sprint. Stuart kept up, rowing mechanically, not seeming to exert himself at all.

"Here's how it will work," Ainsley said, panting. "Drew comes to dinner. You get a few beers in him—you told me he's into those pricey craft beers. We'll get some that will really tempt him. He crashes on the couch for the night. We stage a break-in and take a swing at him, just enough to sideline him for a few weeks. It'll look like the work of the thief. Drew won't suspect us, and neither will the police."

"You've lost your mind. We can't pull a stunt like that."

"You know how Drew is always wanting the window open, even in bad weather—especially if he's been drinking? He'll be sure to ask us to open a window. That'll be an easy way for the 'thief' to enter."

Stuart increased his speed, tipping his paddle from one side of the kayak to the other so rapidly that he shot through the water.

Ainsley stopped paddling to give her aching arms a break. Stuart would eventually turn and come back for her, but the fact that he was agitated was good news. Laughing her off would have been bad news. Getting upset meant he saw this was a real possibility and was scared of it. Scared because he coveted Drew's position.

Scared because he knew if he listened to her, he could have it.

After a moment of rest, she started paddling again, slowly, following the tree-crowded shore. Stuart was far ahead, his yellow kayak small in the distance. Ainsley maintained her measured pace until he finally swung his kayak around and began paddling toward her.

When their kayaks had nearly reached each other, Stuart spoke in a stone-hard voice. "We're not talking about this anymore. I'm calling Drew to tell him the dinner and camping trip are off, that you haven't been feeling well and we'll do it another time."

"Don't," Ainsley said. "You are *not* going to miss this opportunity. When will you have another chance to jump into Chapman's wallet? If you don't have the guts for it, I'll . . . get Drew out of the way myself." Saying those words made her feel like her lungs had filled with lake water. She'd never physically attacked anyone. *Could* she do it?

You can. You can do it. Being a woman doesn't mean you're a wimp.

"I won't let you," Stuart said. "Get real."

"I am being real." Her lungs burned. "You could have *this*, and instead, you'll waste your life taping sprained ankles. I'm sick of how we live. I'm sick of not having money. I'm sick of my family treating us like we're trash."

"You're sick of me? Wish you'd married some snob your dad picked for you instead?"

"I'm not sick of you! I'm trying to help you. I'm not being horrible. You've done worse than this before. How many times have you taken a swing at someone who got you angry? How many times have you taken a swing at *Drew*?"

"That's different."

"You've broken someone's bone before."

"That ref had been cheating the whole match, and he started it anyway. Drew is—"

"Your cousin, but he's also a jerk. If you don't have the guts to push him out of the way and take what should be yours, I'm done. You live your cheap life. I'm going to find something better." Ainsley slapped her paddle into the water, splashing herself with her sloppy technique, and rowed away from Stuart.

After several minutes, she checked over her shoulder.

Stuart sat with his paddle across his lap, his kayak drifting aimlessly toward the middle of the lake.

* * *

"Sit down." Regina waved Natalie to one of the leather-upholstered chairs that faced her desk. "Would you like anything? Coffee? Water?"

"No, thank you."

Regina sat behind her desk, picked up a stylus, and opened her tablet. "How did it go with Kenton Lowery? Was he helpful?"

Natalie tried to quell her discomfort. None of this was confidential, but it *felt* confidential. Wanting to get the report over with, she briskly shared Kenton's insights on his sister. Regina's hand moved at top speed, taking notes.

"Kenton gave me her contact information," Natalie finished. "I'm not sure how far you want me to take this, but I'm willing to try to meet with her if you'd like."

"Yes, absolutely, if she's willing. But don't put yourself in danger. I don't want her dragging you out a fourth-floor window along with her."

"I don't get the sense that she's a threat. I'll keep you updated."

"We appreciate it. I know Bob will be grateful. To switch gears, any progress in identifying the creeper Baxter Quincy complained about?"

"Not yet." Yesterday's call from Regina, asking about the incident Baxter had related at the dinner party, hadn't surprised Natalie. Despite the woman's desire not to make an official complaint about the incident, Natalie had figured Baxter would report it to building management at some point. "Considering that Baxter won't identify the woman and gave us almost nothing to go on, no. Don't quote me, please, but this woman's information—at least as related by Baxter—was so vague that it's possible someone walked past her, smiled, and said, 'Nice weather,' and she panicked. We'll keep our eyes open, but that's the best we can do."

Regina sighed. "I *won't* quote you on that, because if anything does happen, it will look terrible if we didn't appear to take early warnings seriously. Baxter's been talking to others in the building, creating ripples, and not just about this creeper. I've had half a dozen people come to me and vent concerns relating to things Baxter has said about the clinic."

"I'll try to calm him down." Natalie controlled her voice and hoped she could keep controlling it when she talked to Baxter.

"I appreciate it," Regina said. "We love Nefesh Bria, but we do have a lot of people we're trying to keep happy here."

Natalie wanted to suggest that the best way to keep people happy would be to hire the dentist on the third floor to shoot Baxter's tongue full of Lidocaine. "I understand."

Regina's desk phone rang. "I'll let you go," she said. "Let me know what happens with Heather."

Natalie nodded. Regina picked up the phone, and Natalie headed into the quiet hallway, musing on how best to deal with Baxter. No matter what she said to him, she couldn't seem to dislodge the perceptions he'd picked up from cultural stigmas, lurid news reports, and outlier stories. How would talking to him again make a difference?

Nearly at the interior entrance to Nefesh Bria, she stopped and walked back toward the lobby. She didn't want to confront Baxter right now, but if she went to the Parisi Gallery, maybe she could talk to Lauren Bell. From the conversation at Baxter's dinner, it was clear Lauren and Baxter were dating. Lauren seemed diplomatic and sensible, and if Natalie could gain her support, Lauren would have far more influence in dissuading Baxter's rumor mongering than Natalie would.

On the opposite side of the lobby from the corridor that led to Nefesh Bria, a spotless glass door opened into the gallery. At the delicate tinkling noise from the bell over the door, the click of heels moved toward Natalie.

A woman with sleek blonde hair and a silk sheath dress moved fluidly from among freestanding wall panels displaying watercolor paintings. Vanessa Parisi. "Good morning, Natalie. May I help you?"

"Good morning." Natalie made an on-the-spot addendum to her plan to speak with Lauren. Vanessa had always been polite to her, but Natalie knew through Regina that she wasn't happy about sharing the ground floor of the Stoker with the clinic. Maybe if Natalie showed more interest in the gallery . . . and opened her purse . . . she could encourage positive feelings toward the clinic and help inoculate Vanessa against Baxter's rumors.

"I'm thinking of buying some artwork for my office," Natalie said. She cringed at the thought of paying gallery prices, but if it led to getting Vanessa on her side, it would be worth it. "I have wall art already. I'm thinking of something for my bookshelf."

"I'm happy to help you with that." Vanessa indicated the pedestals displaying sculptures formed of glistening strands of glass. "As you see, we're currently featuring work by Anaya Burton. Many of these are very fragile, but there are some sturdier pieces you might like."

"Fragile is fine. I won't be putting it in a spot where it's likely to get bumped."

"These are one-of-a-kind, handmade pieces." Vanessa touched a fingertip to a cylindrical sculpture created of intertwined strands of blue and gold. "The artist is a lifelong friend. Immensely talented."

"Her work is beautiful," Natalie said.

Vanessa moved to a sculpture fashioned of countless clear-glass threads. "The prices reflect their unique nature. It would be a shame for one of them to get broken."

"Yes, of course." The purse hanging over Natalie's shoulder was starting to feel oddly light and empty. How exorbitant *were* the prices? "As I said, it will be in a safe spot."

Vanessa hesitated. "We have some hammered metal pieces in the west showroom. They aren't indestructible, but they're certainly sturdier than glass."

Irritated but not wanting to jump to conclusions as to why Vanessa was steering her away from delicate pieces, Natalie said courteously, "I'm more interested in the glass."

"Would you like to see our watercolor collection? We have some beautiful wraparound canvases that would look elegant on any wall."

"No, thank you." She'd already told Vanessa she wasn't looking for wall art. "I'll have a look around and let you know if I need more information on any of the pieces."

Vanessa's smile went crisp around the edges. "I do recommend that customers think carefully about how well a given piece will suit the location where—"

"Natalie, how lovely to see you." Lauren emerged from among the displays. "I heard you say you're in search of a piece for your office. Forgive me for stealing your customer, Vanessa, but I was browsing Anaya's catalog just now and saw some lovely nature-themed sculptures that would be the perfect complement to the décor at Nefesh Bria. I'll take Natalie into the office so she can have a look. Natalie, please come this way."

With a two-for-one sense of relief—not only could she escape Vanessa, but here was her chance to talk to Lauren—Natalie followed her into the gallery office.

Lauren closed the door. "Please, sit down."

Natalie sat in a chair that had a swirled back in turquoise and white. It coordinated with the abstract curves of the white table.

"I apologize for Vanessa," Lauren said. "She's a tad possessive of our artwork, wanting it adopted into good homes . . . which I'm sure your office will be."

"I'm not sure I understand her determination to steer me toward 'sturdier pieces,'" Natalie said. "Does she think a therapist's office should only be decorated with pillows and padded walls?"

"Gracious, I hope not." Lauren opened a cupboard and removed two fluted, asymmetrical glasses. "May I offer you some juice? We have a delicious cold-press tangerine-raspberry."

"Thank you," Natalie said.

From another cupboard—a fridge—Lauren took a bottle of juice. "I suspect Vanessa is feeling a tad insecure at the moment. She's concerned about making the gallery a success."

"Is she new to the business?"

"Oh, no, she was born into it. She's worked all her life at the Cascata Sculpture Park. Maybe you've visited it? On the south end of Kemper Park?"

"I've been to a couple of weddings there."

"It's unique, isn't it? An intertwining of nature and art. It was her mother's brainchild, and it's named for her, Cascata Parisi. But Vanessa's responsibilities there were different, and now that her parents have retired, she's in charge of the sculpture park *and* this new gallery." Lauren filled both glasses. "She's carrying heavy responsibilities."

"She's fortunate to have your help."

"I'm afraid I'm not very experienced, but I do what I can." Lauren handed Natalie a glass and sat in the chair next to her. "In confidence, she was exaggerating when she told you she's a lifelong friend of Anaya Burton's. Anaya was her mother's friend, not Vanessa's. From what I've witnessed, she still views Vanessa as a child. Anaya only signed a six-month contract with this new gallery, wanting to see how successful it is. The contract will be up for renewal in December, and Vanessa is terrified of losing it."

"That must be very stressful for her."

"Oh, yes. I suspect that's why she got strange with you when you were interested in Anaya's pieces. After that scare with poor Heather, Vanessa is hypersensitive to the threat of bad publicity. She was probably imagining a lurid news report of trouble at the clinic with the remnants of Anaya's shattered sculpture shown in the background."

"For the record," Natalie said, "I've never seen anything shattered anywhere I've worked, except for the time in grad school when my supervisor tripped over his own shoelace and dropped his favorite Freud coffee mug."

Lauren laughed. "You're marvelous. It was a pleasure to meet you at Il Giardino the other night. I apologize if Baxter came across as curt at times. He's genuinely grateful for your help."

"I know. Please don't feel you need to apologize for him. His behavior is not your responsibility."

"Oh, I know." Lauren sipped her juice. "To be honest, I'm embarrassed on his behalf."

Natalie smiled. There couldn't be a better opening for what she wanted to discuss. "I'll be honest too. I came here this morning hoping to talk to you, though I'd love to look at your catalog as well. If now isn't a convenient time for a nonbusiness discussion, we can meet later."

"Now is fine. With the door closed, Vanessa won't know *what* we're talking about. Here, let me get the props in place." She opened a three-ring binder labeled *Anaya Burton, Sculptor* and set it on the table in front of Natalie. "What can I do for you?"

"I'm hoping you can help me with Baxter. He's been stirring up opposition to Nefesh Bria, and it's causing problems."

"Yes, he's worried. In fact, he mentioned the possibility of a petition—gathering signatures of Stoker tenants who want your clinic gone."

Natalie's hand tightened on her glass. "Wonderful. Would you sign it?"

"Gracious. You aren't shy about cornering people."

"If you'd prefer not to answer, don't. I'm just frustrated. Baxter complained to Regina—the building manager—about the situation he mentioned to us at dinner, the one where a woman got followed by someone from the clinic. But he won't provide any information that would help us identify the culprit. Does he want the problem solved, or does he want there to be an ongoing problem so he can have more ammunition against us?"

Lauren absently turned a page in the binder, even though neither of them was looking at it. "I'm so sorry. This is mortifying, but I'm the woman who got followed. He didn't give my name because I asked him not to tell anyone. I had no idea he'd get so upset about it and talk about it at dinner the other night, let alone complain to Ms. Santiago."

Impressed at Lauren's poise when Baxter had caught her off guard by mentioning the incident, Natalie said, "I understand why you were uncomfortable. I don't want to make you more uncomfortable, but if the man who harassed you was from the clinic—either client or staff—I'd like to find out who it was so we can take action."

Lauren fidgeted with her goblet, tracing a fold in the glass with a rose-pink fingernail.

"I overreacted. I don't want to cause trouble for anyone."

"Someone from the clinic followed you as you walked home, tried to engage you in conversation you didn't want, and evoked fears for your safety," Natalie said. "Is that correct?"

"Well . . . when I told Baxter about it, I said the man came from the clinic, but I confess I was making an assumption. I thought I saw him coming from that side of the building, but he might not have come from Nefesh Bria."

Natalie's hopes that Lauren wouldn't make the same type of assumptions as Baxter wilted a little, but at least she seemed sheepish at having jumped to conclusions. "What did he say to you?"

"He said . . . he liked the way I walked. He was behind me then. I kept walking and didn't look back. He caught up to me and said I was beautiful. He said he'd like to make a wax figure of me and put it in a museum."

"How did you respond?"

Lauren nervously stroked her seed-pearl choker. "I ignored him, then ran into the nearest building, a medical office building. He didn't follow me inside. I waited in there for a while, then went out the back and took another route home. I didn't see him again. As I said, I overreacted. He wasn't crude or threatening. But talking about wax figures . . . I felt like I was in the presence of a killer who . . . makes memorial statues of his victims."

"I would have been uncomfortable too, wondering what his intentions were. If you can give me any information about his appearance, maybe I can figure out who he is—if he did come from the clinic."

"I'd feel so guilty if he got in trouble. He was only trying to flirt. I'm a nervous Nellie."

Lauren's old-fashioned attitude toward putting up with street harassment matched her retro style of dress. "We're not trying to lock him up," Natalie said. "But if he's a client, his therapist can discuss this incident with him— why it was inappropriate, why it made you uncomfortable. If he's staff or a volunteer, *I'll* deal with him. Could you estimate his age? Dark hair, light hair, bald? Tall? Short? Skinny? Heavy?"

Giving the door a pleading look as though wishing Vanessa would barge in and save her, Lauren said, "I never took a close look at him. Caucasian, maybe? Average build? I didn't notice him being large or small. Hair . . . He had hair. I don't think he was bald. But please, I truly don't want you to hunt him down. I'm embarrassed by it all. Please forget about it, and I'll tell Baxter he needs to stop holding my ridiculous experience against Nefesh Bria, because I don't even know if the man came from there. I'm so sorry my telling him has caused trouble for you."

"You had an experience that alarmed you. You don't need to apologize for confiding in someone."

"I've been reading about your clinic, and I know it's something you've worked hard to establish, something very important to you. I didn't intend to cause trouble. Forgive me."

"You haven't done anything wrong," Natalie said. "You're not responsible for how Baxter used a story you wanted kept confidential."

"I'll speak to him," Lauren said. "I know he's given you a negative impression of himself, but he is truly a kind and intelligent man. All of us have blind spots, and I'm sure I can help him see past his blind spot about Nefesh Bria. I'll try to get him to drop this silly idea of a petition."

"I'd appreciate that. Thank you."

"Would you like to look at Anaya's inventory so you can sound knowledgeable if Vanessa asks what you thought of her work?" Lauren turned a few pages in the binder and touched a photo of a tree sculpture with glass leaves in multiple shades of green. "This is one of my favorites."

"It's exquisite." Natalie eyeballed the information printed below the photograph. "Do you have anything with fewer digits in the price?"

Lauren laughed and turned the page. Natalie commented pleasantly on the sculptures while most of her mind dealt with what she and Lauren had discussed. Thank goodness, Lauren was willing to help her settle Baxter down—that was a win—but the street-harassment incident still troubled Natalie. If Baxter shared Natalie's suspicion that Lauren was downplaying her story so she wouldn't make waves, no wonder he wouldn't let go of it. If Lauren told him of Natalie's visit and he filtered it through his preconceptions, he'd be in Regina's office with a new complaint: *"Natalie Marsh cornered Lauren and bullied her into keeping her mouth shut. She's protecting predators."*

Something evil is there. Wicked hearts. Heather Osbourne's warnings played like a song stuck in Natalie's head. *Something evil.*

What if something terrible, something related to the clinic *did* happen to Lauren—or to someone else?

CHAPTER 6

A DELIVERYMAN APPROACHED THE RECEPTION desk, carrying a vase of white and blue roses interspersed with sprigs of lavender. Ainsley slid aside the window that separated the reception desk from the waiting room and coerced her mouth into a smile. "May I help you?"

"Yeah, delivery for . . . uh . . . Annie MacKerron."

The words electrified Ainsley's cold mood. "That's me," she said, not bothering to correct her name. He handed her the vase. She set it on her desk and signed the receipt. As soon as he walked away, she whisked the window shut and snatched the envelope tucked into the plastic cardholder. Her name was written on the front in Stuart's handwriting.

She ripped the envelope open. The message read, *You're right, Lamb. Let's do it. I'll meet you after work tonight, and we'll go eat somewhere and talk.*

Ainsley felt as though she were whooshing downhill on a roller coaster. *Let's do it.* After two silent, frigid days, Stuart had finally realized she was correct. And once he decided something, he'd be even more dogged than Ainsley in finishing it. *Let's do it.*

Footsteps approached from behind her. Ainsley quickly closed the card and shoved it into the envelope. She'd have to start being careful in a way she never had before. She didn't feel guilty about what they were planning—Stuart definitely deserved this opportunity, and Drew could afford to miss it—but she couldn't show any unexplained emotions, even cheerful ones.

"Beautiful flowers," Natalie said as she stopped next to Ainsley's chair.

"Thank you," Ainsley said. "They're from Stuart."

"What a sweetheart."

"We had a fight the other day," Ainsley said, then wished she hadn't tried to explain. She didn't need to justify her husband's choice to send her flowers.

"He has excellent taste in apologies," Natalie said. "Any sign of Oliver Wharton?"

Ainsley shook her head. "And yes, he got the automatic text reminder, *and* I called him yesterday, and he swore he'd be here." She checked her computer screen. "That's three no-shows for him."

"All right. If he calls back, don't schedule him. Tell him he needs to talk to me directly, and send him to my voice mail."

Ainsley typed a note into the schedule.

Natalie stood for a moment looking through the glass window into the waiting room, where a mother and teenage daughter sat, both staring at phone screens.

"For Dr. Avery," Ainsley supplied.

"She's running behind again?" Natalie asked.

"Yes, always," an energetic voice behind Ainsley said. Ainsley glanced over her shoulder, and Marianne winked at her.

"Every practice has a problem child, right, Dr. Marsh?" Marianne ran her fingers through her short gray hair. "Or in this case, a problem grandmother."

"You're worth the trouble you cause," Natalie said.

"Thanks, boss." With her fast, athletic pace, Marianne approached the door to the waiting room and opened it to summon her clients.

Natalie headed down the hallway.

Relieved to be rid of both Natalie and Marianne, Ainsley rubbed her neck, loosening tight muscles. She'd been afraid Natalie would stand there and continue chatting about clinic scheduling while Ainsley's heart all but ruptured with the need to text Stuart.

Before any other clients could enter the waiting room or the phone could ring, Ainsley snatched her own phone and texted, *Thanks for the flowers. Pick me up at 6:00. We'll leave my car here and get it later.*

Stuart's *ok* came so fast that clearly he'd been monitoring his phone.

For the rest of the afternoon, Ainsley couldn't concentrate. A few irritable, repeated questions and puzzled looks from clients told her she wasn't faking it well. When quitting time finally arrived, she grabbed her purse and fled out the door.

Stuart was already waiting in the Stoker parking lot, his truck gleaming in the early evening sun. He wiped spots off that truck every day. It was shinier than the cheap gold band on Ainsley's finger.

She hopped into the truck and banged the door shut. "Hi," she said. "The flowers were beautiful."

He leaned over the center console and kissed her, the first affection they'd shown each other since the kayaking trip. "Takeout?" he said. "I'd do something fancier for dinner, but we need privacy."

Ainsley nodded. Fifteen minutes later, they were sitting in the parking lot of a beach on Lake Ohneka, eating falafel and grilled chicken kabobs. There were too many people at the beach for them to have this conversation in the open, but the cab of the truck was comfortable, and the air conditioning was a bonus.

"I know I caught you off guard when I told you my idea." Ainsley leaped to the point of their meeting. "Thank you for listening to me. This is a perfect opportunity. You deserve it."

Stuart faced her. From the unfaltering determination in his eyes to the hardness of the muscles in his shoulders to the tension in his powerful legs, he looked strong. Ready. "*You* deserve it, Lamb. You deserve more than what I've given you. You're what matters to me. Whatever you need to make you happy, I'll get it for you."

"I love you," Ainsley whispered.

"I love you too." Stuart relaxed in his seat and resumed eating.

Heart beating crazily, Ainsley dunked a triangle of pita bread into a cup of hummus. "I really don't hate Drew," she said. "You know that, right?"

"Yeah." Stuart wiped yogurt sauce off his chin. "Neither do I. But the pig called me at lunch to gripe about how Chapman is now talking about hiking in Australia and wants Drew to fly out there as soon as they get back from California to scout things out, and how even with flying first class, that long of a flight will give him leg cramps."

"Poor baby," Ainsley said.

"Yeah, and he gave this monologue about how mad Baxter will be if Drew has to quit Quincy Travel because of Chapman. Drew says they'll have a hard time staying in business without him, even though he's only been there a couple of months. That guy's head alone is going to exceed the pack weight limit."

"Baxter thinks Drew will get on Chapman's nerves after awhile," Ainsley said. "I ran into Baxter in the Stoker gardens at lunchtime yesterday."

"What did he say?"

"I chatted him up about Chapman and Drew and the trip, and he said Drew's tops at his job, but he's arrogant, and pretty soon he'll rub Chapman the wrong way. In fact, Baxter hinted that after the JMT trip, he thinks *he* can edge Drew out and get his nephew into the spot with Chapman."

"Yeah, Drew told me about Baxter's nephew. Baxter just hired him to work for the travel agency."

"Is he any good?"

"He's a stupid kid who spends all his time climbing mountains and has about twenty minutes of real-world experience. But if Baxter can sell him to Chapman, that's a nice commission to Baxter. The contract with Drew was private, but if Baxter's nephew gets it, it'll be with Quincy Travel."

"I didn't tell Baxter fat chance on getting his nephew in as Trekmeister—that the job will be yours," Ainsley said.

Stuart fidgeted with the stereo controls, even though the stereo was off. His jaw stiffened. "After what we're doing to get it, it better be."

* * *

Gideon hooked the strap of his briefcase over his shoulder and exited the redbrick and white-columned building housing the city government offices. As he walked toward the parking lot, he unbuttoned the cuffs of his shirt and rolled up his sleeves. A long-sleeved, button-down shirt had been comfortable in his air-conditioned office but didn't work so well outdoors on a sunny, humid July evening.

Nearing his car, he took out his phone and checked for messages from Natalie. How had her meeting with Regina gone this morning? Eyes on the screen, he reached absently for his keys and pressed the button to unlock the car. The car beeped, but he heard no click of locks disengaging. He looked up. Had he forgotten to lock it? Good thing there was nothing valuable inside—like Fabergé eggs. He opened the door and started to slide into the seat but halted, half his body still out of the car.

Heather Osbourne was sitting in the passenger seat, deep blue eyes staring at him.

He sprang backward, bashing his briefcase against the steering wheel. He nearly slammed the door, ready to call the police, but stopped himself.

Natalie wanted to connect with Heather, settle things down, prevent another crisis. Getting Heather arrested wouldn't settle anything down—it would fuel more conflict. He could at least try to talk to her before he summoned law enforcement.

Gideon didn't reenter the car but leaned over so he could look through his open door. Heather was still watching him, seemingly unfazed by his panicky retreat and his return.

"What are you doing in my car?" he asked.

"Waiting for you."

"Yeah, I guessed that part. How'd you know this is my car?"

"It's not hard to figure out," she said. "I pay attention. I go places. I see things."

"See things at places like Innes Hill?" Gideon thought of her showing up the night Stuart had received his truck. How much time had she spent wandering around the apartment complex, spying on the MacKerrons, on him, on who knows who else? "Heather, get out of my car, please."

"It's the right place to be," she said.

Gideon refrained from asking if she'd gotten that tip from her deceased great-great-great-grandmother. "It's not the right place to be. You're breaking the law."

"Do you want to talk to me, Gideon Radcliffe?"

Gideon debated how to answer, trying to conceal how unsettled he was by the fact that Heather had identified him, identified his place of work, identified his car, and broken into it.

He didn't *want* to talk to her. He'd prefer to push her into the arms of an expert like Natalie or Marianne Avery. Or, in a pinch, the arms of a cop. But she seemed calm, and he didn't want to pass up this chance to learn more about her, vital information he could pass on to Natalie. Information that might help the experts prevent Heather from attempting another dive out a window. "Yes," he said. "I want to talk to you."

She beckoned to him.

He scanned the parking lot. It was sparsely occupied; many people had already left for the day. "Not in my car," he said. "Somewhere in the open."

Heather raised both hands and showed the palms to Gideon. She had narrow hands with long fingers. "No weapons."

"Weapons aren't the only thing I'm worried about." Gideon skimmed over the rest of her. She was wearing a fitted yellow T-shirt, white capri pants, and sandals. No visible sign of a weapon, but she could have a knife slipped in the back waistband of her pants or a disassembled M-16 buried in that thick, long ponytail.

She smiled, the eerie smile he'd seen on her face when she'd mocked Stuart MacKerron's gift from Chapman. "You're scared of me."

"I'm cautious. I don't like sitting in an enclosed space with a woman I don't know. And I'd be wary of anyone who tracked me down and broke into my car."

"It was unlocked."

"I doubt that. And whether or not it was unlocked is immaterial. You can't make yourself at home in someone else's vehicle. That doesn't go over well with the cops."

"You're seeing Natalie Marsh?"

"That's not your business."

"My brother told me Natalie came to visit him. He allowed it. He talked to her about me. He never talks to anyone about us. Why did he talk to her?"

"Probably because he's worried about you and wants to help."

"He knows her. He said he only met her when Beelzebub Chapman sent her, but he's lying. How does she know him?"

"I don't think she does." Gideon wrestled an urge to grin at Heather's dubbing Chapman *Beelzebub*. "She didn't say anything to me about knowing him."

"She's lying to you." Heather's midnight eyes shifted side to side and up and down as she studied him. "You're a handsome man. But you can't match Kenton. Have you seen him?"

"No."

"He's gorgeous."

"Lucky guy."

"He's divorced," Heather said. "He won't talk about it, but his ex told me he had an affair. It broke her heart."

The awkwardness of leaning over to look into the car was making Gideon's neck ache. "I'm sorry to hear that."

"You should ask Dr. Marsh how she knows Kenton. If she didn't tell you, that's a bad sign."

"I trust her." Gideon rode out an irrational pulse of jealousy. If Natalie did know Kenton Lowery but hadn't mentioned it, he could guess what the connection was. Chances were Heather wasn't the only member of her family in need of psychological services. "How about you get out of my car and we go for a walk? It's too hot for you to sit there. You'll get heatstroke."

"You want to walk me to the police station."

"No, I don't. But in the future, if you don't want to get arrested, you ought to avoid breaking into cars."

Fear started to thicken in Heather's eyes, blotting out her enigmatic confidence. "I'm trying to understand."

"Trying to understand what?"

"The clinic. The evil at the clinic."

"What evil?"

"I don't know." She scrutinized him. "You're a good man."

"Uh . . . I try to be."

"You'd help stop it if you could."

"Help stop what?"

"Evil."

Sweat rolled down Gideon's back. "Heather, how about instead of doing the revolving-door thing with law enforcement and doctors, you take real steps toward getting better?"

"I'm not sick."

"Sorry, but the things you've done are sick by any standard." That probably wasn't the right thing to say, but Gideon didn't know how to soft-pedal a ghost-prompted suicide attempt.

"I was wrong about trying to jump out the window." Heather folded her arms and picked at her short sleeves. "I thought it would help Tabitha, but I was wrong."

"Good. I'm glad you see that. No way would your grandmother have wanted you to kill yourself."

"She warned me about the clinic," Heather said.

"Tabitha?"

"Yes."

"What did she tell you about it?"

"She doesn't know much. She has trouble getting in there. She used to be able to go anywhere in the building, but something is blocking off the clinic."

How had Heather ever convinced her doctor to release her? "Here's the deal," Gideon said. "I've been involved with Nefesh Bria since before it opened, and I know a lot of behind-the-scenes stuff. Nobody there is perfect, but there's nothing 'evil' going on. Staff and volunteers are there because they want to help people."

A bead of sweat trickled down Heather's heat-flushed face.

"I can take you to Nefesh Bria," Gideon said. "I'm heading over there anyway. I'll text Natalie and tell her we're coming. If you can talk to her and have a look at the place for yourself, you might feel better about it."

"You know I'm banned. If I set foot on the grounds, I'll get arrested for trespassing."

"Funny you're worried about getting arrested there. That didn't seem to be an issue when you broke into my car."

"I knew you wouldn't call the police. I can read people. I know a lot about you."

Gideon felt a mounting urge to call the cops just to prove her creepy discernment false. "If we walk into Nefesh Bria together, I guarantee no one is going to enforce the ban, unless you flip out, which I'm assuming you won't do. Nobody at the clinic wants the cops showing up. It would cause a lot of stress. Bob Chapman and his people have been bending over backward to resolve your concerns with as mild of consequences to you as possible."

"He's afraid of Tabitha," Heather said softly.

"No. He's not." Gideon took out his phone. "I'll let Natalie know we'll be there in about fifteen minutes."

"Don't do it." Heather's pink face was fading to white. "I don't want to talk to her."

"I promise you, she's not evil. She's one of the kindest, most compassionate people I've ever known."

Heather grabbed the door handle and swung her door open.

"Heather, wait. Don't run away. We honestly want to help you."

Heather sprang from the car and fled, black ponytail whipping her spine.

CHAPTER 7

AT THE BEEP OF AN access card unlocking the outer door, Natalie stopped straightening magazines in the waiting room and went to meet Gideon.

"Hey." Gideon let the door shut behind him. He stepped toward her, paused, and looked past her to the glass reception window. Was he checking to make sure no lingering staff members were watching? Was he hoping there *were* witnesses—an excuse to keep his distance as he greeted her?

She started to close the distance between them but stopped, wanting to see what he'd do. "Thanks for coming."

He took another step toward her, froze in place, and shifted the paper bag he held from one hand to the other. "Glad to be here."

We need to talk, Natalie thought again. Why did she keep thinking that but not doing it? It was important, more important than the other things allegedly keeping her too busy for a candid discussion with Gideon. Was *she* giving off mixed signals?

"I appreciate your help," she said.

"Not a problem. I am Olympic-grade talent when it comes to sitting on my backside and surfing the Internet."

"We should pay you more."

"Heck yeah, you should. I demand a four-percent raise."

"Done. That'll raise your salary to . . . zero dollars annually."

"*Sweet.*"

Natalie laughed and used her ID to unlock the door to the office area. She still felt strange about the level of security here. The door that led to the parking lot locked automatically at six o'clock each day, regardless of whether or not the clinic had evening hours, and the staff door that led to a corridor inside the Stoker was always locked. There was a second locked door between the waiting room and the offices, a sliding reception window made of bullet-resistant glass, and a policy that no staff member could be alone in the clinic while clients were present—hence, Gideon's stint at chaperoning tonight. She'd tried to argue that this much security was over the top for Ohneka, but Regina had insisted, and Chapman had backed her up. So be it, but Natalie still tried to keep costs down with measures like having trained volunteers play chaperone when necessary.

"Dinner?" Gideon held up the paper bag. "Got you a grilled something-or-other. Some kind of cheese. I think apples are involved too and maybe bacon."

"Sounds delicious." They walked into the break room. A smear of ice cream and a scattering of crumbs marred the table, and several coffee mugs and a Tupperware container filled the sink.

"You saved work for me," Gideon said happily. "I'll get this place shiny."

"You're the best. Some people here struggle with the concept of cleaning up after themselves. Ainsley usually straightens up before she leaves, but she seemed to be in a rush tonight."

"People shouldn't leave their messes for Ainsley, the lazy slugs."

"I agree. We'll be talking about that in the next staff meeting." Natalie opened the fridge, took two water bottles, and joined Gideon at the table.

"I just had a strange visit." Gideon passed Natalie her foil-wrapped sandwich. "From Heather Osbourne."

"Heather!"

Gideon handed Natalie a bag of potato chips. "I came out of work and found her sitting in my car. She claims it was unlocked, but that's unlikely. She's skilled at grand theft auto. I can't find any marks that indicate she broke in."

"Did you call the police?"

"No. I decided it would be better to talk to her." He related his conversation with her. Natalie ate while he talked. She was ravenous, and this was her only chance to eat before she spent ninety minutes doing an intake.

"Sorry I couldn't get her to come see you," Gideon finished. "I tried, but Nefesh Bria spooks her."

"Spooks her because Tabitha can't spook *us* and report on what we're up to?"

"Hey, at least you know those anti-ghost spells you paid big bucks for are working."

"Better not say that in public. People will think you mean it."

"Yeah, it'll be headlines." Gideon crinkled his unopened bag of chips. "'*New mental health clinic hired exorcist to rid office of vengeful ghost.*'"

"Just what we need. Are you going to eat?"

Gideon hadn't started on his sandwich, though he'd picked it up and set it down a few times while he was talking. He lifted it now, took one bite, swallowed it, and set the sandwich back on the foil. "Heather insisted you know her hot brother," he said. "Know him beyond your Chapman-ordered contact. She said Kenton denied it."

"I'll leave that between Kenton and her." Natalie deliberately spoke in the same matter-of-fact tone she'd used throughout the conversation. "Does she think I'm plotting evil against Kenton?"

"I don't know. She threw something out about how he was divorced and he won't talk about it, but his ex claimed he had an affair."

"What Kenton tells Heather is his business," Natalie said. "There is nothing in my life—past or present—related to any man or to any man's marriage that I am ashamed of or that I would conceal for personal reasons."

"I know that." Patches on Gideon's neck and jaw flared scarlet, a reaction Natalie had expected to see. He always felt profoundly embarrassed if he let hints of jealousy or insecurity slip.

For a few stretched-out seconds, they looked at each other. Natalie felt her face start to flush. "*Do* you know that?" she asked quietly.

"Yeah, I do." Gideon broke eye contact and quickly picked up his sandwich. "Did you talk to Regina this morning?"

"Yes." Natalie surrendered to this awkward subject change. With a client on the way, she didn't want to force a discussion with Gideon that they couldn't finish. She updated him on her talk with Regina, her experience with Vanessa at the gallery, Lauren's admission that she was the one who'd been followed by the alleged clinic creeper, and Lauren's vow to calm Baxter.

"I think Lauren is sincere," Natalie said. "She's mortified that—" The faint buzz of the intercom at the receptionist's desk distracted her, followed by a banging that made both Natalie and Gideon spring to their feet. A voice shrieked something incoherent.

Natalie rushed out of the break room, Gideon with her. The buzz came again, a signal from the locked outer door. The new client must be early—

Another buzz and a screechy voice: "Let me *in*! Help me! *Open the door!* He might come back!"

Natalie glanced over her shoulder at Gideon. Gideon grabbed his phone from his pocket.

"Hold off on calling the police until we see what the problem is." Natalie hurried through the waiting room and pulled the door open.

A middle-aged woman wearing a flowered sundress hurtled into the waiting room. "Call me a taxi," she shrieked. "I don't want my appointment anymore."

"Daisy Frederiksen?" Natalie let the door close.

"Yeah, and some crazy pervert followed me from the bus stop!"

"I'll call the police," Gideon said.

Natalie nodded at him. "Can you describe him or her?" she asked Daisy.

"Him." She pulled a tissue from her pocket and blotted sweat off her forehead. "Did you lock that door again? You'd better lock it."

"It's locked," Natalie said. "Please sit down and let me get you some water."

The woman thumped into one of the upholstered chairs and pointed at Gideon. "You, guy with the phone, tell the cops he was . . . I don't know, maybe thirties. Taller than me, but so is everyone. Brown mustache and sunglasses, mirrored ones. A hat. Not a cowboy hat but something with a brim all the way around it. A black shirt, or maybe navy. A T-shirt, I think."

Gideon nodded acknowledgment. Natalie filled a cup at the water cooler in the corner and brought it to Daisy. She gulped the water.

Natalie took the empty cup, refilled it, and brought it back to her. "I'm Natalie Marsh, and that's Gideon Radcliffe, one of our volunteers."

"You're Dr. Marsh? You're young."

"Do you need anything else? Are you injured?"

Daisy poured a drizzle of water on her palm and splashed it on her neck. "Why do you schedule regular people on the same days as the axe murderers?"

"I'm afraid I don't know what you're talking about," Natalie said.

"This crazy guy. He was at the bus stop across the street. When I got off the bus and started over here, he followed me. Asked me where I was going. I told him to mind his own business. He asked if I was going to the mental health clinic, and I didn't answer. He said it was his favorite place, that he's here every week. He said you people were fun to play with, thought you were helping him but didn't know anything about him, really. He kept saying, 'They think I'm harmless,' and telling me to lie to you, that it was fun. 'They have no idea what I'm planning,' he said." She pointed at Natalie with the hand holding the cup, splashing water on the floor. "You need to sic the cops on that psycho. He's planning some horrible crime."

Natalie grabbed a handful of tissues to wipe the water off the wood floor. "Anything you can tell us about him would help us find him."

"I told you what I know. He followed me across the street, and when I got close to the Stoker, I started running. He didn't keep up. I don't know where he went."

"Did he harm you or threaten you in any way?"

"What, it doesn't count unless he stabbed me?"

"I didn't say that. Clearly his behavior was inappropriate and distressing to you."

"You must know who he is. He's a regular. Brown mustache!"

"I'll check if any of our clients fit your description."

"Don't you know off the top of your head? Don't you *look* at your patients?"

"We have multiple clinicians working here," Natalie said. "I don't personally—"

The intercom buzzed. "Ohneka Police."

Gideon strode past Natalie and Daisy to open the door. Two uniformed officers entered.

"Thank you for coming so quickly," Natalie said. "I'm Natalie Marsh, the clinic director."

"I'm Daisy Frederiksen, the target," Daisy snapped.

"I'm the guy who called 911. Gideon Radcliffe." Gideon finished the introductions as he tucked his phone back in his pocket.

"I hope you have officers out there searching for that monster," Daisy said.

"Yes, ma'am, officers are searching the area using the description Mr. Radcliffe passed along to us," the female officer said. "I'm Officer Kalili, and this is Officer Daveneau. Dr. Marsh and Mr. Radcliffe, if you could wait in the back while we speak to Ms. Frederiksen."

"Of course." Glad to escape Daisy's evil eye, Natalie headed into the office area and closed the door behind her and Gideon.

She tossed the wet lump of tissues into the trash can, sat in Ainsley's chair, and logged into the computer. Gideon stood to the side, a discreet distance away.

"Checking the schedule?" he asked quietly.

"Yes." None of Natalie's clients fit the description. She skimmed through the listing of all appointments from the past week, but nothing caught her eye.

"I'm guessing you can't give the names of potential creepers to the cops," Gideon said.

"Not unless I think someone is in imminent danger, and I don't think we're at that point. But I'll contact the staff, tell them what we're dealing with, and see if it rings any bells for anyone. We'll go forward from there." She stood. "Excuse me for a few minutes. I need to make some calls."

"I'll hold down the fort," Gideon said.

Natalie retreated to her office, shut the door, and dialed the first name on her list: Marianne Avery.

Twenty minutes later, Natalie returned to the reception area. Gideon stood by Ainsley's desk, talking to a tall man who looked like a college-freshman basketball player in a suit. Recognizing him, Natalie approached and extended her hand.

"Detective Bartholomew," she said.

His bony fingers gripped her hand. "Dr. Marsh." Abe Bartholomew's sonorous bass voice always sounded incongruous to Natalie, given his skinny frame and young face. "Nice to see you again. Congratulations on the clinic." He waved a lanky arm, gesturing from wall to wall. "High-class place."

"Thank you."

"I got the report from Ms. Frederiksen," Bartholomew said. "Officer Kalili gave her a ride home. Do you have anything that can help us?"

"No. By which I mean I genuinely have nothing, not that there are things I can't say. I've spoken to my staff. None of them had any relevant information."

"Mustache, hat, mirrored sunglasses?" Gideon said. "Sounds like a garden-variety disguise."

"It wouldn't be the usual MO for a creep like she described," Bartholomew said. "But who knows? Thanks for checking with your people, Dr. Marsh. I understand that even if you learn something, you can't give us names without either imminent danger or a judge's order."

"Pardon me," Natalie said, "but does it usually take multiple officers and a detective to deal with street harassment and vague mention of 'plans'?"

"No," Bartholomew said.

The simple answer weighted Natalie like he'd handed her a boulder. "That's not good news for us, is it?"

"We understand there have been multiple issues here at the Stoker Building," Bartholomew said.

"Issues like Heather Osbourne? I assume you know about her. That's a totally different type of problem."

"We've received a variety of complaints."

"Complaints related specifically to Nefesh Bria?"

"Yes, ma'am. When I heard of Ms. Frederiksen's experience, I figured it was time to drop by and say hello."

"I appreciate the visit." Natalie wanted to ask if all the complaints were from Baxter Quincy, but she refrained. "I don't think there's much for the police to be concerned about. Most of the complaints I've heard have no substance. They're assumptions and rumors and stereotyping."

"I understand this is not the first time there's been an issue with someone from your clinic following a woman."

"I'm not sure there have been any instances of that at all," Natalie said. "The man who harassed Daisy Frederiksen may not even be a client here. Maybe he just thought it was funny to scare her by pretending to be 'crazy.' And I'm familiar with the other incident you're talking about. Baxter Quincy told me about it. I'm guessing you've heard from Mr. Quincy?"

Bartholomew smiled slightly but didn't confirm her assumption.

"I spoke to the woman who was followed," Natalie said. "She wasn't even sure the man came from the clinic—she assumed that when he approached from this side of the building."

"What's her name?"

Natalie didn't want to embarrass Lauren, but if her experience combined with Daisy's had stirred enough concern that a detective had come to check out the clinic, she'd better send Bartholomew to the source. "Lauren Bell. She works in the Parisi Gallery. She's embarrassed that Mr. Quincy made such a production out of her experience. If he's the one who called you, I don't think Lauren knows it. If you talk to her, please do so with my apologies and explain why I felt it necessary to share her name."

Bartholomew took his notebook out of his pocket and scrawled something.

"How about footage from security cameras?" Gideon asked.

"Neither of the incidents took place within range of the building's exterior cameras," Bartholomew said.

"And there are more discreet ways of figuring out what's going on than trashing confidentiality with a wholesale viewing of everyone who entered or exited Nefesh Bria," Natalie added.

The phone on Ainsley's desk began to ring.

"Feel free to answer it," Bartholomew said.

Normally, Natalie would have let the call go to the answering service at this time of evening, but worries that this was related to Daisy's experience led her to pick up the phone. "Nefesh Bria Mental Health Services."

"This is Kyla at Lakeview Jewelers here on the second floor. A customer told us there were police cars outside your clinic. What's going on?"

Natalie wanted to tell Kyla that was none of her business, but rudeness would provoke hostility, and she had enough opponents already. "A woman was alarmed when a man at the bus stop followed her for a short way. She came to the clinic for shelter, and he left. Reassure your customer that there's nothing to worry about."

"I hope not." Kyla lowered her voice. "I've been hearing weird rumors."

"Rumors with evidence to back them up?"

"Weird people wandering around the building, trying to talk to people or doing odd things."

"Odd things?"

"Like coming into businesses and offices but not buying anything or having any reason for being there. I don't want to be a complainer. I think the clinic is great, but please tell Dr. Marsh that people are nervous."

"This is Dr. Marsh."

"Oh, hello. I'm sorry. I hope you're not offended."

"Can you give me specifics about these 'weird people' and what they've done?"

"Um . . . I can't remember exactly who said what. Somebody from the law firm down the hall told my coworker that a woman walked in, didn't say anything, just stared at the receptionist in this freaky way, then walked out. Oh wait, maybe it was a man who did the staring. No, that one was a woman. I heard something about a man, scruffy guy, going into a different office—financial planner's office or maybe a tax accountant's, I don't remember—and doing this ritual with pennies."

"A ritual?"

"Like lining them up on the floor and refusing to leave until the guys threatened to call security. And a customer told me this old lady was watching her in the Parisi Café, not eating anything—"

"Thank you," Natalie cut in, done with this recital of vague hearsay. "There is *no* evidence that any of these so-called incidents have anything to do with Nefesh Bria. If you hear more rumors like this, please tell the person sharing them to come talk to me rather than making assumptions and perpetuating ignorance. I'm happy to speak with anyone who has concerns or questions."

"Sure, thanks. Bye." Kyla hung up hastily.

Natalie set the phone back in the cradle. Bartholomew and Gideon were both watching her.

"Everything okay?" Bartholomew asked.

CHAPTER 8

WITH BLEARY-EYED APPROVAL, DREW grinned at the row of mostly empty bottles on the table. "Fancy lineup, Stu. Didn't know you could afford it."

"Try this," Ainsley said. "Flower Power. Ithaca Brewing Company." She popped the cap off and split the bottle between two glasses, one for Drew and one for Stuart. Stuart hadn't drunk much, only taking a swallow here and there and sneaking chances to tip most of the beer into the pottery vase Ainsley had moved into the corner of the kitchen next to his chair. She'd lined the vase with towels to absorb the noise of liquid hitting pottery—though Drew had been so busy babbling about lager and ale and American Imperial stout that Ainsley doubted he would have heard anything even without the towels.

Drew took a sip, contorted his mouth, and tried another sip. "Dunno how much I like this one." He took a bigger sip. "That's a fancy necklace. You look hot tonight, Ainsley."

Ainsley straightened the strands of crystal beads. "Shut up, Drew. You're hammered."

"No booze on the John Muir Trail," Drew said. "Total abstinence. But it'll be worth it. I am *der Trekmeister*! Betcha he gives me another bonus after we get home."

"I hope you spend some of it on us," Ainsley said as Stuart pretended to swallow a mouthful of Flower Power.

"Sure, babycakes, take you both on vacation. Where ya wanna go?"

Ainsley tapped her feet lightly against the floor, resisting the desire to imbed the toe of her shoe in his shin. *Babycakes*. Drew was doing a fantastic job of getting on her nerves—and Stuart's nerves—which made her even more elated about their plans. It was about time Stuart knocked a chunk off Drew's pride.

"I'd like to visit Eastern Europe," she said. "What's your favorite tour that Quincy Travel does there?"

On cue, Drew started rambling in tedious detail about river cruises to Poland, Lithuania, Latvia. Ainsley refilled his glass and tried not to yawn. It was almost midnight.

Stuart smashed chocolate cake crumbs with the flat of a knife and asked Drew questions, though Ainsley knew he found the idea of cruises lethally boring. He didn't look tense, to her relief. A little too patient with Drew's babbling but not tense.

"You did good on the cooking, sweetie." Drew reached for an open bottle next to him and dumped the remainder into a glass. "Could you open a window? Bring the outdoors indoors."

"Sure," Ainsley said, careful to smile, not smirk. Drew was obnoxiously predictable. She went to open the kitchen window.

"Don't wake me up early, Stu, or I'll break your nose," Drew said.

"Stuart's not in any shape to get up early either." Ainsley gathered empty bottles. "Sleep in late. The mountains aren't going anywhere. You guys go watch TV. I'll clean up."

"Thanks for letting me crash here. Great to relax. Been so busy." Drew pushed back from the table and shambled to the couch. Stuart joined him and turned on ESPN.

"Hey, you been playing shinty?" Drew picked up the curved wooden stick Stuart had deliberately left on the floor near the couch after a trip to the park yesterday. "Shoulda invited me. Did I tell you I was talking to Bob about sponsoring a Gaelic games club?"

"Won't happen," Stuart said. "Not enough local interest."

"You can recruit for it." Drew jiggled the caman as though bouncing a ball on it. "Get your high school kids to try it." He swung the caman, nearly knocking over a lamp. Ainsley wanted to rush over and snatch her crystal vase out of harm's way, but the vase needed to be prominent in the room, and the coffee table was the best spot.

"Gimme that." Stuart grabbed the caman and set it on the table. "C'mon, man, you're going to give me a concussion."

Ainsley cleared the table as quickly as she could. With dessert and the craft-beer fest finally over, apprehension was spiking inside her, and as soon as the dishes were in the dishwasher, she said good night and hurried toward the bedroom, leaving Stuart and Drew slumped on the couch watching baseball highlights.

Wishing she hadn't eaten so much greasy pork and triple-layer chocolate cake, Ainsley changed into her nightgown, brushed her teeth, and slid into bed. Blinking at the darkness, she took deep breaths, hoping her stomach would calm down. This was going to work. *Don't let me go all girly and helpless now. We have to do this.*

She was still wide awake when Stuart entered the room at quarter to two. "Everything go okay?" she whispered.

"Yeah, he's snoring out there. Can't you hear him?" Rather than turn on the overhead light, Stuart activated the light on his phone and set it on the nightstand while he changed from his T-shirt and shorts into pajama pants. He pulled dark jeans over the pajama pants, then put on a dark, long-sleeved shirt and gloves. He took the ski mask and flashlight from the closet shelf where Ainsley had left them ready for him.

"Okay, Lamb." He bent over her and kissed her. "Time to depose *der Trekmeister.*"

"Good luck," she whispered. He popped the window screen loose, set it on the floor, and stepped out of their ground-level apartment.

Ainsley lay in bed and listened, blood storming through her body, the night breeze wafting through the room.

* * *

It took over an hour of pulling his bedcovers up and pushing them down again, zombie-eyed phone scrolling, and flipping his pillow from warm side to cool side before Gideon fell asleep. The restful stretch didn't last; he woke up sweating three hours later. He got out of bed, switched on the ceiling fan, and opened his window—the night was cool enough that he preferred a fresh breeze to cranking the AC. Back in bed, he tried to doze off, but his brain started rerunning the worries that had provoked insomnia in the first place. What was happening at Nefesh Bria? Natalie had worked so hard to bring the clinic to life. She'd been so excited, so eager to reach out to the community. And now problems and rumors were mushrooming.

Would the bus stop creeper turn out to be a client? Gideon guessed no. As Natalie had suggested, more likely, he was some nitwit who, inspired by the proximity of the clinic, thought a clichéd psycho impersonation was a funny way to scare a stranger. All the other complaints Natalie had received were ridiculously vague—

A woman screamed, her cry loud enough that she had to be close. Instinctively, Gideon launched himself out of bed and yanked on a pair of sweatpants he'd left on the floor.

A shriek. "*Stuart!*"

Stuart MacKerron. That was Ainsley screaming one level down. Gideon snatched his phone off the charger and sprinted out the front door barefoot. He galloped down the stairs and along the walkway toward the MacKerrons' apartment.

Stuart lurched out the door and lunged in Gideon's direction. Gideon speedily flattened himself against the wall to get out of the way.

Stuart slowed and pointed past Gideon. "Did you see anyone running that way?"

"No. I heard Ainsley scream—"

Stuart whirled and sprinted in the opposite direction.

Gideon hurried toward the open door and peeked cautiously into the apartment. The lights were off, but in the dim illumination from the security lights in the walkway, he saw a shadowy Ainsley kneeling on the floor, leaning over something—someone. Someone groaning.

"Ainsley?" he said.

With a yelp, she vaulted to her feet and spun toward him.

"It's Gideon Radcliffe," he said—with him backlit in the doorway, she probably couldn't identify him. He reached for the light switch and flicked it on.

On the floor near Ainsley's feet lay a man, his expression warped by pain. Gideon recognized him from the dinner at Il Giardino, but his name wasn't surfacing.

"I don't know where he's hurt." Ainsley was pale, her red hair a voluminous mess. "Someone was here—we heard a thud—maybe from that?" She pointed at a kitchen chair that lay on its side. "Then we heard Drew say something—he sounded upset, but . . . but he . . . he's had a lot to drink, so we didn't think . . . But there was someone in here . . ."

Drew. Drew Drummond. Stuart's cousin. "Have you called 911?"

"No, we just found him. We'd better—"

"Got it." Gideon tapped his phone. Given how often he seemed to be calling 911, he ought to list it in the favorites section of his contacts.

He gave the dispatcher the MacKerrons' address and a summary of the situation. Phone still at his ear as he awaited further questions or instructions, he walked to where Ainsley was kneeling next to Drew, tucking a pillow under his head. Drew mumbled a stream of words, but the only ones Gideon could pick from among the profanity were "My leg."

"An ambulance is coming, Mr. Drummond," Gideon said.

Footsteps thumped on the walkway, and Stuart reentered the apartment, panting. "No . . . sign of anyone . . . don't know where . . ."

"Drew's leg is hurt," Ainsley said. "I don't know if he fell or—"

". . . *hit* me . . . attacked me—" Drew touched his left thigh and moaned.

"Can you describe the intruder?" Ainsley asked.

". . . dark . . . *dark* in here . . . Couldn't tell . . . couldn't see . . ." Drew rolled onto his side and gagged. Stuart ripped a sheet off the couch and got it on the floor under Drew's head a millisecond before Drew vomited. When his heaving stopped, Stuart wadded up the soiled sheet and shoved the whole thing in the kitchen trash can.

Ainsley wiped Drew's mouth with a napkin. "It must have been that thief, the one the police warned us about."

"Is anything missing?" Stuart returned to the living room. Gideon glanced around. Silk tulips were scattered over the carpet next to some kind of wooden hockey stick. A blanket was crumpled on the floor in front of the couch. He couldn't see anything else out of—

"My vase!" Ainsley cried out. "Stuart, my vase!"

Drew yelled a profanity-encrusted dismissal of Ainsley's missing vase. Flashing red and blue lights showed through the open door. Gideon stepped outside.

A police car, an ambulance, and a fire truck were all pulling into the parking lot. At the dispatcher's orders, Gideon ended the 911 call and jogged to meet them.

While paramedics and police officers headed into the MacKerrons' apartment, Gideon stayed in the walkway, leaning against the wall, keeping himself out of the way, and not touching the window screen propped against the wall under the kitchen window—probably left there by the thief. He wanted to return home, but the police might have questions for him. Not that he could tell them anything. "I heard Ainsley scream" wouldn't add to the investigation.

A few other doors along the walkway had opened. A woman leaned out of the doorway next to the MacKerrons', saw Gideon, and called, "What happened?"

"Looks like another burglary," Gideon said, afraid that even this sparse information was too much to offer. He didn't want to spread rumors, and he definitely didn't want to freak everyone out by announcing that a man had been attacked.

From the end of the walkway near the stairs that led up to Gideon's apartment, a woman approached, a long, wispy skirt fluttering around her legs. Gideon squinted at her in dismay. Was that . . .

Heather Osbourne.

She reached him and stopped. Her eyes were wide, so wide her expression was strained.

"What are you doing here at"—Gideon checked his phone—"quarter to three in the morning?"

"This is the MacKerrons' apartment," Heather whispered.

"What are you doing here?"

"Ainsley MacKerron works at Nefesh Bria. I told you something was wrong there. I told you there was evil."

"This has nothing to do with Nefesh Bria. It looks like a burglary—another one. Why are you prowling around here in the middle of the night?"

"Why is an ambulance here? Who's hurt?"

"A friend of the MacKerrons, but it's not life-threatening. You need to go home unless you want to chat with the police." Gideon's finally slowed heartbeat began to accelerate again as he surveyed Heather—Heather, who was obviously adept at breaking and entering and had no compunctions about doing so if she thought it was "right."

"Where do you live?" he asked, switching his voice to a friendlier setting.

"Nearby," Heather said.

"Where?"

"Drew Drummond . . . Is he the friend who's hurt?"

Gideon's hammering heart added a few more beats per minute. "I'm not in a position to give out information here. I'll go find a police officer for you. The cops will have more accurate information."

"No, thank you." Heather flitted past Gideon, past the MacKerrons' apartment, and toward the sidewalk that led either to the parking lot or the back of the building. For a few seconds, Gideon wondered if he should grab her, but that didn't seem necessary. If Heather did have anything to do with this, the police could find her. His only responsibility was to tell them she'd been here.

What if, in his decision not to report Heather's breaking into his car, he'd left her free to break into the MacKerrons' place and attack Drew?

Nice job, idiot. He'd better report her actions immediately. He stepped through the doorway into the MacKerrons' apartment and scanned the room for the cop who appeared the least busy.

CHAPTER 9

MORNING SUNLIGHT BURNED THE SHADOWS from the room as Ainsley sat at the kitchen table stabbing her uneaten eggs with a fork. Too exhausted to care about food but too jittery to go back to bed, she kept reliving last night: talking to the police, the paramedics wheeling Drew away, the investigation of the crime scene. She'd been so nervous while Stuart had walked the police through the apartment that she'd gotten lightheaded. What if Stuart's initial exit and final reentry through their bedroom window had left any traces? But the police had said nothing about the bedroom window. With the kitchen window open and its screen removed, plus Drew's testimony that he'd seen the burglar escape out the front door, the police *should* consider the points of entry and exit as no-brainers.

Once the police had left, Ainsley and Stuart had gone to the hospital to be with Drew. Neither of them had wanted to go, but it would have looked suspicious if they hadn't. They'd ended up waiting with him for a couple of hours in the ER until Drew was admitted to a room—his broken femur would need surgery. He'd been groggy, but from what he'd been able to say, it was plain he didn't suspect any dirty tricks from Ainsley and Stuart.

"We did it." Ainsley smiled at red-eyed Stuart. "It worked."

Stuart nodded absently. Ainsley couldn't tell if he was too tired to pay full attention to her or if he was preoccupied with something else.

"I didn't know you were going for the thigh bone," Ainsley said. "That's a hard bone to break."

"I hit hard."

"He'll have super strength now, with a rod in his leg." Ainsley fought off guilt. This had been *her* plan, and she couldn't lose her nerve now that it was done. "As soon as it's a decent hour for phone calls, we need to call Mr. Chapman and Quincy Travel."

Stuart didn't respond to Ainsley's unneeded reminder. Drew had given Stuart Chapman's number, asking him to pass along the news of his injury to both Chapman and Quincy Travel. As soon as Drew was out of surgery and coherent enough to make a call, he'd call Chapman personally as well, and he'd for sure recommend Stuart to replace him. He'd already been mumbling about it in the ER, how Stuart needed to sub for him while he healed so he didn't lose the Trekmeister job altogether. Drew was cooperating so perfectly that Ainsley almost wanted to thank him.

Stuart stared silently at the living room, where fingerprinting powder dirtied the coffee table. His caman was gone—the police had taken it as evidence since it seemed likely it was the weapon that had fractured Drew's leg. She hoped Stuart would get it back eventually. Losing his beloved shinty stick bothered him.

Silk tulips were piled on the seat of a recliner. Ainsley had gathered them and set them aside so police boots wouldn't stomp on them. "My vase," she said, remembering as she looked at the tulips. Stuart had hidden the vase under thick ivy behind the building. "The police didn't say anything about it. They must not have found it. Should we get it back?"

"Later," Stuart said. "Too dicey right now. That Radcliffe guy. What did he tell the police?"

"What do you mean?"

"He pulled an officer out of here so he could talk to him. Didn't you notice?"

Ainsley shook her head. She'd been focused on Drew.

"I want to know what he told that cop," Stuart said. "What was the guy doing up at three in the morning?"

"You said he heard me scream."

"Why would he need a private audience with the cops to tell them that?"

Ainsley's lungs felt achy. Gideon had been so nice, wanting to help in any way he could and assuring her she didn't need to worry about work; he'd let Natalie know what had happened and that Ainsley wouldn't be at the clinic today. "You think . . . he might have seen something?"

"Why was he sticking around at all? Why didn't he give the cops his phone number and go home?"

Stuart's questions amplified her sleep-deprivation headache. "Ask him," she said tersely.

"If he knows something he shouldn't, do you think he's going to tell us?"

Ainsley poked her fork through her cold toast. "You're being paranoid."

Stuart didn't reply.

* * *

For a better view of any straggling branches, Natalie stepped back to inspect the bush she'd been trimming. Her elbow bumped someone standing behind her. Startled, she spun around.

Heather Osbourne's haunting blue eyes glared at her. "You told Gideon Radcliffe to call the cops on me."

Gripping her pruning shears harder in case she needed them as a weapon, Natalie edged to the side so she wouldn't be pinned between Heather and the landscaping. Violence wouldn't have been a strong worry, except for what Gideon had told her when he'd called this morning to report on the break-in at the MacKerrons'.

"Hello, Heather," Natalie said. "What are you doing here?"

"An unlisted address isn't that secure," Heather said.

"I didn't ask how you found me. I asked what you're doing here."

"Gideon Radcliffe is a kind man," Heather said.

"Yes, he is."

"He didn't call the police on me before. You made him do it this time, didn't you?"

"I had nothing to do with his decision to speak to the police about you."

"They came to my apartment this morning and questioned me like they think I'm the thief. Like they think I attacked Drew Drummond."

"You were near the MacKerrons' apartment when Drew was attacked. As a matter of routine, they'd need to question you. They questioned Gideon too. That doesn't mean they don't have other suspects."

"I told them if they wanted to search my place, they'd need a warrant."

"That's your right."

"I'm not hiding anything."

"I didn't say you were." Natalie evaluated Heather's appearance. Despite the fact that she was standing in clear, early-evening sunlight, she looked shadowy and colorless. "Would you like to sit on the porch for a few minutes? You're pale. Are you feeling ill?"

"I'm not supposed to trust you."

That was an interesting way to phrase it. "Why aren't you supposed to trust me?"

Heather gathered her hair and twisted it into a rope that she draped over her shoulder. It unrolled, spreading over the front of her yellow T-shirt. "It comes back to your clinic. What happened to the MacKerrons, I mean. To Drew Drummond. Evil and death."

"It has no connection to the clinic. I spoke to Ainsley this morning. She and Stuart are shaken up, but they're coping, and Drew will be all right."

Heather retwisted her hair. "What did you do to my brother?"

"I don't know what you mean."

"He knows you. You mean something to him. I can read him."

Natalie couldn't help eyeing Heather's slim arms, wondering if she could strike hard enough to fracture Drew's femur. "If you have questions, ask Kenton."

"It was you, wasn't it? Who broke up his marriage? He was so faithful, and then"—she gave a sharp clap—"it was over. She was devastated, and he wouldn't even talk to her."

"I have never been romantically involved with your brother." This would have been a much easier conversation if she could have stated, *I was his therapist. He divorced his wife because she was emotionally and physically abusive, but he's too ashamed of getting battered by a woman to tell people the truth, and he doesn't think they'd believe him anyway.* "I'm sorry, but I'm not going to discuss Kenton. If you have questions, ask him. If he doesn't want to discuss it, let it go. Why don't we sit on the porch for a few minutes? I could use a break from yardwork."

Heather's eyes narrowed. Slowly, she lowered her gaze to the large, pointed shears in Natalie's hand.

Natalie dropped the shears onto the grass and removed her gardening gloves. "Would you like something to drink? I have some fresh strawberry limeade."

Heather took a step backward, her expression wary—maybe frightened? Did she think Natalie intended to poison her?

"Gideon made it last night," Natalie added. Clearly Heather had a higher opinion of Gideon than she did of Natalie, so maybe identifying him as the maker of the drink would ease Heather's apprehension. "I'd appreciate a chance to chat with you. We don't have to be enemies. Maybe talking would help us understand each other."

"Where is Gideon? He's not here?"

"No. A friend from work is remodeling his kitchen, and Gideon is helping him. But if you'd like to talk to him, I can call him right now. I know he'd be willing to explain why he felt it was necessary to tell the police you were at Innes Hill last night."

Heather looped her rope of hair around her hand. "What are you trying to do to me?"

"Get you to sit down, have a glass of limeade, and tell me why you're so worried about Nefesh Bria, apart from not wanting the Stoker occupied at all."

Heather's eyes seemed to catalogue each part of Natalie: her hair held off her face by a ratty workout headband, her grass-stained T-shirt, the scratch on her arm from a branch, fraying Bermuda shorts, canvas tennis shoes. Natalie hoped her summer-evening-yardwork dishevelment would help Heather see her as approachable, not as an intimidating clinic director and psychologist.

If she could earn a little of Heather's trust, that breakthrough might counterbalance the uneasiness she felt at Heather's stalkerish tracking of her to her house.

"If there's evil and you're not stopping it, maybe you're the source," Heather said. She turned and hurried toward the street.

Natalie resisted the urge to follow her or call her back—not that she'd come. She watched as Heather trotted down the street and turned the corner, probably heading for wherever she'd parked her car.

Troubled but not sure what to do about Heather, Natalie picked up her pruning shears and resumed trimming her bushes. She deeply hoped Heather *wasn't* the thief who had attacked Drew—not only because she'd rather see Heather get help than a prison sentence, but because if she *did* turn out to be guilty, Baxter Quincy would jump on that as more evidence that "your kind of people" were dangerous. The last thing she needed was new fuel pumped into the rumors ravaging Nefesh Bria's reputation.

Baxter. She should try harder to build trust with him and with the others at Quincy Travel. She could send flowers or a different get-well gift to Drew at the hospital, and she could call Baxter right now and express her sympathy regarding the attack on his employee. She set her pruning shears on the porch, took her phone out of her pocket, and found Baxter's cell number too easily, from the last time he'd called to complain.

"Natalie." Baxter sounded surprised. "I'm guessing Radcliffe told you the bad news."

"Yes," Natalie said. "I'm so sorry. To have your friend and employee get hurt like that must be extremely upsetting."

"Yeah, broken leg. That poor sucker is going to be laid up for a while. Bad timing. He was supposed to be Bob's trail guide on a three-week hike next month."

"Will Bob delay the hike until next summer?"

"No need for that. Quincy Travel can cover it. My nephew has plenty of hiking experience. Have you talked to Ainsley?"

"Yes, briefly, this morning. She's very shaken up."

"No kidding. Lucky it was Drew's leg that got whacked, not his skull. Did she tell you what the thief took?"

"Yes. A Baccarat crystal vase."

"Weird thing to steal."

"Ainsley said it's valuable."

"Yeah, but what meth addict can tell the difference between pricey crystal and a glass vase worth five bucks? All the stuff stolen in that part of the city has been fancy stuff, pretty stuff. Jewelry, yeah, that's always a favorite with thieves. But vases? Knickknacks? Sounds like the thief is one of yours, a nutcase who thinks he's King Henry VIII and needs to decorate his palace. Are you keeping your eyes open at the clinic? The thief might show up there, and the cops need to nail him before another victim gets pummeled."

Natalie wanted to tell Baxter how tiresome he was but moderated the comment to, "I'd appreciate it if you wouldn't turn your theories into rumors."

"I don't spread rumors. The only thing I spread is facts."

"I didn't call to argue with you. I truly want to express my sympathy over Drew." She almost added the ritual *Let me know if there's anything I can do* but didn't want to risk it. If she offered, Baxter would tell her in harsh detail what she could do to help, and it would involve Nefesh Bria relocating to a wrong-side-of-the-tracks building with warped linoleum floors, rusty plumbing, and a water-stained acoustic ceiling.

"Thanks for the sympathy," he said. "I'll pass it on to Drew. But when he's clear in the head, if he can tell us anything about the attacker that identifies him as one of your people, you'd better not stand in the way of the investigation."

Natalie gritted her teeth to keep herself from responding, *Oh! Now that you mention it, Iris, my intern, did an intake this afternoon with a client wearing a black ski mask and a crown.* "Of course I hope the thief is caught before any more damage is done. I'll talk to you later." She hung up, not waiting to see if Baxter would say good-bye or would launch another diatribe.

Natalie picked up her shears and hacked a few more branches off her azaleas. If Baxter learned Heather had been at Innes Hill last night and Natalie had withheld that information, he'd assume Heather was guilty *and* he'd accuse Natalie of covering for delusional, violent people.

Give Baxter twenty-four hours and he'd ensure that those rumors flooded the Stoker like Niagara Falls gone rogue.

CHAPTER 10

"THIS SOUP IS DELICIOUS." AINSLEY sprinkled more chopped dill into her bowl. "I need your recipe, Natalie."

Natalie smiled, glad to hear Ainsley's comfortable tone. She and Stuart had both appeared so edgy when they'd arrived at Natalie's house for dinner Saturday evening, moving cautiously, as though not certain Natalie truly wanted them present, pausing awkwardly before responding to questions. "You'll have to ask Gideon," Natalie said. "He made it. It's his stepmother's recipe."

"Way to make sexist assumptions, Lamb," Stuart said.

Ainsley blushed. "Sorry."

Gideon laughed. "If I hadn't seen myself make it, I would have guessed it was Natalie's handiwork too." He glanced toward the rain dotting the kitchen window. "Seems like appropriate weather for a soup night."

"Thanks for having us over," Ainsley said. "I hope we weren't too pushy, inviting ourselves."

"Not at all," Natalie said. When she'd called Ainsley to ask if she could bring them dinner, Ainsley had agreed and had asked Natalie if she could bring herself and Gideon along with the dinner—Ainsley and Stuart wanted company. They'd ended up deciding to meet at Natalie's house.

"Our pleasure." Gideon took another slice of the bread Natalie had picked up at the local bakery. It wasn't nearly the quality of Kenton's bread, but an hour-long round trip to the Playful Otter wasn't something Natalie had wanted to add to her Saturday. Even if she'd wanted to make the drive, surprising Kenton by spontaneously showing up at his bakery was an atrocious idea from every standpoint. She'd texted him about Heather's encounter with the police and suggested he check on her, but Kenton had responded with only *Thanks.* In other words, *I'm acknowledging your text, but I don't want to talk to you about whatever happened and I'm not sure I want to talk to Heather about it either.*

"You guys need any help putting your place back together?" Gideon asked. "I know it can be a mess after a police search."

"There wasn't really a search," Ainsley said. "The thief didn't have time to do much. When he saw Drew in the living room, he must have panicked. After he . . . fought with Drew, he grabbed my vase and ran. Nothing else is missing. Well, except Stuart's caman. The police think that might have been the weapon the thief used on Drew, so they took it as evidence."

"Caman?" Gideon asked.

"It's a curved wooden stick," Ainsley said. "From the game of shinty. They play it in the Scottish highlands."

"Ah, okay. I saw it on your living room floor that night."

"Yeah, I'd had it at the park," Stuart said. "Wish I'd put it away instead of leaving it where some greedy dirtbag could grab it."

Ainsley used her fork to roll an olive around her salad plate. "We'll never be able to replace our vase. Our insurance deductible is a thousand dollars, and that's two-thirds of the value of the vase."

Gideon appeared flabbergasted that any vase short of a Ming antique could be worth fifteen hundred dollars. Natalie wasn't surprised at its value; Ainsley had mentioned the vase at work one day when the discussion in the break room had included talk of luxury items.

"Baccarat crystal," Ainsley explained in response to Gideon's astonished expression. "It was a wedding gift from my aunt. She has a lot of money."

"Then its sentimental value must be even higher than its list price," Gideon said. "I hope the police find it."

"Me too," Ainsley said.

Gideon reached for the bottle of olive oil. "I'll bet the thief will make a final mistake soon. Things are going downhill. First break-ins to empty places, then breaking in when someone was home, and now a break-in plus an assault. The guy's getting cocky, and he's going to get busted."

"Did you see anything that could help the cops?" Stuart ladled another serving of egg-lemon soup into his bowl. "You were out there right after it happened."

"Sorry," Gideon said. "It took me a few seconds to yank on some sweats and get out the door. I didn't see anybody running out of your apartment until a crazy guy in pajama pants almost mowed me down."

"You didn't see *anything* useful?" Stuart dunked bread into his soup. "You came inside and grabbed that officer like you had big news."

Gideon's head twitched slightly toward Natalie, then back toward Stuart. Natalie knew he'd wanted to make eye contact with her and silently ask whether or not to mention Heather. She sympathized with his dilemma. She'd been worried enough about how Baxter would react if he learned she'd withheld mention of Heather. Hiding information from Stuart was even more problematic. He'd want to rip apart anyone he thought was protecting the thief—or who might *be* the thief, which was a compelling reason not to tell him about Heather.

Stuart's expression went taut. "You're holding back. You'd better have a solid reason for it."

"While I was standing outside your door, after the police arrived, someone walked by and asked what was happening," Gideon said. "I felt their behavior was questionable. I reported the incident to the police."

Natalie expected anger from Stuart, but his hostile demeanor softened. "Did you find out who it was?"

"I know who it was, but I'd rather let the police give you more information if there's information to give. This person might have nothing to do with the break-in, and I don't like smearing reputations."

"That doesn't say much for your opinion of us," Ainsley said coolly. "If you think we're going to spread rumors."

"He didn't say you were going to spread rumors," Natalie said. "But if you were the passer-by, would you want your name handed to the victims?"

"It's still insulting," Ainsley said. "Does he think Stuart will go beat a confession out of them?"

"Maybe," Gideon said. "And on his way out the door, he might beat me to a pulp as a warm-up."

Stuart grinned, to Natalie's relief. "Stand down, Lamb. I get why he's being cagey. Better not to know. If there's anything to it, the cops will tell us."

"How's Drew doing?" Natalie asked. "Any updates?"

"Surgery went well," Ainsley said. "We'll go see him tomorrow. He needs rest tonight."

"How long's the recovery supposed to take?" Gideon asked. "I know he was scheduled to take Chapman on that hike next month."

Ainsley shook her head. "That won't happen. Mr. Chapman will have to find another guide."

"Aren't you experienced with the John Muir Trail?" Gideon asked Stuart. "Could you cover for Drew?"

Stuart shrugged. "Yeah, I know what I'm doing, and I'd be glad to help Drew, but we'll see what Chapman wants."

"You ought to let Bob know if you're interested and available," Natalie said. "He'll want to get things arranged quickly."

"I'll do that," Stuart said. "That way Drew doesn't have to stress about letting him down."

"You can uphold the family honor," Gideon said.

"Yeah, and rub it in Drew's face that I had to save his honor."

"What about your job?" Ainsley asked, frowning.

"I'd have to figure that out."

Ainsley dipped her spoon in her bowl and pulled it out, then dipped and withdrew it again as though evaluating the consistency of the soup. "Three weeks is a long time to be gone."

"Don't stress. Chapman might not even be interested in me. Baxter Quincy will try to nail the contract for Quincy Travel."

A phone rang. Stuart reached into his pocket. "'Scuse me; it's Drew's sister." He stood and exited the kitchen as he answered the call. "Hey, Claire."

"Drew's sister lives in Buffalo," Ainsley said. "She came down yesterday morning."

"Does she need a place to sleep if she wants to stay locally?" Natalie asked. "I have a guest room."

"No, I think she's planning to drive back home tonight."

Gideon refilled Ainsley's water glass. "Do you have other family in the area?"

"Stuart's family is mostly in Albany. I grew up here, but my parents retired to—"

"*What?*" Stuart's voice was loud and harsh enough to make both Ainsley and Natalie jump. "That can't be right. How is it possible?"

Silence. Claire must be answering his question. Ainsley stood and rushed into the living room after Stuart. Gideon glanced at Natalie; they stayed seated. Natalie felt a twitchy urge to grab Gideon's hand and steel herself for whatever was happening.

"I don't get this," Stuart said. "I don't get it. How incompetent are these doctors? It was a broken leg!"

Silence. Gideon and Natalie glanced at each other again and rose to their feet. They moved to the doorway between the kitchen and living room.

Stuart stood with his back to the doorway. Ainsley stood a little behind him, as though wanting to hear the conversation but not wanting to interrupt.

"Okay," Stuart said. "Okay." Silence. "Are you sure?" Silence. "Okay. Thanks, Claire. Yeah, as soon as we can. Bye." Stuart lowered the phone.

"Stuart?" Ainsley's voice quivered. "What's going on?"

Stuart didn't turn to face her. "Drew's dead."

Ainsley gasped. Natalie hurried to stand next to her.

"How can you die from a broken leg?" Ainsley whimpered the question, her cheeks gray. Natalie put her arm around Ainsley.

Stuart finally pivoted to face them. His face was as ashen as Ainsley's. "Claire said . . . said it was a . . . it was a fat embolism."

"A what?" Ainsley asked.

Stuart spoke mechanically. "Rare complication. After a traumatic injury."

"I'm so sorry," Natalie said. "May we take you to the hospital? Is that where Drew's sister is?"

Abruptly, Stuart moved toward Ainsley. "We need to go." He took her arm, and the two of them headed toward the door.

Gideon started to follow. "Let us drive—"

"We've got it." Stuart opened the door, drew Ainsley out, and clapped the door shut.

A blank, black sensation spread through Natalie, nothingness clearing the way for pain. She knew too well how it felt to get a phone call with news that tore you to pieces.

"It's murder." Gideon drew Natalie into his arms, steadying her. "I really hope Heather had nothing to do with this."

Without lifting her head from Gideon's shoulder, Natalie nodded.

* * *

As Stuart drove, Ainsley kept her mouth pinched shut and watched the windshield wipers sweeping rain off the glass. As soon as they arrived at the hospital to meet Claire and her husband, Ainsley could release her tears. If she cried now, it would break the fragile silence in the car and Stuart might start talking. She didn't want him to talk. She didn't want to know what he was thinking.

After a few minutes of driving, she registered that Stuart wasn't heading toward the hospital. Not wanting to ask his destination, she watched wordlessly as he drove until they reached the parking area of an isolated, wooded trail in Kemper Park.

Stuart parked near the trailhead, his truck the only vehicle in the lot. Rain tapped the roof of the truck and trickled down the windows. The boughs of trees drooped with waterlogged leaves.

Ainsley pushed a question out. "Why didn't we go to the hospital?"

"Claire's not there. She and Greg were heading home when she called. There's nothing to do there now. Her parents are making flight arrangements to get here as soon as they can."

"Oh." Ainsley wanted to scream at Stuart that he shouldn't have hit Drew so hard, but if she did, he'd yell back that this was her idea, that she'd pressured him into it.

Was Drew's ghost watching them now? Would he take revenge? *Could* he?

Thunder boomed, making Ainsley start. They shouldn't be sitting here surrounded by trees in a thunderstorm, but she didn't want to go home. Home, where Drew . . .

Ainsley released her seat belt and forced herself to turn toward Stuart. Beads of water slid down his angular face. For a senseless moment, Ainsley glanced upward, thinking the roof of the new truck was leaking.

It wasn't rain. It was tears. She'd never seen Stuart cry.

"This is horrible," Ainsley said.

Stuart's voice shook like the damp rustle of branches in the storm. "I've broken four different bones in my life," he said. "Four. I was always fine."

"It's bad luck. His leg should have healed without a problem."

"We killed him."

Ainsley tried not to cringe. She couldn't help picturing Drew's ghost sitting in the cab of the truck with them, listening to them discuss their crime. "We didn't do anything that should have killed him. We're not murderers."

Stuart wiped his face with his hands. Tears reappeared; he wiped his face again.

"Bad luck," Ainsley repeated. "We can't control bad luck. Should we go to Buffalo to be with Claire?"

"She doesn't want to see us tonight. She's too upset. She hero-worshipped that guy."

Ainsley's control fractured. Tears gushed from her eyes.

Stuart folded his arms and stared at the trees, his tears stopping as though he'd passed the baton to Ainsley.

Sweaty, sick to her stomach, Ainsley struggled to control herself. "We can't let . . . can't let this change anything. We . . . go on. Reach out to Chapman. Get you hired."

Stuart didn't respond.

Ainsley kept crying. Stuart's cousin. She'd badgered him into attacking his own cousin. Drew was dead, and it was her fault. What would happen now? Would Stuart even care about the Chapman job anymore?

"The person Gideon saw outside our apartment," Stuart said gruffly. "Someone else probably saw them too."

True, Ainsley thought. Her screams, the arrival of the police—people would have been opening doors and peeking out windows. "It's nothing to worry about. Gideon doesn't suspect us."

"He said he knows who it was. Couldn't have been a neighbor. It had to be someone who didn't belong there, or it wouldn't have been worth reporting to the police." Stuart met Ainsley's gaze. The expression in his bloodshot eyes was transforming from anguish to flinty objectivity. "Heather Osbourne, maybe? She's been lurking around."

"Who cares?" Ainsley sniffled. "If she was there, she didn't see anything dangerous either, or the police would have asked us about it."

"Unless she hasn't told them yet. I want you to ask around. You're less intimidating. You can get people to talk to you. Find out if anyone saw that crazy Osbourne chick near our apartment on Thursday night."

"Can't you drop this?"

"The cops are searching for a murderer now. They're going to push. Put a lot of resources into the investigation." Stuart used his thumb to rub a few specks of dust off the dashboard. "That woman notices things. We need to know what we're dealing with. Need to be prepared in case the police come back."

Ainsley's thoughts barreled through a terrifying time line: the police returning, interrogating them, grilling neighbors and friends in search of clues and motives, accusing Ainsley and Stuart, arresting them. A trial. Decades in prison, separated from each other, their marriage ruined, their lives ruined.

"If Heather saw something, why wouldn't she have told the police immediately?" Ainsley asked.

"Maybe she's waiting for Granny's ghost to give her marching orders. Or maybe she did tell them and they didn't believe her. They know she's a nut. But now that Drew's dead, they'll dig deeper."

Tingles burned Ainsley's scalp. He was right. He was being practical, evaluating threats and dealing with them. She needed to do the same, not weep uselessly while he worked to protect them. "If Heather *was* there on Thursday, she doesn't have an alibi. She . . . Stuart . . . if the police think they've found the killer, they'll end the investigation."

Stuart's brow furrowed. "If they think Heather is the killer?"

"She'd be a perfect red herring." This mess was Ainsley's fault. She couldn't let it destroy them. She had to fix whatever she could fix. "She knows how to break into places—she was haunting the Stoker for years before Chapman renovated it. She's crazy, so she won't be credible when she denies things."

"Are you saying we frame her?"

"She'd be safer and happier locked up anyway." Ainsley blinked what she hoped were the last of the tears out of her eyes. "Don't you think so? It would be a better situation for her."

"Yeah, for sure. They shouldn't have let her go."

"We need to confirm she was there on Thursday, like you were saying. And we need to find out where she lives."

"I know where she lives," Stuart said. "After we saw her hanging around our complex, I looked up her address. Wanted to know if she lived in the area—how easy it was for her to stalk us. She lives close by."

"Okay, great," Ainsley said. "I need to get my vase back. I have an idea for how to handle this."

CHAPTER 11

"Hang on. I think I did something wrong." Gideon studied the printout he'd placed on his kitchen table next to tidy piles of Legos and the beginnings of St. Patrick's Cathedral. "This isn't lining up."

Absently, Natalie separated the last few Legos they'd put together. She doubted Gideon had muffed the design. It was more likely neither of them were concentrating well. Working on one of Gideon's personal Lego designs should have been a relaxing way to spend a Sunday evening, but Natalie was starting to wonder if the only entertainment they could handle tonight was watching cat videos.

She'd left Ainsley a message this afternoon, checking in and letting her know that Natalie and Gideon wanted to bring over the leftovers from last night, along with a few other meals they'd prepared. She'd also told Ainsley that if she didn't feel up to coming to work this week, they could cover for her. Ainsley hadn't yet responded. How were she and Stuart doing? Natalie hadn't heard from Kenton either—had he decided to talk to Heather? How was Heather doing?

"I can't imagine Heather grabbing a hockey stick and smashing Drew Drummond's leg." Gideon's gaze was on the schematics, but plainly his thoughts were in the same realm as Natalie's.

"Shinty stick," Natalie said. "Ainsley told me once that Stuart and Drew both played. Stuart's caman belonged to his father."

Gideon grimaced. "Now it's in police custody as a murder weapon." He set the printout aside. "What do you think Heather's up to?"

"I don't know." Natalie pressed two random Legos together. "I'm worried about her."

"You don't think Grandma Tabitha will tell her to escape police attention by jumping out another window, do you?"

"I don't know. I doubt it. I hope not." Natalie checked her phone in case she'd missed any calls or texts, even though she'd had her phone at her elbow the whole time they'd been sitting here. "I'm going to try her brother again."

"Maybe call instead of texting?" Gideon suggested.

Natalie shook her head. "He hates phone calls. He won't pick up." She texted, *Have you heard from Heather? I'm worried about her,* and set her phone on the table.

"You said you had Heather's information," Gideon said. "You could contact her directly."

"I've tried," Natalie said. "She hasn't responded."

Gideon rapped two Legos against the table, one in each hand. His expression was troubled. Uncertain.

"No," Natalie said. "I don't think it would be wise for you to call her."

"You have impressive mind-reading skills." He tapped a faster rhythm. "I feel like I should do something, and I think she trusts me. Sort of."

"Trusts you enough to track you down and break into your car. Trusts you enough that when you told the police she was fluttering around the MacKerrons' place at the time of the robbery, she accused me of forcing you to call them, because you wouldn't have betrayed her on your own. Does that sound like healthy trust to you?"

"It sounds like . . . potential disaster." He stood. "Do you want gelato? There's some of that salted caramel left."

Natalie opened her mouth to answer, but her attention looped immediately back to Heather. Maybe she and Gideon together could stop by Heather's apartment. It might be easy for her to ignore Natalie's messages, but it might be more difficult for her to ignore Natalie and Gideon on her doorstep, especially if she was stressed enough to be desperate for someone to talk to. If they could see Heather, they could get a feel for how well she was coping.

"Is that a no?" Gideon asked.

"What?"

Gideon gave a wry grin. "Distracted much? I asked if you wanted caramel gelato."

"Definitely. But first . . . should we stop by Heather's apartment? She's only about a mile away. She probably won't let us in, but your good name might cancel out my evil vibes."

Relief brightened Gideon's face. "Yeah, let's check on her. I feel bad for her."

Natalie nodded, thinking of what she knew about Heather's traumatic childhood but couldn't share.

"Want to hoof it?" Gideon asked. "I could use a walk."

"Me too." Natalie stuck her phone in her purse and stood up.

The evening was muggy but not too hot, and Natalie enjoyed the walk to the apartment complex where Heather lived and worked. They located her apartment near the clubhouse and rang the bell.

No answer, no footsteps, no signs of anyone home. At Gideon's suggestion, they entered the clubhouse, attempting to look casual.

A man with a ponytail and a blue polo shirt embroidered with the apartment logo was sitting behind the reception desk. His name tag read *Rhett*. "Good evening, folks."

"Good evening," Natalie said. "Is Heather working tonight?"

The friendliness in his face fogged up. "Uh . . . She should be here. Not sure where she is. She's usually on time."

"How late is she?" Natalie asked.

He checked the clock on the wall behind him. "Coming up on two hours. She should have been here at five. I tried calling her a few times, but she didn't answer. You friends of hers?"

"Yes," Natalie said, imagining how strongly Heather would object to that claim.

"If you get in touch with her, can you tell her to call Rhett? If Sumi— boss lady—shows up and finds that Heather flaked out, that's going to be a problem. I hope she didn't get hit with a relapse after that flu she had a couple weeks back. Even ended up in the hospital. Did she tell you?"

"Yes," Natalie said. "We're worried about her too."

"Maybe she's at the ER. She's not home, and her car's gone."

A crushing feeling started in Natalie's throat and spread down her rib cage. "We'll see if we can track her down. Thanks, Rhett."

"No prob. Hope she's okay."

Natalie and Gideon exited in silence. When they reached the sidewalk outside the complex, Gideon said quietly, "This can't be good. She's usually reliable at work, and today she didn't show up?"

"Usually reliable unless she's on an involuntary psychiatric hold." Natalie kept her voice quiet as well.

"Do you think she's been arrested?" Gideon asked. "She could have gone to turn herself in."

From what Natalie had witnessed and from what she'd heard about Heather, Heather didn't seem like someone who'd surrender—unless messages from a ghost were guiding her to that decision.

Natalie started speed walking. "Let's go to the Stoker. That's where she's gone for years when she's upset."

Gideon caught up with her. "She seemed skittish about the ban when I suggested taking her to Nefesh Bria."

"If she needs to be there badly enough, she won't worry about getting charged with trespassing."

"You're worried she's going to toss herself out a window."

"I'm worried about a lot of things related to Heather Osbourne." Worried and frustrated at being railroaded into a situation where she felt responsible for Heather but didn't have enough knowledge or insight to know what she was dealing with or even a clear idea of what role she should be playing. She should have refused Chapman's assignment, but it was too late now. She couldn't make herself unworry about Heather, and considering the tension in Gideon's body as he now outpaced her, he couldn't make himself unworry either.

Vulnerable, damaged Heather who might be a thief and a murderer.

Both of them were sweaty and out of breath when they reached the parking lot at Innes Hill and flopped into the seats of Gideon's car. Gideon hurriedly started the engine, turned the AC on full, and backed out of his parking space.

"You know," he said, "we're acting like idiots. If we think Heather's at the Stoker and in danger, why aren't we calling the cops?"

"Excellent question." Should they call? All they knew was that Heather hadn't shown up for work and her car was gone. At this point, it seemed an overreaction to summon a squad of officers to scour the Stoker. If Natalie needlessly stirred negative publicity, Regina would have her head on a platter—a solid gold platter provided by Chapman. "We have no idea where she is or what she's doing," Natalie said. "But I'll feel better if we can verify she's not at the Stoker."

"Uh . . . dumb question . . . Is the building even unlocked on Sunday evenings? Could she get in?"

"The only thing open is the Parisi Gallery and the café. In the summer, the main doors are open until nine, and so are the gardens. Yes, she could get inside but shouldn't be able to get into any of the offices unless she's filched another card, and I doubt she could after the way Regina read everyone the riot act about keeping access cards safe."

"And the security guys are keeping an eye out for her," Gideon said. "But she could throw on a hat and sunglasses and sneak into the gardens. We're not talking about high-level security here."

When they arrived at the Stoker, only a dozen or so cars were parked in the lot. "Do you know what her car looks like?" Gideon asked.

"It's an old white Ford Fiesta. I don't see it, but she could have parked elsewhere and walked so security wouldn't notice the car."

Gideon parked, and they headed toward the main doors. The lobby was empty. On the left, the doors to the Parisi Gallery stood open. At the tap of their shoes on the lobby's parquet floor, Lauren peered out of the gallery.

"Oh, hello!" She approached them. When she was close enough to speak in a soft voice, she said, "Vanessa ordered me to linger near the entrance and check every time I hear someone enter the building."

"To invite them into the gallery?" Natalie asked.

"No. To see if they look 'crazy and dangerous' and to call security if they do."

"Do we look crazy and dangerous?" Natalie asked.

"Oh, yes." Lauren winked. "I don't know how she expects me to tell if someone is dangerous by looking at them, but I want to keep my job, so here I am spying on guests. Did you . . . did you hear the terrible news about Drew Drummond from Baxter's agency?"

"We did hear, from the MacKerrons," Natalie said. "I'm so sorry. This must be terrible for Baxter."

"It's heartbreaking. Baxter considered him a friend as well as a stellar employee. Poor Ainsley and Stuart. I didn't know Drew was Stuart's cousin until Baxter told me. How are they doing? Have you spoken to Ainsley?"

"We were with them when they got the news that Drew had died," Natalie said.

"Oh my goodness! Those poor dears. Fate can be so vicious." Lauren glanced at the doorway to the gallery. "I'd better get back to work. May I invite you in? We have four new watercolors by Jennifer Lacombe, and they're breathtaking. Or do you need to hurry to the clinic?"

Natalie debated for a moment whether to confide in Lauren. Lauren did seem to have common sense and control of her tongue. "We're actually searching for Heather Osbourne. Have you seen her come in? Or rather, seen anyone who *could* be her?"

"Oh mercy. If she's skulking around, Vanessa will have a stroke. And if I let her slip past me and don't call security, I'll be job hunting."

"If she's here, we're not planning to tell Vanessa," Natalie said. "We'd prefer Baxter didn't find out either. How long have you been keeping an eye on the main doors?"

"Since I got here at two. I know she hasn't come into the gallery, but I've seen a handful of people head straight out to the gardens." Lauren fingered the sash of her polka-dot swing dress. "I do remember a woman wearing a hat, a white straw hat with flowers on it, who arrived not long ago. I noticed the hat—charmingly vintage. I couldn't see her face. But she was with a group."

"Thank you," Natalie said. "We'll check the gardens."

"Gracious, so many odd things going on," Lauren said. "Poor Drew, and a murderer on the loose, and now that sad girl haunting us again."

"She probably isn't here," Natalie said. "Don't worry."

"Good luck." Lauren glided back into the gallery on her red baby-doll pumps.

Natalie and Gideon walked toward the doors that led to the gardens.

"I think I saw Lauren Bell in a movie playing opposite Cary Grant," Gideon remarked.

"She does have that old-style movie-star persona," Natalie said as Gideon opened the door for her.

In the summer evening, the gardens were tranquil and scented with roses. A father and his young daughter were the only people in the patio area; the girl was tossing coins into the air so they'd splash into the fountain. Natalie nudged Gideon toward the walking path that branched off the patio area. As soon as they were out of sight of the father and daughter, she and Gideon both started walking fast, their steps instantly in sync. Gideon scanned the left side of the trail while Natalie scanned the right.

"I shouldn't be this worried," Natalie murmured, eyes scouring every tree, every bench, every bed of flowers. "I'm overreacting."

"It's contagious," Gideon said, and she knew he too was picturing worst-case scenarios—Heather hanging from the branch of a tree or bloodless and lifeless on the ground.

In the most secluded area of the gardens, sitting on a granite bench with her back to the pathway and her face toward the trees was a woman wearing a white straw hat decorated with yellow roses. Natalie gripped Gideon's elbow, and they both stopped on the path. Though the woman must have heard their footsteps approach and halt, she remained motionless, her back bowed and her shoulders curved inward.

With cautious steps, they advanced until they were directly behind the bench. A few strands of long black hair had escaped the hat and hung down the back of the woman's yellow dress.

Natalie spoke gently. "Heather?"

She didn't move. Natalie sat next to her. Gideon remained standing behind them.

With the big brimmed hat the woman wore, Natalie could see only a glimpse of her profile, barely enough to confirm it was Heather. In her lap, she held something about the size of a football, wrapped in a white bath towel.

"It's Natalie Marsh," Natalie said. That hat would block most of Heather's peripheral vision, and she hadn't turned her head to see who had invaded her sanctuary. Natalie set her purse on the opposite side of her from Heather. Keeping her movements small and slow, she slipped her phone from the outer pocket and set it on the bench where she could snatch it in a hurry. "Gideon Radcliffe is with me."

Heather turned to face Natalie. She was pale—not white and stony with determination the way she'd been on the night of the Stoker party but wan. Depleted. She lifted the bundle in her lap and hugged it against her chest as though protecting it. "The police sent you."

"No," Natalie said. "We came because we're concerned about you. You weren't at your apartment, so we thought you might be here."

"That beanpole detective knows you. Bartholomew. And his partner, the black man. The professor."

"Detective Turner." Natalie agreed with Heather's description: Jeffrey Turner's bookish appearance and pleasant-but-stern personality always took her back to her college days.

Heather lowered the bundle to her lap. "You know them both."

"Yes. But they didn't send me."

"You have scars," Heather said. "Injuries in your soul."

Considering the things Kenton had said about Heather's researching her, this comment didn't surprise Natalie. "This isn't about me."

"Your scars are about you. You look perfect, but you have scars."

Gideon's hand rested on Natalie's shoulder. "I do have scars," Natalie said, appreciating his supportive touch. "So does everyone, to some degree.

But I'm doing everything I can to heal. I wish you'd let people help *you* heal."

Heather shifted the bundle, positioning her palms on either side of it. "Someone's trying to destroy me." She twisted on the bench so she could look up at Gideon. "Someone's trying to destroy me." With her elbow, she pointed at Natalie. "Is it her?"

"No," Gideon said. "She wants to help you. We both do."

"Tabitha said not to trust her."

"Did Tabitha give you a reason for not trusting me?" Natalie asked.

Heather focused on Natalie, her dark-blue eyes seething with disarrayed emotions. "You think I'm hearing voices. You think I'm insane."

"I don't have enough information to think anything at all about you except that you're hurting. Please let us help you."

Heather lowered her eyes. For a few silent seconds, she played with the edge of the towel.

"What do you have there?" Gideon asked.

Her thin fingers unwound the towel, moving carefully as though she were trying to open a present without tearing the paper. The object inside was a vase.

She held the vase up. Evening sunlight slipping through the trees sparkled through intricately cut crystal.

CHAPTER 12

A GUSH OF DARKNESS FILLED Natalie. She looked questioningly up at Gideon and saw a composed expression too stiff to be genuine. He nodded at her, confirming that this could be Ainsley's vase. Natalie had never seen it, but Gideon had.

Natalie spoke without any trace of accusation in her tone. "Where did you get the vase?"

"I found it," Heather said.

"Where?"

"In my bedroom closet. On the top shelf. Behind a box. When I opened the closet, I could tell things weren't right, that someone had messed with them. I searched and found this."

Gideon sat on the other side of Heather, positioning himself where he could instantly intercede if Heather swung the heavy vase at Natalie—as she must have swung the caman at Drew.

"Why do you think it was in your closet?" Natalie asked.

Heather up-ended the vase. Etched into the bottom was a circle including the words *Baccarat* and *France*. "The thief stole a Baccarat vase from Ainsley MacKerron. The thief. The murderer." Her voice was flimsy. Breakable. "Drew Drummond died from his injuries. Did you know that?"

"Yes," Natalie said.

Heather peered at the upside-down vase, both hands curling around the narrowest portion before it widened into a pedestal base. It resembled a ready-to-swing grip, but before Natalie could react, Gideon spoke.

"May I hold the vase?"

Heather's fingers went paler as she clutched it.

"I'm going to rephrase that," Gideon said. "Hand me the vase, or I'll take it from you. Let's keep this friendly."

"You think I'm going to attack her with it."

"It's a possibility," Gideon said. "Neither of us wants to get clocked by the world's most expensive club."

To Natalie's surprise, Heather laughed, a scratchy, tiny chuckle. "You're going to give it to the police."

"What else can we do?" Gideon said. "It's evidence in a homicide investigation."

"I didn't steal it." Heather arched forward, hunching her body around the vase. "You told Dr. Marsh I was at the MacKerrons' the night the vase was stolen."

"Yes."

"You told her I was there. Now the vase shows up in my closet."

"What are you saying?" Gideon asked.

Heather's neck curved downward, her hat completely hiding her face. Natalie touched the screen of her phone.

"If you're implying Natalie is trying to frame you, I promise you that's not true," Gideon said. "She'd never do that."

"She has scars." Heather straightened. "She's calling the police." In an abrupt movement, she pivoted toward Natalie.

As Natalie sprang off the bench, Gideon's arms lashed around Heather. The back brim of her hat hit his chest, and the hat landed on the ground.

Heather slouched in Gideon's arms. "I wasn't going to attack her. Let go of me."

Gideon shifted his hold, locking his hands around her wrists. "Let Natalie take the vase."

Natalie stepped forward and used the towel to remove the vase from Heather's now slack fingers. She wrapped the towel around the vase and set it on the ground, out of Heather's range.

"Tabitha . . . warned me not to trust you?"

Natalie couldn't tell if she was repeating her statement or restating it as a question. "She's wrong." Natalie scrolled to find Detective Bartholomew's number, which she—unfortunately—still had in her contacts.

"Don't call the police!" Heather squirmed, panic heating her voice. "Gideon, stop her! They won't understand."

Natalie lowered her phone. "We have to call, but if there's anything you'd like us to understand before we do that, we're listening."

"Tell Gideon to let me go. I'm not going to hurt you. Or him. I've never attacked anyone."

"Glad to hear it," Gideon said.

"I don't have any weapons. Dr. Marsh can search me if she wants."

"I do." Natalie didn't want to risk a surprise knife in the ribs. She stepped forward. Heather closed her eyes and stoically endured a pat down.

"All right," Natalie said. "If you'll agree to stay seated, keep your hands together in your lap, and not make any sudden moves, Gideon will let go of you. Agreed?"

"Yes."

Gideon released her. She edged away from him and put her hands in her lap, one fisted, the other gripping the fist. "I can't go to prison. I'll go crazy."

Natalie resumed her seat on the other side of Heather, ignoring Gideon's warning glare. As long as Heather didn't have a weapon, Natalie figured if she tried anything, they'd be able to subdue her before she did much damage.

"Tabitha warned me about you, Natalie Marsh," Heather said. Natalie wondered if her repetitions of this message were her attempt to convince herself Tabitha was right. Did Natalie's reasonable behavior have her doubting?

"How does Tabitha communicate with you?" Natalie asked.

"You're making fun of me."

"I'm not making fun of you. I'm asking a sincere question."

"No one's ever believed she communicates with me. Except Sophia. Sophia believes me."

Natalie doubted Kenton's manipulative ex-wife believed Heather, but she'd have feigned belief if she'd wanted to get her sister-in-law on her side. "This isn't a matter of my believing you or not. I'm asking about *your* experience."

"Why should I tell you?"

"You might feel better sharing it. Considering that you managed to get yourself released from the hospital fairly quickly, I'm guessing you hid things from your doctor when he or she asked you about Tabitha. I'm also guessing you don't like lying about something so important to you."

Confusion billowed in her eyes. "What are you trying to do to me?"

"I'm trying to listen to you."

"So you can report to Beelzebub Chapman. Or to Bartholomew the Giraffe and Turner the Professor so they'll arrest me for murder."

"Heather," Gideon said. "We found you sitting here with what looks like Ainsley MacKerron's stolen vase. That's what the police will want to know about. Keeping silent about Tabitha or anything else won't make the vase disappear. And you don't have to tell us anything. We just wanted to offer you the chance to talk to us since you're worried the police won't understand."

Heather swapped the position of her hands, the left hand now a fist with the right hand clutching it. "I didn't steal it. Someone hid it in my closet."

"So you wrapped a towel around it and trespassed your way into the Stoker gardens so you could sit here holding it," Gideon said. "Why?"

Heather lurched forward, but Natalie and Gideon each caught an arm, keeping her on the bench.

"Running away is not an option," Gideon said. "We're going to talk to the police without making them track you down."

Heather slumped. Natalie released her.

Gideon kept his own grip tight. "Are you done with the conversation? We can call the police now if you don't feel like talking."

"Wait," Heather whispered. "I still don't know what to do."

"Did Tabitha tell you to bring the vase here?" Natalie asked.

"No. I was hoping . . . at home . . . that she'd tell me what to do . . . give some advice. But this time . . . nothing. So I came here. I hoped she'd speak to me here."

"But she hasn't?"

"No." Heather glared at Natalie, her eyes teary. "You want to ask if she told me to attack Drew Drummond. She didn't. She's never wanted me to hurt anyone. She's always kind. Loving."

"You thought she'd told you to hurt yourself," Natalie said gently.

Tears skidded down Heather's face. "That wasn't her. I . . . wanted that for myself. I thought if I died that way, she'd be proud of me and I'd be with her. I . . . I made a mistake. She'd never want me to get hurt."

The ghost of a loving great-great-great-grandmother. The only way Heather could think of to repay the love she'd conjured up was to obsessively defend the turf Tabitha had died on.

At the chatter of female voices, Natalie checked behind her. Three middle-aged women were ambling along the trail, sipping from glasses embossed with the Parisi Gallery logo. They all aimed curious looks at Natalie, Heather, and Gideon.

Natalie turned away and spoke quietly to Heather. "If Tabitha wants to help you, she and I have the same goal. I don't know why you feel she's warned you not to trust me. Yes, Bob Chapman wanted me to stay informed on your actions as they relate to the Stoker Building, but that has nothing to do with the fact that I care about you as a human being and I don't like it that you're suffering."

Heather squirmed on the bench and stretched her foot toward her hat that lay on the ground. She couldn't reach it.

"We'll get the hat in a minute," Gideon said. "Has Tabitha told you any specific reasons not to trust Natalie?"

"Just . . . to be wary of her." Heather's wavering voice steadied and sharpened. "She had an affair with Kenton. She broke up his marriage."

"Did Tabitha tell you that?" Natalie asked.

"I have a brain. I can figure things out."

"I did not have an affair with your brother."

Gideon interceded. "Heather, how does Tabitha speak to you?"

"I . . . don't *hear* her voice." She looked at Gideon, who still had his hand clamped around her arm. "Not in words usually. I sense she's there, and she sends thoughts to me. And . . . recently . . . right after I . . . after I almost died . . . she started writing me letters."

"Letters?" Gideon asked.

"Yes. I know her handwriting. I have letters she wrote when she was alive. I *know* her handwriting."

"Did she say why she started writing letters to you now?" Natalie asked.

"Yes. In the first letter, she said she was worried about me and worried about the building and needed to communicate more clearly."

"How does she deliver them?" Natalie asked.

"She leaves them in the box where I keep her other letters. On my nightstand. The first one was there when I got home from the hospital, then there have been more. When I found the vase today, I checked the box to see if there was a new letter, but . . . no."

"Do you keep her new letters?" Natalie asked. "I'd love to see them."

"She said to burn them, that . . . that she wasn't supposed to be sending them. I guess there are rules for the dead. I have a candleholder. Brass. It wasn't hers, but it's one she could have owned. It's from her era. I put a candle in it and burn the letters in the flame, one scrap at a time. She likes that; I can tell—likes that I use my candleholder, the one I used to carry when I'd visit her here." Heather lifted sweaty strands of hair off the back of her neck. She'd pinned her hair into a knot, but more strands were drooping free. "I . . . I did . . . I saved the first letter. I hid it under the old ones. I hope she's not mad at me. I . . . I didn't want to burn all of them."

"What has she told you in the letters?" Natalie asked.

Heather closed her eyes. "That she loves me. That she's grateful I tried to protect this building for her. She said . . . now she's okay letting it go, except for . . . except she's worried about the clinic. There's evil there. She doesn't know exactly what's happening though. You've blocked her. She can't get in. What did you do?"

"Nothing," Natalie said. "I've never done anything to block Tabitha. Has she asked you to do something about the clinic?"

"She asked me to spread the word, to warn people against it before awful things happen." Heather slouched again, her head bowing. "I messed up. Something awful did happen. Drew Drummond is dead."

"Drew's death is a terrible tragedy, but he's not connected to Nefesh Bria," Natalie said.

"He was at the MacKerrons'. Ainsley works with you. There's a connection, like Tabitha predicted."

More footsteps approached. Natalie checked over her shoulder. Two of the three women they'd seen before were walking past. They must have circled all the way around the garden path. Were they deliberately keeping an eye on the scene on the bench? Natalie imagined it from their perspective: Natalie's hyperalertness, Heather's disheveled hair and slumped posture, Gideon gripping Heather's arm in what plainly wasn't an affectionate gesture. And the odd towel-wrapped object and Heather's hat on the ground.

"We're going to get the police called *for* us," Natalie muttered to Gideon.

"I don't want to talk to the police yet." Jerkily, Heather scooted forward and backward on the bench, probably wanting to free herself but knowing if she did break loose, she'd get tackled. "I don't know what to do."

Out of the corner of her eye, Natalie watched the women pass them. "You tell the police the truth," she said softly.

"Let me go. I could have both of you arrested for kidnapping."

"We'll take that risk," Gideon said. "We'd rather get arrested than let you run off and dive out a window."

"I won't!"

"Take it easy." Gideon raised a questioning eyebrow at Natalie and tipped his head toward the building. She nodded and picked up her phone. Heather was getting overwhelmed and agitated. It was time to pass everything into the hands of law enforcement. She'd rather leave the Stoker security guards out of it and get Heather away from here before summoning the police, but she wasn't sure Heather would cooperate with that plan.

"We need to take this vase to the police," Natalie said. "Would you rather I call them to come here, or would you like a ride to the police station? If you're worried they won't believe you found the vase in your closet, one thing that could help your credibility is handing the vase over voluntarily."

Heather wriggled her trapped arm. "Voluntarily?"

"Call it semivoluntarily," Gideon said.

"I don't want the police to come here." Fear wiped out indignation in Heather's voice. "Not here. I found out . . . Tabitha likes the gardens, the new gardens. She wouldn't want a scene here."

"Okay, let's go straight to the PD," Gideon said. "That's a better choice." He stood, pulling Heather to her feet. Natalie rose and picked up the wrapped vase and Heather's hat.

"Let go of me," Heather said. "I won't run."

"Here, let's try this." Gideon released her arm and held out his elbow. "You hold my arm. Keep a firm grip. If I feel you letting go, I'll turn from Victorian gentleman to linebacker. If you cooperate, we can do this whole deal with dignity."

Heather twitched her weight from foot to foot, transparently gauging the odds of a getaway. Natalie didn't doubt Heather was fast, but with Gideon on alert, an attempt at escape wouldn't work. Finally, she rested a trembling hand in the crook of Gideon's elbow. He laid his own hand on hers. "Take it easy," he said. "I know these cops. They're good guys."

Natalie handed Heather her hat. Heather pulled the hat as low on her brow as it would go.

In silence, they walked through the lobby. Summoned by their footsteps, Lauren peeked out the gallery doors and immediately retreated. Natalie was confident she wouldn't tell Vanessa or anyone else what had happened, not when failing to spot Heather sneaking in could get her fired.

"I didn't kill Drew," Heather said as they exited the building. "Are you framing me?"

"No," Natalie said. "Don't panic. The police won't jump to conclusions, and they're experienced at figuring out the truth. Tell them everything."

"Admit you had an affair with Kenton."

"*Did* Tabitha tell you we had an affair?"

"Not . . . not specifically. But she warned me not to trust you. That there's evil at your clinic."

"If Tabitha has issues with me, tell her to come talk to me herself instead of burdening you with those messages."

"She won't."

"That's too bad," Natalie said. "Because if she's willing to let the rest of her claim on the Stoker go, I'd like to know why she's holding a grudge against my clinic."

CHAPTER 13

Natalie drove Gideon's car. Gideon and Heather sat in the backseat with the child locks engaged so Heather couldn't open her door. She spent the trip in silence, eyes shut, arms folded, chalky face sweating around the hairline until perspiration trickled down her forehead. Every time Natalie glimpsed her in the rearview mirror, she wanted to repeat the same set of questions Heather had already ignored: Was she dizzy? Did she need to lie down? Did she need water? Did she feel sick to her stomach? For Gideon's sake, she hoped the answer to at least the stomach question was no. To be safe, she would have tossed him the towel around the vase, but she didn't want to handle evidence more than necessary.

Before leaving the Stoker parking lot, Natalie had sent two texts: one to Bartholomew, informing him they were bringing Heather in with what might be Ainsley MacKerron's stolen vase, and one to Kenton with a similar message. After she parked at the police department, she checked for replies. None from Kenton, but Bartholomew had answered: *Thanks for your help. We'll be there ASAP.*

"Detective Bartholomew is on his way," Natalie said.

Heather didn't react.

She texted Bartholomew: *We're at the PD in the parking lot.*

Bartholomew responded immediately. *How is she?*

Scared but quiet. We found her in the Stoker gardens. She says the vase was planted in her apartment.

Bartholomew's next question appeared on the screen. *She came with you voluntarily?*

This wasn't the moment to mention Heather's threat to file kidnapping charges. Natalie typed, *She knew it was her best option.*

Almost there. Meet you in the lobby.

Natalie assessed Heather. Her eyes remained closed, but she was fidgeting, uncrossing, then recrossing her arms, slumping against her seat, then stiffening and pressing her shoulder against the passenger door.

Natalie texted Bartholomew. *Meet us at Gideon's car. Silver Accord parked halfway down the row nearest the street. I don't know how she'll react if we try to take her inside.*

Ok.

Natalie set her phone on the passenger seat next to the towel-wrapped vase. "They're nearly here."

Heather opened her eyes. "They won't believe me."

"Give them the facts, and let them investigate," Gideon said. "They might already have information that points to someone else."

Heather's gaze struck Natalie, hard and wild, like hands flailing blindly at an attacker. "You hid the vase in my closet. You're setting me up."

"That's not true," Natalie said. "Why would I do that?"

"I tried to mess up your plans. Stop you."

"Stop me from doing what?"

"The clinic," she said. "Keeping the clinic open."

"You aren't the only one who objects to the clinic." In Natalie's peripheral vision, she saw rangy, young Bartholomew and older, heavier Turner stepping out of a blue sedan a few parking slots away. "Do you honestly think I'd commit a crime and frame you simply to get you out of my hair?"

"Why doesn't Tabitha trust you?"

"I don't know."

"Why—?" Heather noticed Bartholomew approaching and stopped speaking. Turner remained standing behind Gideon's car.

Bartholomew opened Heather's door. "Hello, Ms. Osbourne." His voice was friendly, and rather than his usual suit and tie, he wore cargo shorts, a T-shirt, and a light jacket that he couldn't possibly need for the weather. Natalie figured it covered a holstered gun.

"Thank you for coming in," Bartholomew said. "Finding that vase must have scared you. Thanks for turning it in instead of tossing it. Step out of the car, and we'll find a better place to talk."

Heather's gaze shot to Natalie. Natalie waited for her to tell Bartholomew that Natalie had framed her, but she didn't say anything. She stepped out of the car, legs wobbling.

Bartholomew grasped her elbow. "Let me help you."

Natalie picked up the wrapped vase, opened her own door, and carried the vase to Detective Turner.

"Thank you, Dr. Marsh." He took it. "Could you and Mr. Radcliffe come inside, please, and wait in the lobby?"

"Yes, of course."

Bartholomew guided Heather toward the front door of the police department. Turner followed.

Gideon stepped out of the car. "Whew," he said under his breath. "Got any Valium?"

Natalie handed him his keys. "You handled her well. Thank you."

"Kidnapping—a skill I never knew I had. Visit me in prison, okay?"

"I'll go down as an accomplice." Natalie remained by the car, observing Heather as she and the detectives passed into the lobby.

"I can't figure out whether or not she really thinks you framed her," Gideon said.

"Neither can she." The tension of escorting Heather here was easing, but a different, too-familiar tension was intensifying. She didn't want to go inside the police department.

"You okay?" Gideon asked. "Raw deal that you'd end up back here."

Natalie adjusted Camille's tourmaline ring on her finger. "At least this time they aren't asking questions about my best friend's murder. Let's get this over with." She started toward the lobby.

Behind her, a car door closed and a male voice called, "Dr. Marsh."

Natalie turned. Kenton was walking toward her.

She backtracked to meet him. "You got my message."

"Yeah. I was in town already. I'd come to . . . see what Heather was up to."

Natalie gestured to Gideon, who was lingering a few feet behind her. "Kenton, this is Gideon Radcliffe. Gideon, Kenton Lowery, Heather's brother."

Gideon approached, and they shook hands. From Kenton's faux-friendly smile, Natalie knew he was wondering how much Gideon knew about him and hoping he knew nothing.

"Heather went inside with the detectives on the case," Natalie said.

"Thanks. Uh . . ." Kenton glanced uncomfortably at Gideon.

"Would you like me to step away?" Gideon asked politely.

"Uh . . . whatever . . ."

Natalie knew Kenton wanted privacy but wasn't sure it was appropriate to ask for it. "Gideon, if you don't mind waiting for me inside, that would be great," she said.

"Not a problem." Gideon strode toward the lobby doors. Natalie hoped he wasn't wondering if she wanted time alone with Kenton to discuss their alleged affair. *Relax. He's smarter than that.*

Smart but insecure.

When Gideon was inside the building, Kenton asked, "Did she admit anything?"

"To us, you mean?" Natalie fleshed out the information she'd offered Kenton in her text, explaining how Heather claimed to have found the vase, how she'd gone to the Stoker to seek Tabitha's counsel, the new letters she thought she'd received, her suspicion of Natalie. Kenton stood with his shoulders hunched—a pose Natalie kept seeing in Heather—and his body angled to one side, eyes focused more on the ground than on Natalie.

"She accused *you?*" Kenton asked. "Because of a ghost message?"

"I don't know how much she believes it. Her behavior with me is inconsistent. One moment she's confiding in me, the next she's panicking and calling me evil."

Kenton hid his hands in the pockets of his board shorts. "She hounded me about you. Says I'm hiding something." He flipped a nervous glance at Natalie. "What did you tell her?"

"That I have never been personally involved with you. That's all."

"Nothing else?"

"No. I told her if she had questions to ask you."

"Have you told your . . . friend? Gideon?"

"No."

"Should I tell Heather?"

"That's up to you. If you want my opinion, telling her how we know each other might help her see that mental health professionals aren't the enemy, and specifically that *I'm* not the enemy."

Kenton frowned at his white-speckled shoes. Even though he wasn't dressed in his Playful Otter baker's clothes, his shoes were still sprinkled with flour.

"I'm not trying to pressure you," Natalie said. "But here's one thing to consider: treating the fact that you saw a therapist like a dirty, humiliating secret isn't going to encourage Heather to seek help."

"I . . . worry she might be in touch with Sophia. I don't want Sophia to know."

Natalie restrained her instincts to explore with him why he couldn't risk letting his ex-wife learn he'd sought professional help to get him to the point where he could walk away from her abuse. "It's your choice whom you tell."

He swallowed, still examining his shoes. Kenton was skilled at faking confidence when he felt he had to, and it had taken a lot of work for Natalie to persuade him to lower that facade. She was glad he didn't seem inclined to raise it in her presence now. She'd rather see him openly floundering and frightened than grinning like a breathtaking movie star while inside, everything was bruised and dying.

"When was the last time you talked to Heather?" Natalie asked.

"Right after she was released from the hospital. But she texted me yesterday to tell me about the break-in and that guy's death and to say Tabitha had been right about the evil at your clinic."

"Did she tell you the police questioned her about being near the MacKerrons' apartment that night?"

"No. I learned that from you."

She empathized with Kenton and Heather, both isolated, both hurting, struggling to figure out—with no family role models—how to reach out to each other in positive ways. "Would you like to come inside and wait with Gideon and me? I hope it won't be too long before you can talk to Heather."

"Do you think she killed that guy?"

Natalie wished she could lie, but it wouldn't help Kenton. "I don't know. What do you think?"

His anxious mien answered the question before his words did. "I was reading about the thefts. The thief never took electronics—always stuff like jewelry and decorations. Like that vase. Heather . . . she's always liked pretty stuff."

"A lot of people like pretty stuff. Let's take it one step at a time. All we know is that she had a vase that looks like Ainsley MacKerron's."

"She's smart. Why would she do something stupid like break into an apartment where people were home?"

Natalie guessed that either breaking into empty residences wasn't enough of a rush anymore or that subconsciously Heather wanted to get caught. She didn't want to share either of those theories with Kenton. "I don't know."

"Did they already arrest her?"

"No. She came here voluntarily."

"Do you think they'll arrest her?"

"I have no idea." What Natalie wanted was Heather back in the hospital, compelled to stay there until she really got help. That might happen; if she now thought she was receiving letters from Tabitha, the power her delusions had over her life was expanding. Natalie doubted she'd be able to fake stability well enough to fool Turner and Bartholomew.

"Let's go inside." Natalie started walking toward the police department. Kenton followed.

In the lobby, Gideon was sitting in one of the padded vinyl chairs, grimly fiddling with his phone. He rose to his feet as Natalie and Kenton entered. Natalie took a seat. The men filled the seats on either side of her.

None of them spoke. Gideon scrolled through a news website; Natalie doubted he was doing more than skimming headlines. Kenton stared with blank eyes at the reception window. Natalie thought of trying to make conversation and decided it was better to keep silent.

By the clock on the wall, twenty-two minutes passed before Kenton said, "Do you think she's okay?"

"She was fairly calm when we arrived here," Natalie said.

"She's smarter than I am," Kenton said. "She'll handle it."

Natalie didn't point out that all the intelligence in the world wasn't enough when your brain was misfiring and you couldn't discern fantasy from reality.

"Can I get anyone some water?" Gideon indicated the cooler on the opposite side of the lobby.

"Thank—" Natalie cut off her answer as the door that led to the back of the department opened and Bartholomew stepped out.

"How's everyone doing?" Bartholomew glanced at Kenton. Natalie waited a moment to see if Kenton would identify himself, but he didn't.

"Kenton, this is Detective Abe Bartholomew," she said. "Detective, this is Kenton Lowery, Heather's brother."

"Mr. Lowery." Bartholomew came forward and extended a hand. "Thank you for coming, sir."

Kenton stood and shook his hand. "How is Heather?"

"She's nervous. Having a difficult time talking to us."

Kenton shaped his expression into picture-perfect brotherly concern. "Is there anything I can do to help?"

Bartholomew inspected Kenton, contemplating him for long enough that Natalie could feel Kenton's concealed agony. He'd hate being scrutinized by a cop. It was a miracle he'd been willing to come to the PD at all.

"Would you like to come sit with your sister for a little while?" Bartholomew asked. "Your presence might help calm her. We'd like to keep this as low-stress for Heather as possible."

This time, Kenton didn't do as well creating his mask—he looked alarmed. Natalie was surprised herself. Didn't the police usually want to isolate and intimidate suspects, not comfort them with the presence of family members? Maybe they thought Kenton could persuade Heather to confess.

"Sir?" Bartholomew said.

"Okay, yeah," Kenton said, so much apprehension in his demeanor that Natalie questioned how much comfort he'd be. Maybe his nervousness would cancel out Heather's.

"Dr. Marsh, if you could come with me now too, I'd appreciate it," Bartholomew said. "Mr. Radcliffe, please forgive the wait."

"Not a problem," Gideon said.

Bartholomew touched his ID to a scanner, letting them through to the back of the department. "Dr. Marsh, if you could go through that door on your left and have a seat, I'll join you in a moment. Mr. Lowery, this way."

Natalie entered the room Bartholomew had designated. The inside was familiar—blue industrial carpet, an oak table, upholstered chairs, walls painted soft green. She had to hand it to the Ohneka PD for making their interview rooms more pleasant than the metal tables and bare tile floors she would have imagined before coming here last year, but being in this room still kicked her stress level through the roof. She pulled out a chair, sat down, and waited.

Several minutes later, Bartholomew entered and closed the door behind him. He set a chilled water bottle on the table in front of her. "May I get you anything else? Coffee? Food?"

"No, thank you."

He sat across from her. "You've had a few messes to deal with lately. How are you holding up?"

"I'm all right. What can I do for you?"

"You can exercise better judgment in the future. I understand you're leery of generating more bad press for the Stoker or for Nefesh Bria, but when you found Heather Osbourne there with that vase, you should have called us immediately."

He was right. She should apologize, but she wasn't sorry she'd had those few minutes to connect with Heather.

"Tell me about finding Heather," Bartholomew said. "What brought you to the gardens?"

"Gideon and I were searching for her because we knew she was distressed about being questioned following the break-in at the MacKerrons'. We checked her apartment then the clubhouse where she works. Her coworker told us she was supposed to be at work two hours ago but hadn't shown up, which wasn't like her. We thought she might be at the Stoker, which turned out to be true."

"How did she react when you confronted her?"

"She was nervous. Agitated. She'd gone there hoping for advice from her great-great-great-grandmother's ghost on what to do about the vase."

"She told you that?"

"Yes. She was . . . ambivalent about confiding in us. A few times, she would have bolted if she could have, but we didn't give her that choice. We'd gone there afraid she might have returned to finish her earlier suicide attempt. Letting her run off when she was scared and irrational seemed like a poor idea."

"I understand," Bartholomew said. "Again, I'd like to emphasize that you should have called us rather than handle her yourself."

Glad he hadn't announced that Gideon and she were under arrest for unlawfully detaining Heather, Natalie said, "When she knew she was stuck with us, she did open up a little more." She filled Bartholomew in on the other things Heather had said.

"Letters, huh?" Bartholomew leaned back in his chair, his long legs stretching all the way under the table and out the other side. "Do you think she's burning actual pieces of paper or just imagining she is?"

"I have no idea."

"What's your take on the brother? I know Mr. Chapman personally asked you to establish him as an ally in helping deal with Ms. Osbourne."

"Yes. Kenton is worried about Heather but doesn't know how to help her. They aren't close—he doesn't see her often, as far as I know. He did come to town to try to see her today, so that's a positive sign."

"What's your impression of him? Firing on all cylinders?"

"He seems to be," Natalie said, disliking this awkward part of the conversation and hoping it would end naturally before she had to cut it off. "He's a baker, part owner of the Playful Otter Bakery in East Rochester."

Bartholomew leaned forward and braced his sharp elbows on the table. "He's in with Heather now. Heather hasn't eaten all day, so we're offering her dinner. Officer Kalili is keeping an eye on things. She's a pro at giving out calm vibes."

"You're stalling Heather," Natalie guessed. "Playing for time so you can get a warrant and search her apartment. You're looking for any of the other items reported stolen in the area."

Bartholomew responded with a noncommittal half smile.

"If she demands that you let her go before you can do a search, will you have to do it?" Natalie asked.

"We'll make sure she's safe, if that's your concern."

"It is." Relief cooled Natalie's anxiety. Heather wouldn't be able to scurry back to her apartment to burn imaginary letters and tumble farther—maybe fatally far—from reality.

"Dr. Marsh. Natalie. I apologize for keeping you here when I'm sure you're more than ready to leave, but I need to ask you some questions. You said Heather accused you of planting the vase in her apartment."

"Yes. I did not plant the vase in her apartment."

"Did you know Heather was at the Innes Hill Apartments the night Mr. Drummond was attacked?"

"Yes. Gideon told me."

"You said she accused you of having an affair with her brother and breaking up his marriage."

"I did not have an affair with Kenton Lowery. Did Heather tell you the root of the reason she distrusts me is because her ghost grandmother warned her there was evil at Nefesh Bria?"

"She didn't mention that."

Natalie rubbed her forehead. "She needs help. Can you please do everything legally possible to see that she gets it?"

"Yes, ma'am. Why does she think you were involved with her brother? Did Grandma tell her that?"

"Not specifically." Toying with the unopened water bottle, Natalie debated how to phrase her explanation. "She said she can tell he knows me, but he won't talk about it."

"*Do* you know him, outside of your Chapman assignment?"

"I have never been romantically involved with him. That's all that's relevant here."

Bartholomew gave her the same extended, searching look he'd used on Kenton. "I see."

Natalie unscrewed the lid of her water bottle and gulped half the water. Feeling less parched and cranky, she set the bottle on the table. "Any luck in tracking down the man who followed Daisy Frederiksen?"

"Not yet."

"May I ask a favor? If Heather does get arrested, can you keep the Stoker and Nefesh Bria out of the press as much as possible? We have enough negative publicity."

"I'll do my best, but I doubt we can keep a lid on it. We've already received a call asking if it was true that you were hobnobbing with Heather in the Stoker gardens this evening, and were we going to arrest Heather for trespassing and you for enabling it."

"Who called you? Never mind; you won't tell me. The caller wants me arrested for 'enabling trespassing'? Is that a thing?"

"Serious charge," Bartholomew deadpanned. "Felony enabling."

"I have some clients whose family members need to be charged with that." Natalie pressed her cold water bottle against the back of her neck.

Bartholomew rose to his feet. "I'm going to call Mr. Radcliffe in for a few minutes, then you two can leave. Go home and relax."

Natalie stood. "Let me know if I can—"

A muffled screech came from somewhere in the station, followed by shrill words. The only words Natalie could discern were *no* and *liar.* Bartholomew sprang past her, yanked the door open, and rushed into the hallway.

Knowing she shouldn't follow him, Natalie did it anyway—that was Heather yelling. Bartholomew flung open another door.

In an interview room similar to the one Natalie had exited, Kenton was sitting at the table, his face so immobile that Natalie thought of the wax figures Lauren's creeper had mentioned. Heather was backed against the wall, and Officer Kalili stood between her and Kenton, speaking calmly.

"No need to shout, Heather. Let's discuss this. Your brother is doing his best to help—"

"He's setting me up!" Heather shrieked. "He's trying to make me look like a murderer! He planted the vase himself, he and his lover—*her!*" She pointed at Natalie.

Two officers brushed past Natalie and Bartholomew in the doorway and entered the room. Kalili held up a hand in a stay-back gesture. Plainly she wanted to calm Heather if she could rather than having a group of officers tackle her.

"Mr. Lowery, it would be best if you leave for the time being," Bartholomew said. Kenton stood.

"Help me. Kenton, please." Heather crumpled, her back sliding down the wall until she sat on the floor. Tears streamed down her face. "*Please.*"

Bartholomew glanced at the uniformed officers. "Escort Dr. Marsh and Mr. Lowery out. They can leave, along with Mr. Radcliffe. We'll contact them later."

Kenton walked robotically toward the door and passed Natalie with no eye contact. An officer with the build of a weight lifter followed him.

"Natalie." Heather sobbed her name. "There's evil. *Evil.*"

"Dr. Marsh." The other officer gestured into the hall. "This way, ma'am."

"I don't know what's wrong," Heather sobbed. "I don't know."

The officer's hand touched her elbow. "Dr. Marsh."

"Don't leave me," Heather sobbed. "Don't leave me here."

"Wait." Natalie didn't move. "Detective, she—"

"You need to go," Bartholomew said.

"She needs a medical doctor, a psychiatrist. You can't—"

"Avino, take Dr. Marsh out."

"*No,*" Heather shrieked. "Don't take her; don't go." She pushed herself to her feet as though to intervene but stumbled. Deftly, Kalili caught her. Bartholomew and the already returned weight lifter officer moved forward to help.

Officer Avino grasped both of Natalie's arms and propelled her into the hallway. Ears and attention preoccupied with Heather's cries for help, Natalie lapsed into absentminded cooperation as, with one hand gripping her upper arm, Avino walked her to the heavy door that separated the back of the PD from the lobby.

"She'll be okay, ma'am," he said as he released her and opened the door. "We'll take care of her."

Natalie stepped reluctantly into the lobby, where Gideon waited. Kenton was gone.

The door closed and locked behind her, muting Heather's hysterical pleas.

CHAPTER 14

WEARILY, NATALIE SWIPED HER CARD to open the main doors of Nefesh Bria. She was the first to arrive on what should have been a fresh, cheerful, and sunny beginning to a new week. It *was* sunny on this Monday morning, but Natalie would gladly have swapped out the good weather for even a fragment of good news. News like Heather was innocent. News like whoever had seen Heather with Natalie in the courtyard and called the police about it had now sworn not to share that report with anyone else. News like Baxter Quincy had suddenly moved to the South Pole.

News like Drew Drummond's death had been a bad dream.

The light citrus smell of the solution the janitors used on the wood floors and the scent of new paint and new furniture was welcoming enough to make Natalie's mood a few shades brighter. She settled into one of the comfortable chairs and studied every detail of the waiting room, from the silk plants in the corners to the art-glass ceiling fixtures. It was beautiful. Peaceful. Hopeful. Nefesh Bria. Healthy Soul.

The way things were going, she'd need to learn the Hebrew words for frazzled, stressed-out, frustrated soul. She'd come early today, seeking a few meditative minutes to nourish herself emotionally, to be alone in the clinic, to remember why she'd worked so hard for this, contemplate whom she could help.

Not Heather Osbourne, apparently.

Her phone beeped in her purse. Gingerly, she reached for it.

The text was from Regina. *Come to my office. Bob wants to see you.*

Regina must have seen her car enter the parking lot. Natalie stuffed her phone into her purse, her hopes for a peaceful moment breaking into stale shreds. Chapman was here? She'd hoped he'd be too busy to come to the Stoker anytime soon. How much did he and Regina know?

She exited the clinic and headed to Regina's second-floor office. Her door was ajar. Natalie tapped on it, then pushed it open.

Chapman bounced to his feet and came to greet her.

"*Guten Morgen*." He clasped Natalie's hand and bowed to kiss it.

At least he seemed to be in his usual jovial mood. "Good morning."

Chapman straightened, his lively eyes examining her face. "You look tired, *mein Schatz*."

"*Mir geht's gut*," Natalie said. "I'm fine," she added for Regina.

"Please sit down," Regina invited. Chapman waited until Natalie sat, then followed suit.

"Have you seen the local paper this morning?" Regina asked.

"No." Natalie had avoided it.

Regina slid a tablet across her desk. Displayed on the screen was the front page of the paper.

Natalie picked it up. The headline read "Ghostly Delusions Lead to Theft and Murder: Stoker Stalker Arrested in Death of Ohneka Travel Agent."

The burning in Natalie's face told her she was too flushed to feign calm about this. "'Ghostly delusions lead to theft and murder'? Where is their evidence that Heather's delusions had *anything* to do with what happened to Drew Drummond?"

"That's hair-splitting, and you know it," Regina said. "The facts are the woman is bonkers, and she killed someone. Read on and find your name."

Thumbs sweating on the screen, Natalie skimmed the article. *Osbourne was detained in the Stoker Building gardens by Nefesh Bria Mental Health Services Director Dr. Natalie Marsh and Nefesh Bria volunteer Gideon Radcliffe. Eyewitnesses report that Osbourne and Marsh were arguing, and Osbourne made personal accusations regarding Marsh's conduct, accusations Marsh denied. Marsh and her companion took Osbourne to the police, where she was found to be in possession of stolen property, including property taken from the apartment where Drew Drummond was attacked—*

"Personal accusations," Regina quoted, interrupting Natalie's reading.

Natalie remembered the Parisi Gallery guests who'd wandered by twice. They must have repeated whatever they'd overheard. "Heather is under the mistaken impression—"

"That you had an affair with her brother," Regina said. "Vanessa Parisi told me."

"Heather is mistaken," Natalie said. At least the newspaper had had the sense not to repeat Heather's specific accusation. Natalie scrolled to the comments beneath the article and found what she'd expected: rants about the dangers of putting a mental health clinic in an office building, interspersed with a few sensible comments. But not even the positive commenters seemed to have noticed that Heather's connection with the Stoker wasn't with Nefesh Bria. "I already told you I've never been personally involved with Kenton Lowery."

"That's what I told Baxter Quincy when he called me late last night," Regina said. "He'd heard the rumor."

Natalie set the tablet on the desk. "How did he respond to you?"

"As you can imagine, he wasn't satisfied. He went and talked to Kenton Lowery."

"He talked to Kenton! When?"

"Early this morning. Very early at his bakery. Baxter wanted to check the story with Kenton, so I told Baxter how to find him."

"Regina! Kenton is very private. You know that. How could it be a prudent idea to send Baxter stomping over there to interrogate him, especially after his sister just got arrested for murder?"

"Kenton didn't want to talk to Baxter, but he did, briefly. Kenton said yes, it was true that you two had an affair, but it was over and leave him alone."

Horrified, Natalie writhed mentally, wanting to stomp over to the Playful Otter herself to chastise Kenton. What was he doing to her? She'd thought he appreciated the help she'd given him; he'd seemed deeply grateful at the time.

Grateful. And mortified that he'd ever needed her help, that he'd ever been in a position where a woman with a fraction of his physical strength had left him with cuts and bruises and cracked ribs and he didn't know how to free himself from her control any more than he'd known how to escape his mother. Mortified enough to confirm the rumor of an affair rather than admit Natalie had been his therapist.

Did he realize what that lie would do to Natalie's reputation?

She looked straight at Chapman. Though Regina was serving as spokesman, it was Chapman who truly held the axe. "If Kenton did tell Baxter we had an affair, he was lying."

"Why would he lie?" Regina asked.

"You'd have to ask him."

"You let us assume he was a former client," Regina said. "If he was your client, why won't he own up?"

The answer to that question was spilling over with confidences Natalie couldn't break. "I have never been romantically involved with Kenton Lowery. That's all I've ever said on the subject. That's all I have to say now."

Regina rolled a sleek, silver pen between her thumb and index finger. "I'll put it this way. Prior to Bob's asking you to contact Kenton, when did you . . . interact . . . with him? Was it recently?"

"It was a couple of years back."

"Did he live in Ohneka at the time?"

"How is that relevant?"

"How is it secret?" Regina retorted.

The answer ran through Natalie's mind, but she didn't speak it: he'd been living in Syracuse, but had come to Ohneka because he'd wanted to find a therapist he was certain had never met Sophia, in a place where neither Sophia nor her friends would have any chance of seeing him slinking into a psychologist's office. He'd picked Ohneka because he'd grown up here, and it was familiar. Kenton had difficulty with new experiences, and starting therapy was excruciating enough without having to find his way around a strange city. "Do you have any other questions for me?"

Eyeing Chapman, Regina shifted her pen so she held it in a writing grip, as though preparing to sign a formal request to ban Natalie from the Stoker.

Natalie switched her focus back to Chapman as well. He usually took command in any meeting he attended. Why was he so quiet today? Quiet and studying her.

"Mr. Quincy spoke with me this morning," Chapman said. "He confided that he is mightily concerned about the incidents and rumors that touch on you and Nefesh Bria."

"I am mightily concerned about the rumors myself," Natalie said. "If Mr. Quincy is concerned, maybe he should keep his ignorant mouth shut and stop spreading gossip."

"Ah, *mein Schatz*, that is an uncharacteristically prickly response from you. You may sheathe your sword. I trust you are telling the truth—and if that trust is not warranted, be aware that people who deceive me once are permanently deprived of the opportunity to deceive me again."

"Noted," Natalie said, pretending she wasn't stinging and furious.

"I am partaking of the marvels of air travel and leaving the country this afternoon on business," Chapman said. "I'll be unavailable for a week or so, and I trust that when I return, matters at this glorious edifice will be *glücklich und friedlich.*"

Natalie knew the first word meant *happy.* She had no idea what the second meant, nor did she care. Any demands for the future that started with *happy* weren't likely to be fulfilled in a week's time. "You said you spoke to Baxter this morning. Is he here already?"

"Mr. Quincy is already slaving away at his travel agency."

"I hope he's not too busy to get interrupted because that's what's about to happen." Natalie rose to her feet. "Excuse me." Not lingering to see if Chapman and Regina were done with her, she marched out the door and up the two flights of stairs to the fourth floor.

The door to Quincy Travel was locked—it wasn't even eight o'clock—so Natalie knocked on it, viciously enough and long enough to hurt her knuckles.

The door finally swung inward. "We don't open until—oh." Baxter's impatient expression soured into disgust. "Here to kill the messenger? You should have been honest in the first place. Do you know how embarrassing it is for everyone at the Stoker that you were sleeping with—"

Natalie entered the office and closed the door. "I did not have an affair with Kenton Lowery."

"Uh-huh."

"You cornered Kenton because you were hoping for dirt on me. He lied to get rid of you. I'm sick of this, Baxter. You've been stirring people up, spreading rumors, blaming Nefesh Bria for every odd thing that happens here. If you say one word to anyone about this alleged affair or about anything else you can't prove—"

"What do you mean 'alleged'? Lowery admitted you two were involved. Sounds like Heather resented you for wrecking his marriage. How much did her feelings about you fuel her campaign against the Stoker? You brought us this trouble, lady. Go ahead and sue me if you want. Your story will sound great in court."

"You're not getting rid of Nefesh Bria."

"I don't need to do that. Chapman will. I thought you were trained to understand crazy people—how did you miss the fact that Heather Osbourne is a killer? You were so ga-ga over her brother that you couldn't see how dangerous she was. If you'd opened your eyes and warned us, Drew would be alive. By the way, one of my people is in the break room and can hear every word you're saying. Get out of here, or I'll have her call security."

Natalie's frustration with Baxter, Vanessa, Regina, and Kenton fought to free itself, but with every combative word she spoke, she made things worse. She tamed her voice, making it conciliatory. "I owe you an apology for crashing in here like I did. I'm tired and worried and frustrated. I promise you, I did not have an affair with Kenton, and I hope he comes to realize that lying about it isn't helpful to anyone. Can we reach a truce?"

"Nice try. If by truce you mean you're ready to take all the trouble you've caused to a place that won't ruin my business, then sure. Let's make a truce. Otherwise, you have five seconds to walk out of here or I'll summon security to haul you away. You're sick of this? So am I. The problems you—"

A gentle tapping at the door interrupted him. Baxter's angry demeanor transformed to eagerness, and he hastened to open the door. "Good morning."

"Good morning." Lauren stepped inside and kissed him on the cheek. "I brought you this." She held out a lidded coffee cup decorated with the Parisi logo.

"You're an angel." He took it.

"It's the best coffee in the city," Lauren said. "Oh, good morning, Natalie . . ." Her greeting died, and Natalie knew her attempt to hide her tumultuous emotions wasn't working.

"Natalie is leaving," Baxter said.

Even Lauren's frown was elegant. "Baxter . . . you aren't arguing about those silly rumors, are you?"

"I talked to Heather Osbourne's brother. The rumors are true."

"They're not true," Natalie said.

Lauren's eyebrows puckered.

"Natalie came storming in here to ream me out," he said. "I've asked her to leave, and if she doesn't, I'll call security."

Lauren laid a regal hand on Baxter's arm. "Please, let's all settle down. You need to begin your work, and all this fussing is distracting you. Natalie, come to the gallery with me. We have a heavenly box of pastries, and Vanessa won't be in until noon. Excuse us, Baxter. I'll see you at lunch."

Knowing there were no better options, Natalie accompanied Lauren out the door. As soon as they reached the elevator, Lauren said, "Oh my word, how awkward. Guests at the gallery heard your argument with

Heather and related it to Vanessa. That's how it got to Baxter. He actually talked to her brother?"

Natalie pressed the down arrow. "Yes."

"Baxter can be so arrogant. In confidence, it's the one part of his personality that makes me want to slap him. Whether or not you had an affair with that man is none of his business. Or Heather's business."

"I didn't."

"Of course you wouldn't do that." Lauren's words were too instantly gracious, too facile. Natalie could tell Lauren didn't know whether or not to believe the rumors, but either way, it was the best reaction she'd gotten this morning.

The elevator doors opened, and Natalie and Lauren stepped inside.

"Things have been ludicrously tense around here." Lauren pressed the button for the first floor. "That poor girl. I read that when the police searched her apartment, they found some of the jewelry that's been stolen recently."

"Yes," Natalie said.

"I never guessed poor Heather was the thief we kept hearing about. I hope they can help her. I have a hard time believing she meant to hurt Drew. Don't you think it must have been accidental?"

"I don't think she expected to get confronted."

"Yes, and she panicked. I feel so sorry for her. And for Stuart and Ainsley. And Baxter. I know he's given you a negative impression of himself, but I hope you give him another chance. He's devastated by what happened to Drew."

Natalie's anger sagged, weighted by empathy. When she'd stalked into Quincy Travel, she hadn't been thinking about how Baxter must be grieving over the murder of his employee.

"We have lovely frangipane tarts topped with local blueberries," Lauren said. "Come relax for a few minutes."

"I should get to the clinic. Ainsley is probably already there. I tried to get her to take time off, but she insisted on coming in."

"How is she doing?"

"I saw her for a few minutes last night when Gideon and I dropped off some meals for them. She seems . . . very determined to act normal."

"While her heart is crushed. The poor girl. Some people are so shy about letting others see their grief. Let's go collect her as well. If anyone could use a delectable pastry, it's Ainsley."

"Excellent idea," Natalie said.

The elevator doors opened. "We're due for good luck around here," Lauren said. "I'm sure it will come soon."

"I hope so."

"I'm relieved that the issue with Heather haunting the building is over, but I keep thinking how tragic it is that it didn't resolve before . . ." Lauren sighed. "She didn't seem dangerous. Dangerous to others, I mean."

Natalie nodded.

"Do you ever wish you could foretell the future?" Lauren said pensively as they walked down the corridor toward Nefesh Bria. "See what people are going to do so you could warn those in danger?"

"Yes," Natalie said. "Desperately."

CHAPTER 15

GIDEON SANK ONTO A BENCH outside the city offices. He drew his phone back a little to allow blood circulation to return to his ear and loosened his grip on the phone before he shattered the screen. "That guy is going to trumpet the story to every tenant in the building."

"Yes," Natalie said. "And the story will get worse and worse."

At the raw anguish in Natalie's voice, Gideon pictured himself punching Baxter Quincy. And getting arrested and charged with assault. *Steady. Keep cool.* "You need to talk to Kenton. He needs to know how much trouble he's causing."

"No . . . not now. It won't help. He's shaken over Heather; he's shaken over being dragged into a situation that's getting so much publicity; he . . . I *told* Bob it wasn't a good idea for me to meet with him, that he should send someone else—" Natalie stopped herself, and Gideon knew she'd been about to stumble into saying something confidential. "Lauren promised to try to persuade Baxter to keep quiet about what Kenton said. I don't know if he'll listen, but if anyone can charm him, Lauren can."

"Unless by 'charm' you mean 'FedEx him to Pluto,' that's not going to stop him from spreading rumors. Natalie, listen. I think I know what situation you're dealing with when it comes to Kenton, and there is no way any code of professional ethics would require you to keep your mouth shut while he trashes your reputation. Tell Baxter and Regina exactly how you know this guy."

Natalie didn't respond.

"Am I out of line?" Gideon asked.

"No, you're not out of line. I appreciate the input, but I have to go. Ainsley buzzed me to say my client is here. I'll talk to you soon."

"Let me know how I can help you." Hating to end the conversation, Gideon waited until Natalie had hung up before shoving his phone back in his pocket and heading toward his office. When Natalie had called, he'd come outside for privacy, not wanting to risk starting rumors among his coworkers.

Rumors would blast through the office anyway. Gossip of ghostly hallucinations . . . a psychotic murderer . . . and soon the tale would get even juicier with rumors of an illicit love affair and a home-wrecker psychologist whose unscrupulous behavior had pushed unstable Heather into criminal activity. Meanwhile, Natalie was hurting, scared, and silent. Even if she did risk crossing an ethical line to clarify her relationship to Kenton, would it help? It might make things worse. Baxter and the rest either wouldn't believe her or would think she'd had an affair with Kenton *while* he was her client.

An affair. Fear shoved against his rib cage, hindering his heartbeats. Heather was perceptive and clever at discovering information about other people. Could she—

Leave your insecurities out of this, you jerk. Natalie wouldn't—

"Gideon."

He turned to see coworker Belle Ewell hurrying toward him.

"Hey, Belle." He held the door for her and followed her into the building.

Belle paused so she could walk beside him. "I heard you helped catch a murderer. Way to go, hero!"

"Uh . . . there wasn't any hero action involved."

"What happened? You and Natalie saw her and pounced on her?"

"We talked to her. She agreed to come to the police department."

"That's all?"

"Pretty much."

"What's she like? Is she spooky? Like . . . completely out there?"

"No. She has issues, but she's a regular person. Keep in mind that she's been charged with murder but not convicted. She might be innocent."

"They know she's the thief though. The police found stolen goods in her apartment. Not all of them though. I wonder where she hid the rest of them? Or do you think she fenced them?"

"No clue," Gideon said, glad they'd reached the City Engineering Division. Once they were inside, he could rush to his cubicle and hide under a heap of work. Or hide under his desk.

"So this woman has a problem with Natalie?" Belle asked. "I read that she was accusing Natalie of doing something illegal, or something like that?"

"Heather is confused about a lot of things. Excuse me, Belle, I need to get to work."

To his relief, she took the hint and walked past his cubicle. "Crazy times," she said over her shoulder.

Gideon lowered himself into his chair, calculating how much force it would take to crack his desk with his forehead. This was intolerable. He couldn't passively watch rumors metastasize and grow, damaging Natalie, enlarging Baxter Quincy's arsenal of complaints, and eroding support for Nefesh Bria.

He should talk to Kenton himself. Natalie was constrained by professional limitations, but Gideon wasn't, and Kenton needed to understand how his lie would hurt her. At the very least, Kenton could tell Baxter the truth. If Baxter stopped fomenting trouble, that would slow the damaging rumors.

If Kenton refused to admit the truth to Baxter, Gideon would have to . . . have to . . .

Okay, he didn't have a plan beyond that. One step at a time.

He didn't know Kenton's address or phone number, and neither was listed online. No way would he ask Natalie for them. She wouldn't give up that information, and he didn't want to forewarn her of what he was doing anyway. She *had* mentioned where Kenton worked. Gideon could approach him there. Fearing Kenton wouldn't be there near the end of Gideon's work day—if Baxter had visited him at work early this morning, he must start and end his day early—Gideon told the department admin he'd be gone for a few hours and drove to East Rochester.

The Playful Otter was small, with wide-plank wood floors, exposed wood beams in the ceiling, and an aroma of baking bread so mouthwatering Gideon figured it had the power to lure and capture people fairy-tale style. A gray-haired couple occupied one of the tables near the window, and a teenage girl stood by the counter. The lunch rush obviously hadn't started yet.

Gideon stood behind the girl and pretended to study the menu while concentrating on what he'd say when he reached the counter. The woman behind the counter had a wide smile and moved with skillful efficiency. She reminded him of Michelle Obama, a little older.

"Want herb butter with that, hon?" she asked, handing the teenager a paper bag.

"No, thanks." The girl headed for the door.

Gideon stepped forward.

"Good morning," the woman said. Her name tag identified her as Josie. "What can I get for you?"

"Any recommendations?" Gideon asked. "What's your favorite sandwich?"

"First time here?"

"Yep. Novice."

"Go with today's special. Roasted red peppers, red onions, kalamata olives, and grilled chicken on garlic and asiago sourdough."

"Sold," Gideon said. A plump woman with short reddish hair emerged through a swinging door behind the counter. She was carrying a tray of rolls.

"Anything to drink?" Josie asked. "We have a house-made kiwi-white-grape juice."

"I'll take it." Gideon pulled out his wallet. "Is Kenton Lowery here?"

Josie's expression changed from welcoming to concrete barrier. She glanced at the other woman, whose name tag read *Jenny*.

"Kenton is busy," Jenny said.

"Would you like to add a fresh-baked chocolate-chip cookie to your order?" Josie asked curtly.

From the hostility in their faces, Gideon suspected they'd like to add a police escort out of town to his order. He docked himself a few points for cluelessness. Even though Kenton's name hadn't been mentioned in the news, Gideon should have known reporters would find him. Who else besides Baxter had shown up here asking for him?

"Yeah, add a cookie," Gideon said. "I'm not a reporter, and I'm not the cops, and I need to talk to him."

"That'll be $13.89, and we told you he's busy," Josie said.

"That's fine." Gideon handed her a twenty. "I'll wait until he has a break."

Josie hesitated, her gaze focused past Gideon. He assumed she was checking on the couple chatting at their table to see if they'd noticed what was becoming an argument. "You can't loiter here," she said, her voice low.

"I won't be loitering. I'll be eating. Slowly. Tell him Gideon Radcliffe is here."

"He's not in the mood to talk to anyone." Josie handed Gideon his change.

Gideon dropped all of it in the tip jar. "This isn't a conversation he'll ever be in the mood for, but it's important. I can wait. Let him know I'm here."

The women exchanged another glance. Behind Gideon, chair legs grated across the floor. Footsteps and conversation moved in the direction of the door.

Once the door had shut behind the exiting customers, Jenny spoke. "You need to leave. We have the right to refuse service to anyone."

Josie opened the cash register drawer and removed Gideon's twenty. She held it out.

He didn't take it. "I'd really like that sandwich."

"We asked you to leave," Josie said. "If you refuse, you're trespassing. We could call the police."

"Okay. The police show up. Lights. Uniforms. Drama. Reports to fill out. Maybe news coverage, if it's a slow news day. I'm game. Is Kenton?"

Josie flung the twenty onto the counter. "Leave that boy alone. How would you feel if your sister . . . if you were in his shoes? He doesn't need vultures flapping around him."

"Tell him who I am." From the fact that neither Josie nor Jenny had reacted to his name, he assumed they hadn't read the news report of Heather's arrest. "If he's forgotten my name, tell him I'm a friend of Natalie Marsh's. He'll know why I'm here. I'm guessing he'd rather work something out than have me come up with a way to fix this myself."

"Let *me* guess," Josie said. "Your lady took one look at Kenton and booted you out the door, and now it's his fault. Honey, your woman problems aren't Kenton's to deal with. He never encourages any of these girls. Don't you have any decency, pestering him at a time like this? Leave him alone."

"Your guess is wrong," Gideon said. "It's not a jealous boyfriend problem. It's a problem he created, and it's going to get worse fast unless he intervenes. I'll sit here and wait for him. I can save seats for the cops, just in case."

Josie and Jenny looked at each other again, two angry and confused mother bears. "Fine, I'll tell him you're here," Jenny said. "You're Joshua Radcliffe?"

"Wrong Israelite general," he said. "Gideon."

Jenny pushed through the swinging door into the back of the bakery.

Scowling, Josie picked up a large Styrofoam cup and filled it from a beverage dispenser. She handed the drink to Gideon. "You'd better not give that boy a hard time."

"I hope I don't have to," Gideon said.

Josie slid a cookie into a paper bag and passed it over the counter. "If we hear you haranguing him about a woman, forget the cops. Jenny and I will pitch you out the door ourselves. If this isn't a jealous boyfriend thing, who's that girl you mentioned?"

"Natalie Marsh is the director of the Nefesh Bria Mental Health Clinic in Ohneka. She and I are the ones who found Kenton's sister yesterday and drove her to the police department."

"*You* took her to the cops?"

"Yes."

Josie gave him a once-over, probably debating if she could throw him into the gutter without Jenny's help. "It'll take a few minutes for your sandwich."

"Thanks." Gideon retreated and sat at a table while Josie assembled his sandwich. Before she finished, the door behind the counter opened and Jenny emerged.

"He'll talk to you in the office," she said to Gideon. "This way."

"Thank you." Gideon rose and walked through the staff-only door. Jenny led the way; Josie followed as rearguard. Gideon figured he was one misstep away from a kidney punch.

Dressed in white and dusted with flour, Kenton stood in a cramped, paperwork-crowded office. Warily, he watched Gideon enter.

"Gideon Radcliffe." Hoping this could start and stay civil, Gideon extended his hand. "We met last night at the Ohneka Police Department."

Kenton shook his hand. His fingers were like refrigerated dough—chilled and limp.

"Sugar, if you need anything, yell for us," Josie said to Kenton.

"Thank you. You can close the door."

Josie and Jenny retreated. When the door was shut, Kenton gestured to a chair. Gideon sat.

Kenton sat on the edge of the desk. "What do you want?"

"I'll cut to the chase," Gideon said. "Your personal life is your business, and I know you want to keep aspects of it private. But there's a difference between keeping your mouth closed and lying. Do you have any idea how much grief you're causing Natalie by claiming you two had an affair that broke up your marriage?"

Kenton picked up a baker's catalog from the desk and rolled it between his palms, looking at the furled pages instead of at Gideon. "What did she say?" he asked. "What did she tell you?"

"Only that she has never had a personal relationship with you. She keeps professional confidences, if that's what you're wondering."

Splashes of red marked his neck. "If she keeps confidences, how do you know I didn't . . . that we . . . that I'm a liar?"

"For starters, I know her well enough to know she'd never have an affair with a married man. Also, she's usually open with me, so when she holds back, we're generally dealing with professional conflicts. I can put the pieces together. You've put her in a cruel situation. You can claim whatever you want, and she's so dedicated to her professional ethics—and so concerned about *you*—that all she can do is deny it. She can't share anything that backs up her word."

Kenton sat mute, rolling and unrolling the magazine.

"Look, Lowery. It's your own business why you don't want anyone to know Natalie was your therapist, but if you value her at all, don't make her collateral damage in whatever personal war you're fighting."

"I never wanted to be in this mess," Kenton said. "I have no control over Heather, but that guy, the Chapman flunky, he twisted my arm, wanting me to keep them updated. I haven't spoken to the press at all, and I won't."

"Great. But you spoke to Baxter Quincy, and he'll speak to everyone he can. That guy's worse than the press. He's been opposed to Nefesh Bria from the beginning and wants to see Natalie gone and the clinic closed. He'll push Robert Chapman to believe she lied about your relationship. Chapman hates getting lied to, and if he believes Quincy, things won't go well for Natalie. And the story will get worse as it spreads. How long until people start gossiping that maybe Natalie *did* plant that vase on Heather because Heather objected to her fling with you?"

"No one's going to listen to Heather's fantasies."

"They'll listen to Baxter, and I wouldn't put it past him to latch on to Heather's accusations."

Kenton flipped the magazine over and started rolling it in the opposite direction. His face was flushed and his lips sealed shut.

"Consider this," Gideon said. "If someone comes forward and tells the press you were Natalie's client and you hold to the affair scenario, that could put her license in danger. Are you willing to destroy her career?"

"I never told anyone I was her client."

"That doesn't mean no one knows."

Kenton swore under his breath. "This is the twenty-first century. How can an affair cause such a ruckus?"

"That clinic means the world to Natalie. She's fought for a long time to bring it to life. Don't do this to her. Tell Baxter Quincy the truth."

"I don't know how to contact him."

"Not a problem." Gideon reached into his shirt pocket, took out his own business card, and flipped it facedown on Kenton's desk. On the back, he'd already written Baxter's name and the phone number he'd found on the Quincy Travel website.

Kenton picked up the card, read it, then turned it over to scan Gideon's info.

"I get that Chapman's people hauled you into a situation you didn't want to be part of," Gideon said. "Natalie didn't want to be part of it either. Don't make things worse. Do damage control while you can. Talk to Baxter."

He slid the card into the pocket of his apron. "Okay. I'll call him."

"Thank you."

"You're afraid I won't have the guts, but I'll do it." He started fidgeting with the magazine again, this time curling individual pages. "Dr. Marsh was . . . a huge help to me. Got me to a place I didn't think I could reach, helped me more than anyone ever had. I didn't mean to cause trouble for her."

"I get it," Gideon said. "Thanks for helping fix this. I'm sorry about your sister."

Kenton nodded.

Gideon stood and opened the office door. Startled, he jumped backward. Josie was standing about an inch outside the doorframe.

"Your sandwich is done, Mr. Radcliffe," she said sweetly, holding out a foil-wrapped plate.

"Uh, thank you." Gideon took the plate and eyed Kenton. "You have serious security around here, bro."

"Someone has to protect him," Josie said.

Kenton snorted. "You can back off. The guy's okay. He's not like that Quincy guy you almost beheaded."

Josie patted Gideon on the shoulder. "Lucky for you we got that endorsement. Want another cookie for the road?"

CHAPTER 16

"*THANK* YOU." PHONE TO HER ear, Natalie rested her head on the back of her office chair and focused on the decorative plasterwork on the ceiling. "I can't tell you how much I appreciate your doing that." *And how much I appreciate your faith in me.*

"Not a problem," Gideon said. "He'd better keep his promise to call Baxter."

"I think he'll follow through." Natalie contemplated what Gideon had told her about his conversation with Kenton. "I hope Baxter doesn't hassle him and try to interrogate him."

"If he does, Kenton has two apron-wearing female bodyguards who'll make spaghetti out of him. I barely escaped the bakery without a cleaver between my shoulder blades."

Natalie laughed. "Yes, he mentioned that Josie and Jenny are a bit overprotective. Thank you again, Gideon. This will make it easier to relax and enjoy the lecture tonight. I hope you're not too behind on your work after taking a chunk out of your day."

"I'll catch up. You sure you don't need me to come with you tonight? I'm happy to do it if you want company. Or can Marianne go with you? You said she was interested."

"She can't come. Her husband's sister is throwing a family picnic. If she skips it, she'll be in the doghouse."

"Oh yeah, I've heard stories. Tyrant Theresa and her seven-course outdoor banquets. Sounds terrifying. And fantastic. I hope it doesn't rain on the prime rib and caviar tonight. But seriously, would you like me to come to the lecture?"

"I always love your company. But you've had a long day—a long week—and you don't need to spend three hours in the car for a lecture that will bore you out of your mind."

"Hey, I might learn something. What's the topic again? 'Personal Hygiene for Psychologists'? I could use personal hygiene tips."

Natalie laughed again, grateful Gideon could relight her sense of humor after a day of dark frustration. "The topic is 'You're Not the Exception: Self-Care for Mental Health Professionals.' Thanks for the offer, but please, take your evening to relax. Do something fun, something nonstressful."

"I'll probably go help Junyoung with his drywall. Which might or might not be nonstressful, depending on how many times I drop a panel on my foot."

"Good luck. Follow up with something salty and deep-fried."

"Will do. Enjoy your lecture and forget about all the garbage that's been going on here, or at least let it take second place in your mind."

"Thanks, Gideon."

"Talk to you soon. Drive safe."

"I will." She hung up and rose to her feet, grateful it was the end of her workday, eager to hear from a lecturer she admired—even if it did mean driving all the way to Ithaca—and intensely grateful for Gideon's efforts to help her. She hoped Baxter would believe Kenton's retraction, not conclude that Natalie had manipulated or threatened him.

Don't worry about it now. Relax and focus on the lecture.

Ainsley was tidying the reception area. "Heading to Cornell?" she asked as Natalie approached.

"Yes." Every time Natalie had faced Ainsley today, she'd wished she could help Ainsley deal with her shock and grief over Drew's death. Ainsley did a decent job of acting cheerful, but when she was in repose, anguish shrouded her face and tightened her posture. Natalie had tried to send her home early, but she'd refused, saying she'd rather stay busy—which Natalie could relate to.

"Have fun." Ainsley used a tissue to rub a pencil mark off the desk. Her hands were red and dry around the knuckles. Natalie hadn't noticed them being so chapped previously. "Marianne was telling me what a fascinating speaker Hilary Strickland is."

"Yes, I've heard her before." Natalie didn't mention that she'd heard this exact lecture a year and a half ago in Manhattan. She didn't want to discuss with Ainsley why she wanted to hear it again—how much she hoped the refresher would help her manage a piercing sense of vulnerability that deepened day by day. "Have fun at the Cascata party."

"Lauren was sweet to offer those tickets," Ainsley said. "It's too bad you can't make it."

"I'm glad you're going," Natalie said, not adding that she was glad she wasn't. Tonight, chitchatting at a party would be excruciating.

"I've never been to an outdoor sculpture park," Ainsley said. "I'm curious to see it. I'm trying to talk Stuart into coming with me."

"How's Stuart doing? Did he get a chance to talk to Bob about accompanying him on the trail?"

"I'm not sure."

"I hope it works out," Natalie said. "I'm sure Stuart would enjoy doing that for Drew."

"He'd love it." Anguish flared in Ainsley's face, a candle lit and immediately extinguished. "Thanks, Natalie. Have a good evening."

Natalie had nearly reached the doors of the clinic when they opened and a short, middle-aged woman stepped inside.

"Dr. Marsh." Daisy Frederiksen glowered at her. "No wonder the police haven't caught the creep who harassed me. You're shielding him. Don't want the bad PR."

"I'm sorry, Ms. Frederiksen, but I don't know what you mean. We've fully cooperated with the police, but unfortunately, there isn't much evidence as to the man's identity."

"Is your list of pervert patients so long that you can't narrow it down?"

"We've been unable to identify any current clients as matching the man's description."

"How about sending pictures to all of us businesses here? The cops could get you pics from the DMV if you don't have them already."

"You work at the Stoker?"

"Yes, I work here, part-time, for Dr. Spiros. Ophthalmologist. I've had coworkers who've had to deal with scary people too, though they're too chicken to report it. Don't want to make it a 'big deal.' But give us pictures to pick from and someone will recognize that creep. I doubt I'm the only one he's terrorized."

"I'm sorry, but our client lists are confidential." At the vigorous tap of footsteps behind her, she glanced back to see Marianne approaching.

"So their privacy is more important than all of our safety," Daisy said.

Natalie faced Daisy again. "Neither the man's behavior nor his appearance is consistent with anyone we're currently working with. It's possible he wasn't a Nefesh Bria client at all but was playing on mental illness stereotypes to shake you up."

"Get the pictures and pass them around. Let us judge that."

Marianne stopped next to Natalie and smiled at Daisy. "Not happening, my dear. We don't publicize client identities, which you would appreciate if you were a client here."

"Who are you?" Daisy asked irritably.

"Dr. Avery." Marianne offered her hand. "Clinic psychiatrist."

Daisy shoved her hands into her pockets. "You people don't care about catching the creep. I heard about Dr. Marsh sleeping with the brother of that crazy Osbourne woman. That's why she wigged out and came after all of us."

"Vet your gossip sources," Marianne said. "That rumor is top-grade, non-GMO, organic hogwash."

Daisy rolled her eyes. "I heard it from someone who heard it from a guy who talked to the brother himself."

"The rumor is false," Natalie said. "Some misinformation went out, but it should be cleared up soon, and I'd appreciate it if you wouldn't spread it around."

Heavy footsteps reverberated through the waiting room. Natalie turned to see assistant director Erik Kozlov approaching.

"Excuse me, I need to leave," Natalie said to Daisy. "I have an engagement. Mr. Kozlov here is the assistant director. He'll be able to help you with anything you need."

Daisy shot Erik a narrow-eyed glare. Erik was wearing his Russian-mafia demeanor, and Natalie felt uncharitably pleased at having an excuse to hand Daisy over to him.

"Erik, this is Ms. Frederiksen," she said. "She has some concerns." She strode past the angry woman and out the door, leaving her face-to-face with burly, six-foot-four-inch Erik.

Struggling against an unsettling desire to sprint away from the clinic, Natalie controlled her pace as she walked to her car.

* * *

Ainsley opened the takeout bag and passed Stuart a foil-wrapped burrito as thick as his arm.

"Thanks, Lamb." He unwrapped it and took a hungry bite. Ainsley sat at the kitchen table with him and unwrapped her own burrito but was too restless for an update to start eating it.

"How did it go?" she asked. "Did you talk to him? Did he sign you on?"

Stuart kept chewing. Ainsley waited, nervously breaking a tortilla chip into pieces.

He swallowed. "I talked to him. He's interested but no commitments."

"But the trip is in four weeks! Is he thinking of canceling it?"

"No. But he hasn't decided for sure what he's doing for a new Trekmeister."

"Baxter's after him, isn't he?"

"Yeah." Stuart took another big bite. Ainsley picked at a shred of cheese that had melted onto her burrito's foil wrapper.

Stuart guzzled Coke from the bottle in front of him and set the bottle down. "If Baxter can nail this for Quincy Travel, it'll be a big windfall for him."

Ainsley cursed. She'd known all this before, but she'd assumed Baxter and his kid nephew wouldn't be much competition. Hearing Stuart say that Chapman was debating what to do stirred a squall of panic inside her.

"Don't worry," Stuart said. "I won't let him edge me out. Not now."

Ainsley tore a strip off the foil wrapper and rolled it into a little ball. "Baxter's persuasive. He's a salesman." She formed another foil ball.

"Chapman won't get manipulated by a salesman." Stuart dunked a chip into the cup of salsa. "I won't fail you, Lamb. Baxter's not taking it away from us. We've put too much into it."

The reference to how much they'd put into it made Ainsley sure that any bites of burrito she swallowed wouldn't stay swallowed. "I . . . asked Natalie about what happened with her and Heather."

Stuart scooped a glop of salsa onto another chip and said nothing. Ainsley could tell he didn't want to talk about Heather. She ought to stay quiet, but words broke out. "Natalie said she talked to the police this morning to find out what was happening. They wouldn't tell her much, but they did tell her Heather's being held in jail, in a mental health unit. It looks like she'll be charged with . . . a lot of things. Burglary and murder . . . The charge is worse, I guess, because the . . . the murder occurred as a result of her trying to rob—"

"Quit thinking about her. Come on—they found stolen goods in her apartment. She was the real thief! Figures, the way she was always slinking around here."

Ainsley lowered her eyes and tore off another scrap of foil. "They didn't find all of the stuff. Just some of the jewelry."

"Who cares? The police will figure out what she did with the rest of it. You did a smart thing, planting that vase. Got a thief off the streets." Stuart patted her arm. "We did her a favor. If she'd kept robbing places, sooner or later she would have gotten blasted by some homeowner with a 12 gauge. She needed to be locked up. Now she is."

Locked up. Locked up and charged with a murder she hadn't committed. *There was no murder*, Ainsley reminded herself. *It was an accident.*

"This is a better situation for her," Stuart said, and Ainsley realized he was quoting what she'd told him when she'd proposed the idea of framing Heather. "She's safe. Eat your dinner."

Ainsley crammed a few mouthfuls of burrito down her throat. "Come to the party at the Cascata Sculpture Park tonight. Lauren said Melanie Chapman will be there."

Stuart grunted. "You told me that."

"You'll have a chance to impress her."

"I don't need to kiss up to the missus. She doesn't have anything to do with Chapman's hiking."

"It can't hurt."

"Staring at weird stone carvings and blobs of metal and pretending it's art? Not interested. You go and schmooze. I'm not up for it."

Ainsley didn't feel up for it either, but she was determined to go anyway. She couldn't waste the chance to rub shoulders with Mrs. Chapman and her friends.

"Claire called me today," Stuart said. "She wanted to know if you'll sing at Drew's funeral."

Ainsley stomach constricted, pushing the bites of burrito toward her throat. "I can't."

"What do you mean you can't?"

"How can I get up there and sing like . . . like . . ."

"Like what? You can do it."

"Stuart!"

"Lamb, it's too late for doubts. We have to do everything the same as if we'd had nothing to do with Drew's accident. Sing at the funeral. Do whatever Claire asks."

Sing at Drew's funeral. She imagined herself beginning "The Lord Is My Shepherd" only to look into the congregation and see Drew watching her with dead, knowing eyes.

"I told her you'd do it," Stuart said.

"No. I feel like if I sing that Drew . . . won't like it."

"He's dead. He doesn't care who sings."

"I'm talking about . . . He might . . . be there."

Stuart sighed in annoyance. "He won't be there."

"Ghosts are real, Stuart. My mother used to see people who'd died in our house decades ago. From a broken furnace. Carbon monoxide poisoning."

"Your mom is loony." Stuart grasped her hand. "Stop channeling Heather Osbourne."

Ainsley contended with the urge to tell him he'd better wash his hands after touching hers. Her hands felt so dirty, even though she'd washed them as soon as she'd gotten home from picking up dinner. "Maybe Heather's dead grandmother does talk to her."

"Do you need a doctor? You're losing it."

"People don't disappear when they die. Their souls still live. You know I'm right. You believe it too."

"Their souls mind their own business. Keep talking crazy and they'll lock you in a padded cell next to Heather's. We're an inch away from getting what we want. Don't turn into your ghost-seeing mom and freak out about how Drew will take revenge on us. That's not how it works."

He was right. She couldn't be weak now. They had to finish this, had to do it right. "Okay."

"You making bullets just in case? They won't work on a ghost."

Ainsley looked down. A dozen foil pellets sat beside her burrito. "Just fidgety," she said.

"You going to sing at Drew's funeral?"

Ainsley picked up a pellet and flattened it. "Yes."

CHAPTER 17

NATALIE SCRIBBLED SO MANY NOTES that her hand cramped. Dr. Strickland's lecture was even better than she'd remembered, and every helpful and informative word Strickland spoke nudged her mood further and further into optimism. When she checked her phone after the lecture, she found a text from Kenton that brought another gust of optimism: *Sorry about Quincy. I didn't mean to cause trouble for you. I called him tonight. He didn't pick up, so I left a message saying there was no affair and to leave you alone.*

At least there was hope for getting Baxter to back off, though he might decide the retraction was the lie. But it was movement in the right direction, and that was worth optimism. She replied to Kenton's text, thanking him for his honesty and curbing her urge to qualify "honesty" with "belated." Admitting to Baxter that he'd lied and thus stirring Baxter's curiosity as to why he'd done so must have been agonizing for Kenton. He had difficulty simply making a phone call to someone he didn't know well, let alone making a call about such a sensitive matter. He'd accomplished what was, for him, an extremely challenging task, and she wanted to give him credit for that.

On the drive home from Cornell, she let her mind drift, refusing to let herself concentrate on anything except the requirements of maneuvering safely in traffic. Other thoughts and observations came and went: the glitter of headlights and taillights on the rain-wet road, Heather's confused accusations, Daisy Frederiksen's insults, the dented bumper of the truck in front of her, Kenton's lie, the flute concerto on the stereo, a tiny chip in the windshield that she needed to fix, Gideon's intervention.

Gideon's intervention. Thoughts of Gideon kept entering her mind until finally they washed away all attempts to think about anything else.

Gideon and the way he'd trusted her word and gone to battle for her with Kenton. His support, his good humor, his kindness. His recent inconsistency about aspects of their relationship that marked it as more than a close friendship. Instead of confronting him, she'd allowed the confusion, letting it taint comfortable communication with don't-rock-the-boat silence. How much had she avoided discussing their relationship because it was easier to tell herself she was being patient with his insecurity than to face her own insecurity?

How hard was she trying not to notice that sometimes she yearned to be with him—forever—more than she'd ever wanted anything and other times she was petrified at the thought of emotionally entrusting herself to another person?

With the mixed signals they were both sending, it was a wonder they could communicate at all.

She'd talk to him about it this week. She'd invite him to dinner at her house on Friday, and she'd forewarn him what she wanted to discuss so he wouldn't feel ambushed. Even if his answers weren't what she wanted to hear, she needed to hear them. No more procrastinating the discussion, hoping Gideon—and she—would naturally float past whatever issues were swamping their relationship.

Porch lights, landscape lighting, and living room lights were illuminating her house when she pulled into her driveway. Putting lights on timers had been a wise move. It seemed surreal now that coming home to a darkened house hadn't used to trouble her.

She parked in the garage and entered her comfortably lit house. Tomorrow morning, she'd update Regina on what Kenton had said and also follow up with Baxter. Sometime this week, she would take Ainsley to lunch to give them private time to talk. Maybe Natalie could coax her into opening up instead of resolutely concealing her trauma.

She set her purse on the table in the entryway, stepped out of her shoes, and debated for a moment how hungry she was. In her rush to leave for the lecture, her dinner had been a granola bar and an apple in the car.

Definitely hungry. Hungry and too tired to make anything that took effort. Toast and scrambled eggs sounded like the right ratio of energy expended to tastiness of food produced. She padded barefoot into the kitchen and switched on the lights.

The scene in front of her kicked her brain with such savagery that her thoughts shattered. Her muscles jerked, yanking her backward; her elbow slammed into the doorframe. She wanted to scream, but she stared in silence, eyelids fixed open by the same paralysis freezing her vocal cords.

Baxter Quincy lay on his back in the middle of her kitchen floor, his face toward her, his eyes closed. Red stained the front of his shirt. Next to him lay a knife—her razor-sharp carving knife.

Was he alive? He might still be alive. She needed to help him, stop the bleeding. She stumbled toward him, knees alternately buckling and stiffening. She meant to squat next to him but lost her balance and fell forward onto her hands, her fingertips nearly touching a puddle of blood—a near miss that shook the trapped scream from her throat. She inhaled, rallying, but the deep breath brought nausea. She could smell the blood. Taste it.

Battling dizziness, she spoke his name. "Baxter. *Baxter.*" She shifted so she was resting on her knees and leaned over him to press her fingers against his carotid artery. At this angle, she could see a bloodied bruise on the back of his skull.

No pulse. His chest wasn't moving. He was gone.

Her phone. She had to call the police. She tried to stand but wavered and fell sideways, landing on her hip. She tried to crawl, but her knees caught in her ankle-length skirt, and she ended up dragging herself along on her elbows, then crumpling facedown on the tile, her ability to function lost in an opaque, chilly fog. How could Baxter be here, in her kitchen, dead? Murdered.

Murdered with her knife.

The unfamiliar car—was it black? Dark blue?—she'd seen parked at the curb in front of her house when she'd arrived home . . . was that Baxter's car? She hadn't worried about it; people visiting her neighbors often parked there.

Baxter had never been to Natalie's house before. He didn't even know where she lived.

Who had killed him? Were they still here? Was the killer hiding, waiting . . . Natalie sat up, hauled herself to her feet, and staggered through the kitchen doorway into the living room. She snatched her purse off the entryway table and sped out the front door.

As she rushed off the porch, her feet slammed too heavily against the sidewalk, and she lost her balance. She crashed to her knees, purse falling into the grass, concrete scraping her skin through her skirt. She grabbed the purse and forced herself upright on legs now shaking with both fear and pain. Hurrying toward the street, she rooted in her purse for her phone.

Not there . . . She didn't remember taking it out when she'd arrived home. She'd been thinking about how hungry she was . . . the phone *must* still be in her purse . . .

It wasn't. While she'd been distracted by the discovery of Baxter's blood-soaked body, the killer had stolen it, leaving her unable to call for help—

Natalie seized control of her illogical thoughts. She wasn't isolated or trapped. She was running free in a suburb, and houses on both sides of the street had lit windows. Neighbors were awake. They'd hear her scream, or she could hammer on a door. Her phone must have fallen out when she'd dropped her purse.

Already on the opposite side of the street and halfway down the block, she stopped and spun toward her house. No sign of a pursuer. The killer had probably fled immediately after attacking Baxter.

Attacking Baxter in Natalie's house. *Why? Who?*

Natalie stumbled back across the street to her yard, her bare feet making pops of sound against the wet asphalt. Near her porch, she clawed through the grass in the area where her purse had fallen. Her fingers touched a pen and the case for her sunglasses. No phone.

The pulse of footsteps triggered a blast of adrenaline that whirled Natalie in a circle as she searched for the intruder.

On the sidewalk, approaching from the right, was a woman with a Boston terrier on a leash. Relieved, Natalie hurried toward her. The woman halted and backpedaled. The dog barked.

Natalie stopped. "Wait!" she yelled. "I need help! Do you have a phone? I need to call 911. There's been . . . My home has been broken into, and someone is . . ." Shouting the news of a murder didn't seem wise, but she needed the woman to comprehend that this was urgent.

The woman stared at Natalie's skirt. Natalie looked down and saw wet, torn fabric and splotches of red. She hadn't realized she'd scraped herself so severely—or was that Baxter's blood?

"Someone is dead," she said. "Murdered." She took another step toward the woman.

The woman quickly backed up. "I'll call for you." She pulled her phone out of the pouch she wore around her waist and hastily tapped the screen, retreating as she did so, her dog's leash twined between her fingers. The dog let out a few more anxious barks.

"My name is Natalie Marsh. My address is . . ." Natalie waved toward her house and sank dizzily to sit on the sidewalk. She drew her knees up to her chest and rested her head against them, ignoring the stinging of raw skin, her agitated breaths muffling whatever the woman was telling the emergency operator.

Baxter Quincy, her nemesis, dead in her home, slaughtered with her knife. The police would think she'd killed him. How could the evidence point in any other direction? The scenario would seem obvious: she'd met with Baxter to try to persuade him to drop the rumors about her affair with Kenton and to get him to lay off Nefesh Bria; they'd argued; she'd lost her temper, lost control, knocked him over the head with . . . whatever tool was at hand, probably a heavy pan, then snatched a knife . . .

She'd get sentenced to life in prison while helplessly protesting that she was innocent, that she had no idea why her enemy was sprawled on her kitchen floor, his destructive, rumor-mongering mouth finally silenced by a knife plunged into his chest.

Why had he come here? Why had *they* come here—Baxter and his killer? Natalie tried to sort through possible answers to that question, but every thought blurred into smears of horror.

Baxter was dead.

Not until she heard a car stopping at the curb did Natalie lift her head off her knees. Two cars. The glare of flashing red and blue lights made her turn her head to the side. The woman with the dog stood several houses away, either afraid of Natalie or afraid of the killer. Afraid Natalie *was* the killer.

An officer exiting the first patrol car, a dark-haired woman, advanced toward Natalie—a familiar face, but she couldn't remember the officer's name. Natalie pressed her palms against the sidewalk, intending to stand up, but changed her mind. Her skirt was already dirty and damp, and standing up sounded like preparation for falling over.

"Dr. Marsh." The officer bent over her. "What's going on?"

Natalie blinked at the officer's name tag. The streetlight was bright enough that she could read it: Kalili. *That's right.* One of the officers who'd come to Nefesh Bria in response to Daisy's call. The officer who'd been trying to calm Heather. "There's a . . . in my kitchen . . . A man. Dead. I just got home."

"Do you know who he is?"

"His name is Baxter Quincy. I don't know why he was here. We didn't have an appointment. He was . . . He's been murdered. There's a knife next to him. Stabbed."

"Is anyone else in the house?"

"I don't think so. I didn't search . . . ran out the door. I was going to make scrambled eggs. I just got home. I was at a . . . at a . . ." Where *had* she been? She could picture Dr. Strickland's face, the lecture hall, but couldn't unearth the right words to explain it to Kalili. Why was her brain muck, her tongue numb? She was trained to deal with crises. She'd thought she was calm and rational under stress—

"Ma'am, are you hurt?"

Natalie touched her bloodied skirt. "No. It's . . . scrapes, from the sidewalk . . . I tripped . . . I'm fine."

"Would you like to sit in my car?"

Sit in a patrol car. Practice for when she was arrested. "No."

"Please stay right here."

Natalie nodded. Kalili walked toward the other officers. Natalie watched for a moment as they spread out, approaching the house, weapons drawn, then she rested her arms on her bleeding knees and lowered her head again. She had to get back on keel, be ready to offer clear, organized information when the police questioned her.

Clear, organized information. A clear and organized explanation for a murder victim in her kitchen.

The combination of rain-soaked concrete beneath her and humid air around her was both hot enough to make her sweat and cold enough to make her shiver. She couldn't stop rubbing her tongue against the roof of her mouth, sure she could still taste blood.

What was happening inside her house? Was there evidence that could explain what Baxter was doing there? Evidence that could identify the killer? She strained to remember how things had looked when she'd walked into the house. Had there been anything wrong? No. Nothing she'd noticed. Everything normal and orderly and serene until she'd plummeted into a nightmare.

Again, she backed up mentally and imagined herself walking into the house. Hadn't there been *any* clue? Over and over, she relived the scene, an obsessive loop of desperation.

The clomp of shoes on concrete approached her, finally unsticking her thoughts. She raised her head, this time determined to stand and deal composedly with this hideous situation. Did Baxter have family? How serious were he and Lauren? Would she be devastated? At the thought of

Lauren learning where and how Baxter had died, Natalie felt a new surge of queasiness. Lauren, the voice of reason, Natalie's defender. She would think Natalie had stabbed Baxter.

The towering figure of Detective Bartholomew stopped next to her. She looked up at him. His face seemed high enough and pale enough to be a star in the night sky.

"Natalie." He squatted, lowering his altitude so she could see him better. "Are you all right?"

"Yes." She should stand. She'd been planning to stand. She rotated to the side, pushing one palm against the concrete to lift herself. Bartholomew grasped both her arms and hoisted her to her feet.

"Thank you," she said. He kept a steady grip on her, waiting to make sure she had her footing. Her body was heavy and her limbs so cramped that she wondered how long she'd been sitting there, but she didn't feel like she'd collapse. "Thank you," she repeated. "I'm okay."

Bartholomew glanced at an ambulance among the vehicles crowding the street.

"No." She tugged slightly against his hold. "I don't need medical attention. I'll be fine."

He released one arm but not the other. "You up to talking with me?"

"Yes."

"Can you make it to my car?"

Another invitation to sit in a police car. But they needed a place to talk, and anywhere was better than inside the house. Intellectually, she knew the scent of blood wouldn't have permeated the whole place, but she felt if she stepped through the door, the odor would suffocate her.

Bartholomew escorted her to his unmarked car, walking at what must have been a tenth of his usual speed to coordinate his long steps with her sluggish gait. He settled her in the front passenger seat, went to the trunk, and returned with a fleece blanket that he unrolled and draped over her.

"Thank you," she said. He must have noticed her shivering. He shut her door and came around to seat himself behind the wheel.

He started the car and switched the temperature control from air conditioning to heat. She should tell him he didn't need to do that—she knew it wasn't cold anywhere but inside her, and he didn't need to swelter through their conversation—but fear at the thought that it was time to explain something she couldn't explain made her not want to speak at all.

"What happened?" he asked, his deep voice kind. Kind because he wanted her to trust him. Kind because he wanted her to confess.

Did he know how sharply she'd been at odds with Baxter? Did he know Baxter had contacted Kenton and Kenton had confirmed the rumor of their affair—a rumor Baxter had already spread all over the Stoker, as witnessed by Daisy Frederiksen? Did he know that this morning she'd confronted him angrily at Quincy Travel? Did he know Gideon had confronted Kenton? Would he think Natalie had sent Gideon to threaten or bribe—

"You look like you're debating how to spin this," Bartholomew said. "That's not a look I like to see when I'm asking questions. Let the words out, and we'll sort through the tricky parts. What was Baxter Quincy doing at your house?"

"I have no idea," Natalie said, realizing how abysmally she was managing this interview. Bartholomew had asked for basic facts, and she'd responded by wallowing in guilty silence. "I didn't invite him. I've never given him my address, and it's unlisted, so he'd have needed to put in work to find it. I haven't been home all day. I went straight from work to . . . I was in Ithaca, at a lecture. When I got home, I found him."

"What time did you get home?"

"About ten thirty."

"What lecture did you attend?"

"Dr. Hilary Strickland. Psychologist. I don't know if anyone can vouch for my being there. I did see a few people I know, but I didn't speak to anyone. I don't know if they noticed me. I took notes though, if that helps in proving I was there. They're in my notebook, in my purse . . ." Where was her purse? She must have left it on the sidewalk.

"Thank you." Bartholomew didn't specify if he wanted the notes or not. "Natalie, you mentioned Mr. Quincy to me once before in the context of assuming he'd called us to complain about your clinic. Why did you assume he'd done that?"

"He's been a relentless opponent of Nefesh Bria." There was no point in being anything but candid about that. If Bartholomew didn't already know it—and he probably did—he'd learn it the instant he talked to anyone at Quincy Travel. "I'd heard a lot of complaints from him."

"Did anything happen between you that might have led him to confront you tonight?"

"He didn't confront me. I wasn't home."

"That might have led him to *try* to confront you."

Knowing no lawyer would have advised her to answer these questions, Natalie did it anyway, hoping a flood of truth might erode suspicions that she'd killed Baxter. She detailed her recent interaction with him up through Kenton's text tonight, where he'd reported leaving Baxter a message admitting he'd lied about their alleged affair. Talking about Kenton magnified her anxiety for him. He'd get questioned by the police, pressed to explain why he'd lied, interrogated about Baxter and Natalie. How well would he cope with that? She ought to suggest he start seeing a therapist again, a different one—

Stop. He's not your client anymore, and his lie to Baxter is what's aiming the spotlight at him. That was his choice. He'll have to deal with the consequences.

So would Natalie. Whether or not she was arrested and charged with murder, the press would devour the story that Baxter's body had been found in her house. Plenty of people—like Daisy—would be thrilled to enlighten reporters about the ongoing conflict between Natalie and Baxter.

"Were you expecting anyone to stop by your house tonight?" Bartholomew asked.

Yes, Jack the Ripper, Natalie wanted to say, but she was in enough trouble without annoying Bartholomew with sarcasm. "I wasn't expecting anyone. No one mentioned stopping by, and I can't think of anyone who'd have been likely to stop by tonight without calling or texting me first."

"Does anyone else have a key to your house?"

"Gideon Radcliffe." Already close to drowning in stress, Natalie felt this realization drag her under water. Was Gideon a suspect? Would the police think he'd confronted Baxter for Natalie's sake and an argument had led to murder? No . . . Why would Gideon meet Baxter at Natalie's house, leaving Natalie to find the body and take the blame?

"Do you know of anyone who might have had a reason to hurt Mr. Quincy?" Bartholomew asked.

"No. Beyond our dispute over Nefesh Bria, I didn't know him that well. You might talk to Lauren Bell. She was dating Baxter. Please . . . break it to her gently."

"Of course," Bartholomew said. "Was their relationship serious?"

"I don't know."

"Do you know of anyone who might want to hurt you?"

"Hurt me? No." Her shivering intensified. How could she be in the middle of a murder investigation again? This was absurd.

Excruciatingly, shatteringly absurd.

"Was your front door locked when you got home?" Bartholomew asked.

Natalie thought about it. She'd entered through the garage but exited through the front door. Had she needed to unlock it first?

No. She didn't remember twisting the dead bolt before fleeing. "It wasn't locked. I'm positive I left it locked when I went to work this morning."

"The door leading from your kitchen to your patio was also unlocked," Bartholomew said. "Did you leave it that way?"

"No. Are there any signs of forced entry?"

"No," Bartholomew said. "There aren't."

CHAPTER 18

"You sure about this?" Gideon monitored Natalie as she unlocked the door to Nefesh Bria. He was anything but Sherlock-Holmes-level observant, but even he could tell she'd used makeup to try to camouflage puffy eyes and hide how pale she was. He noted the guarded expression on her face, the stiffness in her posture as though she *would* carry this burden even if it collapsed every load-bearing beam in her psyche.

"I have responsibilities here," she said as he pulled the door open for her. "I have clients scheduled. Do I hide and leave them in the lurch?"

"You take a nap, is what you do." He followed her into the empty clinic. "Did you sleep at all last night?"

She said nothing. He'd bet a year's salary the answer was no. She'd called him from a hotel at six thirty that morning, shared a terse report on finding Baxter Quincy dead in her kitchen the night before, and insisted she was fine and getting ready for work. She didn't want a ride; she didn't need anything. From her flat tone and the horrific facts of the situation, Gideon knew she was anything but fine. He'd insisted on meeting her at the clinic before it opened.

They walked down the hall toward her office. "Thank you for bringing breakfast," she said.

"Not a problem. I can pick up bagels with the best of them."

She unlocked her office door. He trailed her inside and, without asking permission, shut the door. She set her computer bag on her desk. He set the bag of bagels and the carrier holding two insulated cups on a side table.

"If there's a cinnamon chocolate-chip bagel in there, I claim it." Natalie immediately took out her laptop and opened it as though even a thirty-second delay in starting her work would put her behind schedule. Never mind that it was an hour until the clinic even opened.

"There's cinnamon chocolate chip," he said. "Also lemon-strawberry, new flavor for summer. Could you turn around and look at me?"

She drew her hands away from her keyboard and pivoted, a polite, businesslike expression on her face.

Gideon looked steadily into her eyes. "Nice mask," he said. "That's all I get? First you didn't call me when all hell broke loose last night because you're too courteous to wake me up, and now we're playing business-as-usual. For crying out loud, will you let me help you?"

"If there were anything you could do to help, I'd let you know." She shifted her gaze away from his and squinted at the wall as though assessing the paint color. "The police are investigating. They don't know anything yet. None of us knows anything. The best thing I can do is keep working, keep things normal."

"The best thing you can do is stop thinking your mission in life is to fix everyone else while never admitting you need help yourself. It's okay to be human, Natalie. Nefesh Bria won't shut down if you need a few days to get your feet on the ground after a guy gets murdered in your kitchen."

"My feet are on the ground."

"Do you have a lawyer? Not your business lawyer. A criminal defense lawyer."

She folded her arms. "That's premature."

He stepped toward her. Her body was straight, strong, but apply enough compressive stress and even a steel beam would buckle. "You're the prime suspect in a homicide. You can't deal with that on your own."

"I didn't say I was the prime suspect."

"I know you didn't." He rested his hands on her rigid shoulders. "Why not? Why didn't you tell me your alibi is lousy, that you don't have proof you were at that lecture?"

Her expression twitched between obstinate calm and overwhelming fear. "Detective Bartholomew called you."

"No." Gideon massaged her shoulders, trying to loosen tight muscles. "He and Detective Turner rang my doorbell. Right after I hung up with you this morning, in fact. Early birds hunting for worms."

Fear settled in her eyes. "What did they say?"

"They wanted to know what I was doing last night—i.e., could I prove I didn't stab Baxter."

"Could you?"

"Depends on what time they determine he died, but I was over at Junyoung's most of the evening. His wife fed us pizza around six, and we worked on the drywall until ten."

A little of the tension in her shoulders gave way under his fingers. "You have multiple witnesses, then."

"But you don't."

"Someone might . . . I did see a few colleagues at the lecture, from a distance. The police will check with them. What did Turner and Bartholomew say about me?"

"They wanted to know if I could verify that you were where you claimed last night. They also wanted to know about your conflict with Quincy and about your state of mind overall."

"You mean, have you witnessed me sinking into homicidal rage toward Baxter?"

"That's where it was heading. I told them you handled Quincy with patience and class no matter how boneheaded he was, that I've never seen you lose your temper with him or with anyone, and there is no way you would have killed him."

"And they thanked you politely and didn't believe you," Natalie said.

"I'm pretty sure they want to believe me. They know you. They like you. But they have to focus on evidence."

Her muscles loosened further, arms unfolding and falling to her sides. "I didn't kill him."

Gideon couldn't restrain an eye roll. "I know that. What do we do to convince the police?"

For a long moment, she stared at him, terror radiating from her silence.

Gideon wrapped his arms around her and pulled her close. She leaned heavily against him, her body instantly slack, as though his embrace had cut power to her muscles.

He tightened his embrace, and she remained limp in his arms, her head on his shoulder, her uneven breath touching his neck.

He rested his lips on her hair. "We'll figure it out," he said softly. "It doesn't make sense now, but it will."

"He died in *my* house," she whispered. "The blood . . . it was . . . I never wanted him to die."

"Natalie, I know that."

"Drew Drummond," she murmured. "Heather claims I framed her, planted the vase . . . Now Baxter, but Heather's in jail; she couldn't have . . . I have no idea why he was at my house. If he wanted to discuss the clinic, he'd talk to me at work."

Gideon nearly asked if she was positive Baxter had never said anything about stopping by or anything indicating he knew where she lived, but he suppressed the questions. Natalie would have already wracked her brain for any explanation for Baxter's presence and even if the man had hinted he might visit, nothing explained why he was *in* her house, not waiting outside.

"The killer knows why he was there," Gideon said. "There are answers."

"No matter what . . . even if they don't arrest me, the rumors . . . when Bob hears . . ."

"We'll knock down rumors with the truth. Who knows Baxter? Who might have valuable information? The fifties movie star in the Parisi Gallery, for starters."

"Lauren. She was at a party at Vanessa's sculpture park in Kemper Park last night."

"Why wasn't Baxter with her?"

"I don't know. I don't think she said." Natalie's voice was difficult to hear, even though his ear was only inches from her mouth. "I already gave her name to the police."

"Okay, good. She might know what his plans were. That will help a lot. Who else?"

"I'm sure the police will question the people at Quincy Travel. They'll be devastated. First Drew, now Baxter . . . Drew's funeral is on Wednesday—" Natalie's phone began to ring. She lurched backward out of his arms and rushed toward her purse, plainly frantic to answer the call, frantic for news. She grabbed her phone.

"Regina," she told Gideon. She lifted the phone to her ear. "Hello, this is Natalie."

Impressed that she'd managed such a solid imitation of her business voice but worried at her white-knuckled grip on the back of her chair—would she face-plant onto her desk if she let go?—Gideon took her elbow and guided her toward the couch so she could sit while she talked.

Or rather sit while she listened. Natalie wasn't saying much, and whatever Regina was saying was changing Natalie's countenance from anxious to cornered-animal fierce. Gideon didn't sit next to her—he didn't want her to think he was trying to overhear Regina's words—but before he could decide whether to sit on the other side of the office or step outside, Natalie drew the phone away from her ear, switched it to speakerphone, and set it on her lap.

". . . get in touch with Bob until next week, and we can't wait that long to act." Regina's words were fast and firm. "You're not getting removed from your position. It's only a leave, fully paid, of course. We don't have a choice. I'm sorry. Erik agrees with me, and so should you if you care about Nefesh Bria. Do you want reporters snooping around here or photographers trying to get a shot of you? How will the clinic function?"

"I'll stay in the background as much as I can," Natalie said. "But I have clients. I have responsibilities."

"Responsibilities we can perform for you." The accented voice of Erik Kozlov spoke. "We will contact your clients and explain that you cannot work for the next few days. Depending on the individual situations, we can reschedule or transfer them to other therapists."

"I don't want to reassign Iris to another supervisor—"

"Don't worry about your intern. I'll take care of the situation. Dr. Omar can cover temporarily."

"Erik. I have not been charged with any crimes. If I go on leave, that will give the impression—"

"The impression that you're traumatized by what you experienced and need time to recover," Erik interrupted. "It's true. Be sensible, please, Natalie."

Natalie's white face had darkened to fever red. Gideon sat on the couch. She reached for his hand and clutched it, hard. "You know that's not how people will interpret it."

"It's our best option," Regina said. "You don't need to come in to turn in your access and clinic ID cards. I'll send someone to pick them up from you. Where are you? I'm assuming not at home."

Natalie's free hand curled around the cards she wore on a lanyard. Gideon had the feeling that whoever tried to take them from her would end up with a broken nose. "I'm at the clinic," she said coldly.

"Oh!" Regina sounded dismayed. "Erik will be right over to meet you."

Natalie squeezed the cards. "I'll contact my own clients, Erik."

"We would rather you didn't," Erik said. "With this complicated of a situation, better if you keep a low profile and let us manage it. I'll see you in a moment."

The clicks of a door opening and closing came through the phone.

"I'm sorry," Regina said. "I know this is hard on you, but this option will do the least damage to Nefesh Bria, the whole Stoker community, and Chapman Development. Besides, you *do* need to rest. You work yourself too hard. Erik will take care of things at the clinic. Don't worry."

Natalie lowered her hand from her ID badges. The edges had pressed red lines into her palm. "I understand," she said calmly.

"Thank you for cooperating. Of course, we'll do anything we can to help you through this miserable time."

"Thank you."

"We'll talk soon." Regina hung up.

Natalie met Gideon's eyes, her expression bleak.

"They don't have the right to do that," Gideon said. "Regina doesn't have authority over Nefesh Bria, and *you* outrank Erik."

"Regina is Bob's representative here," Natalie said. "He owns the building. He owns and funds the clinic. Regina is his voice. And she's right. He'd agree with what she's doing."

"You can't be sure of that," Gideon said but knew his protest was nonsense. He didn't know Chapman nearly as well as Natalie did, and even he knew Chapman wouldn't okay Natalie's presence here while she was under suspicion of murder.

"If I get arrested for murder, Bob will shut Nefesh Bria down entirely." Natalie drew the lanyard over her head and threw it onto the table next to her. "If people believe the clinic founder and director slaughtered a man in her own kitchen, that's a stain on the clinic's reputation that will never wash out."

CHAPTER 19

TOO DEADENED BY EXHAUSTION to do something as decisive as open her car door and walk into the hotel, Natalie sat in the parking lot and watched summer-green leaves fluttering on an oak tree. She'd driven away from the Stoker, afraid that if she lingered she'd get a security escort off the grounds, but she didn't know what to do now. She should go to her room and nap but doubted she'd be able to sleep, though she'd told Gideon that was her plan to persuade him to go to work rather than stay with her. His department had a meeting with the city council today, and she couldn't stand the thought of his missing it, getting himself in trouble with his boss, and feeding rumors among coworkers who knew his connection to Natalie and would assume his being AWOL had to do with her. Her attempt to go to Nefesh Bria and carry out a normal day had gone down in flames, but maybe Gideon could pull it off at his office.

She'd checked the local news website, an activity she hoped no one else in Ohneka was engaged in. The information on Baxter's death was still sparse and factual: he'd been found dead in an apparent homicide in the home of Nefesh Bria Clinic Director Dr. Natalie Marsh. She was grateful to see the story reported as she'd told it to Bartholomew—she'd returned home last night to find the body—but as soon as reporters started digging, they'd learn of the tension between Baxter and her and report it eagerly, feeding what would become a universal assumption that she'd murdered him.

Why hadn't she talked to colleagues at the lecture last night? Why had she chosen an isolated seat off to the side? Was there *anyone* who'd noticed her there? If only Marianne had been able to attend, they would have driven together and sat together.

If only. What a useful phrase. She felt as though she were clutching a rope that had already frayed down to two or three flimsy strands. She needed to get herself together and do as Gideon had said: find leads for the police, people they could talk to.

She took out her phone. Marianne would probably be with a client right now, but Natalie could leave her a message.

When the ringing changed to voice mail, Natalie did her best to sound levelheaded, even as she started begging. "Marianne, it's Natalie Marsh. Could you call me back as soon as possible? I need to know if you can think of anyone who might have been at Hilary Strickland's lecture last night who would have recognized me and might be able to verify I was there. Anyone at all, even if it's a long shot. It's important. Thanks."

She hung up and stuck her phone in the cup holder. Who else might—

Her phone rang. She snatched it.

Not Marianne. Bartholomew.

Bracing herself, she answered the call. "This is Natalie."

"Abe Bartholomew," he said. "How are you?"

Still the nice guy. "I'm fine," she fibbed. "Have you learned anything?"

"A little. Can you come to the PD?"

Icy adrenaline swished through her bloodstream. "Is that code for 'You're under arrest'?"

"If it comes to that, it won't be in code," he said. "Judges don't like that. This is voluntary on your part. Are you willing?"

"Yes."

"Great. When can you come in?"

She rubbed her eyes. The eye drops she'd used this morning had a short lifespan. Her eyes were already parched and burning. "Whenever."

"Great. How about now?"

"Fine."

"See you in a few minutes."

Natalie drove to the PD almost by rote, wishing she didn't know the way, wishing she'd never had cause to go there at all, wishing she'd done something different—she had no idea what—in handling Baxter. Something that would have kept him alive.

How could she have changed her behavior to keep him alive when she had no idea why he'd been murdered?

Bartholomew was waiting for her in the lobby. He greeted her, thanked her, shook her hand. She tried to match his normalcy but doubted her effort was credible. Her self-control had cracked at the sight of Baxter lying in a pool of blood, and those fractures kept widening. After this morning's eviction from Nefesh Bria and now Bartholomew's summons, red-hot panic must be visible inside the fissures.

Her scraped knees stung as he led her into the all-too-familiar interview room. Standing by the table, holding a manila folder, was Detective Turner. Turner and Bartholomew side by side made Natalie imagine that the two men had perused a menu of physical attributes and made opposite choices on everything: thin, tall, snow-pale, young, and friendly Bartholomew versus older, rounder, shorter, black, pleasant-but-stern Turner.

"Thank you for coming in, Dr. Marsh." Turner's keen gaze sized Natalie up as he reached to shake her hand. Those were new glasses, she thought absently, with thicker rims. Why was her life crammed with enough catastrophes that she had opportunity to notice when a police detective updated his eyewear?

Bartholomew pulled out a chair for her. She sat and placed her car keys and phone on the table. She'd left her purse in her car.

Bartholomew sat on the opposite side of the table. Turner remained standing. "You're free to leave at any time," Turner said. "You're not under arrest."

Not yet, Natalie thought.

"We've spoken to your associates you mentioned seeing at the lecture last night," Turner said. "Unfortunately, none of them noticed you there."

Natalie wanted to ask him to check again, but her tongue felt dry and stuck in place. She hadn't really expected anyone to notice her, at least not more than momentarily, which wouldn't have provided a strong alibi—she could have shown up for a few minutes, then slipped out to commit murder. Humiliation scorched her as she thought of the pathetic message she'd left Marianne. *Did any of your friends notice me? Anyone? Please?*

Turner opened the folder and removed the pages she'd ripped from her notebook and given to Bartholomew last night. "Thank you for providing your notes. Is this the first time you've heard Hilary Strickland speak?"

Natalie swallowed, trying to clear the adhesive sensation from her mouth. "No."

"A favorite of yours?"

"Yes."

Turner read the title she'd written on the first page of notes. "'You're Not the Exception: Self-Care for Mental Health Professionals.'"

"Yes."

"Is this the first time you've heard Dr. Strickland speak on this topic?"

He must already know the answer to that question. Who had told him? Had they talked to Marianne already? Or questioned colleagues at the practice where she'd worked pre-Nefesh Bria? "I heard her give the same lecture about a year and half ago, in Manhattan. I enjoyed it and found it helpful. I wanted a refresher."

"The material was familiar to you. But you still took notes."

"Taking notes helps me concentrate."

"Then you have two sets of similar notes?"

"No." Even if she tried, she couldn't make her alibi sound weaker. *I swear, I took these notes last night. No, I don't have the notes I took at the same lecture last year and* these *certainly aren't those old notes.* A snarky remark about carbon dating the ink from her ballpoint pen wouldn't be wise. "I usually don't keep notes like that long-term. I take them, learn from them, and toss them the next time I clean out my desk."

Without comment, Turner studied Natalie. Bartholomew stayed quiet too, spiky elbows resting on the table. The silence made Natalie want to say anything at all to break it, but she repressed the urge. She used silence to encourage clients to open up; she wasn't going to fall for the same tactic at the hands of Turner and Bartholomew. She looked at Bartholomew, hoping to see compassion. To her relief, she found it. He gave her a sympathetic smile.

"May I get you anything?" he asked. "Water? Coffee? Food?"

"Water, please," she said.

He rose to his feet and exited the room.

"We spoke to Lauren Bell," Turner said. "Ms. Bell didn't see Mr. Quincy last night. She said she'd invited him to an event related to her work at the Parisi Gallery, but he'd declined, telling her he had an appointment that evening."

"What kind of appointment?"

"He didn't say."

This second hope for a witness who could offer exonerating evidence shriveled up. Lauren's knowing that Baxter had had "an appointment" didn't help at all. The police would assume the appointment had been with Natalie.

"Where were you on the night of Thursday, July 19, between 2:00 and 3:00 a.m.?" Turner asked. "The night the MacKerrons' apartment was invaded and Drew Drummond was attacked."

The fact that she didn't have an alibi for that night hadn't frightened her until now, despite Heather's accusations—the police must know Heather was not a reliable source. "I was at home, asleep."

"Can anyone confirm that?"

"No."

Turner picked up Natalie's notes, tucked them back into his folder, and closed it. "Heather Osbourne remains adamant that she did not rob the MacKerrons or attack Drew Drummond. She insists the vase was planted in her apartment."

"Heather is not mentally stable, and part of her delusions involves distrusting me." Natalie glanced at Bartholomew, who was reentering the room with a water bottle in his hand. "I've already discussed Heather's accusations with Detective Bartholomew."

"Before the night of the theft, were you aware that Mrs. MacKerron owned a valuable crystal vase that she displayed in her living room?" Turner asked.

Scorching blood flowed into her cheeks. Here was another question to which Turner already knew the answer. Ainsley must have listed her as one of the people she'd told about the vase. Did Ainsley suspect Natalie? No. That was ludicrous.

What about this line of questioning *wasn't* ludicrous?

Bartholomew set the water bottle in front of her and returned to his seat.

"Thank you," Natalie said. "Yes, Ainsley mentioned the vase at work. It was a wedding gift from her aunt. Could we please keep this conversation on target? I understand that you have to investigate my whereabouts last night, given that Baxter Quincy died at my house, but you have no evidence beyond Heather's irrational accusations that I had anything to do with what happened to Drew Drummond. Why would I want to frame Heather? What does that get me?"

Turner leaned over the table. Natalie wanted to scoot backward—or make a break for the door.

"Ms. Osbourne was causing trouble for you," Turner said.

"At the Stoker Building, you mean? She was causing trouble for all of us there."

"But more so for you specifically. Accusing your clinic of being 'evil.' Accusing you personally of being evil. Spreading the word that you engaged in a sexual relationship with a client."

"I have never been inappropriately involved with any of my clients."

"We spoke with Kenton Lowery this morning," Turner said. "I understand he's a former client of yours."

"I can't confirm that."

"He said you were his therapist at the time his marriage broke up."

"I can't confirm that." Natalie swallowed again, her throat drier. "Did he claim we were involved?"

"No," Turner said. "As you know, he retracted the story he told Baxter Quincy. A story he changed after a visit from Gideon Radcliffe."

Natalie licked her lips, but they remained so dry that she felt her blood had evaporated. Had Kenton's mother hens/bodyguards, Jenny and Josie, talked to the police, making it sound as though Gideon had barged in and threatened Kenton into changing his story?

Bartholomew lifted the water bottle from Natalie's inert hands, unscrewed the cap, and passed the open bottle back to her. "Drink it."

Water. She had water. She raised the bottle and let cold water flow over her tongue and down her throat.

"Where were you between 5:00 p.m. and midnight this past Saturday, July 21?" Turner asked.

"On Saturday?" Why did they care what she'd been doing Saturday night? Rattled by the fear that another terrible crime—a crime they thought she'd committed—had occurred at that time, Natalie couldn't recall what she'd done on Saturday. Memories heaped in her brain, fragmented and out of sequence. Last night had been . . . last night she'd found Baxter murdered . . . The night before, she'd—

"Saturday was the day Mr. Drummond passed away," Bartholomew supplied.

"Oh. Thank you." Memories sorted themselves out. "Ainsley and Stuart MacKerron were at my house for dinner. Gideon Radcliffe was there as well. We were together when Stuart got the call telling him Drew had died."

"What time did your guests arrive?" Turner asked.

"Gideon arrived around three. The MacKerrons arrived at six."

"What time did your guests leave?"

"Ainsley and Stuart left after the call from Drew's sister. That was about seven, I think, or maybe seven thirty. Gideon and I left about eight thirty. We wanted to take the leftover food to his apartment so he could deliver it to the MacKerrons later."

"He needed help transporting the food?" Turner asked.

"No. We'd decided to make a couple of other meals for them to use later, and it was convenient to do it at Gideon's. Since he and the MacKerrons are neighbors, we wouldn't need to pack the meals up and drive them over there."

"Did you and Mr. Radcliffe drive together?"

"No. I took my own car."

"What time did you leave Mr. Radcliffe's?"

"Around . . . eleven? Quarter past eleven?"

"Did you go straight home?"

"Yes."

"What were you doing between eleven and midnight?"

"Getting ready for bed. Going to bed."

"Can anyone confirm that?"

"No."

"Ms. Osbourne claims the Baccarat vase must have been planted in her apartment on Saturday, July 21, sometime between 5:00 p.m. and midnight, while she was at work. We have a witness who can verify that a woman carrying a tote bag entered Heather's apartment that evening between eleven and midnight. A coworker has verified that it couldn't have been Heather."

Natalie set her water bottle on the table, nearly tipping the bottle over. She'd thought she was offering a strong alibi. Instead, not only had she established that she'd been in the area the night someone had allegedly broken into Heather's apartment but also that she had no alibi at all for the most critical hour of the evening. Who had entered Heather's apartment? A woman similar enough to Natalie in build that Turner was questioning her about it. Had the woman been wearing a hat or hood to keep her face hidden? The darkness would have helped as well.

"A woman?" Natalie asked. "That's all the witness can confirm?"

"On your way home from Mr. Radcliffe's, did you drive past the apartment complex where Heather Osbourne lives?"

"Yes."

"Is that your usual route home from Mr. Radcliffe's?"

"I take it occasionally."

"Why? It's a longer route."

"I'll take it if I have an errand in that direction. And no, I didn't have an errand on Saturday night. I don't know why I took it. I wasn't concentrating on it. I was thinking about Heather, hoping she wasn't the one who'd attacked Drew Drummond. Maybe the choice was subconscious."

"Yet you remember it clearly enough to pin the cause on thoughts of Heather."

"When I realized I was driving past Heather's complex, it stuck in my mind." Natalie kept her tone level. "I heard you found stolen jewelry in Heather's apartment. Are you accusing me of planting that as well? Of being the thief who's been operating in that part of town?"

"Are you?"

"No."

"Do you know who the thief is? A client of yours? A compulsive thief who told you where he or she stored stolen property and you decided to use that to—"

"*Don't* go there." Sharp words sliced through her vow to stay calm. "I would never use a client in *any* way, and if you're going to waste time with ridiculous theories, don't create them based on the assumption that criminal behavior is a common element of mental—"

Turner lifted his hand. "Let's stay on track. Did you stop at Heather's apartment?"

"No."

"Did you plant Ainsley MacKerron's vase in her apartment?"

"No."

Turner rose to his feet. "Let's summarize what we've got here. Heather Osbourne and Baxter Quincy had both been causing trouble for you, endangering your work, endangering your reputation, threatening Nefesh Bria—an organization you're devoted to. Have I stated things accurately so far?"

Even agreeing to these basic facts felt like a confession. Not sure what to say, Natalie couldn't stop herself from throwing an exasperated glance at Bartholomew.

"Ease off, Turner," he said. "We all know Quincy and Osbourne were stirring things up. You don't need to make her state the obvious."

"Fine," Turner said. "They were stirring up trouble. You were frustrated. Angry. Scared. Heather Osbourne was an oncoming disaster. Framing her for theft would get her safely locked up, and you're a psychologist; you knew how to manipulate her. But things escalated when you stumbled into Drew Drummond."

You knew how to manipulate her. Fury spiked again, but Natalie stayed silent. Turner wanted to upset her. She didn't want to play along.

"Baxter Quincy wouldn't shut up, wouldn't stop searching for ways to kick your clinic out of the Stoker Building," Turner said. "The rumor about your affair with Kenton Lowery was the last straw. You invited Baxter over, hoping you could convince him to back off. You lost your temper."

"No."

Turner leaned over her. "If you didn't kill him, explain why he died at your house."

"I can't. I don't know what he was doing there."

"We have a witness," Turner said. "A witness who saw Quincy's car pull up to your house. Who saw him walk to your door and ring the bell. Who saw the front door open and Mr. Quincy walking inside. Besides you, who would have opened your door and invited Mr. Quincy in? He didn't break into your house. He was an expected guest."

Her brain froze. Burned. Froze.

"I'm waiting for an explanation," Turner said. "If you have one, let's hear it. Was the ghost of your great-grandmother playing hostess at your front door? That would be a better story than anything you've given us so far."

"Turner," Bartholomew said firmly. "For the love, take it easy on her. You know Natalie. You know what she's been through. She's not a monster. You can bet that whatever happened wasn't anything she wanted."

Turner straightened up. "Fine. Dr. Marsh, take a break. While you're relaxing, psychoanalyze yourself and figure out how you can reconcile your passion to help the mentally ill with the fact that to protect your clinic, you maliciously framed a delusional woman, then fractured a man's skull and drove a knife—five times—into his chest because he dared suggest anything about your clinic was dangerous."

These accusations, now bluntly stated, drilled past fear and struck deep pain. Her mother's accusations: Natalie was a hypocrite. Natalie didn't care about helping her. Natalie only wanted power, wanted control, wanted money, and psychology was a weapon she used to get it.

"In fact, you can go home." Turner stepped back from the table. "We're done with your house. Go home and think about things. Make yourself a nice meal. Your carving knife and your cast-iron skillet have been taken into evidence, but you have plenty of nice knives and pans left. Eat. Sleep on it." He walked out of the room, leaving the door open.

CHAPTER 20

Shifting in her chair, Natalie gazed at the open door. Go home to where Baxter had died. Go home knowing what Turner and Bartholomew—and Regina and Erik and soon Bob Chapman and all of Ohneka—thought she'd done. That she was worse, horrifically worse, than her mother had ever accused her of being.

She didn't want to leave with Turner's accusations ripping her up. She wanted to sit here until she'd convinced the police of the truth.

Which was a stupid strategy. It wasn't working, and she should get out of here as fast as she could move.

Bartholomew hadn't followed Turner out the door. "Have you had anything to eat today? I could bring you a sandwich. Early lunch."

Natalie hauled scorched and frostbitten thoughts back into service. "You two are good-cop-bad-copping me," she said wearily. "Stop it."

Bartholomew didn't look fazed. "Turkey or ham and cheese?"

Ham and cheese. Bread, tomatoes, lettuce, all sliced with steel blades. *We've taken your carving knife into evidence.* Her fingerprints would be all over that knife and all over the pan. Her fingerprints and possibly Gideon's. No one else's. She couldn't imagine the murderer had been sloppy enough to leave prints.

"Or if you want to go the breakfast route, how about some fruit and a muffin?" Bartholomew asked.

"No, thank you." If they were sure she was guilty, why hadn't they arrested her? Either the evidence Turner had blitzed her with wasn't as definitive as they wanted her to believe or they thought the unhurried give-her-rope-to-hang-herself approach was a better strategy.

Or maybe they knew her well enough to calculate that, given time, she wouldn't be able to endure the guilt. She'd crack and come staggering back to them, desperate to confess all to good-cop Bartholomew. She'd confess it all now, except she had nothing to confess. She picked up her water bottle and drank a few gulps.

"How is Heather doing?" she asked, setting the bottle down. Bartholomew would think the question had sprouted from guilt, but she couldn't see how asking it would make things worse.

"She's focused and consistent in stating she's innocent," Bartholomew said. "Other than that, her delusions have become pretty overwhelming."

Natalie couldn't discern a "You did this to her" inflection in his words, but by design, he'd leave that attitude to Turner.

"She's afraid her grandmother's mad at her," he continued. "Because she didn't burn all the letters like she was supposed to."

"Did you find any of these alleged letters?"

"There were ashes in the trash can in her kitchen, so she burned something. She said she put the one unburned letter in a safe place but won't tell us where."

"She told me she'd hidden the new letter under the old letters. In a box on her nightstand." With only friendly Bartholomew in the room, Natalie felt less like she was getting clawed apart from within. Even knowing this was part of their strategy didn't incline her to fight it. A lessening of pain wasn't a change she wanted to resist.

"Yeah, we didn't find the real letters either, the original ones," he said. "They weren't in her apartment. Interesting, isn't it, that she'd be so convinced Grandma wanted her to burn the new messages. Why do you think she believes that?"

"I have no idea."

"Maybe the person who wrote the letters wanted evidence destroyed," Bartholomew said.

"You think someone actually sent her letters? In Tabitha's name?"

Bartholomew shrugged. "It would be a clever way to manipulate her. Tell her what you want her to do and order her to destroy the proof that someone was behind the scenes. Doesn't leave much for her lawyer to work with. Even though she saved one of the letters, she's so sure it's a message from Tabitha that she won't help us find it. I suspect the last thing she wants is anyone telling her the letter is a fake." He paused, his sympathetic gaze holding Natalie's. "It's a rough situation for her."

Natalie steeled herself. It was time for the good cop to take his shot at extracting a confession.

"Natalie." Bartholomew's bass voice was gentle. "If you know anything that can spare Heather suffering, you'll feel better if you share it. You're too good of a person to do anything else."

"I hope you believe that," Natalie said. "Because it's true. If I knew something, I'd tell you. Under no circumstances—*none*—would I use Heather or anyone else in the way you're suggesting, nor would I have stabbed Baxter Quincy. If your evidence has enough holes that you haven't arrested me, then it has enough holes for you to consider that I might be telling the truth."

"We're considering that." He spoke with calm authority, but Natalie picked up on the subtle uneasiness in his tone. He *was* considering it, likely bothered by the fact that circumstantial evidence clashed with his own experience with Natalie and his assessment of her character.

But no matter what he thought of her, his opinion was useless without evidence.

"You look worn out." He stood. "If you're not up for the sandwich, I'll get you the muffin."

Natalie didn't object. A private chance to get her thoughts together was appealing. Bartholomew exited.

She picked up her phone. Out of the corner of her eye, she'd noticed the screen light up a few times while she'd been talking to Turner and Bartholomew.

A text from Gideon: *How are you doing? Any word from the police?*

Yes. Plenty of words.

Two missed calls from the same client, probably worrying his therapist was a murderer. She'd call him back as soon as she left here. No matter what Erik said, she wasn't immediately handing client concerns over to him or anyone else.

A text from Kenton: *Please call me.* Gladly, as soon as she left the PD. If she left the PD. She wanted to know precisely what he and Jenny and Josie had told the police. If he was requesting a phone call as opposed to a text, he must be frantic to talk to her as well.

A voice mail from Marianne Avery. Natalie tapped the screen to play it. "This is Marianne, and what in the deepest pit of brimstone-barbecued demons is going on? Call me *now*, and I mean *now*."

Natalie debated for a moment, then tapped the screen to return the call. If Bartholomew returned while she was talking, so be it. He couldn't arrest her for poor cell phone etiquette.

Marianne answered on the first ring. "Where are you?"

"I'm at the police department. I assume you heard about—"

"Yes. Did they arrest you?"

"Not yet. I came here voluntarily, but they're trying to get me to confess. I'm alone at the moment. The detectives have stepped out of the room."

"I hear Regina and Erik conspired to toss you out of the clinic."

"Regina figured it was what Bob would want. She's right."

Marianne snorted. "You should have had the sense to take a break without their having to banish you. What time did Baxter Quincy die?"

"I don't know. Sometime yesterday evening."

"And you don't have an alibi because you were being antisocial at the lecture. Listen up, girl. I was there. I saw you hiding in your notebook, writing like a fiend. I can tell that to the cops."

A tide of hope swept Natalie to her feet. "But you weren't coming. You had a family commitment—"

"A picnic. With Tyrant Theresa and her pastry-wrapped salmon. A *picnic*. What was the weather doing last night?"

Natalie thought back. Thought of herself hunched on the sidewalk, water soaking through her skirt. "It rained."

"Yes. Forty percent chance of rain, and Tyrant Theresa was holding out hope that the show could go on, but the odds failed us. She canceled, and I jumped into my car and high-tailed it to Ithaca. I would have called you to carpool, but I was leaving late and knew you'd be long gone."

"You saw me there?"

"Yes, I saw you there. Do you think I'm lying? You were sitting on the right side of the hall, toward the back, with empty seats all around you. Boss, what kind of train wreck are you involved in? Why was Quincy at your house?"

"I have no idea. None. I wish I did. Could you please call Detective Bartholomew directly and tell him you can confirm I was at the lecture? Let me get you his number—"

"I'm here." Bartholomew's voice made her jump. She pivoted to see him standing behind her, holding a plate containing an apple and a blueberry muffin. How long had he been in the room, eavesdropping on her conversation? Those giant shoes didn't step noiselessly by accident. *The longer the better.*

She spoke into the phone. "Do you have a minute? He's here now."

"Yes, yes, put him on. I can come in later today to make an official statement or whatever they need."

Natalie offered her phone to Bartholomew. "Dr. Marianne Avery from the clinic needs to talk to you."

* * *

Legs weak as though she'd overexerted them—strange when the most physically strenuous thing she'd done was to walk out of the PD—Natalie reached her car and unlocked it. In the driver's seat, with the door closed and the air conditioning running, she called her anxious client and reassured him, called Gideon and gave him a bare-bones update—she'd give him a detailed report later when she wasn't so shaken—and called Kenton. She got Kenton's voice mail and left a message saying she'd call him again later. Then she drove to the hotel, silenced her phone, collapsed into bed, and slept for three hours.

When she awoke, she checked her phone and found a lengthy, formal voice mail from Regina expressing relief that Marianne had been able to "partially exonerate" Natalie, but since "shock levels are high" and "nothing is officially resolved," it was better if Natalie remained on temporary leave. Natalie was tempted to respond that maybe shock levels would drop if the public could see that Natalie was at work, had the confidence of her colleagues, and was clearly not in legal trouble.

Except she *wasn't* out of legal trouble. Even if the time of Baxter's death coincided with the time Marianne could testify Natalie was in Ithaca—and Natalie wasn't yet sure Marianne's testimony covered that whole window—there was still the question of Drew Drummond and framing Heather. She hoped, feebly, that Turner and Bartholomew didn't genuinely suspect her of doing that but had used those accusations as part of their strategy to shake loose a confession about Baxter: *Okay, I killed him. But I didn't do anything to Drew or Heather!*

At least there were no messages asking her to return to the PD. She'd had enough of the police today. The last voice mail was from an unfamiliar number. She tapped it.

A quiet feminine voice spoke. "This is Lauren Bell. Please return my call as soon as you can. Thank you."

The mental recharge she'd gained from her nap drained instantly, leaving her thoughts tired and gray. Lauren must think she'd killed Baxter, but would she leave a polite message with "please" and "thank you" if she thought

Natalie had knifed her boyfriend? Maybe, knowing Lauren. Or maybe she'd already heard Marianne's testimony that Natalie had been at the lecture. Marianne would do everything she could to spread that around the Stoker.

Natalie rose from where she'd been sitting on the edge of the bed. She stretched aching back muscles, got a drink of water, and settled in the bedside chair. Hoping she could respond with clearheaded empathy no matter what Lauren said, she returned the call.

"Hello?" Lauren said.

"Lauren, it's Natalie Marsh."

"Thank you for calling me back." Lauren started to choke up. "Natalie, I know you didn't kill Baxter. I wanted to tell you that."

Gratitude poured through Natalie. "Thank you."

"The police talked to me this morning, and, of course, they're suspicious of you since Baxter died at . . ." Lauren hesitated. "I told them you would never have attacked him, that there must be another reason why he was found at your house."

"Thank you. I know you must have had a wealth of reasons to doubt me."

"You, doing something so . . . savage? I know you were frustrated with Baxter, but you were so calm about it. You wouldn't . . ." Her voice caught.

"I was away all yesterday evening at a lecture at Cornell. I have a witness who can confirm that."

"Yes, thank heavens," Lauren said shakily. "I went over to Nefesh Bria to see if anyone knew anything, and Ainsley MacKerron told me."

"How is Ainsley doing?"

"Oh my word, not well. The poor girl got so upset while talking to me that Dr. Avery all but dragged her away from the reception desk, telling her to go take a long break. I think she tried to send her home, but Ainsley is so dutiful. She didn't want to leave. I don't think she knew Baxter well, but having this happen so soon after Drew's death . . ."

"Lauren, how are *you* doing? I'm so sorry for what you must be going through, losing Baxter."

"You're very kind. I feel . . . stunned. It's difficult to believe it's real. I suppose that's . . . normal?"

"Yes, it is. Is there anything I can do for you?"

"Oh, no, but thank you. Please don't worry about me. To be frank, we hadn't been involved very long and I doubted it would work out long term, but I did enjoy spending time with him. I lost a sweet friend."

"I'm so sorry."

"The police asked me about Baxter's plans last night, but all Baxter had told me was that he had an appointment. I did wonder if he was making up an excuse to get out of the party at the Cascata park. He wasn't a fan of abstract art."

"To be clear, the appointment was not with me," Natalie said. "I have no idea why he ended up at my house or even how he knew where I lived."

"I did tell the detectives that if he *had* had an appointment with you, it wouldn't have been at your house. You're both so professional. You would have met in a work setting, at his travel agency or your clinic."

"Thank you."

"I didn't talk to him after lunch yesterday. I headed straight from work to a dentist appointment, of all the silly things. Then to the party at the sculpture park, which, because of the rain, was not nearly as lovely as it should have been. The guests had to spend much of the evening under the pavilion and in the gazebo." She sighed. "I hope the police figure this out quickly. It's hard to . . . hard to adjust to it when we have no idea what happened."

"Yes, it is," Natalie said.

"I'll do what I can to make sure people—especially Vanessa—know you weren't even home at the time he . . . was attacked."

"I appreciate that."

"I'll let you go. I hope to see you back at the Stoker soon."

"I hope to be back soon. Thank you, Lauren."

After ending the call, Natalie remained slouched in her chair for a moment, floppy with relief. When floppy started to slide toward sleepy, she sat up straight and picked up her phone. She couldn't doze off now. She needed to try Kenton again.

Kenton answered on the second ring. "Hi, Dr. Marsh. What happened with Baxter Quincy?"

"I have no idea." She was sick of repeating that phrase. "I didn't kill him, if that's what you're asking, and I have no idea what he was doing at my house. I know the police came to speak to you. What did you tell them?"

Kenton didn't answer, and Natalie realized how brusque she'd sounded. She closed her eyes and let herself return to a slump in her chair. "I apologize for being abrupt. I'm on edge."

"I get it." Judging by Kenton's tone, he was edgier than she was. "They asked about our relationship."

Natalie switched her voice into controlled, clinical mode. "What did you tell them?"

"I told them we didn't have an affair. They asked why I told Quincy we had. I said because I wanted him to go away. They wouldn't take that as an answer, so I . . . told them the truth."

"Thank you for doing that. I know that was difficult for you."

"Yeah, it's okay. Sorry about the affair rumors."

"You told them about Gideon Radcliffe's visit?"

"I didn't bring it up, but they asked me about it. Maybe Jenny or Josie told them. I said I promised him I'd talk to Baxter and clear things up. Never did talk directly to Baxter—I didn't have a chance. I did leave him that message though."

"I appreciate that."

"The police also asked about you and Heather."

Natalie hated that the police were giving Kenton more reasons to doubt one of the few people—maybe the only person—he'd dared fully open up to. "What did they ask?"

"They wanted to know what she'd said about you. What you'd said about her. I said I know Heather accused her of planting that stolen vase, but Heather's messed up, and no way would Dr. Marsh do that. I asked how Heather was doing, and they said she's okay. Jail nurse keeps tabs on her. I hired a lawyer for her."

"I'm glad to hear that. Did they ask you about the new letter from Tabitha, the one she says she kept?"

"Yeah. They asked if I knew where Tabitha's letters were, that Heather said she'd put the new letter with the old ones. They didn't find any letters at all in her apartment. Stupid old letters. I wish she'd never found them. Maybe she wouldn't have gone cuckoo."

"The letters aren't the source of Heather's difficulties."

"Okay, yeah, I know. Why do they want to see that new letter? They know she's nuts. It's probably a blank piece of paper or a letter she wrote to herself."

"They're investigating the question of whether someone might have written the new letters to manipulate Heather."

"Like writing to her pretending to be Tabitha?"

"Yes." Natalie was glad Kenton sounded surprised. Apparently, he hadn't connected the questions the police had asked about Natalie to their questions about the new letter.

"To manipulate her to do what?" Kenton asked.

"I'm not sure. If there's any way to find the letters, that would be helpful. Were you able to give the police any guidance?"

"I . . . told them I didn't have a clue. But after they left, I was thinking about Heather, about where she might hide the letters. When we were kids, she had this spot where she'd keep stuff she didn't want Mom to break, like this old teapot she loved. She didn't hide Tabitha's letters there—she kept them close to her, like under her mattress or in her backpack. But if the letters aren't in her apartment now . . . maybe if she was scared of getting arrested and wanted to make sure they were safe . . . I don't know if she still uses it, but it was a clever hiding place."

"Where is it?" Natalie asked. If Heather still used the hiding place, there might be other important items there besides the letters, like stolen jewelry and knickknacks. Not all of the stolen items had been found in Heather's apartment.

"It's . . . there's this wooded area in our old neighborhood. She dug this hole, lined it, hid it below rocks and branches and stuff."

"Can you tell me how to find it?"

"I couldn't really give directions."

Natalie wanted to ask if he could show the police the location but hesitated. Returning to his childhood neighborhood would be challenging for Kenton, and he'd had enough struggles lately. "Can you describe the place?"

"I'd need to . . . see the area. Walk around, I guess. See what's familiar."

"If it's too uncomfortable for you to go back there, I understand. But any direction you could give the police might be helpful."

"I'm not talking to the police about this," Kenton said shortly. "I've answered enough of their questions. I don't want them rooting through Heather's kiddie treasures in search of some worthless letter."

"I understand. Would you be willing to give *me* whatever directions you can?"

He didn't respond. Natalie waited, letting him work through it. He wouldn't have mentioned the hiding spot at all if he weren't at least partly open to guiding her there.

"Do you think it could help Heather?" he asked.

"If it helps prove someone was—or wasn't—forging letters from Tabitha, it could be helpful. And it might give her doctors or the police insight into her mind and activities."

"I don't think I can tell you how to find it. I'll have to take you there."

"If you're willing, I'd appreciate it."

"Let's get it over with. Can you go this evening before it gets dark?"

"Yes. Thank you. And I know you want privacy, but you or I need to bring a friend along. I can't take the risk of someone seeing us slipping off into the woods together."

"I get it."

"If you don't have anyone you'd like to bring, I'll bring Gideon Radcliffe."

After a stretch of uncomfortable silence, Kenton said, "Don't bring Radcliffe. I'll see if Jenny or Josie can come. Is that enough? I don't want a bunch of people there."

"Jenny or Josie is fine."

"I'll text you my old address. Meet there at seven?"

"Fine," Natalie said. "I'll see you tonight."

Kenton hung up.

Natalie wandered to the curtained window. She opened the drapes and observed the sunny day, thinking gratefully about last night's rain. If not for Marianne's canceled picnic, Natalie would likely be in jail right now.

Maybe she should have pressed Kenton to tell the police about the hiding spot, but she'd rather search for the letter on Kenton's terms than insist they notify the police and have Kenton refuse to cooperate at all. Besides, right now, Natalie didn't want to deal with Turner or Bartholomew any more than Kenton did. If Kenton and she found anything relevant tonight, Natalie would convince him they needed to turn it in.

No matter how tonight's search turned out, hunting for the letters sounded more worthwhile than hiding helplessly in a hotel room. She picked up her phone and called Gideon to update him, hoping he wouldn't get the wrong idea when he learned Kenton had banned him from the treasure hunt.

If she lost Gideon's trust now, her last shreds of sanity would go with it.

CHAPTER 21

KENTON INTRODUCED HIS COMPANION AS Josie Tate. At first, Natalie was pleased to meet one of the mother figures who'd helped give Kenton the confidence to step into an emotionally healthier life, but her response to Natalie's hello came with words well chilled and all humor omitted: "I'm here to keep an eye on you, girl." Did she think Natalie was manipulating Kenton or even setting a trap for him? Natalie vowed to be completely amiable and professional with Josie, no matter what. The last thing she needed was another enemy.

Ample daylight remained, but the mercurial weather had layered clouds over the sunshine. With the overcast sky and branches loaded with leaves, the light was dim as Kenton led Natalie and Josie through the forested land behind his childhood neighborhood. For the first fifteen minutes or so, he followed trails—hard-packed dirt, muddy in spots and bulging with tree roots. Natalie tried to keep track of where they were, but when he stepped off the path and started weaving between trees, her sense of direction failed entirely.

If she'd had full confidence in Kenton, her lack of orientation wouldn't have bothered her, but her reservations about her escorts were intensifying—not because she feared Kenton would get them lost but because she worried about his mental state. He didn't speak unless she addressed him, and when he looked back at her, he had a tight, brooding expression that made her want to sit him down and help him process what was happening inside him. Josie followed Natalie, and when Natalie glanced back at her, Josie fired her a glare that reminded Natalie of Gideon's joke about a cleaver in the back. After what had happened to Baxter, that quip didn't seem funny anymore, especially considering how ready Josie looked to wield the cleaver.

After repeated zigzags, Kenton stopped, squinting at two trees with tilting trunks fused together at the bottom. "I think I came too far," he said. "Wait here. I'll check." He backtracked rapidly, passing Natalie and Josie.

Tense and tired, Natalie would have liked to wait in silence, but she couldn't pass up this opportunity to connect with Josie. "Thank you for coming with Kenton. I know it's a lot of time to take out of your evening."

"Give me a break," Josie said. "You didn't want company."

Had Kenton given the impression that it was he, not Natalie, who had mandated a chaperone? Natalie decided not to correct this. She didn't want to embarrass Kenton. "I'm actually grateful for the company."

Josie inspected Natalie as though memorizing her appearance in case she needed to describe her to a police sketch artist. "Are you his ex?"

"You mean, did we have an affair?" Natalie asked. "We—"

"I mean, are you his scorpion of an ex-wife?"

It surprised her that Kenton wouldn't have made at least this fact about Natalie clear to Josie. "No. I'm not."

"You using his sister's problems as a way to wedge yourself into his life?"

Natalie noted Josie's toned arms. Josie must be in her midfifties, but she'd have no trouble clobbering much younger Natalie. "I have no interest in a relationship with him."

"Then what *is* your place in his life? You make that boy nervous. I saw you when you came to our bakery the other week, saw you at the door when I was driving away. What were you doing there? He didn't want to talk about it, but ever since you showed up, he's looked like he's bought a condo in Panic City. You're causing trouble for him."

"I'll leave it up to Kenton to answer any questions you have."

"Uh-huh. Who's your Israelite general henchman?"

"My Israelite . . . ? Oh, you mean Gideon Radcliffe. He's a friend helping me deal with a difficult situation. He is not my 'henchman' in any sense, and I didn't ask him to talk to Kenton. As I said, if you have questions, please ask Kenton."

"You're a head doc, aren't you?"

"A psychologist, yes."

"You like playing mind games?"

Natalie drew a deep breath of humid air, hoping the aroma of greenery and damp soil would help relax her. First Turner's accusation that she had the expertise to manipulate Heather, and now Josie implying she was psychologically tormenting Kenton. "I do not play 'mind games' with anyone. If you think that's what I'm doing, I again suggest that you talk to Kenton."

"Say that as many times as you want. It still won't work as an answer."

Natalie controlled the temptation to snap *Think about it, sister.* Josie had been one of the people who'd persuaded Kenton to go for counseling two and a half years ago. She knew Natalie was a psychologist. It shouldn't be hard to figure out where Natalie fit in his life.

Except that Natalie wasn't behaving like a therapist. Or former therapist.

Despising herself, Natalie glanced at the gray sky crisscrossed by tree branches, then checked her watch. It would be dusk soon. The thought of being out here in the woods after dark with grim Kenton and suspicious Josie evoked enough foreboding that Natalie started musing about Baxter's death and how it would feel if one of her escorts plunged a steel blade into her chest.

"You expecting me to sing the national anthem?" Josie asked.

Realizing she'd absentmindedly pressed her hand over her heart, Natalie rested her palm against a tree instead. She had no idea who'd stabbed Baxter. *Could* it have been Kenton? What could his motive have been? Had he spoken to Baxter—not left a message, as he'd claimed—and told Baxter his true connection to Natalie? Had Baxter, with his caveman views of mental illness, responded with mockery, labeling Kenton weak and pathetic and crazy? Had a lifetime's accumulation of rage at being mocked and abused finally exploded?

No. A murder in a fit of fury didn't mesh with a scenario that would have required Kenton to locate and enter Natalie's house and lure Baxter there. Even if she set aside the bizarre fact that Baxter had died at her house, it was difficult to accept Kenton in the role of murderer, though the right motivation could stir violence in just about anyone.

Josie's hand slipped into her pocket and stayed there. Natalie angled her head so she could watch Josie more closely. With every hiss of leaves rattled by a rising wind and every hostile vibe from the side-eye Josie was giving her, Natalie wanted more and more to get out of here. She'd start walking toward her car at full speed, except she was too lost to know which way led to the street. She studied the murky sky. How inept of a city-dweller was she that she had no idea which direction was which?

Wanting to make sure her phone was still there, Natalie slid her hand into the pocket of the well-worn crop pants she'd chosen for their loose fit—after this morning's confrontation with the police, her stress had hit the level where even dressing in nice, fitted clothes sounded too hard. The phone was there, though if this went bad, she wouldn't have a chance to call for help.

Stop. You're being paranoid. You're not surrounded by murderers. Kenton has never been inclined toward—

Josie dropped toward the ground, her body spinning in Natalie's direction. Her leg crashed into the back of Natalie's knees, sweeping her legs out from under her.

Natalie landed on the dirt with an impact that punched the air from her lungs. Josie leaned over her and jammed her hands in both of Natalie's pockets, then patted her down. Natalie wanted to knock Josie away from her, but breathing was a higher priority than fighting.

"Shame you aren't armed." Josie took a few steps backward. "I'd love to call the cops and tell them you and a .45 semiautomatic tricked Kenton into coming out here to Bury-a-Body Woods. He told me what happened to that Quincy guy at your house. How'd you not get arrested?"

Gasping for air, Natalie pushed herself to her feet. Her rib cage ached, and she peered dazedly around her, choosing where to vomit if needed. "I have . . . an . . . alibi."

"Uh-huh."

"Ask the . . . police if you want." Natalie stepped closer to a tree and braced both hands against the trunk while she struggled to breathe normally. "While you're . . . at it . . . ask them to arrest you for assault."

"You had murder eyes, and you were reaching into your pocket. Checking you for weapons was self-defense."

Murder eyes? Apparently, she'd appeared as suspicious to Josie as Josie had to her. She didn't dare attempt to tackle Josie and complete the group weapons check. From the skilled way Josie had taken her down, Natalie assumed she had martial arts training.

"You sure you're not Kenton's ex?" Josie asked.

Cautiously, Natalie stood straight and lowered her hands from the tree. "What did Kenton tell you about this trip? You have strange ideas about what's going on."

From the wariness in Josie's face, Natalie knew if she took so much as a step toward her, Josie would knock her down. "He said you wanted information about his sister, info she might have hidden out here. Info the police wanted. I said, sugar, what makes you think she'll take it to the cops instead of burning it? Maybe it's evidence that proves she clobbered that boy and stole the vase, not your sister. He said you'd do the right thing, but he wanted company when he showed you the place. So here I am, the muscle and the witness. I'll make sure he's safe *and* make sure every scrap of whatever we find gets to the police."

"If he didn't trust me, why would he have brought me here?"

"If he did trust you, why would he need a bodyguard? Listen, that boy doesn't like to share his woes, and I'm not pretending I understand everything that's happening, but I know you're trouble."

"Let's establish one thing," Natalie said. "I'm not his ex-wife."

"Too bad. I'd love to meet her and tell her if she doesn't quit hassling that sweet boy, then I'll give her grief like she can't imagine."

"If she doesn't *quit* hassling him? Has she been bothering him recently?"

"If you're not the one doing the hassling, it's not your business, is it?"

At the rustle-snap of branches being pushed aside, Natalie wheeled toward the noise. Kenton was approaching, carrying a round box. When he reached them, he held the box out—a vintage hat box decorated with faded fabric in a rose pattern and tied with a pink ribbon that appeared new.

"Found her hiding spot. The letters were there." He held up the box. "Sorry about missing the turn. I haven't been out here in a long time. I can take you there if you want to see what else she hid, but I think it's all from when she was a kid. Nothing that looks like the fancy stuff the police think she stole . . ." His forehead wrinkled. "Are you okay? You look sick."

Natalie wiped her muddy palms on her pants. "Josie and I had a misunderstanding."

"I had to make sure she wasn't packing heat," Josie said, shrugging. "Or a butcher knife."

Kenton grimaced. "What did you do to her? I told you she wasn't dangerous."

"Yeah, you did. Tell me, angel, what's your track record for recognizing trustworthy girls?"

"Please tell Josie I'm not your ex." Natalie kept her tone even. Bruises and muddy clothes notwithstanding, she didn't want to escalate this. She wanted to examine the box Kenton was carrying and get out of here. "She's having issues with mistaken identity."

"Natalie is not my ex," he said flatly. "We've never been involved."

"Good for you. Now tell me the rest. She's causing problems for you, isn't she? Ever since she showed up at the Otter, you've been one jumpy kid."

Kenton's fingers pressed hard against the sides of the box. "She was there as a representative of the Stoker Building. The place where Heather was having so much trouble."

"You told us you weren't going to talk to anyone from Dracula's lair. Did she bully you into it?"

"I changed my mind. I know Dr. Mar—I know Natalie."

"Yeah, I can tell you do, but I don't think it's in a happy way."

Kenton gripped the box harder, denting the sides of it. Natalie reckoned he was fortunate Heather couldn't see him manhandling her treasure. "Natalie was my therapist," he said. "She helped me break with my ex. That's how I know her."

"Peachy," Josie said. "I'll give her credit for that, but what's she doing hanging around you now? If this is part of her 'professional services,' someone needs to yank that girl's license."

This evaluation of her integrity seared Natalie. She wanted to defend herself, but arguing about the situation would be futile. She *had* been foolish. She should have ignored the pressure from Chapman and Regina and refused to contact Kenton at all.

"It's my fault," Kenton mumbled. "I told the Stoker people I wouldn't talk to anyone except her."

"It's not your fault," Josie said. "No offense, but you're naive. She's not. She knows better."

Natalie spoke in controlled, polite words. "Kenton, please check to see if Heather put a current letter in the box. If we find anything useful, we can take it to the police. Then we're done."

Kenton tugged the bow loose. Josie walked toward him. Natalie stayed where she was.

Kenton removed the lid and handed the bow and lid to Josie. He pulled out a stack of letters tied with the same shade of pink ribbon that had held the box shut. He offered the letters to Natalie.

Taking her chances with mother-bear Josie, Natalie moved forward to take the stack. The edges of the letters were all aged and brown, except for the letter on the bottom of the pile. That paper was new, pale-pink stationery.

Natalie untied the ribbon and unfolded the new letter. It wasn't a blank piece of paper. It was a handwritten note penned in an old-style cursive script. She held it so Kenton could read it along with her.

My dearest Heather,

It seems endless time has passed since I began my attempts to send a letter to you, and at long last, I've succeeded. I fear I'm a rogue in doing so. We're expected to keep to our own affairs and not contact the living, but, my dearest, you and I need each other. I've tried in other ways to tell you of my love, and I know you've sensed my presence. How can I thank you for everything you've done to defend my holy ground and honor my sadly short life? You are my one champion. Even though many generations separate us, I feel as though you are my beloved daughter.

Darling, I'm desperately worried about my sanctuary. I've come to terms with the distasteful fact that the building is now in common use. I would leave it alone, but I fear there is deeper evil there. I cannot discern exactly what is taking place—a barrier that has never been there before blocks my ability to roam freely through the building as I once did. I cannot enter the east wing on the ground floor. When I get close to it, horror swells inside me and I know I am approaching a nightmare made real. If, despite this inner warning, I continue, I collide with an unseen barrier, frigid and impenetrable, and I have no choice but to retreat.

My dearest, I fear innocent people are in danger. May I call upon your courage to explore what is happening and to help me stop it? I cannot let this evil be my legacy. Please spread the word of danger. Brave people will join us in our fight.

I will write again soon. I admit that it is exhausting; putting ink to paper is not a gift naturally given to a woman in my state of existence, but my need to communicate with you is desperate. Please know you are the joy of my heart and my greatest comfort.

All my love,
Tabitha

"The east wing, ground floor," Natalie said. "Nefesh Bria."

Kenton took the letter and cursed under his breath. "Did she write this to herself?"

"Heather told me the new letters were in Tabitha's handwriting, that she recognized it." Natalie lifted one of the old letters off the stack in her hand. She set the other letters in the hatbox. Kenton passed the box to Josie and held the new letter open in front of him. Carefully, hoping her fingertips wouldn't transfer too much dirt to the paper, Natalie opened the old letter and held it next to the new one. The faded ink and yellowed paper contrasted with crisp pink paper and dark fresh ink.

The handwriting was the same.

In the cloudy twilight, Natalie, Josie, and Kenton all stood wordless, gawking at the two letters.

"Hoo boy," Josie said at last. "Anybody else got the heebie-jeebies?"

* * *

It took intense persuasion from Natalie to coax Kenton into accompanying her to the police department with the letters. It took flat stubbornness from Kenton to persuade Josie *not* to accompany them. Natalie stayed out of that dispute. She didn't care whether or not Josie came along, but she was pleased to see Kenton standing up for himself. He argued that Josie had spent enough of her evening helping him, she needed to get back to her family, and there was no reason for her to waste hours at the police department. Natalie knew this wasn't his real motive. Kenton would find it mortifying to have a respected business partner witness him dealing with the police, and he'd already had to endure that experience at the Playful Otter.

She suspected Josie sensed this as well, since she yielded more quickly than Natalie thought she would—yielded after a few smoking words of warning for Natalie if she "did anything to hurt that innocent boy." From the clash between her tone and the uncertain expression on her face, Natalie knew Josie was reevaluating her, but the heap of evidence on the *distrust* side of the scale remained weighty.

As Kenton and Natalie sat in the lobby of the PD, waiting for Bartholomew, the impulse to delve into information that should no longer be her business finally slipped through the fuzzy professional boundaries remaining between her and Kenton. "Has Sophia been bothering you? From what Josie said, it sounded like she's been in contact recently."

Kenton massaged his scarred forearm. "She's texted me a few times. I don't know how she got my number. She uses different numbers when she texts, so I never know when it'll be her."

Please tell me you're not thinking of going back to her. "Are you comfortable telling me what she's said?"

He shrugged. "You already know the worst. She says stuff like, 'I know you miss me' and 'No one gets out of my life clean' and 'I still own you.'"

"How do you respond?"

"I don't respond. I don't answer her at all. I'm going to change my number."

Relieved and proud of him, Natalie said, "That sounds like a smart strategy."

He gave her a slight smile. "Thanks. Thank you."

The door from the back of the station opened, and Bartholomew walked out. "Good evening, Dr. Marsh. Mr. Lowery."

Natalie and Kenton both stood, Kenton holding the hatbox.

"I'm sorry," Natalie said. "I just realized we could have waited until business hours tomorrow instead of making you come to work tonight."

"No, you chose right. I don't work nine to five, and when we're dealing with an issue this serious, I don't like delays. Mr. Lowery, if you'd come with me and bring the letters. Dr. Marsh, if you'd please wait, I'd like to speak with you as well."

Natalie nodded and settled into her seat. Facing Bartholomew again left her a little befuddled at having returned already to the place she'd all but fled this morning. Another round of walking willingly into the PD expecting to walk out again. One of these times, the walking-out part of the scenario wasn't going to happen.

Not wanting to be yapping on her phone in the lobby, Natalie texted Gideon. In lengthy blocks of words, she reported on the events of the evening and fielded Gideon's questions and responses—including his anger at Kenton's bringing along a friend who'd turned out to be more of an overzealous bodyguard than a chaperone.

Thirty-five minutes into the text conversation, Gideon was in the process of insisting that if there were any more treasure-digging ventures, *both* sides should have the right to bring backup when Kenton and Bartholomew returned to the lobby. Kenton hurried toward the door, muttering "Good night" to Natalie as he exited. Bartholomew beckoned to her.

To Natalie's relief, Turner wasn't waiting in the interview room. Bartholomew set the ritual water bottle on the table in front of her. She snatched it and drank eagerly. She'd been too distracted talking to Gideon to recognize how thirsty she was.

"Looks like you had a fierce tangle with nature," Bartholomew said. "How'd you get mud in your hair?"

Natalie reached up and found the crusted spot. "Kenton's business partner got overenthusiastic about making sure I wasn't armed. I assume he told you Josie Tate was with us."

"Are you hurt?"

"Not really. I could use a hot shower and some ibuprofen." And fresh Band-Aids for last night's sidewalk scrapes; new blood had seeped through the knees of her pants. Wanting to finish this interview as quickly as possible, Natalie didn't wait for him to ask more questions. She plunged into her report. Bartholomew listened, took notes, and didn't interrupt.

"Thank you," he said when she'd finished. He set his pen down. "Please explain this: if you knew a possible location of evidence relevant to our investigation, why didn't you notify us instead of going after it yourself?"

"Kenton didn't want police there."

"I understand that. But if you'd tried, I think you could have convinced him that taking us along was important. You knew we were interested in the letter. I told you that this morning."

"When you were insinuating I'd written it? Maybe I didn't feel like pressuring him because I wanted to know if the evidence was worth anything before I volunteered to get interrogated again."

"Had you ever seen the old letters before, the ones in Tabitha's handwriting?"

"No."

"But you knew they existed."

"Yes. Kenton told me about them when I met with him at Robert Chapman's request. After Heather's suicide attempt."

"You didn't know of them before that time?"

Natalie scoured her memory. Had Kenton ever mentioned them before? "No. Not that I recall."

"Were you aware Heather had a hiding place she'd used since childhood?"

"Not until Kenton told me this afternoon."

Bartholomew opened the folder he'd laid on the table in front of him. He took out a pad of paper and passed it to Natalie. Blank white writing paper.

He handed her a pen. "If you don't mind, I'd like a writing sample."

Even though Natalie had thought this might happen, her pulse accelerated to a frenzied beat she could feel in her throat. "You still think I wrote the letter? Why would I set Heather against my own clinic?"

"This isn't an accusation."

"The writer was forging Tabitha's handwriting. How is a handwriting sample going to help?"

Bartholomew didn't reply, but she already knew the answer. Whoever had forged Tabitha's handwriting wouldn't have forged it perfectly. Some of the writer's own characteristics would be evident to an expert.

"This morning, Detective Turner accused me of framing Heather because she was causing trouble for me," Natalie said. "If that's what you think, how can it make sense that I would forge a letter encouraging her to make trouble for me?"

"Are you refusing to give the sample?" Bartholomew asked mildly.

"I'm not refusing. I'm asking what you're thinking."

"I'm exploring possibilities. If you don't want to give the sample now, you're free to leave."

Natalie picked up the pen. "What do you want me to write?"

"I'll dictate." Bartholomew lifted a photocopied paper out of his folder. "Begin with 'Dearest Heather.'"

CHAPTER 22

THE CHAPEL AT HENDERSON FUNERAL Home was full, to Natalie's relief. The bigger the crowd, the easier for her to blend in. She'd debated staying away from Drew's funeral, concerned about drawing attention and being a distraction, but she wanted to support Ainsley and Stuart. After Lauren's report of how distressed Ainsley had been at work, Natalie had called Erik to get his view of the situation. Feeling a shade hypocritical given how much she objected to her own forced leave, she'd instructed Erik—and he'd agreed—to inform Ainsley that she was taking a week off whether she wanted to or not. Natalie had tried several times to call Ainsley, but Ainsley hadn't answered. She'd even looked up Stuart's number in Ainsley's personnel file—at least Erik hadn't cut off Natalie's computer access—and tried calling him, but he hadn't responded either.

From where Natalie sat next to Gideon in a pew in the middle of the chapel, she watched Ainsley and Stuart, seated in the row of chairs behind the microphone. Ainsley was on the program to sing "The Lord Is My Shepherd," and Stuart had been asked to share tales of Drew's outdoor adventures. "Brag on Drew's behalf" was how Ainsley had phrased it, attempting unsuccessfully to sound humorous when she'd shared the funeral plans with the Nefesh Bria staff on Monday.

Monday. The day Natalie had stormed into Quincy Travel to angrily accuse Baxter of causing trouble for her. The night she'd returned from Cornell to find Baxter dead in her kitchen.

Don't dwell on that now. Focus on the MacKerrons. How can you help them?

As the current speaker—Drew's sister, Claire—spoke tearfully about childhood memories, Stuart appeared stonily calm, his face and body immobile. Ainsley, in contrast, kept leaning forward and drooping backward on her chair, rubbing her hands together in convulsive motions, and staring apprehensively at the back of the room. Would she be able to make it through her song? She was scheduled to sing after Claire's remarks.

Gideon touched Natalie's hand. "You doing okay?" he whispered.

"I'm worried about Ainsley."

"Yeah, me too. She's taking this hard. No other way to take it, I guess."

Natalie nodded. The fact that Drew had died from injuries sustained in their home must have injected considerable guilt into the MacKerrons' grief. Natalie should try to convince both of them to get counseling. Who would be the best match for them? She mentally reviewed her list of top-notch therapists who didn't also work or volunteer at Nefesh Bria. Kirk Valdez would be perfect. Or Tori Hendershot . . .

Abruptly, Ainsley clutched Stuart's arm and pointed toward the double doors at the rear of the chapel. Stuart shook his head, leaned close, and said something to her. Ainsley whispered a reply and pointed again toward the doors. Natalie checked behind her but couldn't see anything unusual. Maybe a late guest had arrived, a guest Ainsley didn't want to be there. If Ainsley had been focusing anywhere near Natalie, Natalie would have feared that guest was her.

Natalie eyed the corner of the room where she'd noticed Detective Bartholomew sitting. Youthful Bartholomew in his dark suit didn't stand out as a police officer. Was he partly—or even mostly—here to see if Natalie would do anything suspicious? Had a forensic handwriting expert compared her writing sample and Tabitha's alleged letter to see if she could be the author?

She looked away from Bartholomew and resumed observing the MacKerrons. Stuart had placed his hand on Ainsley's shoulder, but from the rigid curve of his fingers, he seemed to be holding her in place more than consoling her. Restlessly, Natalie fiddled with the double-strand pearl necklace she wore, wishing she could walk to the front of the room, put her arm around Ainsley, and escort her to a quiet, private room. The funeral home must have a place where Ainsley could rest, cry, talk, do whatever would help her vent grief. Singing a solo in front of a large group of family and friends plainly was not what Ainsley found comforting right now.

Drew's sister was expressing her love for Drew, approaching the end of her eulogy. Ainsley kept folding the printed program in her hands, then flattening it, then refolding it. Natalie fidgeted with her own program, crossed her legs, then recrossed them in the other direction. Gideon wrapped his arm around her shoulders.

Claire sat down. Ainsley looked at Stuart. With his hand on her back, Stuart prodded her to her feet. Natalie clutched Gideon's knee.

Ainsley shuffled toward the microphone. Her eyes were tearless and too wide, as though she were straining to see in the dark. An older man settled at the piano and spread sheets of music across the music rack.

Ainsley drew a scratchy breath that the microphone picked up. The pianist began to play, and Ainsley began to sing. Her voice had a haunting, glass-like clarity that awed Natalie. By the time Ainsley began the second verse, Natalie had relaxed in her seat, soothed by the gentle music. Ainsley must be an experienced enough soloist that she could control her emotions while she—

A gasp midword cracked Ainsley's song. She bowed her head in a quick, awkward motion that caused her to bump the microphone. The magnified thud made Natalie start. Stuart slid forward on his seat.

Ainsley inhaled a jagged breath and continued the verse in sync with the piano. She made it through another few lines before her voice jolted as though someone had startled her. She fell silent. The pianist hesitated, slowing the notes. Natalie dug her fingernails into Gideon's knee.

Ainsley fled out the side door of the chapel.

The pianist stopped, and stupefied silence replaced the music.

Stuart stepped to the microphone. "I apologize for my wife," he said gruffly. "Drew was like a brother to both of us. She wanted to sing for him today, but . . . She'll be okay; she just needs time alone. Claire asked me if I'd share a few memories of Drew's adventures. If there was ever a guy who loved to challenge Mother Nature, it was Drew."

As Stuart segued into his eulogy, Natalie scanned the room. Despite Stuart's statement that Ainsley needed time alone, someone ought to check on her. No one was standing up. Natalie caught Gideon's eye. He nodded before she could ask the question.

"Do you want me to come?" he whispered.

Natalie shook her head and picked up her purse. "She'll be less embarrassed with just me. Keep your phone handy. I'll text to update you."

"Okay."

"If I don't come back, go ahead and leave," she whispered. "I'll call you tonight." They'd driven separately to the funeral; Gideon was returning to work after the service.

Glad she was sitting near the aisle so she didn't have to squeeze past a group of people, Natalie rose from her seat, slipped past Gideon, and headed for the back doors, not looking right or left. She didn't want to know if people, especially Bartholomew, were watching her.

Once in the lobby, she headed toward the corridor where Ainsley would have ended up when exiting through the chapel's side door. The corridor was empty. Natalie walked toward the exit at the end. Ainsley might have gone outside to get fresh air or to put more distance between herself and Drew's funeral service. As Natalie passed a restroom, she paused and opened the door to check if Ainsley had retreated there.

The door opened into a luxurious lounge area with plush carpet, peach-colored brocade furniture, and a carved table holding a vase of lilies and a box of tissues. Beyond the lounge was the restroom. Harsh, sobbing breaths mingled with the rush of water, prompting Natalie to hurry through the lounge.

Ainsley stood at the sink, washing her hands. The tap gushed at full flow, and Ainsley's frantic scrubbing was splashing water across the counter, the tiled floor, and the front of her black dress.

"Ainsley?" Natalie said.

Ainsley whirled toward her, spraying water nearly to where Natalie had stopped at the border between the restroom and the lounge. The skin on her hands was bright red.

Natalie took a cautious step toward her. "Is there anything I can do to help?"

Ainsley's crimson hands hung at her sides, water dripping from her fingertips. "Did you see anyone in the hall?"

"No." Steam rose from the water pouring from the faucet. Natalie walked to the sink and touched a fingertip to the stream. The water was hot enough to be painful. She turned it off. Ainsley scrubbed her hands against her skirt. Natalie could all but feel her frenzied urge to turn the taps back on and resume washing.

"Come sit in the lounge with me," Natalie said.

"Did you see anyone?" Ainsley asked. "Standing in the back of the chapel?"

"Standing? No. Did you see someone? You were looking in that direction, and you appeared agitated."

"No. Why do you . . . think I couldn't sing?"

"You've been through a traumatic loss, Ainsley. Wanting to sing for Drew was a beautiful thing to do, but the fact that it overwhelmed you emotionally is not surprising."

"They asked me to sing," she said. "Drew's family."

"You have a beautiful voice. It was kind of you to accept."

Ainsley's hands made a twitchy motion toward the sink, then flinched back.

"Do you feel responsible for Drew's death?" Natalie asked.

Ainsley's face petrified around wild eyes. "Why would I?"

"Feeling unwarranted guilt is common with grief."

"Guilt?"

"Feeling like you should have prevented it? That you should have done more to avert the break-in or to protect him?"

Ainsley's face flushed the same shade as her heat-and-friction reddened hands. "I can't help that someone broke in. Why would you think I had anything to do with that?"

"I was only saying it's not unusual to feel guilty when someone you care about dies. I am *not* suggesting you should feel guilty. Drew's death was not your fault. Please come sit down."

Ainsley took fast, wobbly steps toward the couch. She sank onto the cushions, arms folded, hands hidden under her arms.

Natalie sat beside her. "I'll text Stuart and let him know where you are."

"He's speaking. He won't get the message."

Natalie took her phone out of her purse and switched the ringer back on. "He might check his phone when he's done."

"He won't leave the service. He won't want to make another scene."

"You didn't make a scene. Grief isn't something to be ashamed of." Glad she already had Stuart's number in her phone, she texted him. *I'm with Ainsley. We're in the lounge of the women's restroom in the corridor to the west of the chapel.* Hastily, she sent a second text to Gideon. *Found Ainsley. She's agitated but okay. I'll stay with her until Stuart comes in. Talk to you tonight.*

Gideon texted back: *Thanks. Let me know if I can do anything to help.*

"Marianne said she saw you at Cornell the night Baxter died," Ainsley said.

"Yes." Natalie set her phone aside. "Even though I didn't have anything to do with his death, I feel terrible that he died at my house."

"Is Marianne your only alibi?"

"Yes. Thank heavens for Marianne."

"She and Erik sent me away from Nefesh Bria yesterday."

"They did that on my orders. You need to give yourself time to get through the shock of Drew's death. Will you do that, please? Compelling yourself to act like nothing happened isn't working."

Ainsley's eyes were whorls of fire. "What do you mean?"

"Tell me about your hands. I noticed on Monday that they were chapped. You're washing them a lot. Would you like to talk about that?"

"My hands are fine."

"Ainsley—" Natalie's phone beeped. She glanced at it. The text was from Stuart. *On my way.*

"Stuart's coming," Natalie said.

Ainsley lowered her hands from where she'd concealed them under her arms. "Coming right now?"

"Yes."

Ainsley examined her hands. The redness was beginning to ebb, which made the dry skin and cracks around her knuckles more visible. Natalie was relieved that she didn't seem to have scalded herself.

She reached toward Natalie and wrapped her fingers around Natalie's right hand. Caught off guard but grateful Ainsley trusted her enough to seek comfort in physical contact, Natalie didn't pull away. Ainsley lifted their hands together and folded Natalie's fingers so they formed a fist.

"That's a pretty ring." She tapped the emerald-cut stone that transitioned from pale green on one end to pink on the other. "Is the stone natural?"

"Yes. Watermelon tourmaline."

"A gift from Gideon?"

"No. It belonged to a friend who . . . passed away."

"I'm sorry." Ainsley cradled Natalie's fist in both her hands, then slid one hand so it circled Natalie's wrist. She drew Natalie's hand closer to her and leaned over it, examining the ring. "Do you wear it to honor her?"

"Not to honor her so much as to comfort myself," Natalie said. "To feel a little of her strength. When I—"

With a movement so quick that Natalie had no idea what was happening until it was over, Ainsley slammed Natalie's fist against her own mouth.

"Ainsley!" Natalie shrieked. She tried to pull her hand free, but Ainsley clamped both hands around her wrist and yanked Natalie's fist toward herself, bringing her face forward to meet it. Natalie uncurled her fingers before her fist made contact, but straightening her fingers caused her nails to gouge into the skin beneath Ainsley's eye. Ainsley twisted her head, scraping Natalie's nails across her cheek and over her mouth.

Fiercely, Natalie wrenched free of Ainsley's grip. Ainsley slammed the heel of her own hand into the bleeding scratches below her eye socket. Natalie lunged toward her, reaching for her hands. "*Stop!*"

A knock came at the lounge door. "Ainsley?" Stuart called.

Ainsley froze. Natalie seized both her wrists.

Ainsley threw herself off the couch, dragging Natalie down on top of her. "Help me!" Ainsley screamed.

The door crashed into the doorstop. Natalie released Ainsley but didn't have a chance to get off of her. Stuart seized her from behind and hauled her away from Ainsley.

Ainsley sat up. Blood streamed from a gash in her lower lip and trickled from the gouges near her eye. "She attacked me." Tentatively, she touched her swelling lip. "She was trying to . . . to . . . tell me I killed Baxter Quincy, to get me to remember that I did it, that I broke into her house and I . . . I . . . told her she was wrong, and she . . ."

"Ainsley!" Natalie twisted, trying to escape Stuart's hold. "That's not what happened—"

"Lamb, that cop Bartholomew is in the chapel. We need him."

"I can't go in there like this." Tears flowed down Ainsley's face. "They'll all stare. They'll hate me for disrupting Drew's service—"

"Text him. He's a cop on assignment; he'll be monitoring his phone. I have his number. Let me get my phone." Stuart swung Natalie around and shoved her face-first against the wall. He grabbed her right wrist and pinned her arm behind her. "Move and I'll rip your shoulder out of joint."

Clenching her teeth, Natalie stopped struggling and braced her free hand against the wall. She heard a rustle of movement and the noise of a phone hitting the carpet.

"It's in my recent calls," he said.

Ainsley crawled across the carpet, picked up Stuart's phone, and retreated as though wanting to be out of range if Natalie went berserk again.

"Ainsley." Natalie couldn't make her voice calm. The best she could do was make it quiet. "Why are you doing this?"

Ainsley didn't answer. She was texting, blood dripping off her chin and plopping onto her dress.

"You tricked Marianne into lying for you." Stuart kept Natalie trapped against the wall. "How'd you do it? Did you pay a friend to dress up as you? Won't work for long. Marianne's a smart lady. She'll figure out you're playing her."

"Stuart . . . please listen. I did not attack Ainsley. She staged this. She's not in her right mind—" Stuart jerked Natalie's arm, straining her shoulder. Her explanation splintered into a cry of pain.

"You have her blood on your fingers," Stuart said. "Save the stupid lies."

"Detective Bartholomew's coming right now," Ainsley said.

Her blood on your fingers. Natalie wanted to talk to Ainsley, help her acknowledge what she'd done, but if Natalie spoke, she'd provoke Stuart. The thought of her shoulder joint popping apart like a shattered Lego creation kept her silent.

The door to the lounge swung open, and Bartholomew entered, followed by Turner. *No, please no.* She hadn't realized Turner was at the funeral. It would have been hard enough dealing with Bartholomew alone. With Turner here, she was on her way to jail.

"Natalie Marsh attacked my wife." Stuart's furious voice thundered in Natalie's ears. "Tackled Ainsley and kept punching her in the face."

Bartholomew moved to stand behind Natalie and Stuart. She couldn't rotate her head far enough to look at him, and she couldn't bring herself to make eye contact with Turner. "That's not what happened. Stuart mistook—"

"Mr. MacKerron, please release Dr. Marsh," Bartholomew said.

Stuart let go. Natalie's arm flopped to her side, her shoulder on fire.

Stuart strode across the room and knelt next to Ainsley. She crumpled against his chest.

"I saw it happen," he said, enclosing Ainsley in his arms. "I had to drag Marsh off of Ainsley. Arrest her."

"You saw me trying to prevent Ainsley from hurting herself." Natalie gingerly rolled her burning shoulder and lifted and lowered her right arm, making sure her joint was intact. "If I were beating her up, why would I have texted you to tell you we were in here?"

Bartholomew's hand closed on Natalie's elbow. "Please come with me."

With a weeping, bleeding Ainsley as evidence against her, Natalie knew she'd only make Stuart angrier if she attempted to stay and convince him of the truth. She let Bartholomew lead her out of the lounge. As soon as the door closed behind them, she said, "Stuart is wrong. He walked in late and misinterpreted what he saw. Ainsley is lying to him. I have no idea why."

Bartholomew tightened his grip on her arm and slowed his gait to snail speed, probably in hopes of keeping her on her feet. She was tottering as though she'd lost her already limited ability to walk in heels.

"Are you injured?" he asked.

"No."

"Tell me what happened."

She told him. Flat, truthful words that sounded like lies and madness. He listened without comment as he led her to a small room with a desk, a few upholstered chairs, and tranquil landscape paintings on the walls.

"Have a seat," he said. "Will you wait here, please?"

"Yes."

He exited and closed the door behind him.

CHAPTER 23

NORMALLY, NATALIE ENJOYED THE SCENT of flowers combined in an arrangement, but in this closed office, the vase of roses, lilies, and peonies smelled like her mother's funeral, magnifying her desire to run away. Resolutely, she stayed in her chair and did her best to calm herself to the point where she didn't feel on the verge of emotional disaster.

The effort failed. The more time she had to think, the more her self-control weakened. She couldn't even seek comfort by calling Gideon—her phone and purse were in the lounge. She'd been too flustered to remember to pick them up when Bartholomew had walked her out of there.

Her shoulder ached from Stuart's brutal hold, and her hand hurt from Ainsley's use of it as a weapon. She wished she could go wash Ainsley's blood off her fingers, but she didn't dare leave the office. She didn't want to do anything that might in any way be viewed as suspicious.

Too late. Stuart would fervently swear he'd caught Natalie attacking his wife. Ainsley would swear Natalie had punched her. Natalie would be left offering a defense more absurd than anything she'd told the police so far.

Hitting a new low of absurdity was a spectacular distance to sink.

Judging by the sounds of conversation in the hallway, the funeral service was over. Natalie shut her eyes, rested her head against the wall behind her, and tried again to soothe herself.

Not working. She wanted to burst into wherever the detectives were talking to Ainsley and Stuart, corner Ainsley, and shout, "Why are you doing this to me?"

Think about that. Why is *she doing this?* Were her actions completely irrational? She'd been agitated when fleeing the service, agitated while trying to scrub the skin off her hands, but calmer and seemingly more rational before she'd staged the attack. Had it been a cunning, deliberate action?

What had she meant when she'd claimed Natalie had tried to convince her she'd killed Baxter? After their discussion about guilt, the accusation would have been *almost* decipherable if she'd claimed Natalie had attempted to convince her she'd killed Drew—but Baxter? Was guilt over the miserable fact that Drew had died in her home overflowing into an irrational conviction that she was somehow responsible for Baxter's death as well? Natalie thought of Ainsley's frantic hand washing. Did she struggle with obsessive-compulsive disorder? She might truly think she'd done something to cause Baxter's death. But in that case, Natalie would have expected her to cling to the guilt even as it tore her apart, not try to off-load it onto Natalie—

A knock on the door made Natalie start. The door opened, and Turner and Bartholomew walked into the room. *Good cop/bad cop, part two.*

"Sorry to keep you waiting," Bartholomew said.

"It's fine."

Bartholomew sat in the chair next to her. Turner remained standing in front of the desk.

"You already gave Detective Bartholomew a summary of what happened," Turner said. "Would you repeat it for me?"

Natalie did so. When she finished, Turner said, "Why would Mrs. MacKerron want to make it appear you'd assaulted her?"

"I don't know."

"You 'don't know' much about any of the incidents occurring around you," Turner said. "Which are occurring at a phenomenal rate."

The stone in her ring had rotated, digging into the finger next to it. With her thumb, she poked twitchily at the ring, rotating it to the correct position. Out of the corner of her eye, she saw Bartholomew's gaze shift to her fidgety right hand. Her bloodstained hand wearing the ring that had split Ainsley's lip. "Did Stuart show you the text I sent him? Telling him I was with Ainsley in the women's lounge? How does Ainsley explain my summoning him as a witness if I were about to attack her?"

"How long have you known Mrs. MacKerron?" Turner asked, ignoring Natalie's question. Natalie almost repeated it but decided it wouldn't help. Given the way Turner was treating her, Ainsley's explanation must have been credible. Did the police think Natalie had intended for Stuart to see Ainsley supposedly hurting herself but Ainsley's resistance had prevented Natalie from setting the stage?

"I've known her about . . . six weeks? The receptionist we'd hired originally ended up with a family situation that prevented her from doing the job, so she quit. We hired Ainsley about a week after the clinic opened. That's how long I've known her. Dr. Marianne Avery, our psychiatrist, has known her longer. She's the one who told Ainsley about the opening for a receptionist."

"Were you aware Mrs. MacKerron is superstitious?"

"Superstitious?"

"That she believes in ghosts," Turner said. "That she believes they can interfere with our lives."

"Yes, I knew that. She mentioned it when we were talking about Heather Osbourne and her certainty that her great-great-great-grand-mother's ghost was haunting the Stoker Building."

"Did you tell Mrs. MacKerron you saw a ghost today at Mr. Drummond's funeral?"

"No, of course not."

"Did you tell her a ghost had communicated with you about her?"

"No."

"Did you tell her, 'Watch out for ghosts' and that a ghost would reveal her guilt in Baxter Quincy's murder?"

"*No*," Natalie said, her patience gone. "This is ridiculous. If the rest of your questions are along this line, no to all of them. Until I followed her out of the funeral today, I hadn't even spoken to her since Baxter died."

"You didn't speak to her at work yesterday?"

"I wasn't *at* work yesterday." The first of the explanation emerged quietly, but the volume got louder with each word. "I got kicked out of my clinic—put on 'leave' to avoid the risk of my causing scandal and scaring the clients, the risk of my *destroying* everything I've been building."

"But you contacted Ainsley MacKerron several times yesterday via text and call," Turner said.

"I *tried* to. If she showed you her call list, I assume you saw they were missed calls. She didn't pick up. If you read the texts or listened to the voice mail I left, you know they were messages asking her how she was doing and offering my help."

"What kind of help?" Turner asked.

"What *kind* of help? What do you think—that I was offering to brain-wash her? I called her because I was concerned about her. I wanted to support her, find out if she needed anything. That's why I sought her out today. I didn't attack her. I didn't manipulate her. *I care about her.* Doesn't that make a little more sense than thinking I warned her a ghost will expose her as a killer?"

Neither Turner nor Bartholomew responded, and this time their calculated silence snapped the last thread of her composure, freeing roaring anger. "*I'm done with this.* First, I'm writing ghost letters to Heather, then I'm playing mind games to control Kenton, now I'm using supernatural gaslighting on Ainsley?" As the words escaped, she realized the accusation about Kenton had been Josie's not Turner's, but who cared? "I don't use psychology as a weapon. I've *never* used it as a weapon! I want to *help* people. That's what I do; that's all I want. Whose evaluation of my character are you taking here—my mother's?"

"Natalie," Bartholomew said quietly.

"Is *she* the ghost we're dealing with? Did she tell you I like manipulating people, that I want control? Power? Money? More of *this*?" Natalie curled her fingers around her necklace and yanked it forward to display the pearls—her mother's. Why had she even worn it, like the spoils of conquest, like greed in jeweled form? Pearls dug into her neck and the clasp snapped. Loose strands whipped her arm.

Turner's expression was so keen that he'd no doubt memorized every word she'd shouted. "How do you deal with people who threaten what you want, Dr. Marsh?"

Natalie flung the broken necklace to the floor and sprang to her feet. "I'm not lying to you. I've never lied to you about anything. You *know* I've been proven right before, no matter how bad things looked, but now you think I'm a manipulative killer? I'm sick of this. I'm finished here." She stalked toward the door. "Get Ainsley MacKerron to a doctor because she needs help. I've told you everything I know. If you want me to stay, arrest me." Natalie jerked the door open, slammed it behind her, and fled down the hallway toward the exit. She was nearly certain she was about to get grabbed, handcuffed, and carted to jail, but she wasn't going to stand and wait for it. She was frantic to get out of the building before anger scorched away everything except pain and she was curled on the floor, sobbing, immobilized by anguish she thought she'd dealt with.

Only a few cars remained in the parking lot. She reached her car on the far side of the lot and realized she didn't have her purse. No purse, no car keys or house keys, no phone. If she wanted to drive away, she'd have to walk back into the funeral home and face Turner and Bartholomew, who probably knew what had become of the belongings she'd left in the lounge.

Natalie planted both hands against the hood of her car and arched forward, body shaking. How could she have lost control in there, falling apart in an unprofessional, shrieking mess?

Unprofessional. Did she even have a profession anymore?

Calm down. Calm down. You can handle crisis situations.

Other people's crisis situations.

Footsteps approached her, but they were lighter than either Turner's or Bartholomew's. She didn't turn around. No matter who it was, she didn't want to talk to them or even show them her face.

"Natalie." A woman's voice. A hand rested on her shoulder. "What's going on?"

Marianne. Surprised, Natalie pressed her hands harder against the car, as though pushing downward would cancel out her trembling so Marianne wouldn't feel it. The pressure made her shoulder and her wrist hurt. "I . . . left my purse inside. My keys. I didn't know you were at the funeral."

"I wasn't," Marianne said. "But the funeral director here is a friend. She called and told me you punched the daylights out of Ainsley MacKerron in the women's restroom and the police were here interrogating you about it."

That sounded like a story of two bickering high school girls. Natalie wished she could laugh, but the fact that the funeral director—and who knew who else—was already spreading rumors made her want to find an object she could smash with her bare hands. The hood of her car was too sturdy. *Find some Baccarat crystal to smash. I hear Ainsley has a lovely vase.*

"Natalie?" Marianne's touch evolved from gentle to firm as she forcibly turned Natalie around. "Tell me what happened."

Natalie couldn't meet Marianne's gaze for more than an instant, and she absolutely couldn't explain the whole situation without breaking down. She managed a few curt words. "Ainsley lied to the police. I didn't hurt her."

"Why would she do that? Who *did* hurt her?"

"She . . . hurt herself. I was there."

"She hurt herself! Why?"

Natalie shook her head.

"What did the police say?"

Natalie shook her head again. "Later. I'm going home." *Without keys. Going home to where Baxter died.*

Even without eye contact, she could sense the incisiveness of Marianne's gaze. "Yes, you are going home," Marianne said. "To *my* home." She steered Natalie toward the Mercedes parked in a shady area. "You're exhausted. You're going to sleep, then we're going to talk, and we're going to figure out what in the name of the devil's red satin bowtie is going on."

Natalie thought about objecting as Marianne unlocked the passenger door and guided her into the seat, but resistance would take determination she didn't currently have. Determination and an alternate plan. Right now, her alternatives were to go in search of her purse, which involved facing the cops she'd just screamed at and walked out on, or sit on the asphalt and cry.

"You stay here," Marianne said. "I'll track down your purse." She left the car door open and hastened toward the funeral home.

Glad for the breeze drifting into the car, Natalie wilted against the comfortable leather seat. Ainsley's blood on her hand made the skin sting, pain she knew was psychosomatic. Her hand was bruised but not scraped or cut.

It took longer for Marianne to return than Natalie had expected, but she didn't mind the delay. The longer it took, the longer before she had to talk to anyone. Finally, Marianne approached carrying Natalie's purse. Without handing it to Natalie, she shut the passenger door. She walked to the driver's side, tossed the purse into the backseat, and settled behind the wheel. "It was in Yvonne's—the funeral director's—office."

"Thank you. And wait . . . I can drive myself."

Marianne started the engine. "I'm sure you can, boss." She shifted into reverse. "And I can eat a bucket of habanero peppers, but that doesn't mean either of those things would have positive consequences. Buckle up. I told Yvonne we were leaving your car here for a while, and she's fine with that."

Feeling a stir of empathy for Heather Osbourne, Natalie fastened her seat belt. "You're kidnapping me."

"It's not a kidnapping. It's an involuntary commitment. I've been keeping an eye on you. Worrying about you. You've been bashed repeatedly with a mind-boggling amount of trouble. How many hits can you take without pausing for a moment to heal?"

"Work can be healing."

"Within reason, and your reason tank is running on fumes. Let's talk about effective self-care, shall we? How important is that for a therapist?"

"I know it's important."

"Did you learn anything at Hilary's lecture the other night? No wonder you wanted to hear it twice. You didn't listen the first time. Or, apparently, the second time."

"I did listen."

"How are you doing at applying what you learned?"

Natalie didn't reply.

"Okay, I'll answer for you. If you're at the point of projecting your conflicts with your deceased mother onto a current police investigation, you're not doing well."

Cringing inside, Natalie said, "You talked to the police."

"Of course I did. I asked Yvonne where they were, and I marched up and interrogated them. Asked them how you didn't get arrested, to be blunt."

Searing knots of pain formed in Natalie's aching muscles. "Did they tell you anything?"

"I badgered a few things out of them. They didn't witness the fight. When they pressed Stuart, he had to admit he hadn't actually seen you striking her, and the rest is your word against Ainsley's. If you want my expert opinion, you both sound nuts."

At least Marianne didn't think she was the *only* crazy person in the situation. It was a pitiful victory, but Natalie was grateful for it.

"They asked me about your previous interaction with her," Marianne said. "I told them as far as I knew, you'd never been anything but kind and gracious to her, and she to you. They asked me to again verify that you were at Cornell the night Baxter died, and I said listen, gents, I already made a statement about this, and I don't do perjury, so that stands. Natalie, I need to warn you that my testimony is not viewed as impervious. When I talked to them the other day, I got questions like, was I certain you were there the entire time? Did I ever look away from where you were sitting? Could I swear you never left the meeting? Was I certain it was *you* the entire time? You're bright enough to know how I had to answer those questions."

Natalie groaned softly. The police had been considering the swapped-places-with-a-friend scenario even before Stuart had invented it today?

"I'm not trying to scare you," Marianne said. "I'm trying to help you understand that this catastrophe wasn't anywhere near resolved before you and Ainsley faced off in the restroom. There's a mountain of trouble for you to work through, and if you don't take care of yourself, you're heading for core meltdown. In fact, after what I learned from the cops about your behavior today, I'd say the alarms are wailing."

Natalie had no idea how to fend off that diagnosis, so she kept looking out the windshield, randomly watching a bicyclist pedal through the intersection ahead of them.

Marianne continued. "I told them I don't know a thing about who punched whom, and I don't know anything about Quincy's death beyond what I've already told them, but I do know I'm taking Dr. Marsh home with me, where I'm going to force-feed her a decent meal, dope her, and sequester her in my guest room. No one's going to hear from her until she's slept for about eighteen hours, so hold any further questions until tomorrow."

"Wait," Natalie said. "I didn't agree to all this."

"Which part of 'involuntary' don't you understand?"

"Marianne."

"Do I need to call for reinforcements? I'll start with Gideon. If I told him I was trying to make you step away from this mayhem and take care of yourself, whose side do you think he'd be on?"

Natalie didn't reply. Even without knowing about today's altercation with Ainsley and Natalie's tantrum with the cops, Gideon would be adamantly on Marianne's side.

"So you're ready to admit I'm right?" Marianne asked.

Natalie massaged her forehead. She had a headache. Again. "I swear, I told the police the truth. Ainsley grabbed my hand and used it to punch herself. She caught me so off guard I couldn't pull away in time."

"Okay."

"You don't believe me."

"I don't care about believing or not believing anyone right now. I care about your emotional and physical health."

Words flooded out of Natalie. She wanted Marianne to hear her version of what had taken place in the lounge, not rely simply on whatever Turner and Bartholomew had told her. When she finished, she asked, "Have you ever seen signs of compulsive behaviors in Ainsley? OCD, maybe?"

"No."

"Maybe guilt over Drew's death is exacerbating symptoms she was able to previously keep hidden. The hand washing—maybe she feels dirty, contaminated. Blood on her hands."

"You're suggesting *Ainsley* killed Drew? I hope you didn't suggest that to the police. You have enough check marks in the crazy column."

"No, I'm not suggesting she killed him. She had nothing to gain, and she's devastated . . ." *Was* there anything Ainsley or Stuart had gained from Drew's death? Stuart might gain the job as Bob Chapman's hiking expert, but who would kill over that?

Natalie's thoughts spun at high speed, flinging out snippets of speculation. Even if the attack on Drew had been the point and the vase theft a red herring meant to implicate the serial thief—Heather, apparently—an attacker wouldn't strike someone in the leg in an effort to kill them. Fatal complications with a broken bone were rare; Drew's death had been a fluke. Surgery, physical therapy—in a few weeks he should have been back on his feet, and within a few months, he should have been out hiking again.

A few months. Chapman would have had to hire someone else for his much-anticipated trek on the John Muir Trail. Chapman could be extremely—quirkily, absurdly—generous with people he hired as part of his personal staff. Drew Drummond had struck Natalie as a braggart, so if Chapman was offering him big money, Stuart and Ainsley would have known about it. Ainsley had even mentioned the money . . . When had that been? Not after Drew's death . . .

The party in the Stoker gardens. Ainsley's remark had initiated that conversation about backpacking: *He's paying Stuart's cousin an insane amount of money to be his personal trail guide.*

An insane amount of money. What if Ainsley had decided she wanted that money?

What if she, or she and Stuart, had set up the attack on Drew? What if they'd wanted to take him out of commission but not kill him?

That would give Ainsley ample reason to feel frantic guilt over his death.

Natalie's question sprang out, abrupt and wobbly as though she'd released it too soon. "Do you know how much money Bob Chapman was offering Drew Drummond for serving as his hiking guru?"

"Good heavens, no. Why?"

"Could it have been enough to tempt someone to try to steal that contract from him? To go to extreme measures to put him out of the running?"

"Tell me you're not inventing a motive for Ainsley or Stuart to have attacked him." Marianne's tone was uncharacteristically irritated, and Natalie didn't answer. She concentrated on remembering anything else the MacKerrons had said about the Trekmeister position. In that conversation at the Stoker party, Ainsley had mentioned what an excellent guide Stuart would be. At the dinner at Il Giardino that Baxter had hosted, the MacKerrons had been sitting near Drew. Had they shown any signs of hostility toward Drew's windfall?

And the dinner at Natalie's house after Drew's death . . . Stuart's response when Natalie had mentioned the possibility of his taking over the job for Drew. *"Baxter Quincy will try to nail the contract for Quincy Travel."*

Baxter Quincy.

A chill crawled over her scalp and tingled along her arms. Could Ainsley have concluded that Baxter was a barrier to Stuart's winning the position?

With Drew dead, did she feel she had nothing left to lose morally?

Natalie's heart pulsed with cold, shivery beats. Baxter had died at Natalie's house. Ainsley knew where Natalie lived. Could today's incident be a continuation of her first attempt to frame Natalie by choosing the site of Baxter's death?

Could Ainsley have lured Baxter there? Stabbed him? Was she capable of that?

"*Natalie.* Are you with me?"

Natalie nodded, though she knew she must have missed something Marianne had said to her, or Marianne wouldn't have spoken her name so urgently.

"I asked if you have any allergies."

"I don't."

"What's your doctor's name?"

"My regular doctor? Krista Schulberg."

"Oh, she's excellent. I like Krista."

"I don't need a doctor right now. What I need is a lawyer." Natalie hesitated and tried to make herself hesitate longer—she should wait until she had more information—but the words burst out. "You're friends with Mel Chapman."

"Yes," Marianne said warily.

"Will you give me her number? She'll have a way to get in touch with her husband while he's out of the country. If we can learn from Bob what he was offering Drew, that could help establish—"

"I'm not giving you Mel's number. Once you've had some rest, you'll regret calling her and asking bizarre questions that could get you permanently cut off from your clinic."

"I'll be tactful—"

"There's no way you could be tactful enough not to come across as a lunatic."

"But—"

Marianne shook her head. "Since you seem only half able to listen to me, I assume you aren't listening to yourself either, but trust me, you don't want to talk to Mel right now."

Words kept spilling out. If she held them back, they'd fill her lungs and drown her. "If there was enough money at stake, that could be a motive for Ainsley. I heard Stuart say Baxter was a rival for the Chapman position. First Drew, now Baxter dead—"

"Natalie." Marianne steered into the driveway of her spacious, stone-accented house. "Honey, I understand where you're coming from. You've been hideously betrayed before, but to suggest Ainsley is capable of attacking Stuart's cousin *and* plunging a knife into a man's chest, all so Stuart could steal a *part-time job*? That's completely irrational."

The same fury and frustration she'd felt when getting interrogated by Turner and Bartholomew stormed into Natalie's voice. "I don't *want* to think Ainsley could do this. I didn't pull her name out of a hat and decide to accuse her of murder. I'll set aside speculation; let me tell you what I *know*." Natalie clenched her bruised hand and raised it. "Today, she rammed *this* into her face, twice. Then she lied to Stuart and the police, attempting to frame me for assault and claiming I'd tried to brainwash her into believing she killed Baxter. Those are *facts*, not my imagination."

Marianne parked in the garage, not answering Natalie. The quiet contrasted with Natalie's rant, highlighting how agitated she'd sounded.

Grappling with her anger, Natalie tried to speak with composure. "If you think I'm nuts, *you* come up with a theory to explain why she'd do that."

Marianne glanced at Natalie but still didn't answer. She opened her door and stepped out of the car.

Natalie grabbed her purse from the backseat and exited the car as well. Marianne met her at the front of the car and took her by the arm as though afraid she'd run to hunt down Ainsley and babble crazy accusations.

"A foot in the door with Bob can be worth a lot," Natalie said. "You know that."

"That's true. Bob enjoys being generous."

Relieved that Marianne finally seemed to be considering her theory, Natalie said, "You've known Ainsley a long time, right? How ambitious would you say she is? What about Stuart?"

Marianne escorted Natalie into the house. "I'd rather not make guesses about their ambitions."

"I'd rather the police not make guesses about me being a double murderer," Natalie snapped.

"You're shaken about what happened at the funeral home," Marianne said. "You're angry and needing answers."

This annoyed Natalie. Marianne *wasn't* considering her theories. She was reflecting Natalie's emotions back to her, trying to ground her. "You don't even believe me about what happened there."

"I don't know what happened, but I believe it was upsetting for you." Marianne guided her down a hallway and through a vaulted-ceilinged living room that would have made the Metropolitan Museum of Art look second-rate. She led Natalie down another hallway and opened a door near the end of it.

"Your room and bathroom." She prodded Natalie inside. "Get out of those uncomfortable clothes, and go take a hot shower."

Natalie wanted to yell that this was not a problem a hot shower could fix, but when she looked down at her wrinkled blouse, she noticed flecks of blood on the cream-colored fabric. Her skirt was so askew that the back zipper was now a side zipper, and her feet throbbed in her shoes.

She flexed her bloodstained right hand. A shower did sound wonderful.

"I'll bring in comfortable clothes for you to wear while you rest," Marianne said. "We're close to the same size. My clothes should fit you. Do you remember where the kitchen is?"

"Yes. I promise I don't have it in for Ainsley. But her behavior today—"

"Ainsley was at the Cascata party the night Baxter Quincy died. You know that. I heard her mention her plans to you. I'm sure witnesses can testify she was there."

Natalie had forgotten that. "Maybe she's protecting Stuart."

"I don't know what she's doing. Right now, it's not my job to figure that out." Marianne headed for the door. "After you've cleaned up, come to the kitchen."

"*Wait.*" Natalie took a hasty step in pursuit and turned her ankle. Wincing, she righted herself. "Will you at least consider giving me Mrs. Chapman's number so—"

"Lunch will be grilled chicken, citrus couscous, and green salad," Marianne interrupted. "Dessert will be two milligrams of Ativan. Give me any trouble and I swear I'll bring the entire clinic staff here to gang up on you. I'm not letting you call Mel. You need rest, not an opportunity to self-destruct. Go take a shower." She stepped into the hallway and shut the door.

CHAPTER 24

Turner, then Bartholomew shook Gideon's hand. "Thank you for taking time out of your workday to meet with us," Bartholomew said.

"Not a problem," Gideon said grimly, though he had the feeling it would be a problem soon. An ulcer-causing problem. The detectives wouldn't summon him in the middle of the day and double-team him if they wanted only a scrap of insignificant information. At least they'd invited him to meet them in the park next to the city offices rather than cornering him in his office.

"Have a seat." Turner indicated the tree-shaded picnic table where they'd been waiting for him.

He sat facing the two detectives. "What can I do for you?"

"You were with Dr. Marsh at Drew Drummond's funeral earlier today," Turner said.

"Yes." Stress zapped Gideon's gut, choosing real estate for the ulcer. They had *more* questions about Natalie?

"After Ainsley MacKerron became too emotional to continue her performance and exited the chapel, Dr. Marsh followed her," Turner said.

"Yes."

"Did Dr. Marsh say anything to you before she followed Mrs. MacKerron?"

"Telepathically," Gideon said, then realized a goofy answer didn't belong in an interview with the police. "I mean, after Ainsley bolted, Natalie gave me a look, and I knew what she wanted to do. I asked if she wanted me to come with her. She said no, that Ainsley would be more comfortable with just her, and if she didn't return, she'd talk to me tonight. We went to the funeral in separate cars."

"You say you knew what she wanted to do," Turner said. "What was that?"

"Check on Ainsley, see if she could help her. She'd been worried about her for the whole service. Ainsley looked like she was having a rocky time up there."

"What is your assessment of the relationship between Dr. Marsh and Mrs. MacKerron?"

"Uh . . . I'd like to know what's going on here."

"Please answer the question, sir."

"They get along fine. Natalie was pleased with Ainsley's work."

"Have you ever witnessed tension between them?"

"No. Why?"

"After Dr. Marsh went in pursuit of Mrs. MacKerron today, did you hear from Dr. Marsh?"

"Yes, she texted me to say she'd found Ainsley and she'd stay with her until Stuart came out. I haven't heard anything from her since then." The stress etching Gideon's stomach got hotter. "Please tell me no one's been hurt."

"Why would you ask that?" Turner said.

"For real?" Gideon wanted to turn his back on the cops, pull out his phone, and call Natalie immediately. "Two murders in the past week, and now you're grilling me about potential conflict between two people, and you think it's strange I'm worried something rotten happened?"

"There was an altercation between Dr. Marsh and Mrs. MacKerron," Turner said.

"What kind of altercation?"

Turner explained. Gideon tried not to gape at him.

"No," Gideon said when Turner finished. "No. There is not a chance, not a sliver of a chance, not a microchance that Natalie played malicious mind games with a grieving woman and slugged her in the face."

"Natalie is human." Bartholomew spoke with sympathy. "Good people under stress can do things that surprise us."

"Try being a police officer and you'll understand that," Turner said.

"In that case," Gideon said, "I assume you're considering that Ainsley MacKerron could be the good person doing surprising things."

"Mr. Radcliffe." Turner leaned forward, sealing his gaze with Gideon's. "You've seen Natalie Marsh under stress. Have you ever seen her lose her temper?"

"No."

"Yell exaggerated statements? Break something in anger? Walk out on a discussion and slam the door?"

"No to all of the above. She handles stress better than anyone else I know."

"We witnessed her do all those things earlier this afternoon," Turner said.

Gideon looked at Bartholomew, hoping for a *He's kidding*.

"That was her response when we questioned her about the fight with Mrs. MacKerron," Bartholomew said. "We're not sharing that as evidence of any crime but to show that she's not behaving as she normally does."

Natalie had done those things? Gideon was tempted to accuse Turner and Bartholomew of lying, but he kept his mouth shut, knowing the accusation would come across accurately as frightened and defensive. He realized he was jiggling both legs and fidgeting with the phone he hadn't noticed he'd taken out of his pocket. He wanted to get to Natalie so acutely that it was all he could do not to leap from the bench and sprint for his car. He checked his phone—no missed calls. Why hadn't she called him? Why hadn't she told him what Ainsley had done?

Not behaving as she normally does.

"Any new messages from Dr. Marsh?" Turner asked, a question Gideon conceded was fair play since he was looking at his phone in the middle of police questioning.

"No," he said. Where was Natalie now? Back at the hotel? Home? Somewhere else? "Look, no matter how upset she is, she wouldn't attack Ainsley or play cold-blooded games with her memory. You guys need to figure out why Ainsley's lying. Maybe *she* has something to hide when it comes to Baxter Quincy."

Turner's phone rang. He drew it from an inner suit pocket, glanced at it, and said, "Excuse me." He walked away from the table, not stopping until he was out of eavesdropping range.

Gideon sat pointlessly staring at Turner's back until Bartholomew said, "We're not trying to pin anything on Dr. Marsh. We're exploring possibilities."

"Yeah, I know. If you could explore them a little more gently, I'm sure she'd appreciate it."

"To be frank, we've cut her a lot of slack. I hope that wasn't a mistake."

"It wasn't." Gideon couldn't endure more waiting. "Do you mind if I give her a quick call while we wait for Detective Turner? If she was that, uh, stressed during your interview, I'd like to check on her."

"Go ahead."

Gideon wanted to retreat from the table for privacy like Turner had, but he didn't want it to appear as though he thought Natalie might incriminate herself during the conversation. He tapped the screen to call her. Voice mail. He texted. No answer.

He lowered his phone.

"Not answering?" Bartholomew asked. "She's probably resting. Dr. Avery came to the funeral home upon hearing of the disturbance, and she told us she was taking Dr. Marsh home—to Dr. Avery's home, that is—to rest."

Good for Marianne. "With respect, I hope Dr. Avery also told you guys you're crazy for hassling Natalie."

"She's concerned about all parties. She's not passing judgment on anything. I assume Dr. Marsh must be confident in her objectivity or she wouldn't have gone with her, given Dr. Avery's relationship to Mrs. MacKerron."

"Her relationship?"

"Her family relationship."

"What are we talking about?"

"Dr. Avery is Mrs. MacKerron's aunt," Bartholomew said. "I assumed you knew that."

"No." And if Natalie knew it, she'd never mentioned it.

Turner returned to the table. "That was our handwriting analyst," he said. "She's confident that the new letter from Heather Osbourne's dead grandmother was not penned by Dr. Marsh. Feel free to share that with her."

"Thank you," Gideon said, deeply grateful for a piece of evidence in Natalie's favor. "Did Heather write it herself?"

"No," Turner said. "The handwriting isn't consistent with Heather's script. Thank you for speaking with us. We won't take up more of your day, but if you learn anything remotely relevant to this investigation, contact us immediately."

"I will. I know the drill, sorry to say." Gideon rose from the picnic table. "At least now you have evidence that someone who isn't Natalie was messing with Heather's head. Have you checked the letter against Ainsley's handwriting?"

"Yes," Turner said. "The handwriting isn't hers either."

* * *

The steaming shower—especially in Marianne's spacious guest bathroom, with its slate walls and rainfall shower—felt so soothing that Natalie lingered, letting hot water ease muscle and mind aches. As tension lessened, dismay at her own behavior swelled. Turner and Bartholomew were doing their jobs as objectively as possible. She knew that. Why hadn't she been objective as well? Why had she taken the interview personally, letting their questions slash open old scars?

What had become of the necklace she'd made an object of her anger? She'd started wearing it again a few months ago, proud that she'd been able to wear it without feeling that it yoked her to pain. So much for pride. It was a miracle she wasn't in jail right now.

As soon as she had more information on how tempting the Chapman job might have been to Ainsley and Stuart, she'd pass that on to the police, with her apologies. She had to admit Marianne was right about her not trying to contact Chapman at the moment; that *would* backfire. First, she'd explore a different possibility for learning about the appeal of the job: Lauren Bell. If the position was lucrative and Baxter's company had had a shot at it, there was a chance he'd mentioned it to Lauren.

Reluctant to leave the luxury of the shower but afraid if she stayed longer, Marianne would send a search party, Natalie turned the water off, dried herself on a plush towel, and walked into the bedroom. Marianne had left clothes on the bed—a loose, silky, long-sleeved shirt, drawstring pants of the same material, and thick socks. Grateful for any clothes that weren't heels and a bloodstained blouse, Natalie dressed, ran her fingers through her wet hair as a minimal nod to grooming, and went to grab her purse from where she'd set it on the dresser. She'd call Lauren now. Lauren was probably working and couldn't answer, but Natalie would feel better even leaving a message—one tiny step toward figuring out this catastrophe.

She reached into the pocket of her purse, but the phone wasn't there. She checked the rest of the purse—no phone. Her broken pearl necklace was there—the detectives must have given it to Marianne's funeral-director friend, Yvonne—as were her keys and everything else, but no phone. She'd had the phone out in the lounge. She must have set it somewhere instead of returning it to her purse, and whoever had picked up her purse hadn't noticed the phone.

She slapped her purse onto the dresser. She could imagine how Marianne would react if Natalie asked to borrow her phone to contact Lauren. Better to ask Marianne if Natalie could contact Yvonne about the phone. Marianne would consider *that* a sane request.

Fluffy socks soundless on the carpet, Natalie walked toward the kitchen, disconcerted by how tiring it was to hold a normal pace. She *was* worn out. Marianne had called that right too. If she could speak with Lauren and relay to the police anything relevant, then she'd obediently check out until tomorrow.

As she neared the kitchen, the scents of grilling chicken and orange zest made her mouth water. She stepped into the room, a palace of granite, wood, and gourmet appliances.

". . . being particularly rational, going by what Stuart says." Marianne was talking on the phone while she chopped parsley. "I wouldn't do that yet." She glanced at Natalie. "Excuse me, I need to go," she said into the phone. "We'll talk soon. Yes, thank you. I'll do that." She hung up. "Have a seat. Lunch is ready."

Natalie wanted to ask whom she'd been talking to, but it was an intrusive question, and she didn't want to thank Marianne for her hospitality by being rude. But clearly Marianne had been discussing the conflict at the funeral home. What had she told—

"Have a seat," Marianne repeated. She took a spatula and lifted a sizzling chicken filet off the grill that was part of her stovetop.

Controlling herself, Natalie sat at the table in the breakfast nook. In front of her was a tall glass of chilled water. Sliced strawberries, sliced cucumbers, and mint springs floated in the water pitcher on the table. The drink looked so refreshing that Natalie immediately picked up her glass and took a few swallows. "Your water is better than my meals."

Marianne chuckled and set a plate in front of Natalie. Grilled chicken, couscous, a salad of baby greens sprinkled with raspberries, almonds, and feta cheese.

"Thank you," Natalie said. "This is fantastic. You didn't need to go to this much work."

"How much work could I have gone to? We haven't even been here an hour. It's all fast and easy." Marianne placed a second filled plate on the table, poured herself a drink from the pitcher, and sat with Natalie.

"My phone isn't in my purse," Natalie said as Marianne picked up her fork and knife. "It must have gotten knocked under the couch in the lounge. If I could borrow your phone, I'll call the funeral home and ask about it."

Marianne swallowed a bite of chicken. "It's not at the funeral home. I have it."

"Oh, perfect." Natalie picked up her glass and drank several more sips. Plain water would be a letdown after this fruit-infused deliciousness. "Did Yvonne drop it by?"

"No, she gave it to me when I picked up your purse. I didn't think you needed it back yet."

Natalie frowned. "I do need it, thank you."

Marianne held up a forkful of couscous sprinkled with parsley and flecks of orange peel. "Eat your lunch."

"Why did you confiscate my phone?"

"Why do you think? To give you less disaster cleanup to do later. To force you to let the rest of the world go for a few hours and focus on your own well-being."

"I'd have more well-being if you weren't holding me incommunicado."

"Eat and rest and get yourself to the point where you're less likely to call people and start ranting questions and accusations you'll regret. *Then* I'll let you communicate with the outside world."

Anger reared; Natalie wrestled with it. Losing her cool with Marianne—again—wouldn't get her phone returned. "You are overstepping."

Marianne arched one gray eyebrow. "Overstepping what? Professional boundaries? So fire me. Then we can both look for new practices, because Bob will cut you loose as soon as you start spreading rumors that your receptionist is stabbing people in your kitchen."

Frustration cramped her stomach. She took another gulp of fruit-tasting water, hoping to relax herself physically, at least, but felt worse.

"Eat," Marianne said. "I'm overstepping as a friend. Honestly, I wanted to corner you even before you started shouting at cops and flinging pearls. You have remarkable resiliency, but you don't have superpowers. You're so set on helping everyone else that you don't stop to realize when you need help yourself. I know work is therapeutic for you, but, Natalie, it's not *that* therapeutic. When was the last time you saw a therapist for yourself?"

"Fine, I'll see someone," Natalie said brusquely. "Give me my phone."

"Did you see someone last year after Gideon hauled your nearly dead self out of the lake? Or was almost getting murdered by a friend not enough trauma to shake you?"

"I . . . meant to go for counseling. I was busy trying to get funding and recruit staff for the clinic—"

"Oh, you adorable young hypocrite."

"I said I'll see someone. I know it's important. Give me my phone."

"Eat your chicken. You'll like it. It's one of my go-to recipes."

Natalie cut a bite of chicken and put it in her mouth, but her tongue was dry. Objectively, she knew the chicken was both delicious and tender, but chewing it took her so long she might as well have been gnawing the leather seat of the chair. She stopped fighting her anger; now she *wanted* to feel wrath at Marianne's overbearing actions. That would be more comfortable than the panicky fight-or-flight sensation that had her scanning the kitchen for exits and listening to determine if anyone else was in the house. If she made a run for the door, what would Marianne—

A run for the door? Really? What's wrong with you?

"Who were you talking to about Stuart?" she asked.

Marianne ground a sprinkling of black pepper onto her couscous. "Erik."

"Did you call him, or did he call you?"

"He called because Stuart called him, informing him I was covering for you in Baxter Quincy's murder."

Natalie's fist closed around the handle of her fork. Quickly, she released it so it wouldn't appear she planned to use the fork as a weapon.

"I told him that was nonsense," Marianne said. "I'm not covering for anyone. I told the police the simple truth. And don't panic. Erik won't take any action at the moment beyond what he and Regina have already done, putting you on leave."

"What about Ainsley?"

"The same. She'll remain on leave for now. I told Erik something I'll tell you: Ainsley is my niece. I don't think you knew that."

"Your *niece?*"

"She didn't want me to tell anyone at Nefesh Bria, and I swore on the ghost of Caesar that I wouldn't, but given the circumstances, I don't think that promise holds any longer."

"Why didn't she want you telling us?"

"She was concerned that people would think she got the job because of me, that she wasn't smart enough to get hired on her own, or that she was riding my coattails. She struggles with feeling inferior."

"Are you her 'rich aunt' who gave her the Baccarat vase?"

"Yes, she wanted fine crystal for a wedding gift. I said, 'Don't you want something more practical?' She said no, she wanted a showpiece. She was determined to have a collection someday. She loves crystal."

"Collecting fine crystal sounds like an expensive hobby."

"She's looking toward the long term."

Natalie picked up her fork and skewered a raspberry but didn't put it in her mouth. She wanted to suggest that if Ainsley yearned for wealth, winning Bob Chapman's favor wasn't a bad way to start, but Marianne knew that already.

Ainsley had set Natalie up, lied to the police, and might be connected to Baxter's murder—and Natalie had put herself in the care of Ainsley's aunt?

Another compulsive urge to sprint for the exit made Natalie twist in her chair, her gaze shifting to and from the french doors that led to a covered patio. That would be the quickest escape, unless she couldn't get past the fence that enclosed the backyard—

Stop being paranoid.

But *was* she being paranoid? When Marianne had learned of the fight at the funeral home, she'd come for Natalie, not Ainsley. Shouldn't she have gone to help her niece?

Was she helping her niece—helping her by efficiently spiriting Natalie away and preventing her from talking to anyone? By containing the truth?

"Natalie, you seem agitated," Marianne said. "Tell me what's going through your mind."

"I'm fine." The police thought she'd killed Baxter and maybe Drew. If she supposedly committed suicide while a guest at Marianne's, it would seem obvious that she'd succumbed to unendurable guilt. Marianne could tell smooth lies about Natalie's mental state and about how she'd found her . . . an overdose, maybe . . .

A heavy sensation pressed from the inside of her head outward. She lowered her fork to the table, awkwardly clanging it against the edge of her plate. Her arms felt weighted, her hands weak. Was it fatigue or stress . . . Was her vision blurring? She blinked at the glass in front of her, the nearly empty glass that had been waiting for her, that she hadn't watched Marianne fill. Could Marianne have . . .

Marianne's hand closed around her wrist. Natalie jumped, bumping her plate and sending couscous and baby greens spilling onto the tabletop.

Before she could pull free or stand, Marianne reached across the table and caught her other wrist, her grip tight.

"Easy, sweetheart," she said. "You're not going anywhere."

CHAPTER 25

GLITTERING FEAR WHIRLED THROUGH NATALIE. Struggling to wrench her arms free, she lurched to her feet, yanking Marianne up with her. Marianne's grasp slipped, then tightened again, painfully mashing Natalie's wrists.

"*Natalie. Stop.* Honey, listen to me. *Listen to me.* If you go tearing out that door in my pajamas like you're running for your life, I'll call the police and have them haul you to the ER for your own safety. That's not how you want this to end."

Her urgent words injected uncertainty into Natalie's panic, stalling the fight. Motionless, face-to-face with Marianne over the table, Natalie looked into her eyes and saw deep anxiety.

Marianne spoke softly. "Honey, what do you think I'm going to do to you?"

Natalie couldn't answer.

"I'm so sorry," Marianne said. "I picked the worst moment imaginable to tell you my relationship to Ainsley. I didn't realize how much you . . . Will you sit down, please, and talk to me?"

Fear-petrified muscles still stiff, Natalie settled tentatively into her chair.

"That's better." Marianne sat. She loosened her grip and massaged Natalie's wrists. "You're safe here. Even if my niece *is* Lady Macbeth, *I'm* not."

Natalie could have easily pulled away now, but she didn't. Dazed by comprehension of her own behavior, she stared numbly at a strawberry floating in the glass pitcher. She hadn't been drugged or poisoned by an innocent glass of fruit-infused water. She'd been poisoned by her own paranoia. "I'm losing my mind," she whispered.

"No, you're not. If I were in your shoes—or, rather, in your fuzzy socks—I'd be jumpy too." Marianne withdrew her hands. "But I'm glad we agree that you're a wreck and need to take care of yourself."

Natalie nudged her plate aside and drooped forward, resting her head on her crossed arms. She felt Marianne's touch on her hair, a motherly caress. Tears spilled from Natalie's eyes and dripped onto the table. "I should be roommates with Heather Osbourne," she murmured.

"I've heard worse ideas." From the humor in Marianne's voice, she was teasing, at least partially. Natalie remained head down, muscles slackening further, soothed by Marianne's compassionate touch.

"I'm sorry," Natalie mumbled. "You don't have time for this. You need to be at work."

"In a doctor's life, emergencies happen," Marianne said. "You're an emergency."

"I . . . really don't want to be an emergency."

"People don't usually volunteer for the position," Marianne said drily.

Natalie lifted her head. "Marianne, I *am* in somebody's crosshairs. Baxter Quincy didn't die at my house by random coincidence. Someone chose to kill him there, and they knew that would make me the prime suspect. Today—whether or not you believe this, it *did* happen—Ainsley tried to make me appear manipulative and violent. Do you see why—"

Marianne's phone rang. She glanced at it where it rested next to her plate. "It's Gideon. Do you want me to answer it?"

"Please, yes."

Marianne touched the phone, not lifting it to her ear. "Hello, Gideon."

"Hey, Marianne." Gideon sounded tense. "Sorry to bother you, but is Natalie with you? I was chatting with the cops, and they said you'd taken her home with you."

"Yes, she's right here, listening to you."

"Oh, hey, great. Natalie . . . are you all right?"

Natalie picked up her napkin and wiped her face. She wanted to claim she was fine but feared Marianne would contradict her with the truth or that Turner and Bartholomew already had. "No."

"Can't blame you."

"I would have called you once I . . . left the funeral home, but Marianne confiscated my phone." She couldn't keep her voice even, but at least she could speak without weeping. "She's holding me prisoner."

"Good," Gideon said. Marianne shot Natalie an I-told-you-so look. "Can I do anything to help you?"

"Yes." Marianne intercepted the question. "Two things: Can you ditch work and get your tail over here as soon as possible? Natalie's pretty wound up. I think she'd find your presence reassuring."

"Done," Gideon said. Natalie felt she should object, insist Gideon didn't need to take more time off, but she didn't speak. She desperately wanted him here.

"I also need you to stop at the pharmacy for me," Marianne said. "I'll text you the details and my address."

"Thanks. Natalie, here's some positive news. The police got the handwriting analysis on that so-called letter from Heather's ghost grandmother. The expert says you didn't write it."

Relief steadied Natalie's voice. "Thank goodness."

"Heather didn't write it either," Gideon said. "Neither did Ainsley. I don't know if they compared it with anyone else's writing. Okay, I'm leaving work now. See you in a few."

Marianne spoke. "Thank you, Gideon." She tapped her phone to end the call. "All right, boss, eat fast or you're going to be sharing. I didn't make enough for him."

Grateful that Gideon was on his way, Natalie shakily brushed spilled food into her napkin and tried not to wonder if the police had compared Marianne's handwriting to the penmanship on the ghost letter.

* * *

Gideon moved noiselessly out of the hallway and found Marianne sitting in an armchair in the living room, a computer on her lap. She closed the computer and set it on the alabaster table next to her.

"Have a seat, Gideon." She removed her glasses and folded them. "Is she asleep?"

"Soundly." Gideon sat on a high-backed chair that reminded him of a throne. "I get the feeling she didn't have much choice after whatever that was you gave her."

Marianne laughed softly.

Gideon surveyed the vast living room. This house was spectacular, but if he lived in a place this big, he'd lose things, like a shoe or his car keys, and never find them again. "She asked me if I'd stay here until she wakes up. I promised I would. Hope that's okay with you and Mr. Avery."

"Mr. Avery is in Philadelphia for the week. And I hope you brought a sleeping bag. I'll be astounded if we hear from her before morning."

Gideon checked his watch. It was four thirty. "I can crash on your couch. Or on your floor. Or on a kitchen shelf or on your grand piano or wherever."

"I was joking about the sleeping bag. I have another guest room; you're welcome to it. Unless you'd rather sleep on the floor outside Natalie's door with your sword in your hand."

"I might do that," Gideon said, debating whether or not he was serious.

"You're scared," Marianne said, reading him. "You almost lost her once, and there are terrifying things going on now. You have reason to be protective."

"I wish I knew what—and who—to protect her from."

"Thank you for being willing to trust me. Natalie wasn't so sure about that. I imagine that's why she's requested your bodyguard services while she's sleeping."

Gideon offered a wry smile in place of an answer. He'd never seen Natalie as easily agitated and indecisive as she'd been while he was trying to get her settled. He'd been relieved when the medication had started to kick in. No wonder Marianne was worried enough about her to get bossy.

"I respect Natalie Marsh as a mental health professional," Marianne said. "I admire her as a person, and I love her as a friend. In exchange for room and board for the night, I'd like you to give me your completely candid viewpoint on what happened today. You have my promise that I won't tell Natalie anything you say."

"Okay," Gideon said. "My completely candid viewpoint is that Natalie is telling the truth. Losing control with the cops—that's not like her, but I can see it, given the circumstances. But playing on Ainsley's superstitions, trying to manipulate her? Punching her in the face? No. That's not in her character. She'd be sick, ripped apart, at the thought of hurting someone the way Ainsley claims Natalie hurt her. It would tear right through the core of what matters most to her."

Marianne tapped her fingers on the arms of her chair and scrutinized Gideon. He figured he was getting evaluated on both honesty and objectivity, but Marianne's attentive expression wasn't revealing how he ranked.

"May I hand the question back to you?" Gideon asked. "What do *you* think happened today? I won't tell Natalie or Ainsley anything you say. And yeah, I know Ainsley's your niece."

Marianne pursed her lips and played with the reading glasses she'd set on her computer. Gideon waited, but within a few seconds, the silence had him fidgeting.

"I take it this is a hard question," he said.

"I've been thinking about it all afternoon, naturally." Marianne unfolded the earpieces on the glasses and closed them again. "Gideon, I don't know."

"Okay," Gideon said, not wanting to press her. That was more than enough information: she'd conceded her niece might be a liar—and worse.

"Obviously, I've known Ainsley a lot longer than I've known Natalie, but we're not particularly close. I'm closer to my husband's clan, Tyrant Theresa and the rest. Ainsley's father is my brother, and we don't see eye to eye on much."

"Sorry to hear that."

"He's . . . very materialistic, inclined to look down on anyone who can't match his bank account. I'm not claiming I dislike money"—Marianne gestured at the elegant living room—"but I do understand that dollar signs have nothing to do with a person's value. Patrick, my brother, wanted his children to marry money, and Ainsley's brother and sister did, but lovely little Ainsley went her own way, marrying Stuart. Her family likes to taunt her about her 'poverty,' and she's a bit insecure."

"Ouch." Ainsley's background could potentially strengthen Natalie's theory that she'd craved wealth to the point that she was willing to play dirty to get it. "Does Ainsley's mother feel the same way as her dad?"

"Oh, she's better than Patrick in that way, but we don't have the warmest relationship. She finds it impossible to treat me like a regular person. She's too stuck on the fact that I'm a psychiatrist. I say, 'How was your weekend?' and she says, 'Don't analyze me!'—that type of nonsense."

"That would wear on you."

"It does. Ainsley's mother is extremely superstitious, far more so than Ainsley. She thinks I'm judging her, which I'm not, though honestly, I'd love to get her into Natalie's office because I think there's more than old traditions going on in her head." Marianne sighed. "To warn you, Stuart is coming over."

"When?"

"Any time now. He called about half an hour ago. He wants to talk to me."

"Talk to you about what happened today?" Gideon gripped the gilded arms of his chair. "Maybe Ainsley's come clean with him."

"Actually, I think he wants to rake me over the coals for helping Natalie."

"Ah. Hey, at least he wants to talk. Now that things are calmer, how likely is he to be open to Natalie's side of the story?"

"Not open. He's very invested in defending Ainsley, in fighting her enemies. Stuart has his insecurities, and I suspect one of them is his fear that he's not enough of a hero for Ainsley. I guarantee he won't take sides against her."

"He'd be a lot more of a hero if he'd get her professional help, because it sounds like something's seriously wrong with her."

Marianne didn't comment. Gideon assumed she was thinking, *Or there's something seriously wrong with Natalie.*

"I'd better stay with Natalie while he's here," Gideon said and realized the words implied he either felt he needed to protect Natalie from Stuart or that he considered Natalie a threat to Stuart—not that sedated and slumbering Natalie could pose a threat to anyone at the moment. "I'll stay out of your way so you can talk," he clarified.

"I'd prefer you join the conversation. I'm not taking sides here, and I'm not serving as a messenger between factions. If he wants to hound me, he can do it in front of you. I trust you can behave yourself no matter what he says."

"Yes, ma'am. I appreciate—"

The doorbell rang. Marianne rose from her chair and went to answer it.

When she escorted Stuart into the living room, Gideon rose to greet him but, noting his hostile expression, refrained from offering a handshake. He didn't want to get his arm torn off, and he sensed Stuart was about that thrilled to see him.

"Why are you here?" Stuart asked.

"He was here before you called," Marianne said. "I'd invited him for Natalie's sake."

"*She's* here? I thought you took her to her place!"

"How unfortunate that the gossip network is glitchy. Have a seat."

Stuart chose a chair. "Why are you harboring the woman who attacked your own niece?"

"If Ainsley would like to come over, I'd be happy to harbor her as well. I already told you I didn't witness what happened, and I'll do what I think is wise, not be restricted by the assumptions of others."

"Where is she?"

"Sleeping."

"You had to drug her, didn't you? That's why you brought Radcliffe here—you couldn't control her on your own. You should have called the cops. That girl's a murderer. If she didn't kill Quincy, why would she try to trick Ainsley into confessing to that crime?"

"I don't know what happened, Stuart."

"I know you saw her at that lecture, but the alibi you gave her is full of holes. How many times did you see her face? She could have had an accomplice, somebody in a wig, dressed like her, who took her place while she sneaked home to dice up Quincy."

"That's a theory to discuss with the police, not with me." Marianne eyed Gideon as though checking on his self-restraint. Gideon folded his arms and tried to look stoic. It was easier to endure this conversation knowing Natalie wasn't listening.

"You need to go back to the police." Scarlet blots mottled Stuart's neck. "Make sure they know you can't swear it was her the whole time."

"I've already told them, in detail, precisely what I saw. I have nothing to add to it. Would you like a glass of lemonade?"

"I'll take whiskey."

"The last thing you need is alcohol. Coke? Ginger ale? Mineral water?"

"Forget it, then. Why aren't you helping your family out? If you told the cops to arrest Marsh, they would."

"I have no influence on whether or not they arrest her."

"Tell them she's crazy. They'll have to take her in. You can do that."

"A psychiatric hold is not an arrest, and Natalie doesn't need hospitalization. How is Ainsley doing?"

"Bad. Her lip and eye are all fat and purple, and she was so freaked out after the cops were done with us that she wouldn't even talk to me about what happened. Bawled for a while, then conked out on the couch. What went on between you and Marsh today? What did she say to you? Is she still telling that idiot story about Ainsley faking the fight?"

"Rephrase that question in an objective way and I'll answer it."

Stuart scowled. "Does she . . . say Ainsley staged the fight?"

"Yes."

"You know that's a stupid story."

"I'm not ruling on the stupidity of anyone's story right now. When you get home, please tell Ainsley to come see me, or I'd be happy to come see her. I don't want her to think I'm taking sides against her."

"If you're protecting Natalie Marsh, you're taking sides."

"If you choose to interpret my behavior that way, that's your choice. The correct interpretation is that I'm withholding judgment and offering help to anyone who'll accept it."

"With that strategy, you're going to end up *dead*."

Marianne fired a look at Stuart that would have made Gideon shrink like a kid about to regret his smart mouth. "I'll consider myself warned. Do you have anything else you'd like to discuss?"

"I have a question for Stuart," Gideon interjected. "At the funeral, before Ainsley got up to sing, she looked upset. Not sad but agitated. She spoke to you and pointed toward the back of the room. From what I could see, it looked like you shrugged off whatever she told you. What was that?"

Redness spread along Stuart's hairline. "That was your girlfriend's handiwork. Brainwashing Ainsley into thinking she'd seen Baxter Quincy's ghost."

"She thought she saw his ghost?"

"You mocking my wife?"

"No. I'm trying to understand what happened. When would Natalie have had a chance to plant these ideas about Baxter's ghost in her head? It wasn't immediately before the funeral. I was with her, and she didn't speak to Ainsley before the service."

Stuart gave a surly shrug. "At work, I guess; where else? I don't know the details. The cops talked to us separately, and like I said, she was too upset to explain everything to me afterward."

"Natalie hasn't been at work with Ainsley since Baxter died," Gideon said. "She went in to Nefesh Bria the morning after his death, but I was with her, and she didn't see Ainsley. She left before the clinic opened, and she didn't go in today."

"I told you, I don't know when they talked. Maybe she called Ainsley."

"She tried, but Ainsley didn't answer. Phone records will verify that."

Stuart's hands clamped together, forming a combined fist that could probably knock Gideon through the wall. "If she's clever enough to trick Marianne into giving her an alibi, she's clever enough to contact Ainsley without leaving a trail."

"The police will hunt for that trail. If they know when Ainsley claims Natalie contacted her, they can check to see if Natalie has an alibi for that time. And I don't buy into the idea that Natalie is a clever murderer. She's an intelligent person, but if she killed Baxter, doing it at her own house was award-winning stupidity."

"So she didn't mean to kill him, but she screwed up, lost her temper."

"You already suggested she planned it carefully, recruiting an accomplice to masquerade as her at the lecture. That's not a heat-of-the-moment murder."

"You think you can do the cops' job for them? Cover for Natalie? Or cover for yourself. Did *you* kill Quincy?"

"If I did, why would I do it in a way that would implicate Natalie? Besides, I have an alibi."

"So does Ainsley. Solid. Multiple witnesses."

"Good," Gideon said. "How about you?"

Stuart sprang to his feet and glared at Marianne. "This is useless. If you care about your niece, call her when you've thrown this joker and his murderer girlfriend out." He stalked out of the living room.

Marianne didn't pursue him. Stuart's footsteps thumped in the entryway, and the front door opened, then crashed shut.

She looked at Gideon and raised her eyebrows.

Gideon cleared his throat. "Uh . . . did that qualify as behaving myself?"

CHAPTER 26

"NATALIE?" A HAND SHOOK HER shoulder. "Sorry to wake you. I mean, sorry to try to wake you." Fingers brushed the side of her face, tucking her hair behind her ear. "Okay, sorry to fail at waking you. I'm thinking this is a lost cause."

"I'm awake," Natalie muttered, blinking. Gideon stood next to her bed, leaning over her. The bed. Not her bed. Not her room. Above her hung an unfamiliar ceiling fan with a beaded glass fixture and curving, transparent blades. Puzzled, she looked at Gideon. He wore a Columbia University T-shirt and needed to shave. "You went to Georgia Tech," she said.

"Marianne's husband went to Columbia. I borrowed his shirt."

Marianne. She was at Marianne's. In her guest room, taking a respite from an in-progress nervous breakdown. "What time is it?"

Gideon checked his watch. "It's seven minutes after ten."

Ten o'clock. She'd fallen asleep in the late afternoon. "I . . . took a five . . . four . . . six-hour nap?"

"That plus another twelve hours." Gideon waved toward the window, where morning sunlight blazed through open blinds.

"I slept all night?"

"I would have let you sleep longer, but Detective Bartholomew is here and wants to talk to you."

Too bleary to feel much anxiety, Natalie sat up and pressed her fingertips against her spongy eyelids.

"I stalled him as long as I could," Gideon said. "Sorry."

"Thanks for running interference." She pushed back the bedcovers. "This is perfect. I'm going to get arrested in my pajamas. In Marianne's pajamas."

He helped her out of bed. "If he were here to arrest you, I don't think he'd have come alone."

"Turner and the SWAT team are probably outside."

Gideon picked up a bathrobe draped over the back of a chair. "I don't think you're dangerous enough to qualify for a SWAT team."

"Where's Marianne?"

Gideon took her hand and directed it into a bathrobe sleeve. "At work."

"Why aren't you?"

"I promised you I'd stay until you woke up. Remember?"

"You spent the night here?"

He aimed her other arm into a sleeve and pulled the robe up to her shoulders. "I did."

"Thank you. I'm sorry. I didn't think I'd sleep so long."

"I'm glad you did." He tied the belt of the bathrobe. "You steady enough to walk?"

"Yes, I'm fine." She took a few steps, stumbling a little, bewildered that the carpet was tripping her.

"Let's do this together." Gideon wrapped his arm firmly around her waist and escorted her toward the door. As they passed the mirror over the dresser, Natalie glimpsed herself. She resembled a corpse. An ill-groomed corpse. She ought to get herself together before facing Bartholomew, but even thinking about brushing her hair made her want a nap. Besides, she didn't have a hairbrush with her.

"May I have my phone back now?" she asked as Gideon led her into the hallway.

"Depends. What are you planning to do with it?"

"Call 911 to report a kidnapping, apparently. Are you Marianne's henchman?"

"Absolutely."

"I want to set up a meeting with Lauren to find out if Baxter bragged to her about the Chapman commission."

"Good idea, as long as the meeting isn't today. You are 100 percent grounded today."

Natalie yawned. "I know."

Gideon directed her into the living room. Bartholomew was waiting in an armchair. As Natalie and Gideon entered, he rose to his feet.

"Good morning, Dr. Marsh. I apologize for waking you."

"It's fine," she said.

Gideon settled her on the couch. He squeezed her shoulder and started out of the room.

"Mr. Radcliffe, if you could stay, I'd appreciate it," Bartholomew said. "In case Dr. Marsh needs assistance."

Gideon turned back. "Glad to." He sat next to her as Natalie pondered Bartholomew's request. Assistance, like being shoveled off the carpet and heaved back onto the couch? Yes, she might need that.

"Are you feeling better?" Bartholomew asked Natalie.

Natalie ran her fingers through her hair, untangling it. "Any better than when I was throwing jewelry and slamming doors yesterday?"

"Yes, ma'am."

"I'm feeling much better. Did you come alone hoping I'd be less of a monster without the bad-cop part of the equation?"

"Truth is, Turner hates this whole deal," Bartholomew said. "He likes and respects you, and if the evidence could magically go away, he'd be the first guy to cheer."

"I apologize for my behavior."

"You're under extreme stress. We understand that. I have a few questions for you. Are you up to answering them?"

"Yes."

Bartholomew rose to his feet, phone in his hand, and came to show Natalie a picture on the screen: a man, maybe in his late twenties or early thirties. Spiky, sandy-blond hair, triangular face. The picture looked like one from a social media account; the man was laughing and balancing a tall stack of plastic drinking glasses on his head.

"Do you know this man?" Bartholomew asked.

Natalie scrutinized the picture. Did he look familiar? She didn't want to give a quick, incorrect answer and find herself under even more suspicion of lying when Bartholomew said, "*He's been a client at your clinic for a month.*"

"I don't think I know him." She again ran her fingers through her hair, wondering vaguely how it had retangled itself when she hadn't moved. "Could you give me some context?"

"You'd probably have seen him in the area near the Stoker Building."

Her eyes started to have difficulty focusing on the picture. She closed them and tried to imagine the man in the lobby of the Stoker or on the grounds . . . at the opening party . . . in the parking lot . . . in the clinic waiting room . . . standing at the reception window, handing paperwork to Ainsley . . .

Ainsley . . . What was Ainsley doing right now? Did she regret the lies she'd told? Natalie had been worried about her, had wanted to help her . . .

Gideon jiggled her shoulder. "Natalie?"

Natalie lifted her head from the back of the couch. Had she dozed off? Bartholomew was standing in front of her, slipping his phone into his suit pocket. "I'm . . . sorry," she said. "I'm a little groggy. Dr. Avery gave me . . . What were you . . . the picture? Do I know him? No. If I've seen him before, I don't remember it."

"Thank you." Bartholomew returned to his seat.

Natalie rubbed her thumbs under her eyes, hoping to clear away any mascara smears that made the shadows darker than they had to be. Gideon rested his arm around her shoulders, his closeness offering strong, comforting warmth.

"Who is he?" Natalie asked.

"His name is Simon Cain," Bartholomew said. "Ring any bells?"

"No."

"He's the man who harassed Daisy Frederiksen when she was en route to your clinic."

"You found him?" A shot of relief made Natalie momentarily less sluggish. Simon Cain was not a client at Nefesh Bria, or at least he hadn't been at the time he'd harassed Daisy. Natalie would have remembered his name from her careful study of the client lists.

"Yes, Mr. Cain confirmed that he has never set foot in Nefesh Bria," Bartholomew said, accurately reading Natalie's thoughts.

"How did you find him?"

"A regular passenger who waits at the bus stop across the street from the Stoker was able to help us identify him. Mr. Cain claims he was hired to harass Ms. Frederiksen."

"Hired!" Natalie hadn't expected that. "By whom?"

"He claims he doesn't know. He works in a restaurant in the plaza across from the Stoker. He found an envelope under his windshield wiper offering him a job, describing what he was supposed to do, to whom, and at what date and time. The envelope included a hundred dollars in cash, and the note said if he went through with it, he'd find another two hundred in payment."

Gideon spoke. "He took marching orders from some anonymous goon? How many brain cells does this guy have?"

"Mr. Cain seems impetuous," Bartholomew said. "He has a reputation as a practical joker."

"Whoever left him the note must have known that," Gideon said. "If there *was* a note and he didn't make his story up."

"He claims he carried out what he saw as a harmless prank and got the promised payment. He assumed somebody—maybe one of his customers—was annoyed with Ms. Frederiksen, and $300 for a one-minute acting gig appealed to him."

"This person not only knew Daisy had an appointment at the clinic but knew the date and time," Natalie said.

"Yes," Bartholomew said. "Who had access to that information?"

"Besides me?"

"Yes."

The question had an obvious answer. As the receptionist, Ainsley would have known the whole schedule, but why would she have targeted the clinic's reputation by hiring Simon Cain? Any connection she might have to Drew's death or Baxter's didn't seem to have a logical link with the clinic, not if it the crimes were about the Chapman post . . .

Could creating negative publicity about Natalie's clinic have been an early part of Ainsley's scheme to frame her? No . . . that was ridiculous . . . At what point *had* Ainsley decided to frame her? Baxter's death . . . the incident at the funeral home . . . She couldn't have preplanned the scene at the funeral home . . . couldn't have known Natalie would follow her into the lounge. She could have assumed Natalie would, knowing her personality, but she couldn't have known they'd be alone . . . When had she decided to . . . What had happened right before she'd staged the attack? They'd been talking about Drew's dying at the MacKerrons' apartment, about guilt . . . Natalie had asked about the hand washing . . . No, Natalie had texted Stuart and Gideon first . . . or had that been after they'd talked about guilt? It didn't matter. Stuart had texted back, and she'd told Ainsley he was coming. Ainsley had clasped her hand, pretended to admire her ring . . .

Knowing Stuart was about to arrive. Had her actions erupted from a fear of what Natalie might say to Stuart about guilt and Ainsley's behavior? With Natalie accused of assault and Stuart in a rage, he wouldn't believe anything Natalie said . . .

"You still with us?" Gideon spoke close to her ear.

"Hmm?" Natalie lifted her head from where it had fallen onto Gideon's shoulder. "Yes, mostly. Did I . . . miss something?"

"I asked who besides you knew the date and time of Daisy Frederiksen's appointment," Bartholomew said.

"I'm sorry. I swear I'm coherent. Just sleepy. Ainsley MacKerron is our receptionist." Natalie tried to sound neutral as she spoke Ainsley's name. "She would have known."

Bartholomew twirled long fingers in a few rotations. "You had that wheels-are-turning expression—while you were still awake, that is. Would you share what you were thinking?"

"I was . . . thinking that I don't know of any reason why Ainsley would have hired Simon Cain. Did you ask Daisy if she told anyone?"

"Ms. Frederiksen was vocal about her upcoming appointment. She told people in several different public and private locations that she'd made an appointment so she could see if your clinic was any good. She claimed she had experience with many therapists and was more than qualified to rate Nefesh Bria."

"Did the note instruct Cain to tell Daisy he was our client?"

"Yes. He claims there were specific instructions for what to say to her. He's already destroyed the note, unfortunately."

Had Baxter hired Simon Cain? If the police connected Cain to Baxter or even discovered that more of the strange incidents at the Stoker were scandal-for-hire, that was another reason for Natalie to have been furious with Baxter. Furious enough to murder him?

Maybe this break in the case wasn't good news.

"We're following up to see what else we can learn from the situation with Mr. Cain," Bartholomew said. "Thank you for your input."

"Has there been any progress on figuring out who forged that letter from Heather's ghost grandmother?" Natalie asked.

"We've eliminated a few possibilities. I assume Mr. Radcliffe told you that."

"Yes."

Bartholomew remained quiet, his expression thoughtful. The silence didn't make Natalie edgy this time, but it did make her hope he'd stay silent long enough for her to sneak a quick nap on Gideon's shoulder.

"I have a message for you from Heather Osbourne," Bartholomew said.

Adrenaline roused Natalie. "What did she say?"

"She said to tell you her brother told her the truth about you and him, or rather, he sent the message through her lawyer. She wants to apologize for accusing you of having an affair with him."

"I appreciate that." Kenton had probably assumed the police would have told Heather the connection between Natalie and him, but she was impressed he'd made certain Heather got the message, even if he hadn't felt able to tell her personally.

"Has she apologized for accusing Natalie of planting that vase?" Gideon asked.

"Her opinion on that wouldn't affect the investigation at this point," Bartholomew said.

"She's always seemed to have contradictory ideas about Natalie," Gideon said. "Like she doesn't know what to think."

"I think her own perceptions clashed with Tabitha's warnings about my evil clinic," Natalie said. "Which confused her since she's skilled at reading people but she needs to trust Tabitha."

"Heather said to ask you if Kenton's ex-wife, Sophia, knows who you are," Bartholomew said.

"I'm not sure." Natalie doubted Sophia knew. Kenton had always been adamant about not even hinting to his wife that he was in therapy, let alone sharing the identity of his therapist. But that didn't mean Sophia hadn't discovered it. "Why does she want to know?"

"She says if Sophia knows about you, she'll hate you. Whatever her brother told her about his ex upset her. She wanted to warn you."

"Warn me that Sophia might hate me? What is Heather afraid she might do?"

"She didn't get specific. She kept repeating that she'd been wrong about Sophia and that Sophia was scary. Can you expand on that?"

"No." *Not ethically.*

"Natalie, if you do have an enemy in Lowery's ex, you'd be wise to come clean about it, no matter how uncomfortable or even how professionally damaging it might be. It's to your advantage if we have other options to explore."

Natalie sighed. Heather had believed Kenton's denial of the affair, but evidently the police were still iffy on it. "I have no idea if Sophia Lowery even knows I exist, let alone if she's an enemy."

"You've never met her."

"No."

"Do you know where she lives?"

"No."

"Do you know if she and Mr. Lowery are still in contact?"

Natalie hesitated. "He mentioned that she texted him recently, but he didn't respond to her."

"Did he say anything about the content of the texts?"

Natalie mentally cursed herself for asking Kenton questions that were none of her business. She *could* tell Bartholomew the content of the texts—this was new, not confidential information. But Kenton had been on autopilot as far as confiding in her, and she was sure he hadn't anticipated she'd repeat his words to the police.

"He did tell you but you don't want to share it," Bartholomew interpreted. "Would you prefer we ask Mr. Lowery directly?"

Getting interrogated about Sophia's taunting texts would be agony for Kenton. "Please don't do that, if you can avoid it. If it becomes relevant, I'll give you the information."

"It's relevant now. If you're not constrained by professional ethics, tell me what those texts said, or I'll have to make assumptions."

Gideon's arm tensed around her shoulders. Natalie knew he wanted to order Bartholomew to back off but didn't want to get kicked out of the room. Natalie gritted her teeth, despising herself for what she was doing to Kenton. She wished she didn't remember what the texts said, but the words had stuck in her mind. "The ones he mentioned were 'I know you miss me,' 'No one gets out of my life clean,' and 'I still own you.'"

Poker face unchanged, Bartholomew jotted in his notebook. "Thank you. Anything else you can tell me?"

Natalie wanted to beg him not to track down Sophia, but there was no way to do that without making the police even more eager to talk to her. If Sophia did know Natalie had been Kenton's therapist, it was possible she blamed her—partly, at least—for the divorce. She might even genuinely believe Natalie had had an affair with him. When she learned Natalie was in legal trouble, she'd be thrilled at the opportunity to vilify her and could do it with such finesse that Turner and Bartholomew would walk out of there convinced that murder was the nicest thing Natalie had ever done. "Please, just . . . don't mention this to Kenton unless you have to."

"Understood. Anything else?"

"No." She didn't want to bring up her theory about Stuart coveting the job with Chapman until she had at least a crumb of information suggesting the job had been worth serious coveting. If she tossed what turned out to be a nonsensical suggestion into the conversation, it would make her look desperate—which she was—and even less credible than she already did, if that were possible.

Bartholomew rose to his feet, which took his head an impressive distance toward the vaulted ceiling. When Natalie and Gideon started to stand, he held up his hand. "I'll show myself out. You two stay where you are. Natalie, keep following doctor's orders, please."

"I will," Natalie said. *Today*, she added silently. The last thing she intended to do was ask Marianne's permission before making an appointment to meet with Lauren Bell tomorrow.

CHAPTER 27

"OH MY GRACIOUS, YES, OF course Baxter told me about the hiking contract."
Lauren set her glass of iced peach tea on the café table. "Men are genetically
compelled to brag, don't you think?"

Natalie wanted to contradict Lauren, but she didn't. She didn't want
to do anything to risk Lauren's antipathy or to hinder her willingness to
share confidences. When Natalie had called her last night, Lauren hadn't
said anything about the confrontation at the funeral parlor—though she
must have heard rumors—and she'd cheerfully agreed to meet Natalie for
lunch.

"If he was bragging, I take it the terms were worth bragging about?"
Natalie said.

Lauren leaned across the table. "Two hundred dollars an hour," she
whispered. "And when they're on overnight hikes, he pays that rate twenty-
four hours a day, which means over $100,000 for that trip alone. Not to
mention all the hours spent planning, the hikes to get Mr. Chapman in
shape, shopping for gear, and whatever else it takes to prepare to act like a
mountain man."

"Wow," Natalie said. "I should change careers."

Lauren laughed. "Me too. Isn't it absurd? That kind of money for being
a glorified camping buddy? Of course, I would never have phrased it that
way to Baxter, but I suppose since . . . well, since it can't embarrass them
now, I'll tell you that the reason Baxter recruited Drew to work for Quincy
Travel was *because* of that Chapman contract. When the contract came up
for renewal, Baxter's intention was to persuade Drew, or pressure him, to
go through Quincy Travel, not make a private deal with Chapman. Baxter
would get a commission then, you see. But he decided Drew was . . . Forgive
me; this feels unkind to say . . . but he came to feel Drew was a pain in

the neck. He decided he'd rather coax Chapman into firing Drew after the John Muir hike and hiring his—Baxter's—nephew instead."

"That's interesting," Natalie said. The Chapman contract could have been a motive for Baxter to attack Drew, as well as for Ainsley and Stuart. It had never occurred to Natalie to suspect Baxter. She'd pass that thought on to the police.

"That number I gave you was only the hourly rate," Lauren said. "Mr. Chapman had already given Drew bonuses and expensive gear. Baxter was confident he'd be able to get his nephew into Drew's spot *and* develop the high-end trail guide service into a permanent option for well-to-do clients. His nephew was thrilled, naturally. A cushy future getting paid for doing what he loved."

"It sounds like a dream come true," Natalie said. From the way Lauren described it, this *had* been a job Stuart might have coveted or that Ainsley might have coveted for him. That thought jarred her memory: the night Stuart had prevented Heather from jumping out the window at the Stoker, Heather had said something to Stuart about his becoming Chapman's sidekick. Had the MacKerrons taken that to heart, letting Heather's prediction crystallize into greed? And after Chapman's outrageously generous gift of a truck, had the MacKerrons decided this was their chance to take advantage of his appreciation?

"In fact," Lauren said, lowering her voice, "confidentially, I don't think Baxter was particularly upset about Drew's death. His own employee. Even if Drew got on his nerves, you'd think he would have cared more, wouldn't you?"

"He may not have been comfortable showing his grief," Natalie said.

"You're so charitable," Lauren said. "But truly, Natalie, I think he was so delighted at the thought of snatching that contract immediately that he felt like 'good riddance.' He actually said to me, 'A corpse isn't much of a Trekmeister. This is our contract now.'"

Another scrap to relay to Bartholomew.

The server approached, carrying their meals. When two coconut-shrimp and mango salads sat in front of them and the server was gone, Natalie asked, "Was Baxter concerned the job might go to Stuart MacKerron instead? Bob was impressed with Stuart."

"Baxter did mention Stuart." Lauren lifted a sprig of cilantro on her fork and laid it back on the plate. "He said Stuart would try for it, but Baxter wouldn't have trouble nailing it down. I admire a confident man, but Baxter could be *too* confident. Forgive me, but occasionally he crossed the line into arrogance. Like how he was about your clinic."

"Yes, that was frustrating." Taking Lauren's words as a handy lead-in, Natalie said, "This is an odd question, but did Baxter ever give you the impression that he might resort to . . . creating incidents to make Nefesh Bria look bad?"

"Creating incidents? What do you mean?"

"The police have evidence that someone arranged at least one of the incidents that was blamed on the clinic."

"Arranged it how?"

"Paid someone," Natalie said. "To embarrass us."

"Gracious. What a strange thing to do. That's terrible. He certainly never said he'd use a tactic like that."

"What's your impression?" Natalie asked. "I'm curious if you think it would be in character for him."

Lauren touched the petals of the white carnation in a bud vase that decorated the table. "Well, of course, I couldn't read his mind, but if you want my opinion, it doesn't seem like him at all. He was so confident that he was right. I can't imagine he'd think he needed hired help to prove the clinic was dangerous."

"Thank you. I realize I'm insulting a friend of yours, and I apologize. I'm sure he was a good man."

"Oh yes. Handsome and fun, and he liked to flatter me and spend money on me, which, girl to girl, I'll admit I enjoyed." Lauren tore a poppy-seed roll in half and reached for a pat of butter. "Natalie . . . dear, I know it isn't my business, but why did you ask all those questions about Baxter and Mr. Chapman's hiking contract? Does it . . . have to do with what happened between you and the MacKerrons?"

"What have you heard?" Natalie asked. "I assume rumors have made the rounds."

"Well, yes, Vanessa was talking about it this morning." Lauren set her butter knife down. "Of course I . . . I would never believe . . . It was Vanessa who told me that . . . well, that you . . . well, it's ridiculous. She said something about you blaming Ainsley for Baxter's death and even . . . hurting her? I'm sorry. I shouldn't repeat rumors, and I wouldn't repeat them to anyone else . . ."

"The rumors you've heard are false." Natalie couldn't blame Lauren for being curious. She was impressed Lauren had waited this far into their discussion to ask about the incident. "Since the police are in the process of investigating, I'd prefer not to give details of what happened. I don't know what's going on with Ainsley, but I didn't accuse her of anything nor did I harm her in any way."

"Of course. I didn't think you would."

"Thank you."

Lauren peered at her salad and prodded a cube of mango. "Do you . . . think Stuart and Ainsley killed Baxter so Baxter couldn't take the Chapman contract? Is that why you're asking me about Mr. Chapman's offer?"

"I'm exploring possibilities," Natalie said, quoting Bartholomew. "I don't know what's going on. I wish I did."

"My word, I'm starting to think sad little Heather Osbourne is right and the Stoker Building truly is haunted by a vengeful ghost. So many heart-breaking things have happened!"

"I doubt it's a ghost's fault." It would be wise to change the subject now lest she provoke Lauren into thinking she did have a vendetta against Ainsley, but a question was all but searing Natalie's tongue. "On Monday night, Ainsley was at the party at the Cascata Sculpture Park. You were there too, correct?"

"Yes, naturally. I did see Ainsley, if that's what you want to ask me. Not Stuart though."

"No, he didn't go. By chance, did you notice if Ainsley was present the entire evening?"

"Unfortunately, I wasn't mingling with guests the whole time." Lauren stroked the right side of her jaw. "The dental work I'd had done earlier that day was bothering me, but I didn't want to abandon Vanessa, so I took a painkiller and lay down on the couch in her office until it started to work. I think I dozed a little. During that period, I couldn't swear Ainsley was there, and even when I was mingling, she wasn't always in my line of sight. But I did see glimpses of her."

"Thank you," Natalie said. "I'd appreciate it if you wouldn't tell anyone I was asking you these questions. I don't want to start new rumors. Or fuel old ones."

"Oh, of course I won't share this. I should warn you that . . . well . . . Vanessa is spreading gossip about what happened with you and Ainsley. I've heard her bring it up with visitors in the gallery. With just about *every* visitor. Usually, she's not loose-lipped, but I suppose this is spectacular gossip."

"That surprises me," Natalie said grimly. "I'd think she wouldn't want to spread scandal for fear of contaminating the gallery's reputation."

"Yes, I did suggest that it might not be wise to speak about it to visitors, but she feels like no matter what, it will all be headline news, so she wants to ensure that people know how appalled she is and that there is no connection at all between you and the gallery."

"Does she make it clear she didn't even want one of her glass sculptures trapped in the bedlam of my clinic?"

Lauren sighed. "Goodness, she probably does."

"Maybe I need to talk to her and suggest she keep the gossip under control." While she was at it, she could find out if Vanessa could verify Ainsley was at the party the whole night. If Vanessa would tell her.

"Please leave me out of it," Lauren said. "I don't want to lose my job."

"I won't even tell her we spoke. You get along well with Vanessa. Do you have any advice for me on how best to approach her?"

"Let me think." Lauren toyed with the brooch pinned to her silk blouse—porcelain roses with a gold filigree border, an antique jewelry piece Natalie suspected she wore better than any original owner could have done. "Be polite but not a pushover. Compliment her. She loves compliments— her appearance, her clothes, her taste in art. Anything you can find to praise."

"Perfect. Thank you."

"Also, if you can manage it, arrange to meet with her in person rather than speaking on the phone. She seems to be more . . . How do I describe this? More testy on the phone? No, that's too harsh. More impatient. She does better when she's face-to-face. I think she needs to see facial expressions and body language to help keep her from leaping to negative conclusions. She can be touchy, you see. Does that make sense?"

"Yes, it does."

"I don't recommend showing up without contacting her first. Being caught off guard will make her defensive. Call the gallery. She never picks up the office phone right away, so you can leave a message. That will let her prepare herself before responding to you."

"I'll do that."

"Would you like the number?"

"I can look it up in the Stoker directory. Thank you for your help."

"I hope everything works out." Lauren touched Natalie's sleeve with carnation-pink fingernails. "You must be under so much stress. Have the police interrogated you?"

"Many times. Getting questioned by the police is my favorite activity these days."

"Oh, how humiliating." Lauren patted her arm. "It must be mortifying to be treated like a criminal. I hope it's over soon."

Natalie almost said, *I hope it's over in a good way*, but didn't. There wasn't a purely good way for this to end. Someone she knew was guilty of murder, and the thought of it being Stuart or Ainsley didn't seem to qualify as a happy ending.

Though she'd take it over being arrested and sent to prison for life for murders she hadn't committed.

* * *

Natalie tapped the screen to end the call and nestled more snugly into the passenger seat of Gideon's car. The upholstery was comfortable. Definitely comfortable enough for a nap.

Stopped at a red light, Gideon glanced at her. "Do you think Vanessa will return your message?"

"Out of ghoulish curiosity," Natalie said. "Or out of the hope that I'll give her new gossip fodder."

"Ah. Like, 'Hello, Vanessa. I called because I want to brainwash you.'"

"Exactly," Natalie said. "'Repeat after me: I killed Baxter Quincy.'"

"You should try it."

"I might." Natalie wished she knew how to loosen the anxiety wound around words Gideon had tried to speak lightly. *Hand him over to Marianne*, she thought, holding back a yawn.

"I don't have high hopes that she'll be helpful even if she does call back," Gideon said. "If she's broadcasting Ainsley's version of the story, she's not likely to help you pick apart Ainsley's alibi."

"I know. I still want to talk to her. If she won't return my call, I will show up at the gallery, no matter what Lauren said about her liking a chance to prepare herself."

"That's fair."

"Thank you for playing chauffeur for my lunch date," Natalie said, speaking through a yawn that escaped. "I really could have driven myself. Marianne said twenty-four hours, and it's been longer than that."

"Uh-huh. Nice yawn."

"I'm tired, not drugged."

"Either way, I prefer to drive you. I'll drive you to meet with Vanessa if you get that arranged, but the truth is, I'd prefer you didn't meet with her at all. If you want to verify Ainsley was at the Cascata party the entire night, that's a job for our detective friends anyway."

"I know, but I want to gather as much evidence as I can before I throw this theory at them. I'm sick of looking like a homicidal crackpot making up stories to blame my crimes on others."

"You'd prefer to make it clear they have a selection of homicidal crackpots to choose from."

"That's my goal."

"Natalie . . . after what happened at the funeral home, haven't you had enough of dealing with hostile, irrational people? Give yourself a break."

"I'm a psychologist. Dealing with hostile, irrational people is familiar ground."

"Nice try. This is personal for you. That's different."

"Besides, I want to warn Vanessa to stop spreading rumors. Her gossip is trashing my reputation, and she must be scaring potential clients away from Nefesh Bria."

"She won't stop."

"She might if I make the point that what she's doing is verging on slander and, if I'm proven innocent, could hurt the gallery's reputation. I hope she'll have the self-preservation and the class to keep her mouth shut until . . . things are settled."

Gideon lifted one hand off the steering wheel and reached for Natalie's hand. "The cops will figure out what happened."

"I hope so."

"Where are we headed?" Gideon asked. "My apartment?"

"No, take me home. You need to get back to work."

"I'm edgy leaving you at your house. Even with your shiny new locks and shiny new security system."

"I know. I'm edgy just about everywhere." Since Baxter's death, she'd been home only to pick up clothes and personal items and to deal with the security installation, but it hadn't been *too* stressful going inside. She hadn't felt scared or repulsed. Just unsettled.

"I suppose rolling out your sleeping bag in the lobby of the police department is out of the question?" Gideon said.

"I might be bunking with the police soon enough."

He grimaced. "Sorry. Lousy joke."

"Don't worry—" Natalie's phone rang. She pulled her hand away from Gideon's and pounced on the phone.

"Is it Vanessa?" Gideon asked.

"Yes! That was fast." Natalie swiped the screen. "Hello, this is Natalie."

Vanessa's cool, sleek voice spoke. "This is Vanessa Parisi, returning your call."

"Thank you for getting back to me so promptly. As I said in my message, I'd like to meet—"

"This is the middle of my workday. I don't have time for a discussion now."

"Of course," Natalie said. "I want to set up a time to meet with you, at your convenience."

"I don't know what questions you could have for me, but we all have questions for you. If I answer your questions, I expect you to answer mine."

We all have questions. Did Vanessa consider herself the new spokesperson for the Stoker tenants who opposed the clinic? "If I'm able to answer your questions, I'd be happy to do so. When can we meet? I can come to the gallery after business hours, if that's best for you."

"No, don't come to my gallery."

"You're welcome to meet me at Nefesh Bria or another place of your choosing." After Natalie issued the invitation, she realized they couldn't meet at Nefesh Bria—she didn't have access to the clinic after hours. She didn't correct herself; Vanessa wouldn't want to meet there anyway.

"I have work to do tonight at the Cascata Sculpture Park office in Kemper Park," Vanessa said. "I'll be done around nine. If you want to talk to me, come at nine thirty."

"That's fine. I'll be there tonight at nine thirty."

"Security will be on site."

"I'm glad to hear that," Natalie said. As Gideon braked at a stop sign, she nudged him and mouthed, "Come with me?"

He nodded emphatically.

"Gideon Radcliffe will be with me," Natalie told Vanessa.

"Is this a discussion or an ambush?" Vanessa asked icily. "I'm not interested in getting bullied by you and your angry boyfriend. Is that what this is about? Cornering me so he can threaten me and jump on everything I say?"

"Gideon won't do any of that."

"Spare me. I'm open for a discussion. I'm not open for getting lectured by an overprotective male who thinks you're a saint. Bring him along if you can't handle this without him, but leave him in the car."

Natalie paused, picturing the sculpture park and evaluating her options. "I understand if you don't want him at the meeting, but given my current situation, I'd prefer to have at least one set of friendly eyes watching us. Let's compromise. Instead of meeting in your office, let's meet in the gazebo by the overflow parking area. He can stay in the car and keep an eye on things."

"An *eye* on things? What do you think I'm going to do?"

"I'm not making any assumptions about what you're going to do. I want to bring him to witness whatever either one of us does. I'm happy to talk in the presence of your security guard as well or anyone else you'd like to invite."

"You want to meet out in the gazebo instead of sitting in the office like civilized people?"

"I want to meet wherever my witness can see us."

Vanessa was quiet. Natalie guessed she was debating the appeal of whatever fresh gossip she could wring out of Natalie versus how offended she wanted to be at Natalie's implication that she wasn't trustworthy.

"*Fine*," Vanessa said. "Bring your boyfriend and leave him in the car. Nine thirty at the gazebo. I expect you to give me honest answers."

"I'll see you tonight."

Vanessa hung up.

Natalie stowed her phone in her purse and summed up the conversation for Gideon.

"How many friends do you think she'll bring to the meeting?" he asked.

"I predict one security guard. Too many ears would dilute the exclusiveness of the gossip she hopes to get."

Gideon turned into Natalie's driveway. "I don't like being banished to the car. She brings a second; you bring a second. That's how it works."

"It's not a duel. I'm hoping she'll be less defensive with just me."

"Yeah, I remember you saying something similar when I asked if you wanted company when you followed Ainsley out of Drew's funeral."

Natalie winced. "That's why you're coming along this time. Thanks, Gideon. If you want to come over whenever you're done at work, I'll order takeout. Then you can chauffeur me to my meeting."

"Yes, madam." Gideon mimed tipping a hat. "Just stay where I can see you while you're talking tonight, or I guarantee I *will* coming barging in."

"Agreed. At least Vanessa has no reason to hurt me. Worst-case scenario: she'll insult me with a Picasso metaphor and serve me a rancid bacon-wrapped scallop."

"Sheesh, these art people are vicious." Gideon leaned over and kissed Natalie on the cheek.

Natalie controlled the desire to grab him and redirect the kiss, transforming it into much more than a platonic peck. This wasn't the time to push Gideon like that. What had happened to that conversation she'd planned to have with him about their relationship? When had she intended to do that? This weekend? *Yes, that was your plan before Baxter got murdered in your kitchen, Ainsley tried to frame you, you nearly got arrested twice, Marianne kidnapped you, and Vanessa started spreading damaging rumors about you to everyone she sees.*

Gideon had a point about not adding stress by confronting Vanessa tonight. But if Natalie bypassed an opportunity to gather information about Ainsley's activities *and* made no attempt to mitigate Vanessa's gossip rampage . . . No. She wasn't canceling her appointment.

"Have a good afternoon." Natalie reached for the door handle.

"Go take a nap."

"I will." She opened the door. "When I wake up, I'll learn that the last month has been a bad dream. It's actually the day before the opening gala at the Stoker."

"I like that plan," Gideon said. "Here's hoping."

CHAPTER 28

NATALIE CHECKED HER PHONE AGAIN. Nine forty. Vanessa was running late. The Cascata office was on the other side of the sculpture park, near one of the main parking areas for Kemper Park, but from her vantage point in the gazebo, Natalie had a distant view of its lighted windows. Either Vanessa had left the lights on, or more likely, she was still there. Natalie doubted Vanessa had stood her up, but she should have thought to ask for Vanessa's cell phone number so she could check in with her.

A breeze blew through the gazebo, rippling the loose cotton tunic Natalie had thrown on over the fitted T-shirt she'd been wearing in the heat of the day. The balmy weather was a perk to meeting outside, but other than that, she regretted suggesting this spot. Now that she was at the sculpture park, she realized there were better locations where Gideon could keep watch. In contrast to the brightly glowing office and the well-lit main parking lot at the front of the park, the area where Natalie waited was deserted and darker than she'd anticipated. When she'd been here at night previously, she'd come for weddings or other events, and she hadn't realized how much of the lighting came from decorative lanterns or white Christmas lights twined around tree branches. The lighting in the grass-covered overflow parking area where Gideon waited consisted of two light posts that left 90 percent of the area in shadow. As for the gazebo itself, it had no lighting at all, and the sidewalk lighting was so dim that Natalie would have done better with a candle and Heather's antique candleholder. Weak, individual floodlights shone on the sculptures, but didn't light the areas around them, and under the circumstances, abstract creations of metal and stone lurking on the lawn appeared more eerie than artistic.

No wonder Vanessa had been hesitant to meet here.

From the direction of the office, a female silhouette approached. Natalie sent a hasty text to Gideon: *Here she comes. Wish me luck.*

She walked down the gazebo steps and went to meet Vanessa. As the path lighting tentatively illuminated the woman's face, Natalie halted. It was Ainsley.

Confused, phone clamped in her hand, she glanced toward the parking area for a comforting glimpse of Gideon's car. He wouldn't hear their talking, but if she screamed, he'd be over here instantly. With the poor lighting, he probably couldn't tell it was Ainsley, not Vanessa, approaching.

Trying not to appear as wary as she felt, Natalie waited until Ainsley reached her before saying, "Hello, Ainsley. What are you doing here?"

"You do innocent so well." Ainsley's pale face radiated disgust but not surprise. She had expected to see Natalie. Vanessa must have invited her. Why? Did Vanessa want to see how Natalie would react?

Natalie evaluated Ainsley. Her hair was a mess, half of it straggling loose from a ponytail. The bruises on her face were splashes of black paint in the dimness.

"Did Vanessa Parisi invite you to come here?" Natalie asked.

"Why would she do that?"

"I have an appointment with her, but she's running late." Natalie pointed toward the office. "She'll be out here momentarily. Would you like to sit in the gazebo?"

"No."

"All right. Is Stuart with you?"

"*No*, he's not with me. You told me to come alone. I came alone. Happy?"

"I told you to come alone?" Natalie didn't want to contradict her and risk angering her. Whatever Vanessa was scheming, Natalie didn't want to participate. Never mind getting information. She needed to carefully disengage herself from Ainsley, flee to Gideon's car, and call Bartholomew. "I'm sorry. Could you remind me what I said to you?"

"Do you think you're funny?"

"Maybe it would be better if we talked another time. I'll—" At the cadence of footsteps behind her, she started to pivot, grateful that Gideon—

A dark figure crashed into her, throwing her off the sidewalk and onto the grass. Hands searched her, jamming themselves under her arms, moving down her sides, pawing her legs to the ankles. Natalie screamed, but her cry was a hoarse, winded screech.

The figure rose and stepped back. Stuart. Dazed, Natalie sat up and groped for the phone she'd dropped. Vanessa was playing a spiteful game, inviting the MacKerrons here, setting Natalie up . . . Setting her up for what? It wouldn't work—Natalie had a witness this time. Gideon could see the scene from the parking lot. He'd be on his phone now, calling the police even as he rushed in Natalie's direction.

Where was he? Except for the chirping of crickets, the night was quiet.

Stuart stood in front of her, Ainsley behind her. "You're a cold devil," Stuart said. "At least we didn't want this."

Her confidence skidded on icy black fear. *Where is Gideon?* She couldn't find her phone. Stuart must have taken it. Shakily, Natalie rose to her feet. "Stuart . . . Ainsley . . . whatever you think you're doing, it's a mistake."

"At least we make mistakes," Stuart said. "Not cold-blooded plans."

Natalie wanted to speak firmly, but pain and lack of air made her voice jagged. "Ask Ainsley what . . . really happened in the women's lounge at Drew's funeral."

"That was one of the mistakes," Stuart said. "We worked that out. Ainsley panicked. Thought I'd killed Quincy, and she needed to cover for me. She trusted you too much—didn't realize it *was* you who'd killed him."

That baffled Natalie. Ainsley had been covering for Stuart but Stuart was innocent? "Past mistakes don't make it a smart idea to make new mistakes. You go home. I'll go home. I don't want this to get worse for any of us."

"Go *home?*" Stuart stepped closer to her. Natalie held her ground. If she backed up, she'd bump into Ainsley. "You're the one who brought us here. Now you want to run?"

Natalie wanted to scream Gideon's name but knew it wouldn't help. Either he was already on his way toward her, or something . . . someone . . . was stopping him. "I didn't bring you here. I—"

"Blackmail?" Ainsley spoke in a trembling whisper. "You act like you care, like you want to help, then you *blackmail* us?"

Natalie faced her. "I don't know what you're talking about. Vanessa is manipulating all of us. I—"

A wall of heat blocked the breeze behind her. She started to turn and bumped her shoulder against Stuart's chest.

"Who else knows what Heather Osbourne saw?" he asked.

Grappling with a panicky impulse to shove Stuart back and run—she wouldn't succeed, and she'd enrage Stuart—Natalie focused again on Ainsley. "Please listen to me. I did not invite you here. I do not want to blackmail you. If Vanessa used my name, it was without my permission. I would never—"

"This innocent game is really old." One of Stuart's arms whipped around Natalie, pinning her against him. She thrashed; his other hand lifted a knife and rested the blade against her throat. "Hold still."

Natalie obeyed, fight-ready muscles instantly motionless.

"Who else knows what Heather saw?" Stuart repeated his question.

"What—" The slight vibration of speaking made her feel the edge of steel more acutely. "Gideon is here," she said. "See that silver Accord in the parking area? That's his car."

Stuart swung Natalie around, scanning the area, the blade digging deeper. "If he comes near us, you're dead."

Natalie shrank against Stuart, trying to draw her throat even a fraction of a millimeter away from the blade. "He will have called the police by now."

"You're bluffing." Stuart made another rotation, hauling Natalie with him. The blade shifted with the motion of their bodies, and a stinging pain made Natalie gasp. Ainsley yelped. Stuart's arm quivered, and he released a little of the pressure on the knife.

A warm trickle slipped down her neck, cooling in the night air. Natalie balled her fists to keep herself from grabbing Stuart's arm and futilely attempting to force the knife away before it could sever her jugular. "Let me go. Get out of here before the police arrive. You'll have a head start."

"Radcliffe's not here." Stuart's heart pounded so violently that Natalie could feel it, a wild rhythm competing with her own frenzied pulse. "He would have jumped in already."

"So you could challenge him to a knife fight? He's smart enough to wait for backup. Let me go, Stuart. Do you want to end up in a hostage situation? We'll all get killed."

"We don't even have money." The faint lighting caught tear-streaks on Ainsley's cheeks. "You're horrible. You wanted to use our mistake to take *everything*. We didn't want to hurt you. Drew's death was a mistake, but you killed Baxter in cold blood."

Natalie couldn't decide if denying the accusation was wise, so she ignored it. "Ainsley, please. If you harm me—"

"The police aren't coming," Stuart said. "They'd be here by now. Radcliffe isn't with you. You wouldn't dare get him involved and show him the dirt his cute girlfriend is made of."

A tide of terror made her feel she was drowning. Stuart was right—the police *should* be here. What had happened to Gideon? Had Stuart . . . or Vanessa . . .

"You have ten seconds to start telling us what you wormed out of Heather," Stuart said.

"About the . . . night Drew died?"

Stuart added a trace more pressure to the blade crossing her windpipe. "If you want to die, keep playing stupid."

Natalie drew a deep, cautious breath, inhaling as much oxygen as she could to combat dizziness. "I'm not playing stupid. I honestly don't understand what you want from me. As far as I know, the only thing Heather saw the night Drew died was Gideon standing by your door. She asked him what was going on; he told her it was another burglary and said one of your friends had been hurt. She guessed it was Drew and linked the attack to evil at Nefesh Bria. Then she left before talking to the police."

"You talked to her about it later," Ainsley said.

"Yes, when Gideon and I found her in the Stoker gardens with your vase. She said she'd found the vase, that it had been planted in her apartment, and she accused me of planting it. She said her ghost grandmother had warned her about my clinic. I got the sense she couldn't decide whether or not to trust me."

Stuart's voice thumped against her eardrums. "You call that proof?"

"Proof of what?"

Ainsley reached into her pocket, unfolded a piece of paper, and lit it with her phone flashlight so Natalie could read the plain type.

Dear Ainsley,
You know what I did. I know what you did, but unlike you, I have proof. Heather Osbourne saw some critical things that night, but I'm the only one she'll confide in. I control her mind. If I say talk, she talks. If I say quiet, she'll keep her secrets forever. It's going to cost you $10,000 to keep me from pulling the Heather trigger and sending you and Stuart to prison for murder. Meet me tonight, 9:45, at the Cascata Sculpture Park. Come alone. Park in the main lot and walk through the grounds. I'll be waiting in the gazebo. I know you don't have all the cash now, but bring a thousand, and that will

get us started. If you don't have the thousand, bring some of that jewelry you've been stealing. Yes, Heather knows about that too.

The knife at her throat made it difficult to concentrate on the words. She read the note twice, trying to comprehend it, before Ainsley pulled it away.

"How did she know?" Ainsley crookedly refolded the note. "About the . . . about the . . . Stuart didn't even know . . . Why did you have to tell—"

"*You* should have told me, Lamb," Stuart said. "You should have told me weeks ago. So what if you've been swiping stuff? Who cares now? All I care about is who *else* that weird girl told."

"I did not send you that note," Natalie said. "I have no control over Heather Osbourne. I've never heard her accuse you of anything to do with Drew's death or with the thefts. I absolutely do not want to blackmail you."

"So someone else shoved the note under our door and you happened to be here tonight?" Stuart adjusted the arm curled around her body, constricting his grip until the pressure made it a strain to breathe. "It's all coincidence, eh?"

"I . . . thought I was—" Natalie tried for a deep inhale but could only fill part of her lungs. "I thought I was meeting Vanessa Parisi. I was expecting *her*, not you."

"What would you want with Vanessa?" Ainsley asked. "She hates the clinic."

The truth wouldn't go over well, but Natalie couldn't think up a lie that would go over any better. "You were trying to make it appear as though I'd killed Baxter Quincy. I assumed that meant one of you had killed him. I wanted to know if Vanessa could certify you never left the party here on the night he died."

Stuart grunted. "If you wanted information like that, why wouldn't you leave it to the cops instead of setting up a crazy meeting?"

Good question, Natalie thought despairingly. Bartholomew would lecture her corpse with a fierce *I warned you to call us first* when they found her body buried in the woods or fished it out of the lake. What had she done to Gideon by bringing him with her? Was he dead?

"I don't have much credibility with the cops right now," she said. "I hoped I could get information to take to them. Stuart . . . Ainsley . . . Vanessa is manipulating us. I have no idea why. We need to stop the game, stop hiding, and get all this to the police. If we do anything else, we'll make it worse."

Ainsley rubbed her hands against her jeans in the convulsive movement Natalie had witnessed when she'd found Ainsley at the sink. "We can't make it go away," Ainsley whispered.

"No," Natalie said. "But we can make sure nothing else terrible happens."

Ainsley studied her palms, then rubbed them again on her thighs.

"Ainsley," Stuart hissed. "Stop it."

"She's not doing it deliberately," Natalie said. "She needs help, Stuart."

"She needs this *over*. Which means you gone. If Vanessa is messing with us, we'll deal with her too."

"Wait!" Ainsley said. "Wait."

"Lamb, we don't have a choice." Natalie felt Stuart inhale, felt his muscles loosen for an instant and then tighten. He was steeling himself, preparing to kill her. As subtly as she could, she lifted one foot, ready to slam it onto Stuart's foot with every shred of strength she had. If the pain of a broken foot distracted him momentarily, she might be able to grab his arm and pull the knife back far enough to give her a chance to fight.

"Wait." Ainsley stumbled forward and clutched Stuart's knife arm. "I know we don't have a choice. But . . . let me do it."

"Get back, Ainsley," Stuart said.

"This is my fault. Drew is my fault. You didn't want to hurt him. You tried to tell me no. I pushed you into it." Sobs shook her voice into wordlessness for a moment before she added, "I'll . . . I can . . . I'll take care of Natalie."

Stuart didn't respond; Natalie felt him trembling. She remained motionless. Despite Ainsley's hand on Stuart's arm, the knife was still pressed against her throat, and now she was tightly sandwiched between the MacKerrons. She could kick Ainsley, forcing her back, but attacking Stuart's wife was a surefire way to get her throat cut immediately.

"My hands are already stained." Ainsley picked at Stuart's fingers clenched around the knife. "It doesn't matter."

"Lamb, you don't want to—"

"Let me *do* it!" Ainsley shrieked. "You hate what you did to Drew. You don't have to live with this too. Give me the knife. You hold her. I'll put the knife straight in her heart. Natalie, it won't hurt. I promise it won't hurt. You'll die so fast you won't feel it."

"You . . . are you sure?" Stuart's tone was so relieved that it amazed Natalie. Would he truly let Ainsley—

"I'm sure," Ainsley said. "This is my fault. I'll do it."

Stuart opened his fingers. Ainsley took the knife.

With the blade away from her throat, Natalie instantly smashed her heel into Stuart's foot and wrenched her body to the side. Stuart yelled, losing his grip on her, but her momentum made her stagger. Before she could gain her footing, Stuart's shoulder slammed into her, hurtling them both to the grass. She tried to squirm out from under him, but Stuart sat up, planting his weight on her stomach, and grabbed both her wrists.

She brought her leg to the side, bracing her foot against the grass so she could push upward and roll Stuart off of her, but he scooted back so he was sitting on her thighs, immobilizing her legs. He yanked her arms so they lay straight at her sides and pinned her wrists to the ground. Natalie struggled, but he was so much stronger than she that the fight was ridiculous.

"Do it," he said.

Ainsley moved to stand next to Natalie. Her face was shadowy gray, her eyes lifeless black—two candles gone out. She touched the tip of the knife with her thumb.

"Ainsley, please." Natalie gasped out the words. "Guilt is . . . already . . . destroying you. Don't do this."

Tears flooded down Ainsley's face as she clutched the knife.

"You don't want this. Ainsley, please. You can't live with this."

Ainsley held the knife in front of her, blade pointing toward Natalie's chest. She raised the knife above her head, lowered it to waist level, raised it again as though she couldn't decide the optimal striking distance. Natalie writhed, but the best she could do was lift her shoulders off the ground and twist from side to side. She could throw off Ainsley's aim, but she couldn't avoid the strike.

"Out," Ainsley whispered, taking two steps backward. "I have to get the stain out."

"Lamb—"

In a twitch of motion, Ainsley flipped the blade toward her own chest and shoved it inward.

"*Ainsley!*" Stuart howled her name, springing off Natalie. The knife plopped to the grass. Stuart caught Ainsley.

Natalie threw herself toward the fallen knife, grabbed it, and ran.

CHAPTER 29

NATALIE SPRINTED TOWARD GIDEON'S CAR, the memory of Ainsley's anguished face so dominant in her mind that she could barely see where she was running. She should flee toward the main park road, not the secluded overflow parking lot, but she couldn't follow through on that survival instinct, not when Gideon was in trouble.

Running too fast to stop herself, she skidded on the short-clipped grass and bumped into the hood of his car. The parking area was too dark for her to see the whole interior of the car, so she grabbed the door handle on the driver's door and pulled. The door was unlocked. The dome light lit empty front and back seats.

She wanted to yell his name but didn't want to draw Stuart's attention away from Ainsley. How severely was Ainsley hurt? How deep had the blade gone? It was a large hunting knife, deadly sharp—

Focus. You can't help her. Find Gideon and find a phone.

Find him how? She couldn't see well enough to search—

Flashlight. Gideon had a flashlight in the glove compartment. Knife gripped in her right hand in case Stuart showed up, she knelt on the driver's seat, yanked the glove compartment open with her left hand, and fumbled inside it until she grabbed the mini flashlight.

Through the windshield, she looked in the direction of the gazebo. She couldn't see Stuart or Ainsley. Where had they gone? Was Ainsley still alive?

Focus.

She stepped out of the car and swept the beam of the flashlight across the ground, searching for any indentations in the grass, any hint of which direction he'd gone—which direction he'd been taken.

"Gideon." She could no longer keep herself from blurting his name, her voice crumpling with fear. She couldn't wander around, hollering for him. She needed to get out of here and call for help. There was a gas station—

Something brushed her ankle. Natalie screamed and leaped backward, swinging the flashlight beam toward the car. Feet in canvas loafers protruded from under the car. Duct tape encircled the ankles of jeans.

"Gideon!"

A groan and words too muffled for her to understand came from beneath the car. She knelt and shone the beam under the car. Gideon lay on his stomach, his hands shackled behind him. A dark sack covered his head.

Brimming with relief, Natalie set the flashlight in the grass, folded Stuart's knife, and shoved it down the front of the fitted shirt beneath her tunic. The knife was too big to fit in her front pocket without falling out, and she didn't want it in her back pocket where Stuart could swipe it from behind.

Stuart's knife, now covered with her fingerprints and Ainsley's blood. She'd never be able to convince the police—

Worry about it later. "Gideon, it's Natalie. I'm going to grab your feet and pull you out. If you need me to stop, tell me."

Gideon mumbled something. Hoping it wasn't *Don't move me,* Natalie got a firm grip on his bound ankles and backed up, dragging him. She was too shaky to make the motion as smooth as she wanted. It ended up being a jerky stop-and-start, and she felt part of him smack the undercarriage of the car as she pulled him into the open.

"Your phone." She worked at the knotted rope around his neck that held the bag secure. "Do you have it?"

He muttered something that resembled "I don't know"—with the bag muting his voice and his face in the grass, it was hard to tell. She abandoned the knot and hurriedly checked his back pockets, then slid her hands underneath him and checked his front pockets. No phone, but she did find his keys. She shoved the keys in her pocket, picked up the flashlight and swept the beam under the car, then jogged around the car in a circle, sweeping the flashlight across the ground. The phone wasn't here. Whoever had attacked him must have taken it.

"Are you . . . okay?" Gideon asked, his words a little clearer.

"Yes." Natalie retrieved the hunting knife. "Hold still. I have a knife. I'm going to cut the rope off your neck and the duct tape off your ankles." She couldn't do anything about the handcuffs, but the police could deal with that later. She needed to get Gideon in the car and both of them out of here, which would be easier if he could see and stand.

She opened the knife and held the base of the small flashlight in her teeth to aim the light at his neck. Warring against nausea at the sight of bloodied steel, she wriggled a finger under the rope to pull it away from Gideon's neck and sawed through the rope.

She eased the bag off Gideon's head. Blood had matted his hair in back. *He's alive. Don't panic.*

"I don't . . . remember . . . what happened," he said.

She sawed through the duct tape, ripped it from his ankles, and set the flashlight in the grass. "You got hit on the head. You need a doctor. Let's get you into the car." She closed and stowed the knife.

"What . . . We're . . . Where are we? You were . . . We were . . ."

"We're at the Cascata Sculpture Park." Natalie opened the back door of the car. "We need to get out of here."

"Was I . . . ? I was waiting for you."

"Yes, I was supposed to meet Vanessa. It was a trap. Vanessa set us up. I'm going to turn you over." She leaned over Gideon, grasped his shoulder, and rolled him onto his back. He groaned.

"I'm sorry. I'd be more gentle, but we really need to go." She drew him to a sitting position. He swayed. She hooked her hands under his arms and dragged him toward the car. "I'll hoist you into the backseat," she said, leaning him against the doorframe. "If you can get your footing even for an instant, that would help."

"Got it," he said, but from the expression on his face, visible in the car's dome light, he looked more likely to vomit than to stand. She slid her hands under his arms and heaved upward. He drew his legs under him, his shoes sliding on the grass. Finally, his legs steadied and pushed upward. She lifted and shoved; he landed on his back on the seat.

Natalie raised his legs, swung them to the side and stuffed them into the car. "I'm sorry." She shut the door. He must be miserably uncomfortable, but she didn't have time to fix that. She snatched his keys from her pocket and reached for the flashlight.

Something slammed into the back of her knees, buckling them and hurtling her toward the still-open driver's door. She threw her hands up to catch herself, dropping the keys. A blow to the side of her rib cage knocked her away from the car. She staggered and fell. The car door slammed.

"Hello, Natalie." A female voice spoke softly. Natalie could see the dark silhouette of a masked figure and the dark silhouette of a gun. "You're going to head toward those trees." The muzzle of the gun pointed toward the forested area east of the parking lot.

Between pain and fresh, boiling terror, Natalie could hardly force words from her mouth. "Vanessa . . . why . . . ?"

A baleful whisper was the response. "If we have that discussion here, I'll have to kill any witnesses. Is that what you want?"

Desperately, Natalie eyed the car where Gideon lay shackled and injured. If she could lead Vanessa away from him, she had to do it. She drew herself to her feet and stumbled toward the trees. Her back to Vanessa, she touched the knife beneath her shirt. She was armed. She had a chance.

When they were past the perimeter of the parking lot in an area lit as much by moonlight as by the security lights, Vanessa spoke. "Stop. Turn around. Slowly, please."

Was that Vanessa's voice? Natalie pivoted to face her. She stood only a yard or so away. "What do you want?"

"First?" She extended her free hand. "I want Stuart MacKerron's knife. Please give it to me."

"I don't have it."

"Oh, don't be silly. You have it."

The politeness. The sweetly chiding tone. Natalie squinted through the darkness at the masked woman. "*Are* you Vanessa?"

A refined giggle. "Vanessa changed her mind about meeting with you. When she told me about the appointment, as I knew she would, I warned her it wasn't safe to go near you, that I suspected you planned to set her up. To lie about her like you did about Ainsley."

"*Lauren?*"

"The knife, please."

"Lauren . . . what's going on?"

"The knife. Or I'll shoot you."

"I don't have it." Natalie patted her front jeans pockets, then turned around to show her back pockets. She hoped the blousy tunic wasn't exposing the outline of the weapon. "I picked it up, but I tossed it into the car when I was helping Gideon in."

"No, you didn't. You're not careless. You wouldn't let it go until you finished your getaway."

"How did Stuart and Ainsley . . . Did *you* leave them that note? Telling them to meet me? That I was blackmailing them?"

"It was outrageous, wasn't it? But I knew they'd believe it. They're panicking, not thinking logically."

"How did you figure out they killed Drew? I didn't think you knew the MacKerrons well."

"I don't, but I do check in with Heather occasionally. She craves a listening ear, and after the incident at the opening gala, I called her once she was out of the hospital."

"You called Heather? You know her personally?"

"Yes, I've known her for several years. She told me everything she knew about the MacKerrons and Drew Drummond. She knew a lot. She drifts around, learning things, noticing things. I made a few educated guesses."

"The thefts? Heather—"

"Yes, I knew Heather wasn't the thief. She has a treasure, a lovely little nineteenth-century teapot. When she heard the thief liked jewelry and pretty knickknacks, she told me she'd hidden the teapot so it wouldn't get stolen. Even Heather wouldn't wring her hands over her beloved teapot if *she* were the thief. When the police found stolen jewelry at her apartment, along with the vase, Ainsley seemed the likely culprit. Such an intriguing tidbit of information to add to your blackmail note, wasn't it?"

"Why did you lure the MacKerrons here tonight? So they'd kill me?"

"That was my hope. I didn't expect Ainsley to stop Stuart, the silly girl. She seems to have a weak mind, doesn't she? All that nonsense about ghosts. Honestly, Natalie, do you know *anyone* who is sane?"

"Why are you doing this?"

"Oh, my dear. I don't like it when people stick their nasty hands into my life and steal things that belong to me. Beautiful, perfect things. Things that promised to stay with me forever. He would have stayed if you hadn't brainwashed him with your psychobabble."

He would have stayed . . . Things that belong to me . . . You're still mine. Sophia's texts. Heather's warning. "You . . . are Kenton Lowery's ex-wife?"

"I'm his wife. I don't acknowledge the ex, and neither will he once your claws are out of his brain. You think you have so much control, don't you? Why don't you mind-control this gun out of my hand?"

"Everyone else thinks she's perfect." Kenton's lament spoken repeatedly in therapy. *"If I told the truth, no one would believe it. She's that good, Dr. Marsh."*

Good enough to fool even Heather—Heather, who had a knack for understanding people. No wonder Heather had been so shaken when Kenton had told her the truth, shaken enough to insist that Bartholomew warn Natalie.

"You're Sophia Lowery," Natalie said. "Does Heather know you work at the Stoker?"

"Oh, gracious no, and it *did* take some effort to ensure she never saw me. Heather has no idea I live in Ohneka now, you see. As far as she knows, I'm still in Syracuse. And my name isn't Sophia. That was a nickname, a darling little joke from when Kenton and I first met. He thought I was so lovely, so elegant, like a classic movie star. He was a fan, you see, of Sophia Loren. And with my name, Lauren, it became an inside joke. Sophia Lauren, and eventually just Sophia, and it was adorable, so I kept it. Everyone in his world knew me as Sophia. Until you broke his mind and took him away."

"I did not have an affair—"

"Oh heavens, I know that. I've figured you out. Your weapon is your mind, not your body, though it's a lovely body, and what a darling blouse that is. Now reach under it and pull out that knife you're hiding."

Natalie ignored the command. "I didn't brainwash Kenton."

"He never would have left me without your influence. He wanted to make it work, didn't he? He wanted to stay with me. You tricked him. Manipulated him."

The fact that, even with Kenton's ex holding a gun on her, she couldn't break confidentiality and tell Lauren what they'd discussed made Natalie feel that reality had disintegrated into absurdity. "Lauren, be reasonable. You can't think that—"

"Of course, he didn't have the courage to admit he was seeing a shrink," Lauren said. "But I saw regular amounts of money disappearing from the account and a lot of unexplained miles on his car. It was simple to follow him to figure out where he was going and took only minor detective work to identify you."

"I'm surprised you didn't confront him."

"Oh, sometimes secrets are a delight. You can store them up and wield them when the time is right. I admit that at first, I didn't recognize how poisonous you were. I thought once he quit seeing you, he'd return to me, and that would have been the simplest and sweetest ending. Is there anything more satisfying than a beautiful, humbled man crawling back to beg forgiveness?"

Natalie kept her mouth closed. Speaking her mind would get her shot.

"You damaged him." Lauren took a step closer. "That requires special payback. How best to punish Natalie Marsh? Noble Dr. Marsh and her beloved holy clinic. Let's convince people she and her clinic are evil personified. That's a marvelous idea."

"You . . . the letter to Heather. *You* wrote those letters from Tabitha, urging her to help bring down Nefesh Bria. Yet you accuse *me* of playing with people's minds?"

"Oh, Heather's always been a lost cause. If you can do anything useful with her, it's for the better. I charmed her because she was a convenient link to Kenton, but, my word, she's crazy. Now, you can throw that knife to me, or I can put a bullet or two in your leg and you can ask me the rest of your questions while you're whimpering and bleeding on the ground. I won't shoot to kill yet. This is such a delightful conversation. I'd hate to cut it off early. I'm actually glad now that Stuart didn't kill you. Seeing the look on your face is a memory I'll treasure. It's a shame the light isn't better."

At this point, holding on to the knife was useless. She couldn't ward off a bullet with a blade. She removed the knife from under her shirt and tossed it at Lauren's feet. Lauren picked it up with gloved fingers and tucked it into a deep front pocket.

"Baxter," Natalie said. "You were helping Baxter try to get the clinic thrown out—"

"No, darling. Baxter was helping *me*, but he didn't know it. Controlling an egotistical man is so easy it's comical."

"Until he figured out what you were up to," Natalie said. "*You* killed him. It wasn't Stuart or Ainsley, was it? It was you. You sneaked away from Vanessa's party when you were supposedly resting because of dental pain."

"I didn't want to kill him. Truly, who *wants* to commit murder? So nasty. But he'd figured out I was paying people to cause trouble, and he was so self-righteously angry about it. Did you know dear Baxter had a conscience? A conscience even about the clinic he hated? He demanded I come clean with you. I agreed and pretended I'd arranged to meet you at your house so we'd have privacy. I invited him to come witness my confession." Lauren gave a gleeful laugh. "He showed up. I was there. You weren't."

"You killed him to spare your reputation, and you think it's funny to brag about it."

"I'm not heartless. If I were, I would have killed Gideon instead of knocking him silly and tying him up. It would have been easier, but I didn't want him to die. I hope I didn't hit him too hard. *He* never did anything to me, and he's a nice man. Not that I'm going to take him, darling; don't worry about that. He's not my type. Kenton is my man, and without your toxic influence, he'll be wholly mine. We can start clean."

"Clean?" Natalie said coldly. "The police already suspect Kenton's ex might be targeting me. They're tracking you down. Detective Bartholomew talked to me about it today."

"Did he? I wondered why he left me a message to call him. But I'm not worried. You'll be dead, and I'll have an alibi. Vanessa will swear I was with her tonight."

"Vanessa *is* involved?"

"Oh, my dear, she won't have a choice. I stirred such dreadful fears that you were plotting to frame her for a crime tonight that we've already promised each other to swear we were working together until midnight. She *is* working late at a storage shed on her family's property, sorting through years of old artwork her parents collected and deciding if anything is worthy of being displayed at the Parisi Gallery. I helped her for a while, then told her I was getting a ghastly migraine and was going home to bed."

"If she hears murder is involved, she'll change her mind about lying for you."

"No, no. That's when she'll be even more desperate to lie. It will be self-preservation. Remember, Gideon will swear you had an appointment with her tonight. She's working alone. She'll need me to *give* her an alibi even more than I'll need one *from* her."

"She won't risk—"

"Besides, she was foolish enough to stretch the truth for me the night Baxter died. When the police were coming to talk to me, I begged her to swear I was at her party the entire evening. I told her Baxter and I had had a tiny argument, and I was scared you'd try to blame me for his death. She doesn't like you, and she thinks you killed Baxter. And she thinks I *was* at the party the whole time, so why not tell that to the police?"

"She doesn't realize you left," Natalie said. "She thinks you were lying down in her office."

"Yes, exactly. She'll lie for me; she has no choice. We'll testify we were together at the storage shed, and all will be perfect."

"It won't work out that neatly. Stuart—"

"Stuart is on his way to get help for Ainsley. I'm sure he'll claim you stabbed her, which works beautifully, because your fingerprints are all over the knife. All Gideon will be able to do is testify—*if* he remembers anything that happened after you arrived here tonight—that you returned to the car, helped him inside, then left again. He won't even be able to say whether or not another person was there. I looked at him in the car right before we started over here, and his eyes were closed. I suspect he wasn't conscious, or at least wasn't lucid. The police will assume either you or Stuart attacked him originally. And you'll have stabbed yourself to death in a welter of guilt, so you can't deny anything."

"That last part's not happening," Natalie said. "I'm not helping you frame me."

"You don't have to cooperate." Lauren shifted the gun to her other hand and reached into the backpack Natalie hadn't noticed she was wearing. She withdrew what looked like a dark stick and expanded it to become a longer dark stick.

A police baton. Was that what she'd used to knock Gideon out?

"If you hit me over the head, how are the police going to believe I—"

Lauren lunged forward, the baton held like a bayonet. The tip of the baton slammed into Natalie's gut. A blast of agony sent her to her knees, and her body curled forward until her face almost touched the dirt. She couldn't straighten her spine; she couldn't lift her head; she couldn't breathe.

Lauren seized her shoulders, shoved her onto her back, and sat on top of her as Stuart had done, landing with enough force to knock any remaining traces of air from Natalie's lungs. Natalie reached to push her off, but movement raised the pain to heights where she couldn't perceive anything beyond it. Her arms fell to her sides.

Vaguely, Natalie felt gloved fingers lift her right hand and press something hard against her palm. The handle of Stuart's knife. The blade was open now, reflecting a white glimmer of moonlight. Lauren grasped Natalie's other hand and wrapped it around the handle as well, molding her limp fingers into place like they were putty.

Gasping, Natalie channeled all her strength into resisting as Lauren turned the blade toward Natalie's chest and shoved it downward. She couldn't hold Lauren off; her arms shook, and savage nausea racked her body. The blade grazed her shirt. Lauren lifted herself onto her knees and thumped downward onto Natalie's stomach, again driving the air from her lungs.

Natalie strained to direct the blade off target, to aim it toward the ground or even her own shoulder. She couldn't do it. Under Lauren's power,

Natalie's hands brought the blade closer to her chest. This time it pierced fabric and sank into flesh. Natalie couldn't scream; she had no air in her lungs.

A blare of noise and flashes of light made Lauren jump and twist to look behind her. Scavenging the last of her energy, Natalie pushed the knife upward as ferociously as she could. The handle of the knife slammed into Lauren's masked jaw. Lauren reeled, and Natalie rolled, knocking Lauren off of her. Her breath was returning, and she realized only she—not Lauren— was gripping the knife.

Lauren scrambled to her knees, yanking the gun out of her pocket. Natalie propelled herself toward Lauren and slammed the point of the knife into Lauren's arm. Lauren screamed, and the gun bobbled in her hand. Before Lauren could correct her aim, Natalie hammered the hilt of the knife against her wrist. The gun fell out of Lauren's hand.

Natalie's free hand had been bracing her weight against the ground. She tried to shift and reach for the gun, but Lauren's uninjured hand snatched it first, holding it awkwardly by the barrel. Natalie swiped at her hand with the knife. Lauren yanked the gun upward, and the blade missed her. Frantic to prevent her from aiming, Natalie rammed the blade into Lauren's thigh, then, when she lowered her arm, slashed at her hand. Lauren flung herself backward. The gun hit the ground again, but this time Lauren didn't try to retrieve it. She stumbled to her feet and limp-ran into the trees.

Natalie fumbled for the gun and picked it up in her left hand. She should swap it with the knife, holding the more deadly weapon in her dominant hand, but she couldn't seem to loosen her fingers from the knife handle. Still fighting for breath, she dragged herself to her feet, her body hunched over the blazing pain where Lauren had struck her in the stomach. She had to get back to Gideon . . . get out of here . . . Lauren might come back . . . or Stuart . . . No, Ainsley was injured. So was Lauren. Natalie had stabbed Lauren. Lauren's blood was all over her blouse. Or was that her own blood?

Natalie stumbled into the grassy parking area. The headlights on Gideon's car flashed, and the throbbing honk of a car alarm battered her ears. His car alarm. He'd set it off, distracting Lauren. She could see him wobbling toward her. She was wobbling. The ground was wobbling; the sky swayed. In the distance, past the gazebo, past the office, more lights flashed, blue and red. Police cars. How had Gideon called the police? No phone . . .

Searing light—a flashlight? A searchlight?—hit her. She closed her eyes, but losing her vision was enough to make her lose her balance. She fell to her knees in the grass. Shaking with pain, she stayed there, trying to remember where she'd been going, the knife in one hand, the gun in the other.

The knife. The gun. Both covered with her fingerprints.

CHAPTER 30

TURNING HIS HEAD WAS A lot harder than it should have been. Pain boomed through Gideon's skull, his vision blurred, and he nearly fell over, but the one clear glimpse he'd gotten of the people approaching from the direction of the gazebo was enough. Police officers. Powerful relief made him even less steady as he resumed his slog toward Natalie. He slowed to a shuffle. He didn't want to fall again, and between the knock on the head and his hands chained behind him, staying on his feet was already a hairsbreadth from impossible.

An officer reached him. Another started toward Natalie but stopped. The beam from a flashlight lit Natalie, and the terror that had eased when Gideon had seen her approaching returned. A trickle of red stained her neck and crimson blotches stained her blouse. His gaze was too bleary for him to observe her expression—all he could see was a patch of lifeless white.

Natalie crumpled to her knees, and Gideon recklessly accelerated his unstable steps. Why weren't the police rushing to help her?

The officer next to him caught his arm. "Keep clear, sir."

"She's hurt," Gideon said. "Help her. What are you—" Those dark blurs in Natalie's hands. A gun in one hand, a large knife in the other. From behind Gideon, he heard cars driving into the overflow parking area.

"Drop your weapons!" An officer shouted the command, her gun trained on Natalie.

Natalie didn't react. Her head was bowed, the gun and the knife both resting on her knees.

"Let me talk to her." Gideon tried to shake off the officer's hand. Another officer caught his other arm. "Hey—no—listen to me. She's not dangerous. She's not thinking straight. Let me—"

"Put your weapons down! *Now*."

"*Natalie!*" Gideon yelled, his own voice triggering an avalanche of dizziness. "Natalie, do what they say. They don't know—They think you—" He had no idea what the police thought she'd done; he had no idea what had happened. All he knew was that she'd never hurt anyone unless she had no choice, unless she was fighting for her life . . .

"Let me talk to her; let me *go*—" He struggled, the handcuffs gouging into whatever skin remained on his wrists. Fire shot over his skull and down his spine. His legs buckled. "Natalie—" He was on the ground, face-down, firm hands on his back keeping him there, choking her name into the grass.

* * *

She *had* dropped the gun—hadn't she? She could see it resting on the grass, black metal against green. Where had she gotten a gun? She didn't own one.

Lauren.

Lauren Bell? Why did she think Lauren had a gun?

No. Not Lauren. Sophia. "*She's the best actress on the planet, Dr. Marsh. If I told people, they'd call me a liar, say I must have hurt myself.*"

. . . best actress . . . no one would believe . . .

"Natalie?" A kind bass voice spoke above her. Familiar voice. Detective Bartholomew. She tried to lift her head to look at him, but she couldn't. Her head was leaden, her neck useless. Her blouse was wet, clinging to her skin.

No one would believe me.

Best actress . . . sweet Lauren . . . oh, my dear, no one steals things that belong to me . . .

No one would believe me.

"Natalie, can you hear me?"

She wanted to connect her broken thoughts, but when she tried to hook them together, they floated apart. Sophia. This was about Sophia. What about Sophia?

Does Sophia know who you are? Heather wants to warn you . . .

She's that good, Dr. Marsh.

"You're injured. We're going to get you to the hospital, but you need to give me the knife."

The knife. Lauren's knife. No, Stuart's knife. Ainsley's knife. Ainsley had taken it . . .

"Natalie, can you hear me? Answer me, please."

"Yes," Natalie rasped.

"Good. Give me the knife."

She had the knife? She blinked. One hand resting on her lap was empty. The other hand was clenched, a blade extending from the fist. She couldn't feel it in her palm, but she had it; she could see it. There was blood on the blade. On her hand. On her jeans.

She had the knife. Of course she had it. She'd stabbed Lauren with it.

You brainwashed Kenton.

Brainwashed Ainsley.

I didn't brainwash her. I went to help her. I wanted to help her.

"Natalie, can you look at me?"

Slowly, she managed to tip her weighty head backward. Bartholomew was leaning over her. He stretched out a sinewy hand. "Give me the knife."

Was he real? Was she hallucinating? She couldn't yield up the knife. She had to be ready to fight, to defend herself—

"Gideon is worried about you," Bartholomew said. "He has half the force pinning him down to keep him from running over here. How about you let me take you to him before the guy has a heart attack?"

Gideon. Natalie tried to make her tongue shape words. "He's . . . he's hurt."

"We know. Ambulance is here. You're hurt too. Let us help you."

"I thought I was meeting Vanessa. We had an appointment . . ." She touched her blouse where a soaked red blotch was spreading. "I wanted to ask her about Ainsley. I didn't hurt Ainsley. I wanted to help her."

"You help people," Bartholomew said. "It's what you love. How about you let someone else take a turn? Give me the knife, and let me help you."

Marianne had said something like that. Or was it Gideon? Gideon. He was worried about her. She stared into Bartholomew's face. He looked real.

"Stuart MacKerron tried to kill me," she said. "This is his knife."

"You're safe. We won't let Mr. MacKerron near you. Give me the knife."

She lifted an unwieldy hand and offered the knife to Bartholomew, handle first. Her cramped fingers wouldn't completely open. Bartholomew gently uncurled them the rest of the way and took the knife.

"Thank you." He raised his empty hand and waved someone forward.

"I stabbed Lauren Bell," Natalie said.

"Why did you do that?" Bartholomew spoke so calmly that the miniscule part of her professional brain that was functioning admired his composure.

"She was . . . trying to kill me." Natalie groped through her memories, hunting for pieces. "She . . . tried to stab . . . tried to make *me* stab myself . . . I got the knife . . . attacked her. She ran. She ran . . . You need to find her; she's out there, that way . . ." Natalie tried to gesture behind her, but the motion hurt too much.

"We'll find her," Bartholomew said.

"She had a gun . . . She dropped it . . ." Natalie squinted at her empty hands. "I used to have the gun. I don't remember what I did with it."

"I have it."

"My fingerprints are on it. The gun. And the knife. I didn't want . . . Lauren was . . ." *She has to be in control . . . has to have everything how she wants . . . She's perfect to everyone else . . . can lie about anything, and everyone believes her . . .* "She killed Baxter. Lauren killed Baxter. Stuart and Ainsley killed Drew . . . They didn't want to. Lauren . . . she . . . Kenton . . . you won't believe . . ." Natalie couldn't remember what she was trying to explain. Her thoughts misted over, and her face prickled with lack of blood.

"Don't assume I won't believe you," Bartholomew said as Natalie felt two sets of hands easing her onto her back. "We had a long talk with Kenton Lowery earlier this evening. I'm willing to have a pretty open mind about what the ex-Mrs. Lowery is capable of."

CHAPTER 31

AT A LIGHT KNOCK ON her hospital room door, Natalie opened her eyes. She didn't attempt a verbal response. No one who knocked ever waited for one.

The door opened, and Marianne leaned into the room. "May I come in?"

Marianne. Ainsley's aunt. A trickle of guilt and anxiety spread through Natalie, along with the drip of fluid passing through her IV tubing. "Yes," she said quietly. Quiet was the only volume she could use without magnifying pain.

Marianne entered the room and closed the door behind her. "So here you are in a hospital bed," she said, her voice as soft as Natalie's.

Natalie smiled at her, a smile she hoped didn't appear as breakable as it felt.

"Betrayed," Marianne said. "Manipulated, stabbed, nearly killed. Is this your hobby? Collecting brushes with death?"

"I hope not."

"How are you feeling?"

"Better."

Marianne settled into the chair Gideon had left at the side of the bed. "How long are they keeping you here?"

"I don't know. The knife wounds weren't life-threatening. The biggest concern is internal bleeding." Natalie touched her stomach. "I got . . . punched hard. They're trying to manage it without surgery, and so far, so good."

"I'm glad to hear that," Marianne said. "Gideon's been discharged, I hear."

"Yes. He's staying with a friend's family for a couple days. His doctor didn't want him going home unless someone could keep an eye on him."

The sorrow in Marianne's gray eyes was meditative, and Natalie wondered what she was pondering. "If you're in the mood to tell me 'I told you so,' feel free," Marianne said. "Clearly, your take on my niece was more accurate than mine."

"I'm not in the mood. You were more objective than any of us, and I didn't understand most of what was happening either. I'm sorry I didn't handle it better."

"Do you feel you failed somehow?"

"I don't know." Understanding her own feelings wasn't a task she had the courage or the energy to attempt right now. "I'm grateful to hear Ainsley survived. The police told me Stuart called 911—that's why they showed up at the Cascata park."

"Yes. Thank heavens. Those greedy, foolish kids."

Natalie spoke cautiously, trying to gauge how painful this was for Marianne. "I heard they confessed."

"Yes. I cornered your friend Detective Turner—nice man—and wrung as much out of him as I could. Stuart tried to blame everything on you but kept butchering his story, and Ainsley was too torn up by lies and a hunting knife to even remember to claim you'd stabbed her."

"This must be heartbreaking for you."

"I'm grieving for Drew Drummond's family. I'm grieving for Ainsley and Stuart. I'm not angry with them; that's fruitless. Ainsley is already torturing herself, and the legal system will take care of the punishment. They don't need any chastisement from me."

"I'm so sorry," Natalie said.

"So am I." Marianne touched Natalie's shoulder. "Tell me how you're doing. I'm not asking how many rounds of antibiotics you've had or whether or not they're letting you walk around yet. I'm asking about your soul. Your mind. Your heart."

"I'm all right," Natalie said. "Grateful. I'm grateful Gideon is alive . . . grateful I'm alive . . . grateful the police are figuring out the truth."

"What else?" Marianne tapped Natalie's hand where she'd unconsciously clenched it around the bed rail. "Gratitude is not what's radiating from that fist."

Memory crashed on already eroded emotions. "I . . . There are some things I'm . . . having trouble processing."

"Like the fact that you sank a knife into another human being?"

Natalie grimaced at Marianne's candor. "I don't want to be here." Her throat constricted, and bruised abdominal muscles tightened. "I don't mean here in the hospital. I mean here, where I am in my head." She paused, trying to relax, but everything got tighter. She swallowed.

Marianne took her hand. "Tell me about where you are."

"I really don't want to."

"I know. Tell me anyway."

Tears began to leak. What was it about Marianne's firm compassion that triggered weeping? "I hate this. I hate that I need to talk about it, that it hurts to talk about it, that I'm afraid of it. I hate that I'm crying."

"Why do you hate the fact that you have natural human reactions to mental and physical trauma?"

Her fingernails dug into Marianne's hand. "Because I don't *want* to be traumatized."

"That's strange," Marianne said. "Most of us enjoy it."

Natalie laughed, which hurt so acutely that she stopped the laughter and lay motionless, tears falling. "I don't want to need help," she said. "Again."

"You want to march out of the hospital and get back to work helping other people solve their problems. You don't want to be the one with the problems."

"Marianne, how could I not see . . . *anything*? How could I not have any idea what Lauren Bell was? *Who* she was?"

"You can answer that question yourself."

Natalie drew her hand away from Marianne and let it flop to the bed. Objectively, she did know the answer. Lauren was brilliant at presenting a flawless image. Kenton had never given Natalie any identifying details about his wife—not even her real name—and he'd had no idea she knew Natalie existed, let alone that she would seek revenge. Why *would* Natalie have had reason to suspect Lauren's identity?

"Exactly." Marianne obviously recognized the awareness in her face. "Stop feeling you have to be the all-knowledgeable, mind-reading shrink. I'm giving you a head's up: I'm going to convince Bob to give you three months paid leave—mandatory—from Nefesh Bria so you can take time to rest and recover."

Natalie started to push herself up. Pain or not, she couldn't win this argument while lounging feebly in a hospital bed. "Don't you *dare*. I need to—"

"Heal," Marianne finished. "You need to heal. So does everyone. You waltz back into the clinic immediately and you know what it will be like. Reporters, rubberneckers, gossips. You'll be trying to work with clients who are too sidetracked by what they've read in the news to pay attention to your work together. Take some time, boss. The clinic's not going anywhere. I'll personally ensure we have people to cover for you. Your clients will receive the help they need."

Natalie slumped onto her pillow.

"Everything will be all right," Marianne said. "But it won't be all right *now*. That's not how growth and healing work."

"I know." Natalie let her eyes close. "I know."

* * *

"You can sit." Heather's thin fingers indicated the couch in the meeting room where a staff member had led them.

"Thank you for seeing us," Natalie said, heartened at how composed Heather appeared. She wasn't smiling, but she looked thoughtful, not distant or scared. Her hair was in a glossy braid draped over the shoulder of her yellow knit dress. Her socks had miniature yellow roses woven into the fabric.

"Did they tell you you're the first visitors I've let in besides Kenton?" Heather asked.

"They didn't." Natalie sat on the couch with Gideon. The small room was furnished with upholstered sea-green and coral furniture. A window overlooked tree-covered grounds.

Heather sat in a chair across from them. "That's because the other people who've tried are people who never cared about me on the outside. I think they're hoping to sell stories about me."

"We're not fans of making a buck off gossip," Gideon said.

"No. You *are* the gossip."

Gideon winced. "Yep."

"Mr. Chapman is coming to visit me today as well," Heather said. "I wasn't sure if I wanted to talk to him, but I'm curious what he'll say. So I agreed."

"I'm glad you're talking with him," Natalie said. "I think you'll find he's a good man."

"At any rate, he's a hoot to talk with," Gideon said.

Heather reacted with a tentative smile.

"I want to thank you," Natalie said. "For pointing the police in the direction of Kenton's ex-wife."

Heather bit her lip. "I should have known. Earlier. I should have known earlier. I'm not usually wrong about people."

"I was completely wrong about her too," Natalie said.

"She would contact me sometimes." Heather played with her braid. "She was always so sweet."

"She's an expert manipulator," Gideon said. "Fooled everyone."

"She'd talk to me about Tabitha—she pretended she believed Tabitha communicated with me. She always wanted information on Kenton. She'd tell me she still loved him, even though he'd cheated on her. I'd tell her about his bakery or whatever. I thought she still lived in Syracuse. I had no idea she was in Ohneka. Neither did Kenton. He visited me a few days ago and told me more about what she did to him. She was horrible . . . like Mom, but better at hiding how awful she was. Do you know he has scars from her? That scar on his arm is one of them." She looked at Natalie. "Kenton said she tried to kill you."

"Yes."

"How did you get the police to believe you? Kenton was amazed that anyone would believe the truth about her."

"She made mistakes." Not sure how much Heather knew, Natalie summarized the events of that evening. As she spoke, Heather's midnight-blue eyes examined her so intently that Natalie suspected she was zeroing in on the pain beneath the objective report.

After Natalie finished outlining the confrontation between Lauren and her, Heather repeated, "I should have known earlier. I should have warned you earlier."

"This is not your fault," Natalie said. "Lauren is responsible for her own behavior. You weren't responsible for magically reading her mind and stopping her."

Heather watched Natalie thoughtfully. Natalie heard Marianne's voice in her mind: *Oh, you adorable young hypocrite.*

"You weren't responsible for it either," Heather said, apparently also attuned to Marianne's brainwaves. "Did she get arrested at the park?"

"No." Gideon spoke, resting his hand on Natalie's arm. "The police found her at the ER."

"What happened to the alibi she'd arranged with Vanessa?"

"Yeah, it's poetic how that backfired," Gideon said. "She'd left her phone at Vanessa's house so cell phone records wouldn't contain any evidence to contradict her and Vanessa's story. But after her fight with Natalie, she's bleeding all over her car, needs to get to the hospital immediately, and can't tell Vanessa there's a problem with their alibi—it's not like she can go dripping into a gas station and ask to use the phone. She heads for the ER. The police track her down. She claims Natalie lured her to the sculpture park and stabbed her. Meanwhile, other cops are talking to Vanessa, who has no clue what's going on, and Vanessa tries to stick to the script, claiming Lauren has been with her at the storage shed all evening and just barely went home with a headache, a story the police already know is garbage. The takeaway: even Lauren Bell can't scheme effectively when she's about to pass out from panic and blood loss."

"She's scary," Heather said.

"She is," Gideon said. "The police aren't handing us many details of the investigation, but they arrested her as soon as she was released from the hospital."

"Detective Bartholomew said they told you about the analysis of the new letter that was supposedly from Tabitha," Natalie said.

Heather's face tensed. "Yes. That it was a forgery. That the handwriting expert said there's a high probability that Sophia—Lauren—wrote it. She must have written the new letters I burned too. Using Tabitha against me. *Using* her."

"I'm sorry," Natalie said.

"Things make more sense now." Heather coiled her braid around her hand. "I could feel you were a good person, but Tabitha kept warning me about your clinic, how evil it was—but it wasn't Tabitha. It was Sophia. I'm sorry I accused you of having an affair with Kenton. He never cheated on Sophia, let alone cheated with you."

"I understand. Don't worry about it."

"And I'm sorry I accused you of setting me up. I *did* get set up. Just not by you. Ainsley MacKerron . . . using me. Like Sophia, like *everyone*."

"Not like Kenton," Natalie said.

A flicker of hope lit her expression. "No. He hid the truth, but he didn't play me. What's happening to Ainsley?"

"She's in the hospital," Natalie said. "After she's released, she'll face charges for what she's done. Stuart MacKerron is in jail. The judge denied bail."

"What about you? You're pale. Are you supposed to be traveling here to visit me? Or are you supposed to be resting?"

"I'm taking it easy," Natalie said. "I'll be taking time off work. How are *you* doing?"

"I'm all right. Most of the people here are kind to me. I always dreaded being in a psych hospital, but . . . it's okay here. I feel a lot better than I have in . . . than I have *ever*, pretty much. It's a relief to be out of jail."

"I'll bet," Gideon said. "That's rotten that you had to go through that."

Heather swished her sock-covered feet back and forth over the carpet. "How are you?" she asked Gideon.

Gideon touched the back of his head. "Occasional headaches, but not too bad. I'll be fine. I'm cleared to drive, I'm back at work, all that fun stuff."

"You made a mess of your wrists."

Gideon looked down at the partially healed abrasions and bruises. "Let's say I discovered I'm not Houdini."

Heather scooted to the edge of her chair and held out her hand. "Let me see."

Gideon extended his right hand. Heather grasped it and delicately rotated his wrist. She brushed her fingertips over the worst of the scrapes. "You fought hard."

He flexed his fingers. "I have a bruised nerve, but the doctor doesn't think there's permanent damage."

"You fought hard for Natalie," Heather said. "You'd do anything you could to help her, wouldn't you?"

Pink patches started to develop on Gideon's neck. "I would."

"How did Sophia manage to knock you out?"

Gideon withdrew his hand. "I was in my car, keeping an eye on things, and I heard something thump against the back of the car. Like a nitwit in a horror movie, I stepped out to see what had hit my car. I don't remember anything after that until Natalie found me."

Heather studied Gideon, switched her gaze to Natalie, then looked back at Gideon. "You two are interesting."

"Interesting in what way?" Gideon asked.

Natalie squirmed. She had the feeling Gideon was about to get an answer that would embarrass them both.

"Your relationship," Heather said. "I'm having trouble getting my mind around it. I've watched you. I've heard the gossip. I still haven't figured you two out. I'd like to."

Gideon turned chili-pepper red.

"Our relationship isn't your concern," Natalie said pleasantly, hoping the heat in her cheeks didn't mean she was as scarlet as Gideon. "You have enough to focus on."

"Uh . . . I should get Natalie home," Gideon said. "She does need to rest."

"Thank you for visiting me."

"Our pleasure." Gideon stood and held out a hand to Natalie to help her to her feet. Natalie appreciated it. She was still sore enough that rising from a chair was uncomfortable.

Heather rose too. "I'm glad you're both okay."

"Thank you," Natalie said. "We'll keep in touch."

Heather shook Gideon's hand. She turned toward Natalie and paused. "Is it okay if I hug you?"

"Of course." Natalie embraced her.

Heather clung to her. Her hold wasn't panicky; Natalie sensed trust and vulnerability. How often, if ever, had Heather experienced comforting physical contact with a person she trusted?

Finally, Heather stepped back. "Please visit me again."

"We will," Natalie said.

On the way to Gideon's car, they both kept the conversation superficial: light comments about how well Heather was doing, observations on the modern architecture of this psychiatric facility, admiration for the flowerbeds near the main doors.

When they were in the car with the doors closed, Gideon started the engine but didn't reverse out of his parking space. He adjusted his side mirror. Checked the sunglasses holder for the sunglasses he'd already mentioned forgetting. Fastened, unfastened, and refastened his seat belt as though not sure he'd clicked it correctly on the first try. Pressed the button to set the AC on maximum, then, as warm air blasted them, turned the fan down.

Natalie tried not to let herself tense up. Taut muscles would soon be achy muscles.

Gideon fingered the lid of a water bottle in the cup holder. "So we confuse her, huh?"

"Yes."

"Because I'm confused," Gideon said. "Confusion personified. An artist should make an abstract-sculpture version of me and stick it in the Cascata park to represent 'The Confusion of Man.'"

Natalie smiled nervously. "Trust me, you're a lot less confused than many people I know."

He unfastened his seat belt and faced her. "You've been very patient."

"So have you." She swallowed, wondering if Gideon would mind if she commandeered his water bottle. "I've been thinking we need to talk about where we're at. I'm not saying we need to talk about it right here in the parking lot . . ."

He picked up the water bottle and shook it. It was empty. He stuck it back in the cup holder. "I know I've been . . . What's the right word? Indecisive? Irrational? Irritating?"

"Incredible?"

He laughed. "Nope, wrong word. But I'm done being an idiot. I'm . . . done confusing Heather Osbourne."

Natalie focused on his eyes. Warm, apprehensive, honest eyes. "What does that mean?"

"It means I'm all in, Natalie," he said. "I love you."

Natalie released her seat belt, leaned across the center console—holding that position hurt but not enough to stop her—and kissed him.

Gideon laid one hand on the back of her head to seal them more firmly together and one hand on her shoulder to steady her. Gently, he leaned toward her, repositioning her so she was comfortable in her seat and he was the one stretched over the divider.

A rap on the window distracted Natalie. They pulled apart and saw Bob Chapman standing next to the car.

Gideon rolled down his window. "Uh, hi."

"Ah, Mr. Radcliffe, I apologize for the interruption."

"Welcome—welcome home," Gideon stammered. "How was your trip?"

"Not nearly as riveting as what happened while I was gone." He raised his white eyebrows at Natalie. "*Mein Schatz,* you should spend more time kissing Mr. Radcliffe and less time getting in potentially lethal trouble."

"Noted," Natalie said, her cheeks scorching.

"I'm deeply grateful you are both recovering," Chapman said. "Such sad and bizarre happenings at my beloved Stoker. Dr. Marsh, here is some news for you: this morning, my office received a call from our artistic and very humbled friend, Vanessa Parisi. Ms. Parisi feels significant regret for her actions and for her attitude. She wishes to donate to your clinic and wanted to know how to do so. We gave her that information. She also inquired as to when you'll be back at work. She has a gift for you, a fragile piece of artwork she'd prefer to hand-deliver. William the Prepared told her you were on leave, but he would notify you of her wish, and you could contact her to make arrangements, if you desire. Expect a call from William, if you haven't already received it."

"Thank you," Natalie said, smiling. "That's generous of Vanessa. I'll contact her."

"Ms. Parisi feared you would be too angry to do anything but rip the leaves off any olive branch she offered, but William assured her—correctly, I see—that you have phenomenal patience with struggling humankind. We'll talk later. For now, rest, and be confident that Nefesh Bria is in capable hands."

"Thank you."

Chapman waved farewell and strutted toward the hospital.

"Great news about Vanessa." Gideon rolled up his window. "You know, we just got busted by Bob Chapman for a public display of affection. This is the most romantic moment of my life."

Natalie's hands trembled as she buckled her seat belt. She felt a little punchy and wanted to suggest they stay and try to get busted by Chapman again when he finished his visit with Heather. "If this is the best so far, we need to give you more romantic moments."

Gideon laughed and bent toward Natalie to kiss her. After a moment, he drew back and fastened his seat belt. "I love you."

"You're not the only one who's done being confused," Natalie said. "I love you too."

Gideon grinned at her, his smile so transparently elated that it was the most appealing thing Natalie had ever seen. "I'm starting to think being decisive isn't half bad," he said, shifting the car into gear.

ABOUT THE AUTHOR

STEPHANIE BLACK HAS LOVED BOOKS since she was old enough to grab the pages and has enjoyed creating make-believe adventures since she and her sisters were inventing long Barbie games filled with intrigue and danger or running around pretending to be detectives. She is a four-time Whitney Award winner for Best Mystery/Suspense and a finalist for Best Speculative Fiction.

Stephanie was born in Utah and has lived in various places, including Arkansas, Arizona, Massachusetts, and Limerick, Ireland. She currently lives in northern California, plays the violin in a community symphony but never practices enough, and enjoys spending time with her husband, Brian, and their family. She is a fan of homemade pizza, homemade chocolate-chip cookies, and naps.

Stephanie enjoys hearing from her readers. You can contact her via e-mail at info@covenant-lds.com or by mail care of Covenant Communications, P.O. Box 416, American Fork, UT 84003-0416. Visit her website at www. stephanieblack.net and her author Facebook page at www.facebook.com/ stephanieblackauthor.